MW01245992

The Depresso Trilogy

O. W. Láav

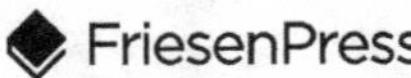

One Printers Way
Altona, MB R0G 0B0
Canada

www.friesenpress.com

First Edition — 2022

ISBN
978-1-03-912832-3 (Hardcover)
978-1-03-912831-6 (Paperback)
978-1-03-912833-0 (eBook)

1. FICTION, FANTASY, ACTION & ADVENTURE

Distributed to the trade by The Ingram Book Company

Table of Contents

Author's Note

THE following work contains adult language and scenes of graphic violence, including violence perpetrated by and against police officers. It also deals with subjects of mental illness and mental health, including depictions of suicide, suicidal ideation, depression, and substance dependence.

If these themes feel too heavy, that's okay. Please put this book away, I promise I won't judge or be offended. There are plenty of absolutely fantastic books out there containing similar superhero and police themes—I can recommend a few. Just off the top of my head, V. E. Schwab's *Vicious* is awesome, or if you're looking for a graphic novel, *Gotham Central* by Brubaker, Rucka, and Lark is amazing.

But anyway.

If you do choose to read this one, well, first off, thank you. But I also want to note that you may feel as though the depictions of mental health and illness don't fit with your own impressions or experiences. And I think that's natural. I wrote this based on my personal struggles, and I imagine my depression isn't the exact same as others'. I hope you'll keep that in mind. The last thing I want is to invalidate anyone's experience.

One thing I do hope we can all agree on is that, as a society, and as a humanity, we need to take better care of our mental health for ourselves and for each other. I mean, life, even the mundane day-to-day life, is fragile and hard enough as it is.

If this book helps, entertains, or distracts you for a bit, then I guess I've done my job.

Hopefully I didn't scare you off. It's actually a pretty fun book, there's lots of action and dark humour and stuff. If you made it this far, I think you'll like it. So, go ahead. Turn that page already.

O. W. Láav, 2021

Depresso I:
Depresso Begins

They're lined up at the window, peer down into limbo
They're frightened of jumping, in case they survive

. . .

I wish I could fly
From this building, from this wall
And if I should try
Would you catch me, if I fall?
When I fall?

— *When I Fall,* S. Page & E. Robertson, 1996

1 — *Twenty-six*

DR. PATEL walked towards one of the ER examination rooms. It was 3:00 a.m. He hated night shifts at the hospital, but then, every doctor hates night shifts. You still had to do them, nothing you could do about it.

The doctor yawned. He resented being called down to the ER, but as the only qualified psychiatrist on-call at the moment, he had no choice. He entered the exam room, took one look at the patient, and sighed.

"So. *You* again. What was it this time?" he asked.

The patient answered in a raspy, laboured voice, coughing intermittently. He was lying on the hospital bed, eyes closed. "Carbon monoxide".

"Ah. Let me guess, you locked yourself in your garage, with the door closed, turned the car engine on, and went to sleep?"

"Something like that".

Dr. Patel sighed again. "How many times does this make now? Ten?"

"Eleven".

"Eleven failed suicide attempts—"

"No. Those are just the ones that ended up with me in the hospital. In total, it's twenty-six".

"Sure. Twenty-six, eleven, whatever. I personally have seen you on at least five of those times, right? And we have spoken about it all—your depression, your . . ." the doctor trailed off, his tired head foggy. "Look, at this point, I honestly do not know what I could say or do to stop you from making these . . . attempts".

Owen didn't respond. He still hadn't opened his eyes.

"I'm beginning to think . . . look, twenty-six attempts. Even if it's just eleven, the fact that nothing worked so far tells us something here. Perhaps you don't really want to kill yourself after all. Maybe this is all just a deranged plea for attention. Maybe you're lonely, or bored".

No response.

Dr. Patel felt himself growing increasingly frustrated. "I do not dispute the fact that mentally, you are *not* healthy. You need help, yes. In my professional opinion, you are in clear need of therapy as well as medication. I don't think I personally can give you the help you need, but I'm certain we can work something out, if you let me. I can refer you to one of our on-site therapists as an outpatient. I can prescribe antidepressants, SSRIs, benzodiazepines. I can try to help, *if you let me try.*

"But you will not let me try, will you? I have asked you this before, we've had this conversation, I've made the offers. I've written prescriptions, but you never took the pills. I set up appointments for therapy, but you cancelled them or just never bothered to show up. I've done what I could. I will do what I can again this time, fully expecting no change, but it's my job to try. I swore an oath as a doctor. I will ask you the same questions, and you will give me the same answers. Yes? Yes. So, please tell me, why are you here tonight, Owen?"

"I'm here because your stupid paramedics drove me here," croaked the patient, his voice still raspy, though a little less so.

"Uh-huh. So, you did not want to come here?"

"No".

"What did you hope to do tonight, with the carbon monoxide?"

Owen finally opened his eyes. "Are you an idiot? I wanted to *die*. I was trying to kill myself".

"I don't believe you".

Owen looked angry. He half sat up. "Okay, so *don't* believe me. What, you think I go through this for fun? It amuses me? Or because I want your attention? How fucking *conceited* are you? You've got records of all the things I've done to myself. I'm trying to die, that's all I want to do".

"If you were really, seriously, trying to die, don't you think you'd be dead by now?" asked Dr. Patel. In a sense, it was a fair question, but the doctor posed it with some malice in his voice, some sarcasm. He was tired and pissed off.

Owen glared at him. They were both angry.

The doctor paused. He knew what he wanted to say, but he also knew it wasn't the right thing, the *proper* thing, to say. As a doctor, he had to try anything in his power to help any patient, anyone who was unwell for whatever reason. But this man before him, with his history of repeated suicide attempts, or 'supposed' attempts—since Dr. Patel didn't entirely believe any of his stories—was clearly just calling out in a series of desperate pleas for attention. The patient evidently had deep psychological, or more likely personality-based problems that required assessing, but Dr. Patel didn't believe he was truly suicidal, or else he would be dead, or at least severely injured after five, eleven, or twenty-six attempts. Therefore, the doctor reasoned, Owen was *not* suicidal and was owed no duty as a patient.

For non-suicidal psychological conditions, where the patient does not pose a danger to himself or others, the patient must be willing to invest in rehabilitation and therapy, or else his condition would not improve. This patient was clearly not interested in any treatment.

Dr. Patel's course was suddenly clear. No, it wasn't the medically appropriate response. And yes, his decision might have been influenced by how tired and annoyed he was, but he felt it was correct. He decided on what he would say, measuring his words carefully.

"Listen, here's what I think. I think you're wasting my time and the time of the paramedics and everybody at this hospital. You are wasting time and money and resources. I don't know why you're doing this, but after having seen you several times, I truly believe you pose no real threat to yourself or anyone else. In the morning, as long as you're physically healthy, I'm discharging you".

"I thought you're legally required to keep me under observation for seventy-two hours after a suicide attempt," Owen said, based on experience.

"Only if you're a danger to yourself. Let's not waste time or money. I already told you, I wrote prescriptions, I suggested therapy, and you don't want any of it. Fine. I have nothing else to offer you. You can go home. If you want help, real help, I'll be happy to try and help you. I'll refer you to some fantastic psychiatric clinics here at the hospital or externally, and we can try any of several drug regimes, antidepressants. You know the options".

"I've tried your options. They don't do shit".

"Okay. See, you're refusing my help. Is there anything else I can do for you, Owen?"

Owen put his head down on the hospital bed and shut his eyes once more. "I guess not," he said in a soft, weary voice.

"Okay then. Feel better. And I don't want to see you back here again," said Dr. Patel as he walked out of the room.

Why did he ever go into psychiatry in the first place?

Owen stayed on the hospital bed for the night. He cried a bit when he could manage it, but it was difficult to really feel anything. There was that crushing sadness, of course, it's been there for years, but he felt pretty numb to it at the moment. There was anger too, which was relatively novel. Owen supposed the anger stemmed from Dr. Patel's dismissiveness, which really pissed him off. Motherfucking asshole. Some people shouldn't be psychiatrists, they do more harm than good. Owen learned this the hard way, having been exposed to several psychiatrists in his lifetime. A lifetime that should have *ended* by now, twenty-six times over.

In the morning, the nurse deemed him perfectly healthy. He was discharged.

So he took a cab home.

. . .

"Hi, Dad. Sorry, I know it's early, sun's not even up yet. My squad's on night rotation for the next couple of weeks. I just figured I'd stop by before going home. I'll probably crash, straight to bed, like you'd always tell me. I'm . . . I guess I'm doing all right. How are you?"

Dinah Borst, captain of the city's 16th precinct, didn't expect an answer to her question.

"Dad, I'm . . . I guess I'm stressed out. I feel really anxious. I don't know. Sometimes I worry I took that promotion too soon. I don't feel like I know what I'm doing half the time and it's . . ." Borst trailed off, then sighed. "Don't get me wrong, I know I have the best damn squad in the city. More than half of them grew up in the 1-6, same as me. Same as you, Dad. I've got me some good police. We're pretty close to closing a couple of major cases. But that's not . . . *that* part of the job is fine. It's what I want to do. I like being a cop.

"It's all the shit around it. I've got to meet up with D'Alfonso tomorrow, my division inspector. He's going to stick it to me with some union bullshit, I just know it. My squad's been hitting the overtime pretty aggressively. And I still haven't decided what to do with Jordan-Dee. He's retiring in a couple of months, and I don't have anyone to replace him with. I don't want to bring in someone I don't know, it'll mess with the dynamic of the squad, but I know D'Alfonso's gonna force . . ."

Borst trailed off again. "It's the politics. I don't . . . I don't know how you always managed to keep it together. I'm sure you hated the bullshit as much as I do, I just never remember you complaining about it. Maybe you did, I don't know. Maybe I'm just weak. But you . . . everyone loved you, Dad. You kept your composure, smiled at everybody. I just wish I knew how to do that. Instead, I get all worked up and I snap. Everyone outside my squad thinks I'm a bitch. I know what they say about me behind my back.

"I *hate* it. And I know, I know. Each time I visit, I say the same things. Sorry, Dad. I think the worst of it—the red tape, the union crap, the defunding—it gets in the way of actual police work. All I want to do is be like you, be a good cop, protect people, save lives, keep the community safe, the 1-6. That's the important thing, I know. But I don't know if . . . if . . ."

For some reason, her eyes burned, a tear rolling down her left cheek. Why was she crying? *Stupid*, she thought. *Emotional. Keep it together.*

"Sorry, Dad. I'm fine. I'm okay, really. I know you'd ask me—you'd change the subject. Ask if I met a guy, or if I'm finally going to get that cat I always talk about. Maybe someday. I just don't want to turn into a crazy cat lady. And I don't . . . I went on a date, actually. Last weekend. It was . . . you'd have laughed. The guy . . . why are men so weak and insecure? I'm pretty sure he was intimidated by my job, so he kept talking about *his*, trying to look like a big man. It turned me right off. I just went home after dinner. And then I felt so shitty I . . . well, I took the leftovers home with me, and I just ended up eating them as soon as I got home. What a crappy date. See, that's where you had it easier. Being a male cop is simple. People get it, no one questions it, no one . . . yeah. Guess I'm just doomed to be alone forever".

Borst chuckled to herself. "Maybe that's for the best, anyway. I'm not exactly dating-material. Anyway, I don't even know why I'm talking about that. Sorry".

She shuffled. A shiver ran through her, and she looked up to the sky, which was starting to brighten from a velvety blue to a light gray. "The days are getting longer, at least. But it's still fucking cold. Oh—sorry. You always hated it when I swore. I swear a lot more now. Anyway, it *is* cold. I remember you always said this city hibernates in winter, like a bear. Then summer comes, and it just explodes". She rubbed her arms through her coat. There was no one else around.

Borst secretly liked night shift duty. Night shift was quieter, safer, which gave her and her officers more time to solve actual cases. Other than the cold of winter, she didn't have much to complain about, really. Her officers did—they had families, schedules to figure out while working nights, school pickups and this and that. Borst didn't have to worry about any of that. It was just her now.

"I guess I'll try to appreciate the winter quiet while it lasts. Okay, Dad, I'm freezing my ass off. I'm gonna go home, take a nice hot shower, then roll into bed. I'm glad we had this chat, though. Always nice talking to you, Dad. I really miss you".

Borst reached into her coat's inner pocket and retrieved a metallic flask. She unscrewed the top. "Here's to your memory, Dad. Keep resting," she said, raising the flask towards the gravestone in front of her. "I'll see ya in Heaven". She took a stiff drink, pocketed the flask again, and walked out of the graveyard, cold, tired, but comforted.

2 – *Now what?*

EARLY in the morning after getting home from the hospital following his latest suicide attempt, Owen sat on his bed for a couple of hours, staring at the wall.

Given his lifetime of dealing with depression, staring at walls was a pretty typical pastime of his.

As he sat, his vision drifting in and out of focus, thoughts went through his mind. *You're useless, sad, pathetic. You can't even* kill *yourself right. You're wasting the time and resources of healthcare providers. Genuinely sick people need those resources. You don't fucking deserve them. Seriously. Just . . . fuck. I'm in so much pain. Just . . . emotional anguish. I just want to die, just fucking . . . why can't I die? Why can it never end? It'd be so much easier. Such a fucking . . .*

Owen tried to deal with these thoughts using the techniques he had developed over years of therapy, acknowledging them without judging, accepting them as counterproductive, then letting them go, checking in with how these thoughts informed his emotions.

He still wasn't really feeling much today. He was mostly just numb, empty. So damn empty.

When he finally looked up to check the time, half the day had gone, and Owen had done nothing. Most days were like this, but today felt worse. That's how it goes—some days were better, some were worse. It made sense that today was worse, to be fair. He *did* try to kill himself last night. And failed. Again. Owen sighed.

He got up and grabbed his wallet, keys, and jacket. He had to get to the bank. The idiots cancelled his debit card by mistake, and he had to come in and show a piece of ID to get it reactivated. What a miserable joke. Had his attempt worked, he wouldn't have had to go to the bank, but since he was still alive, he had no choice. At least it got him out of the house. It got him to do something other than stare at the wall. Could be worse. It could always be worse.

Owen walked. It was February, but it wasn't too cold out. February was weird in this city. Some days were -15°C, some were 15°C. Ups and downs, but always on the cold side. There was a metaphor for Owen's life somewhere in there. Either way, today was walkable, around 3°C, so Owen walked. He could use some air to clear his head. He always felt out of it after getting discharged from the hospital. Cold air and some walking would do him good. Well, maybe not *good*, but better. Or not worse. Or something.

There was a line-up at the bank. There always was. That was fine. The longer this took, the longer Owen was out of the house, doing something, being productive. If you could call this productive. You probably couldn't. Well, it didn't matter, he felt like shit either way. But at least now he had an excuse to feel like shit. The bank cancelling his card and forcing him to stand in line would make anyone feel shitty, right? There was normalcy in that. So he lined up.

Some days you wish something would happen. Anything. Just something different to distract you from how shitty you're feeling, how pathetic your life is. Of course, when something does happen, it's usually something worse than the mind-numbing mundanities of everyday life, and you end up wishing it never happened in the first place. You forget you wanted it, that you had wished for it, for something, anything. It's just how life goes—you get what you ask for, as long as you ask for shit.

And so, as Owen was waiting in line at the bank, a guy walked in wearing a ski mask and a fedora, with a gun in his hand. He locked the branch's main door behind him, waved the gun in the air, and yelled, "Everybody down! This is a robbery!"

You've got to be kidding me, thought Owen. Whoever this robber was, he clearly spent his time watching too many movies. All he was missing was a canvas bag with a dollar sign on it.

All around him, people were panicking and dropping to the ground, while the robber in his stupid ski mask and the freaking fedora—*who the fuck wears a fedora to a bank robbery?*—was rushing towards the tellers, screaming, "Get away from there! Nobody touch any alarms!"

Owen forgot all about the fact that seconds earlier he was hoping for something, anything, to break up the monotony and distract him from how unhappy he was feeling. With this ludicrous, surreal, clichéd bank robbery scene unfolding around him, he just did not want any part of it. He wasn't having it. He just kept standing in line, shaking his head.

A lady next to him, prone flat on the ground, hissed, "What are you doing?! Get down!"

"Yeah, I'll get right on that," Owen replied sarcastically.

The robber was still busy with the tellers. He kept shouting these stupid robber-movie banalities, like "I want non-sequential unmarked bills!" or "If you get a dye-pack in there, I will kill your ass!" He was just missing, "Nobody be a hero and we all get to go home".

How the fuck does this even happen in an actual bank? Owen wondered. *Who* is *this clown?*

And then he thought bitterly, *Why is this happening now, to me?*

The same thought occurred to several other people in the bank at roughly the same time. Nobody appreciated the change in the tedium of a daily bank scene. Other than Owen, they were mostly busy being afraid for their lives. Owen did not share that particular sentiment.

Suddenly, while waving his gun at the tellers, the robber finally noticed him. Owen was still standing nonchalantly, untouched by the chaos unfolding around him, just feeling generally miserable.

"Hey, you! You think I'm kidding around here? Get on the fucking ground, man!"

"No," Owen said simply. He was firm, but he wasn't trying to be provocative, although he may have unintentionally come across as antagonistic, he realized, and immediately felt annoyed about his failure to control his tone.

The robber turned to face him, waving the gun again.

"What did you say? What did you *fucking* say? Get down or I'll shoot you right now, you hear me? I'm not fucking joking!"

Owen started walking forward now, ducking beneath the velvet rope keeping the line in place. For a second, it felt like he was doing something wrong by skipping his place in line at the bank. He shook that off. Guilt was one of his triggers, doing anything wrong always got to him. He knew this feeling stemmed from a deep-rooted belief that he was worthless, which had a lot to do with his father. His thought-journals were full of this pattern. But he didn't have the time to chart his feelings at that exact moment, these were exceptional circumstances, so he let it slide.

"Stay back, hey, what the fuck do you think you're doing? Hey!" shouted the robber. Staff and customers tried to grab at him too, tell him to stop, that it wasn't worth it.

But Owen was already standing in front of the ridiculously dressed robber in his ski mask and fedora.

"Listen," Owen said. "I'm in a bad mood today. So fuck you. I'm not getting down on the ground. I'm just going to stand and wait for you to wrap this nonsense up. I'm not going to do anything. Okay?"

"Get the fuck away. Get out of my face," warned the robber. He started panicking. "This is your last warning. Get on the goddamn ground".

"No thanks".

"Stop it!" yelled one of the girls behind the counter. She was a young teller, and she looked utterly terrified but had managed to muster the courage to speak up and try to stop the crazy man from resisting the criminal with the gun. "He'll shoot you, just . . . just stop".

Owen remained unperturbed.

The robber didn't take that well. "I'll shoot you dead right now. I swear I'll—"

"Then shoot. Go ahead. I want to die anyway. You want to escalate this from robbery to murder? Get life in jail? Go ahead, you fucking idiot. I don't care. Shoot me".

"I swear to God, get the fuck away from me—"

"Shoot me, come on. *Shoot me*!"

And then the robber shot him.

Everybody started shouting at the sound of gunfire, losing their shit. The tellers dropped the money and everything else and ducked behind the counter. The silent alarm had been pressed ages ago. This should have been a simple robbery, no one had to get hurt. And now a gun's gone off and anything could happen, anyone could get shot. This just turned to shit.

Owen was shot. He got hit in the chest. He staggered back a bit. The wound started leaking blood all over the place—*so* much damn blood.

"Fuck. That hurts," Owen said. He pressed his left hand to his chest. "Okay, you shot me. Now what?"

"What the . . . what the fuck, man. I shot you! Why aren't you dead? I . . . what the hell?" asked the robber. He was completely freaking out at the total lack of reaction from Owen, who was still standing there like nothing happened, despite the dripping blood. Then the robber pointed his gun back up. "Get back!"

"Stop it with the gun already," Owen said, and made a move for the weapon with his right hand. The robber squeezed the trigger again, half intentionally and half just as a reflex, out of panic. The second bullet hit Owen in the right shoulder, causing him to lose his balance and fall to the ground.

"Oww! Stop shooting me, it hurts like hell. Give me that!" he complained as he got back to his feet. Owen reached for the gun again. This time, the robber barely put up a struggle as Owen snatched it away.

"What the fuck *is* this?" the robber asked hysterically.

"I don't know. Karma?" Owen said. He put the gun on the counter. "This really does fucking hurt, you know," he said, rubbing his wounded shoulder, which was bleeding profusely, as was his chest.

They finally heard sirens blaring down the street towards the bank. With the exception of Owen and the robber, everyone was still on the ground in varying degrees of shock, still fearful for their lives. The robber took one look at the scene and realized he was screwed. This really had gone to hell. He turned towards the door, intending to make a run for it.

"No, you're staying here," Owen said. He just said it. He didn't block the way or anything.

"I . . . fuck . . ." the robber said, but he was done. It was over. He started to cry beneath his dumb ski mask. The ridiculous fedora had been knocked off during the brief struggle for the gun.

Owen thought, *Now I'll probably have to come back another day to get my card reactivated. Fuck. Oh well, it'll give me something to do later this week.*

. . .

"Sir," said Borst, stepping into her superior's office.

She was tired as fuck. She was still on night shift rotation for the rest of the week, but she was scheduled for her monthly review with Division Inspector D'Alfonso, which had to happen during normal business hours, so she swapped shifts for the day. It really messed with her sleep schedule. She ought to be in bed now, in mid-afternoon. Instead, she not only had to be awake, but be focused, smart, and conduct herself professionally. It didn't help matters that D'Alfonso already had on an exasperated expression, which signalled that he was *not* having a good day. Borst braced herself.

"Captain. Have a seat," said D'Alfonso, himself rising and rubbing his temples while staring out his office window. He had a window. That's how you knew an officer was high-ranking.

Borst didn't have a window. She was one of two serving captains, one of the highest-ranked officers in the 16th station, her home precinct. But this wasn't the 1-6, this was Central Division Command Headquarters. You'd think she *would* have a window in her own office, but she didn't. Maybe one day she'd have a window. But did she even want one? A window would mean she was even farther removed from her officers on the ground, from saving lives and making a difference.

Screw the window, she thought.

"How's the 1-6?" asked D'Alfonso.

"Working hard, sir".

"A little too hard, from what I hear," he said, turning to face her. The pained expression was still there, but maybe it was just a migraine. "The union's busting my balls, Borst".

"What are they on about? Overtime?"

"Oh, union's happy with the overtime. More pay for their folks. My bosses upstairs, they're pissed off about overtime. No, the union's complaining about your squad's tendency to . . . hold on, let me find the right wording," he said, sitting back down and scanning his computer for a few seconds. "Squad is feeling under pressure to jump into situations that pose a danger to officer safety".

Borst almost snorted. "What?!"

"Yep. They're complaining that your officers feel pressured to walk into scenes where they could be exposed to violence and anti-officer sentiment".

Borst felt close to losing it. Violence and anti-officer sentiment? The entire damn *country* was experiencing a wave of violence and anti-officer sentiment because some racist fucks were killing black people. But *those* racist cops down on the other side of the country weren't anything like her officers, they weren't real police, serving and protecting. They were just fuckers with guns who got off on power and thought they were better because of the colour of their goddamn skin.

It's taken so much work, so much effort, to get those fuckers the hell out of the force in this city. And granted, maybe there were still a few bad ones in uniform. But Borst knew, she *knew*, her cops were good cops. Each and every damn one of them. And yet, the general populace still hated them because of the mere fact they were cops. And maybe they were right to—Borst struggled with that question every day. She struggled to work a job she believed was necessary even when the world hated her for it, hated the badge and what it stood for.

It's gotten worse the past few months. The mayor's office was talking about defunding the entire force again, there were constant protests. And when there were protests, there was no one else to keep the peace but the police force, even when they also happened to be the target. But what choice was there? Let the people riot? They had to keep the peace, even if it meant serving as a wave-barrier against the largely justified rage of the world.

Borst and her people knew it. She had given her squad the pep talks. She sat down with her officers regularly, made sure they were okay. They weren't, but they put on a brave face, same as her. How do you work as a police officer when the people of the city don't want you to exist? Still, *they* believed in their jobs, even if no one else did. But the union, the goddamn union . . .

Borst forced herself to take a deep breath before speaking. "Sir, it . . . it sounds like the union is complaining that my officers are *doing their job*. I'm not sure I . . . I don't know what I can do about it. They're cops. Dangerous situations, the protests, anti-police . . . we don't have a choice, we have to—"

"I understand, Borst. Frankly, and pardon my French, this seems fucking ridiculous to me too. But I've got to tell my superiors that I talked to you about what the union wants. Now, I did have an analyst go over your field reports—Borst, as ridiculous as it seems, your squad *does* find itself in volatile, violent situations remarkably often. Your people go in half-cocked a *lot*".

"Sir—"

"Let me finish, please," said D'Alfonso, and Borst felt the blood rush to her head. "I'm not talking about the protests here. Your squad's top of the division and third in the whole *city* when it comes to sanctioned usage of firearm. You're second in the division for injuries on shift, bottom in days off. Your boys—"

"—and *girls*," Borst couldn't help herself.

"—boys *and* girls see more action than most squads in the city, and don't take time off to rest and recuperate".

"We also close more cases, make more arrests, we have the *best* scores when it comes to making sure that our numbers are not racially biased. We couldn't do any of that without seeing more action. We do our job, sir, we're the best—"

Shit, she was talking *very* quickly. She slammed the breaks mid-sentence.

"Captain Borst. I don't dispute your numbers. You're one of the best squads I've got. But I'm worried. I'm afraid that what you're building is a culture that's hungry for action, that goes out looking for it. And from there, you're a step and a half away from . . . from zealots, from action-hero territory. If your officers fall into that mindset, they're a liability".

"Sir, we're not hungry for action, we're hungry for justice. We're saving lives—"

"Listen to yourself. You know what you sound like? You sound like a comic-book character, like . . . Batman. Look, Borst, the unions are bullshit, and I'm happy with your results. All I'm saying is, you need to think about how sustainable your squad's culture and attitude are and the impact on your officers' state of mind in the long-term. You need to be careful. I need to know you're hearing me on this".

She was about to continue arguing, but D'Alfonso's words rang true. "I hear you, sir, but . . . well, what do you want me to do?"

"Right, that takes us to the second item on the agenda. One of your sergeants, Jordan-Dee, is up for retirement, correct?"

Borst was impressed he knew the name without consulting any files. D'Alfonso wasn't a bad guy. "That's right".

"We'll need a replacement, obviously. Now, I'm not sure if you had anyone in mind, but we do have a few potential transfers I wanted to discuss with you. Well, just the one, really".

"I *was* hoping to promote internally, sir".

"Has anyone passed the Sergeant's exam?"

"Not yet, sir".

"Right. Well, do you know Sergeant Akada from Major Crime?"

"Donoghue's team?"

"Donoghue's transferring to Drug and Substance Control, actually. His entire squad is being decommissioned after . . . well, there's been some . . . anyway. They're rebuilding Major Crime, moving some people in, some people out. I've been asked to find a place for Akada".

"Sir, all due respect, it sounds like you're trying to . . ." Borst was about to say, *trying to stick me with some asshole no one else wants*, but caught herself in time. Shit, she hated this politics crap. She started again.

"What I mean is, the 1-6 is a delicate precinct. Most of us have grown up in the neighbourhood, we know the streets. Especially these days, the situation is tricky, in terms of race, and . . . well, I would . . . I would be concerned that an outsider might not fit in with the rest of my squad, and . . . well, if they're coming in as a sergeant, it's a high rank, and people may feel as though . . ."

"I understand, Borst. They'll need the rapport, or your people won't trust them. Look, I'll forward you Akada's file, but it's your squad and your call. If you think you've got someone you want to promote and they pass the Sergeant's exam in the next few months, you have my blessing".

"Thank you, sir".

D'Alfonso nodded, then went quiet again. "One more thing, Borst. And I hate to do this". He sighed deeply. "I've got news on the Finnie trial".

"Oh". Shit.

D'Alfonso licked his lips as if trying to delay saying the words. "He's off on a technicality. It was the warrant. I'm sorry".

"That's *bullshit*!" Borst found herself shouting. She immediately regretted losing her composure like that.

Finnie was a case her squad had worked for weeks. He'd kidnapped a kid and . . . she'd rather not think about the rest. The man was a monster, a fucking animal.

They found him, went in, and arrested him . . . but her people, Chen and Lawson and the others, went in without a warrant. Borst had signed off on it, because she knew Finnie would escape otherwise. They did get a warrant, a few minutes *after* the arrest was made. So technically, they had no right to search the premises. It was legal bullshit.

"I'm sorry," Borst apologized for her outburst.

"It's okay. I completely understand how you feel. This sort of thing happens to all of us. Borst . . . you have a law degree, don't you?"

Borst nodded. Before joining the force, she earned a degree in legal studies. Her father never wanted her to be a cop—he wanted her to be a lawyer, serve justice from a safe distance. But then her father passed away, and she decided that what she really wanted was to follow in his footsteps.

"Well, then you know how this works. I'm not blaming you, criminals get off all the time, sometimes legitimately, sometimes not. But . . . look, you know this better than most. We can't . . . we *have* to follow the law to the letter. We're cops. We enforce the law".

"But—"

D'Alfonso sighed again. "Borst".

"Sorry, sir, I know . . . I'm not arguing with you. I . . . you're right".

"I am. I don't want to see you cutting corners again. Or at least, just be *smart* about it".

"Sir?"

D'Alfonso opened his mouth as if to continue, then closed it and smiled. "You know what I said. Don't play dumb".

"Don't get caught?" she asked, confused. What *was* he saying?

"Don't be dumb, Borst. I'm a division inspector. I *have* to tell you to follow procedures, I have to pass on messages from the union and from my superiors. But damn it if I don't miss just . . . chasing a perp down the street, cuffing him. I'm getting fat. Sorry, musings of a middle-aged man," said D'Alfonso, rising from his desk. "Point is, if it's between waiting five minutes for a warrant and risking the perp running off . . . well, you judge and do the right thing. I trust your call. Anything else, Captain?"

It was clear that the question was really a dismissal. "No, sir. Thank you, sir," she said, rising to leave.

There was so much to dissect there.

What was she supposed to do with her squad? Tell them to tone it down? After all, maybe D'Alfonso was right. Maybe her people were getting too gung-ho, and some of them had accrued a lot of paid leave, but . . .

Well, wait. Did that mean someone on the squad had complained to the union reps? Or did another squad get jealous of the 1-6's numbers and decided to throw a fuss? Either way, that was fucked up. No, she couldn't . . . she wouldn't start suspecting her own squad. That was just a recipe for disaster.

But what if . . .

And what was she going to do about Jordan-Dee?

And . . . fuck. Finnie got off. *Fuck.*

What was D'Alfonso trying to tell her? It almost felt like he was admonishing her not for authorizing a search without a warrant, but for getting caught. Should she have asked her officers to forge the timing of the arrest by a few minutes, so it looked like the warrant came out first? Or was he . . . was he saying the opposite?

Mostly, there was him. D'Alfonso. The ending of their meeting . . . that was *exactly* what Borst was afraid of for herself. Moving up and growing detached from actually making a difference. Getting a window, getting sucked into the politics, and getting farther from the people she was supposed to be serving and protecting.

Poor D'Alfonso.

She was thinking all of this while taking the stairs down to the first floor. She needed . . . she needed a *drink*, she thought. Then her phone buzzed.

"Captain?" it was Santiago, one of her men.

"Yes?"

"Just giving you an update, we had a bit of a hostage situation, but it's resolved. We've got the perp in a box, and we're interviewing a couple of witnesses".

"Any injuries?"

"Well, no, but . . . you might want to get down here. Some of the testimonies we're getting . . . Chen and I have been pulling some files, and . . . you might want to see this for yourself".

"I'm on my way back to the 1-6 right now," she said, disconnecting. Now what?

3 – *A fucking cape, even*

THE next few hours following his witnessing of the world's most idiotic attempt at a bank robbery were pretty bad. Not only did he never get his card reactivated, Owen was forced to stick around for hours on end. First, the cops came by to secure the scene and arrest the perpetrator, then he was seen to by a medic and interviewed by an endless succession of officers of varying ranks, initially on the scene and then at the nearest precinct station, which he was driven to.

What a shitty day this turned out to be, he thought. He started to think it was what he deserved, shit days, because he was an awful, unlovable waste of a human being, but he stopped himself. That wasn't useful thinking.

He was now waiting in an office. An actual office, rather than the interview room, which was plain and poorly lit and practically bare, and stressed Owen out. This office was a marginal improvement. There was no window, but there were diplomas on the wall, two small succulent plants, and a desk with a computer and a phone. There were no personal touches except a small Eeyore plush doll.

Eeyore was Owen's favourite Winnie-the-Pooh character. Maybe whoever worked in this office wasn't the worst person in the world. He could only hope.

Then she walked in. She didn't look like a cop. She wasn't in uniform, for one thing. She wore normal clothes except for a long overcoat, which she hung on a hook behind the door. She seemed younger than Owen would've imagined for a police captain, which was the title on her desk. But then, maybe Owen was misjudging her age—the first impression was mitigated by the fact that she had on an utterly serious expression. And she looked kind of sad.

That part Owen could tell. He knew from sad.

She walked over to her desk, placed the few folders she was carrying on top of it, sat down, and crossed her arms. Before she spoke, she took a minute to size him up. It was pretty obvious this lady was an intelligent, deliberate woman. Owen was already a little scared of her.

"Hi. I'm Captain Borst. Sorry about the wait. You doing okay?" she said, possibly trying to sound compassionate. It was hard to tell.

"Yeah, I'm fine".

"Okay. Good. Mr. Kale . . . can I call you Owen? I'm gonna call you Owen. So, Owen . . ." she said, placing her chin on top of her hands, elbows on the table, staring him down. "What can you tell me about this robbery I've heard so much about?"

"Nothing you don't already know," he answered. No attitude, just fatigue. Too many interviews, too many questions. She could understand that, she knew how it worked.

"Fair enough. According to witness testimonies, you were quite the hero today".

"I'm not a hero".

"No? You stood up to an armed robber. Nothing was stolen. No one got hurt. In my line of duty, that's pretty heroic".

"I thought in your line of duty that's just your job," he countered and regretted it immediately, feeling like an asshole for being snarky.

"Yes. It *is* my job. So, thank you for helping me do my job, making sure no one gets hurt. Except . . . somebody did get hurt, right? Somebody got shot, according to witnesses. Right?"

"Sure. I got shot," Owen admitted. "Twice".

"Right, right. *You* got shot. Well, I'm sorry for that. May I—?" asked Captain Borst, getting up. Owen didn't stop her as she walked around the desk. It was her office, what was he going to do?

"You have a hole in your jacket," she pointed out.

"Yeah".

The police captain stood directly in front of him, looking down. Owen was still wearing his jacket and had a thick sweater on underneath. Suddenly, he felt nervous.

She reached down. Owen managed not to flinch or pull away. She pulled down on the neck of his sweater, surveying the exposed shoulder wound. It had already healed, almost fully. "Lift your shirt, please," she asked, and he exposed his bare torso. "Right in the chest," she whispered, as if to herself.

Owen wasn't comfortable with a strange woman grabbing at his sweater and looking at his chest, but he said nothing.

And then, from inches away, Borst looked Owen in the eye. She felt as if some chord deep inside her was suddenly struck, because his were the saddest she'd ever seen.

It took her a moment to recover. She got up and walked back around her desk. Instead of sitting down, she started pacing back and forth. "I spoke to the medics. You're a very lucky hero, Owen. From that range, this type of chest wound kills, or at least does some serious damage to vital organs".

"Okay . . ."

"Uh-huh. The shoulder wound would hurt like hell, too. Major blood loss. Most people would pass out".

"Right".

"And yet . . . here you are. Awake, alive. Perfectly fine".

"Yeah".

She stopped pacing and approached him again, slowly this time, keeping her distance. "You're walking, you're talking, you don't appear to be in any physical discomfort. Injuries that, if they don't kill you, take weeks to heal. They're basically healed hours later. You seem totally fine to me. You *are* fine, right? Doing okay?"

"Sure".

"Because . . . see, my officers and I, we took the liberty of looking up some records. We wanted to check you out, right? See what we're dealing with. And you know what we found, Owen?"

At this point, she was sitting on the desk, across from him. He was looking up at her.

"We found quite a few very interesting records. For example," she said, reaching back to a folder she had placed on the desk earlier. "Three months ago, you were hospitalized. One witness said she saw you jump from a window of an office building downtown . . . but she was old, and it was nighttime. Must be a mistake, right?

"Or for instance," she picked another folder, "you were pulled out of the water at the pier at 5:00 a.m. in September last year, half-drowned. Does that sound right? Half-drowned? Well, okay.

"How about this, a cop was called to an apartment after the neighbours complained about hearing gunshots. He—"

"Okay, already! You can stop," Owen said.

Captain Borst nodded. She knew she had him now.

"Now, granted, most of these are inconclusive, but on two incidents the reports were filed by *my* cops. I know officers Santiago and Chen personally. So, this tells me . . . there's something about you, Owen. Something special. Something different. So, you can either tell me or I can guess. Do you like playing the guessing game?"

Owen crossed his arms defensively. "Okay, sure. Guess".

"See, my initial guess would be, you get shot, drowned—that means somebody wants you dead. *Very* dead. But then I looked over these some more . . . and it became pretty obvious I was right, but not quite in the right way. Somebody *does* want you dead . . . it's you, isn't it? These are suicide attempts. But then there's something more, something I'm missing. Because when a man tries to off himself—how many times is it actually? I have evidence for four here".

"Twenty-six," Owen said.

The Captain's eyes widened. That was a far higher number than she expected. "Twenty . . . fuck. Sorry, I meant . . . okay, see, when a man tries to kill himself twenty-six times, and then he gets shot, right in the chest, as seen by a bank-full of witnesses, and after all that, he's still sitting in front of me looking perfectly okay, and you are okay, right? I asked that already, you're okay. So. What am I missing?"

Owen took a deep breath and looked up at the Captain. "I can't die".

"You can't die?"

"You wanna try? I've tried everything. I can't die. I want to, goddamn it how I want to be dead, but I can't".

"Okay, well, let's start with, *why* do you want to? Why have you tried everything? Why have you tried *anything*?"

"I'm depressed. Okay? I've had major depressive disorder ever since I can remember. I'm suicidal. Not that it helps me".

"Are you on any . . . therapy, medication? Anything?"

"Not anymore".

"Why not?"

"I tried that. For years. I've tried everything. It did nothing. Pills don't do anything, and therapy just . . . after a while, it stops working, or it just pisses me off. I don't know. It doesn't matter. I'm fine, I'm alive, right? So it doesn't matter".

"Okay. But, so, you're suicidal, and you've tried a whole bunch of stuff, and you're still here. Okay. But there's no actual proof you can't die, right? It's just . . . conjecture, basically".

"You feel like shooting me right now? Cutting my head off? Go ahead".

The Captain, who was still sitting on her desk, jumped off it and pointed a finger an inch from Owen's face. "Don't you fucking talk to me like that, okay? I'm a cop. I don't shoot people for fun".

She looked angry, and that made Owen feel instinctively guilty. "Yeah, okay, sorry. I didn't mean it like . . ."

"Well, it's okay," said Borst, calming down. "So, let's say you can't die, for the sake of argument. What are you doing with yourself, then? Just wasting your life with one suicide attempt after another?"

"Pretty much, I guess. I used to work, but . . . holding down a proper job when you're suffering from a mental illness, depression, it's . . . it didn't work out. So now I . . . I don't know. I do some writing on the side, freelance sort of stuff, but, yeah. Not much of a life, really".

"Right, sorry. So you just . . . you don't work, you watch shows, play video games, jump off buildings a bit, go to the bank, get shot. Is that your deal?"

"Listen, Captain . . . Borst?"

"Let's say you can call me Dinah".

"Dinah. What do you want from me?"

"Owen. What I want is to make you into what you were today, every day. You were a hero".

"I wasn't a hero".

"That's not what at least ten witnesses have told me today".

"They don't know".

"Don't know what?"

"I . . ." Owen looked down. "The reason I did that, stood up to that idiot, tried to get him to shoot me . . . I was thinking, maybe . . . maybe if somebody else shot me, not myself . . . I just wanted to die. And trying to kill *myself* didn't work, but I was hoping . . ."

"Okay, I get it. See? You weren't a hero, you were just trying to commit suicide by robber. Okay, sure. That's it, isn't it?"

He looked back up at her. She was seated on her desk again.

"So, here's my idea. We kill two birds with one stone. I want you to be a hero, you want to keep trying to die. That sound about right?"

"Yes".

"Fine. So we make you a hero. A *super*hero. I mean, look, you got yourself a superpower already, you can't die. We can shoot you, throw you off a building, drown you. And nothing".

"I'm not a damn superhero".

"Maybe not, but you *could* be. I could use someone like you. Look, I'm a cop. I've been on the force a while now, I know how shit works. Just before talking to you, I had a meeting with my division inspector . . . being, look, being a cop today is . . . there's public opinion issues, and on top of that there's a lot of red tape, legal crap. We're here to serve and protect, right? But then we get into situations where I can't—I can't risk lives knowingly, and sometimes it's even messier than that, and I can't—sometimes it's just political bullshit, honestly. I fucking hate it".

Owen was looking at Borst, who wasn't even looking at him, really. She was getting worked up, animated. Then she *did* look back at him as she continued, more enthusiastic than ever. She seemed alive. More alive than anyone he'd interacted with in a very long time.

"But if I had someone like you," she continued, "who's not officially part of the force, but who could go into those kinds of situations where *I* have my hands tied, because they're risky, because of the legal restrictions that just don't make sense . . . in those situations, if I send *you* in, you know, there's two outcomes. Either it works, and you save the day, and you're a hero, or else you die. Either way, one of us wins. Right?"

Owen was quiet for a second. He was thinking about it.

"Come on. It's a win-win. You can be a superhero. We'll get you a fucking cape, even".

"It's not a joke," Owen said.

"I know. I'm damn serious. And listen, if you tell anyone . . . this could ruin my career. But I think . . . having someone like you active—if you really can't die—you can make a difference. A *huge* difference. Let me tell you, this cop thing, I'm a captain now, so I've been through a lot of it, and it's . . . it doesn't work. The politics, the crap, the corruption, whatever. A uniform doesn't mean shit anymore. The world wants to defund us, they don't trust us. And honestly, maybe they're right. I don't know. I trust my own squad, my people, but out there . . . sometimes, I don't know what the force even stands for.

"So, I guess I've been looking for something . . . you know. A way to fix it, a way to make a *real* difference. That's all I want to do, save lives, make this city safer. And the more I read these files, the more I think *you're* my way. Santiago and Chen wouldn't lie, and your records don't lie, and for some reason, when you say you can't die, I believe you—you can't die. I also believe you when you say you *want* to, but I think you can do so much while you're trying. Stop jumping off fucking buildings and jump in front of bullets. It makes no difference to you, right? But it makes a difference to me, it makes a difference to the innocent person who might've been killed by that bullet. You see what I'm saying?"

"I do see what you're saying, but . . . I don't know. It's not me. I'm not a hero".

"Then don't be a hero. Be a suicidal freak who can't die, but helps people. What's the difference?"

"And . . . and what if I do die? Will you be okay with that?"

Now it was Dinah's turn to be quiet for a bit. She pursed her lips. "No. But, the way you're going, you'll be dead soon without my help either way". She lifted the files off her desk, waving them at him. "It's pretty damn clear you've been trying to off yourself for ages. I can't stop you, I don't think anyone can at this point. If you die . . . listen, what I'm asking for . . . is it ethical or whatever? It's probably not. It's insane, and it's definitely illegal as hell. But I'm thinking . . . twenty-six suicide attempts. You'll kill yourself whether I want you to or not. I'm just trying to make sure that, *if* you die, you die protecting lives and doing something worthwhile. Is that really so bad? I think it's a good thing. I really do".

"Okay. Look, I get what you're saying. It makes sense, but . . . I don't know. Can I think about it?"

"Of course," Dinah smiled. "Listen, it's not like you're in trouble. I'm not going to throw you in jail or something if you say no. I'm not crazy, and I'm not . . . I'm good police, okay? You can trust me. Besides, you really were a hero today".

"Right. Do you interrogate every hero like they're some crazy supervillain about to explode?"

"Only the ones who attempted suicide twenty-six times and got shot in the chest just to look like nothing happened hours later".

"Fair enough". Owen got up.

"I have your number. Let me give you my card," she said, and pulled out a card saying Captain Dinah Borst with her numbers on it, both cell and office extension. "Call me if you make a decision. And I'll call you if anything comes up".

"Sure".

"Good".

"Can I go home now?" Owen asked. After hours at the police station, after all those questions and interviews and now *this* crazy woman trying to recruit him into some sketchy superhero operation, all he really wanted was to go home and sleep, or stare at some walls.

Borst smiled at him. "Yeah, of course. You need a ride? I'll get a cruiser to drop you off".

"I'm okay, thanks".

"You sure? It's pretty cold out".

"Thanks, I'm fine. Worst case scenario, I freeze to death. No great loss".

Dinah wasn't sure whether to smile at that or not. "Well, for what it's worth, I know you disagree, but I think somewhere deep inside you *are* a hero. And I think you should let it out. But it's your call. So . . . goodbye, Owen", she said, stepping forward with an outstretched hand. "Hope to hear from you soon".

Owen shook it.

"Yeah . . . bye," he said, and he walked out of the crazy lady's office.

4 – *What am I here for?*

THE very next evening, Borst was in her apartment, just about to head over to the precinct and get night shift started when her phone buzzed. It was Chen, one of her lieutenants.

"Ma'am?" Chen started. Borst hated when her officers called her that. It made her feel old and out-of-touch.

"Don't call me ma'am, Chen. What's up?"

"We've cracked it, ma' . . . sir".

Borst smiled. "Just call me Captain. You've cracked the trafficking ring?!"

"Yes, Captain," answered Chen, and Borst thought she could hear her officer smiling back on the other end of the line. "We placed teams in rotations staking out our lead for 48-hours, and a couple of hours ago, he led us to a building where we're pretty sure the girls are being kept".

"That's fantastic work, Chen".

"I wanted to check in before we bust them".

Borst was about to give her go-ahead before pausing.

Finnie.

Yesterday's meeting with D'Alfonso made her think about the Finnie trial. The bastard got off because her officers busted him without a warrant.

"Chen, I want you to keep at least two officers on the target's location at all times. I wish I could give you the green-light, but I'll need you to file a request for a warrant. I met with D'Alfonso yesterday, and he made a fuss. But he's right, we can't just storm in without a warrant. We do that and we risk losing the conviction in court".

"I thought so, Captain. I've already filled out the forms. I can send them in as soon as someone relieves me at the scene".

"That's . . . very good thinking, Lieutenant," said Borst, impressed. "I'll send someone down. I'm just about to head to the 1-6 to get shift started.

Get the warrant, and I'll meet you on the scene to coordinate the bust. We may need support from Armed Ops. Let's get it done—we've got vulnerable women whose lives are at stake".

. . .

Owen spent the day after the bank incident trying to ignore Captain Dinah Borst's ridiculous proposal. He woke up late, which meant he felt groggy and had a bit of a headache, so he ended up staying home the whole day. That was probably for the best, the last thing he needed was more crazy shit like that dumb robbery.

But try as he might, Borst's ludicrous suggestion kept nagging at him.

She wanted to make him a hero? Life wasn't a comic-book. He wasn't some action movie protagonist, Bruce fucking Willis. He was just a sad, depressed man who wanted to kill himself but couldn't die. Why did the world hate him so much? What did he ever do wrong?

No, stop thinking that. That's not useful.

Borst was crazy, he reasoned. That was it. A guy like him, who couldn't get out of bed in the mornings, who had zero muscles, no training . . . there wasn't much he could do to help anybody anyway. Hell, he couldn't even help himself. He couldn't even *kill* himself, let alone help himself. So, yeah. The whole thing was dumb.

But then why . . . why did he feel guilty, turning her down like that?

Was he feeling some sort of societal obligation to . . . to try and work with Borst? To help people? That seemed to be the right thing to do, but Owen knew—he'd discussed it in therapy before—the *right thing* concept was arbitrary and very subjective. He shouldn't feel guilty about saying no to something that didn't make sense, about refusing to do something he didn't want to do. He was entitled to say no, he was allowed.

He didn't want to try and save people. He just wanted to stay home, lie in bed, and feel sorry for himself. That's what he was good for. Right?

He was sitting and brooding when his cell phone rang. Private number.

Shit.

He didn't want to answer his phone, but he answered it, because . . . well, he didn't know why. Maybe he just wanted the ringing to stop.

"Owen? It's Captain Borst. Dinah. We met yesterday?"

"Yeah, I remember".

"Good. Where are you?"

"I'm . . . at home?"

"Good, I got your address from your file, you're just a couple of blocks away. Listen, I need you to come down here. We have a bit of a situation. I need your help".

"What? I don't . . . what are you talking about?"

"You remember what we talked about yesterday? Delicate situations where I can't do much, but you might be able to? There are people in danger right now, real, innocent people, and I can't do anything about it. *You* can help us save them. So, man the fuck up, put your jacket on, and get down here, now!"

Owen sighed. He knew he didn't want to do this. He *shouldn't* be doing this. He should just say no. Stand up for himself, no need to feel guilty about it.

But . . .

But. There were real, innocent people in danger, she said.

He wasn't heartless. He had a conscience.

Owen was planning on staying in and feeling sorry for himself tonight. And he didn't like it when his plans changed. But what was he going to do, let somebody get hurt? He wasn't a hero, but he was human. Well, if you could call a person who couldn't die human. But anyway.

"Fine. Where are you?" he asked.

. . .

"Okay. We'll be in business in a bit," said Borst, hanging up.

She couldn't believe it, couldn't *fucking* believe it. The judge wouldn't sign off on the warrant.

How could they not approve the warrant? She thought. Her officers had tailed the suspect for two whole days. He finally walked into this building. Other shady characters had walked in and out. No, they couldn't conclusively identify any as potential collaborators or members of the trafficking ring, and sure, when her officers stepped into the building at a couple of points in time, they didn't perceive any suspicious activity, but clearly, there was enough evidence that something was going on.

She even called up D'Alfonso to see if he could try talking to the DA's office and get them to certify the warrant. He tried. He called. Nothing.

Fucking hell.

The whole thing was idiotic. How was she supposed to do her job when the legal system wouldn't let her and her officers do anything? Those girls were *in* there. They were in that building. And since no johns came in or out, this wasn't their final destination. They could be moved at any moment, and when they were, she'd lose them.

The DA's office advised her to keep surveillance. If she witnessed the girls being moved, or could identify any known elements with criminal records coming in or out of the building, then they could bust the ring. Yeah, sure, but who knew what was happening in there in the meantime?

And then she got the idea. All she needed was evidence, right? Evidence that the victims were in that building. Okay. Well, she could get one of her officers to gather the evidence, but that would amount to a search without a warrant.

But if it wasn't an *officer* who got the evidence . . . well. A citizen's tip-off was perfectly legal, wasn't it?

Sure, it was risky, but just a day ago she met someone who seemed not to mind danger. Someone who stood up to it.

So Borst had called Owen.

"Captain, are you sure this is a good idea?"

"I think it's the only way we get our evidence tonight, Chen".

"But won't the DA's office challenge it? Claim we got the evidence ourselves?"

"My guy will testify if he needs to. He's an honest one, don't worry," Borst said before admitting to herself that she actually didn't really know the guy. They had *one* conversation. Instinct told her he was a good one, that she could trust him, but . . . well, it was too late now.

"It just doesn't feel right," Chen said. And Borst understood. Hell, she agreed. It wasn't right. Involving a citizen in bringing down human traffickers wasn't something the police ought to be doing.

But their warrant getting refused wasn't right either.

It was a grey area. Like D'Alfonso said, Borst made her call, and she had to stand by it. End of story.

"Chen, you're a good cop. You've got good instincts. But we're doing this. I'll assume full responsibility. The important thing is to take down these fucking scumbags and save those girls. So . . . let's just focus on that for now".

Chen nodded. Borst crossed her arms and started pacing.

. . .

It took Owen just a few minutes to walk the few blocks over. Owen lived in a part of the city that wasn't too seedy, but in a few years, it probably would be. Or else it'll gentrify. For now, it was full of a multitude of ethnicities taking advantage of the small apartments and relatively affordable rent. Maybe there were some shady characters, and there sure were drugs, but it wasn't like you'd be afraid to walk the streets, even at night.

Not that Owen was ever afraid to walk the streets. Some nights he secretly hoped he'd get mugged, caught in the crossfire between some rival gangs shooting at each other, or something. But that sort of thing only happened in the movies, it didn't happen in real life. And even if it did, it couldn't kill him. Nothing could.

"So, what am I here for?" he asked.

Borst was standing across the street from an apartment building with two other cops. At least, Owen guessed they were cops. They weren't in uniform.

"We have a situation," Borst explained. She was looking up at the building. It was an old building, only about six stories tall, with an old cheap restaurant on the ground level next to an empty commercial unit. The captain looked agitated.

"Yeah, you said that. What *is* the situation?"

She took a deep breath. "Human trafficking".

"Okay . . . what about it?" he asked, since that phrase alone didn't actually explain anything.

Borst continued. "We've been chasing a human trafficking ring for months now. They're here. We know they're here. The problem is, the judge refused to grant our search warrant. He thinks we don't have enough evidence. So we can't go in".

"It's a fucking joke," said one of the cops behind her.

"Yeah, it fucking is. See, there's girls in there. Right now. They could be moved out anytime, and while they're in there, we don't know *what's* being done to them. But we can't go in because—"

"No warrant. Right," Owen interrupted. He was starting to get the idea.

"Yeah. I could send a plainclothes, but that would risk the conviction".

"Okay, so . . . what? You want me to go in?"

"I just need you to get in there, get a photo of something, some evidence, anything incriminating. You can send it to me as an anonymous tip, just text it. Then I can get the warrant tonight, and we get those girls out. If you don't, they could be gone by morning, and who knows when we'd catch up again. Look, I don't think I need to explain the cost of human trafficking, or what's going to happen to those girls. They'll—"

"It's okay, I understand. So, I just go in?"

"Just go in. Take the staircase to the basement, we're pretty sure that's where they'd be keeping them. If anyone stops you, just say you made a mistake and walk out. But if you manage it, find the girls, take a photo. A video or a sound recording . . . I just need something, anything".

"And what if . . . I assume these traffickers are dangerous. What if there's violence?"

"Yes, the gang could be violent. If that happens, you get out. At the first a hint of violence, the first hint of anything—you see a weapon, you see anything out of place, anything risky—you get out. Simple. That's it".

"Right, but I don't . . . look, I have no idea what I'm doing".

"Here," said one of the other cops. She came forward with a bullet-proof vest.

"I'm not taking that".

"You'll wear it!" Borst yelled. She was losing it. "Wear it, and go in there, and just . . . you're helping us break down a trafficking ring. You're saving the lives of innocent girls. So go already. Go!"

Before he knew what was going on, Borst's cop handed Owen the vest. Owen felt like an idiot. He took his jacket off, pulled the vest on, and zipped his jacket over it so it didn't show. *What the hell.*

"Borst, I—"

"It's just in case. I don't expect you to need it. Just . . . there's no protocol here, all right? Just trust me. Get going," commanded Borst.

So he went.

. . .

The lobby was dark, and it took him a few seconds to find the light switch. The stairs to the basement were around the back, and it took a while to find those, too. Everything felt and looked creepy as fuck.

What am I doing here? he asked himself, not for the last time that night.

He made it downstairs and found himself in an empty hallway. He held his breath, trying to listen. He thought he heard male voices coming from the door directly across from the staircase, while softer voices came from the far end of the hall, so he picked a door at random from that direction and tried it. The door was unlocked, and he walked through.

What he saw was pretty awful. Given his long-standing bout with depression, he was emotionally numb and desensitized, but even so, there was a knot in his stomach when he saw those poor, skinny, all-too-young women—girls really—chained up, treated worse than animals.

He knew he was only supposed to take a photo and run back upstairs, but . . .

"Help," croaked one of them. "Please".

Then they all started to speak, begging, pleading.

All that noise. Too much noise.

The door behind him opened.

"What the fuck—!" came a shout, then something hard hit him on the back of the head.

Owen fell down. He remained conscious, but his vision went blurry for a moment.

"Who are you? You a cop?"

"No, I'm . . . it's just . . . a mistake," he mumbled, trying to recall Borst's instructions. What was he supposed to say?

His vision refocused. There were two men standing over him, arguing. One was remarkably large, while the other was shorter and looked about as young as the girls. Both held guns.

"We gotta dispose of him, man. He saw," said the younger man.

"Why the fuck did you leave the door unlocked?"

"Like that matters now? Shoot him. He's getting up".

Owen *was* getting up. "Look, you can shoot me all you want. Just . . . you have to let the girls go".

The two traffickers laughed. "Fuck off! Let them go? Are you a fucking idiot?" asked the larger of the two men. "You know how much they're worth?"

"Dude, just *shoot* him, man".

Then Owen felt himself get shot three times. That made five bullets in less than 48 hours. The impact knocked him back down, but this time he got right back up.

"What the—"

"Fucking hell!"

The two men stood there, mouths agape. The girls were all shrieking now.

Owen was surprised there wasn't much pain. Then he remembered the vest.

"Look, can we . . . can we just talk or something? I don't—"

The men weren't interested in listening to him. "He's wearing a vest, man. I told you, don't aim for the chest," said the young-looking man.

And then Owen was shot in the head.

Once again, he was knocked to the floor before getting back up. He may have blacked out for a second, but he couldn't be sure. His vision was blurred again, this time by his own blood. "Fuck, that hurt. Ow, my head".

"Okay, dude, this is fucked up," said the big man.

"I'm gonna go get A.J.," said the young one, running out of the room.

"I've had enough," said Owen, wiping blood from his eyes.

"How are you still talking?" asked the big man. Finally, someone was conversing with him. "I just shot you in the fucking head".

"Yeah, well, I don't know. I can't die. Anyway, look, unlock these girls, let them go".

"I can't do that, man".

"You have the key?"

"Yeah, but—" said the trafficker, confused.

"Give it to me".

"I . . . no! I'm not doing that," he replied, and shot Owen yet again, to much the same effect. "What the fuck?!"

"Give me the key or I'll kill you," said Owen, trying to sound menacing.

"What?"

"Well, you keep shooting me and I'm not dying. So . . . I can *kill* you. It's . . . magic, let's say. Sure, magic. Now give me the key, unlock these girls, or I'll kill you".

He was improvising. Badly. But it was worth a shot, Owen figured.

Instead, the man dropped his gun like some cursed object and ran off.

Owen sighed. "Stand back," he told the girls, unsure whether they spoke much English, but they seemed to understand. Or at the very least, they instinctively backed away from the man who's been shot multiple times in front of them, was now covered in blood, but was somehow still alive. He tried to pull at the chain, then at the bar connected to the wall. Neither budged, not even a little. So instead, Owen picked up the dropped gun and shot at the chain's connection to the wall behind them, figuring the impact would break it off, releasing the girls.

It was the first time he had ever shot a gun. The recoil was insane. He was knocked down again. He was sick of having to get up off the floor. But, to his credit, the chain did break. The trafficked girls were free now, and without waiting for him, ran out the door.

And then more gunshots rang out.

Without thinking, Owen stepped out into the hallway. At least two girls were on the floor, but several were making their way upstairs. A large group of men stood at the other end of the hall and were now shooting freely at Owen.

He lost count of the number of bullets in 48 hours.

It finally stopped. He got up.

"Told you! It's some sort of dark magic!"

"Who . . . what the hell *are* you?"

Owen coughed. "I'm . . . magic. I don't know. You . . . stop trafficking women, stop being criminals or . . . I'll kill you". He could tell he didn't sound very convincing. "I'm gonna go now," he added, and walked upstairs. No one seemed to want to try and stop him.

He emerged from the building just as the cops came swarming in. There were ambulances and other emergency vehicles outside. Lots of flashing lights.

He saw girls in blankets, being treated. Armed cops in vests with their guns out, storming the building. There was too much noise, too many people, and his head was so foggy . . . so heavy . . . he felt himself fall down . . .

. . .

Owen was waiting down the street, a block away. He should have gone home. He had every right to go home. He was in pain, and it was late and freezing out. He'd been shot more times than he could count, and his shirt and jacket were practically in tatters. The medic said he was perfectly fine, but he didn't feel fine, he felt sick. Well, *mentally* he felt sick. Physically, sure, he was fine. Still. He should have been on his way home.

But he wasn't. He was waiting.

Finally, she came over.

"Hey. Let's take a walk," she said. And so they started walking down the street. Anything to get away from that building.

They walked in silence for a bit. Borst took something out of her jacket. It was dark and half-hidden behind her arm, so Owen couldn't tell exactly what it was until a streetlight happened to shine on it. It was a metallic flask, and she took a long swig out of it. She coughed. Then she spoke.

"They're all alive. Two were shot, but . . . well, nothing serious. And they're all free now".

Owen let this sink in.

"They're safe. And it's all thanks to you".

"*Me*? I almost got them all killed".

"Yeah. You could have. But—look, that's my bad. It's on me".

"On you? If I weren't—"

"If you weren't involved, those girls would be gone. Forced to . . . look, you saw. You know what would have happened".

Owen stopped walking. "You know, I still don't get why you couldn't have just gone in there right away".

"I . . . I didn't think it would go down that way. I was trying to do things by the book, legally. We just had a child murderer's conviction get turned because the warrant was late, so I was trying to do this one right, but I never realized . . . look, it was a mistake. I admit it. I completely misjudged the situation".

"You did. They could have been killed. This could've . . . I shouldn't have been involved".

Borst started walking again. Owen followed. "Look, maybe you're right," she admitted, talking slowly, quietly. "Maybe you shouldn't have. But you were. You saved innocent lives. You really did".

"You're gonna start with that hero crap again?"

"You *did* do a heroic thing. Don't—"

"No, *you* don't. When I was down there, I didn't know what I was doing. Those girls were *this* close to dying, because of me. Two of them got shot. I know you thought I could just sneak in, get a photo, and go back up, but I couldn't do that, because as soon as I saw them . . . Anyone else would have died. I got shot I don't know how many times. I'm not trained for this. I'm not a cop. I'm not a hero. I'm just . . . just a guy who's got major depressive disorder, who you're using for hell knows what. I don't know what I'm doing. I have to . . . I can't do this".

"Owen, listen—"

"No, you listen. I can't do this. I'm not a hero. I just want to die. I don't know what you want, I don't know what you're playing at, but it's not my game. I don't want any part of this".

"You don't want to save lives? To do the right thing? You've already done more than you know, you're *already* a hero. You could—"

"Maybe I could, but I won't. You know what? The truth is, no, I don't really want to save lives. That's *your* job. You picked it. I didn't. I just want to die. That's all I want and all I've ever wanted for a long time, and I can't, I can't get it, I *can't*, I never die. I don't know why, but—"

At this point, Owen started crying. He wasn't even sure why, it was involuntary.

Borst took a long breath. "You almost died tonight. And I mean, I never really thought . . . I never expected it to get that bad. And your whole *can't die* thing, I didn't actually believe it, not really. I thought you could get in and out and no one would get hurt. But look at you, you got as close to dying as you ever did. You were shot multiple times. I never meant for that to happen and I'm *so* fucking sorry that it did—look at me, look at my hand,

I'm shaking—thanks to me, a man, a good, innocent man, got shot multiple times tonight. And that's my fault, and I'm going to have to live with it. But look, you were right, you *didn't* die. And you could have, right? You got into a situation that logically should have resulted in you dying. So, you got exactly what you wanted. And you saved lives doing it. Listen, I know it's hard, I've been in the field. When it gets violent, it—"

"You don't—"

"*Listen.* Please, just . . . You weren't ready for this. I know. I get it. You're right, you shouldn't have been there. You were completely unprepared. But we can prepare you, next time. I'll personally enroll you at the police academy, or if you don't want that I'll refer you to the specific courses or private classes that'll help you get ready to do what we're trying to do here. Emotionally, physically, in whatever way. I have some ideas, I know people. We'll work on it. I promise. We can make a difference, a huge, huge, *huge* difference. We've already made some of it. You . . . you have so much in you, so much to . . ."

They both quieted down again. The Captain pulled her flask out and took another swig.

"For what it's worth, I *am* sorry". She looked at him now, but it was still so dark out she could barely make out his face, which was still stained with blood and tears. "I really am. You shouldn't have been there and . . . and it was entirely my mistake, my fault. I know, and I'm sorry. Okay?"

"I . . . listen, Dinah, Captain Borst, I accept your apology. I understand. And this doesn't have anything to do with you. It's me. This thing . . . this isn't me. I'm not a cop, I'm not . . . I'm sorry too, I'm sorry I have to mess up your plan or whatever it is, but . . . I can't. I can't do this".

"But . . . doesn't it feel good? Even a little? Knowing you saved—"

"Sure," Owen interrupted again. "It's great. But that's the thing with depression. It takes away the good. I don't feel good, I can't. I'm not even sure I want to feel good. I don't *want* to be a hero. I want to die. That's it. Don't you get that? And anything that gets in the way, anything that makes me feel good . . . the depression makes me want to throw it away. Because it doesn't fit. It just doesn't fit. I don't deserve it. I don't deserve good. I just . . . my existence, it doesn't get to amount to anything more than fucking misery".

"That sounds horrible".

"Yeah. It is horrible. It's my life, okay?"

"But don't you . . . can't you change it? Don't you *want* to change it, get better? I don't believe you don't deserve good. That's bullshit, Owen. Get some therapy, or . . . look, here's something that's positive, a good thing you can do, and maybe you can take that, focus on that, maybe it'll make you better, make your life feel like it means something—"

"Sure. But I don't want it. And I can't. It's not me".

"But—"

"It's not me," said Owen with a determined finality.

Borst was silent for a minute. She didn't know what to say. How do you argue with a mental illness? She wasn't a psychiatrist. She wasn't equipped for this, just as Owen wasn't equipped for police work. She realized she felt . . . disappointed.

"So you're . . . you've decided? That's it?"

Owen took a long pause before he answered. "Yeah. Look, tonight, I tried. But I can't. I'm sorry".

"Okay. Well . . . thanks for being honest. I'm really sorry you feel this way, and I think . . . I mean, forget this stuff, the police stuff, I'm talking beyond that now. I think you need help. Proper help, because you're clearly not well, and . . . I think you could be. You deserve to be. You're a good guy, Owen. Please, try to get help. And again, I'm sorry for how things went down tonight. You have my number in case you ever change your mind about helping people".

"Yeah. But, honestly . . . I don't think I'm ever going to call it".

"I understand. Well, can I get you a ride home with someone? I've got to head back to the scene".

"Don't worry about it, my place is just a few blocks that way".

"Right. Good. Okay, well, uh . . . yeah".

Owen started walking away.

"You know what," Borst called after him, and he turned around. She walked up and hugged him.

It was . . . he hadn't been hugged, *really* hugged, in so long. It was . . . nice. Everything else that night was so wrong on so many levels, but the hug . . . the hug was nice.

"Take care, okay? Stop . . . I know trying to kill yourself is your thing, but I like it better when you're alive. So . . . yeah. Think about it, about getting help. Please".

There may have been tears in her eyes as she said it.

Dinah turned around and started walking away. Owen watched her go, and then he went home.

He honestly wasn't even sure what he was feeling at that point. It was all very confusing. Plus, he was still in pain. Damn, what a fucked-up night.

. . .

She walked back to the scene. Her officers were still there, supervising the arrests. Chen was there, and Borst walked towards her.

"We've booked everybody. The girls are getting processed, and I have people going door-to-door for testimonies from the residents".

"That's good work, Chen".

"Look, Captain, we got them. *All* of them. No casualties. It's . . . kind of a miracle. But . . . I'm . . ."

"You're worried it won't hold up in court". Borst let out yet another sigh. "Chen, you're a good cop. You're also smart. What do you think is going to happen?"

"I think the perps are going to testify about that guy, the one you called. They'll claim he got in, tried to save the girls. But I've already heard some crazy, conflicting stories. Apparently, he was shot in the head, something about dark magic . . . it won't hold up in court. Besides, he's not a cop. No one knows who he is. We'll have to try and locate him, but . . ."

"But who knows if we can locate some random individual who slipped out during the chaos and gunfire," Borst said, completing Chen's sentence.

"Exactly. As far as testimony goes, he's just some guy who walked in, and shots got fired. Once we heard gunshots, we *had* to go in. So, I think we're covered. We'll get challenged, but I don't think we did anything illegal. I think you did the right thing".

Borst agreed with Chen's analysis of the legal situation. But in terms of going the *right* thing . . . "Yeah, well. Now I'm not so sure".

"How *was* that guy? Is he okay? Medics said—"

"Let's not talk about that guy, Chen".

"Is he a friend of yours?"

"Chen".

"Sorry," said Chen. She looked embarrassed for a moment. She *was* a good cop, though. Without her, and without Owen, tonight wouldn't have happened. They wouldn't have saved any of those girls.

"Chen, how long have you been a lieutenant?"

"Three, four years, I think. Maybe more".

"Have you thought about taking the Sergeant's exam? Jordan-Dee's retiring," said Borst. It was a spur-of-the-moment idea. But Chen was . . . yeah. It made sense. It made a hell of a lot more sense than bringing some random outsider into the 1-6.

"Uhm, I . . . kind of thought it's too early for me, Captain".

"Well, if you want to take it, I think you should. You're a good officer, Chen. You saved lives tonight, thanks to basic, good police work. And I need . . . I could use more good cops on my side, Chen. Because it's . . . it's a difficult job these days, being on the force".

"I—" Chen started, but she didn't seem to know what to say.

Borst put a hand on her shoulder. "Think about it. The Sergeant's exam. I would fully back up your application if you choose to make it. But it's your call. Right, well, I'm headed back to the 1-6. Scene's yours".

"Yes, Captain," said Chen.

Borst stifled a yawn and walked to her car, taking another discreet swig from her flask. It was the middle of the night, but her shift wasn't even close to being over. And with such a big operation, she'd have a mountain of paperwork to climb. The adrenalin was wearing off, and despite the fact that lives were saved and no one got hurt, Borst wasn't feeling the usual high of a successful bust.

She felt . . .

Ugh. Didn't matter. One last swig, then off to the precinct.

5 – *Don't jump*

"... AND I'm not kidding, we just walked out of the bar, and he grabbed my waist and said, 'We're going back to my place, babe'. He actually called me *babe*. So I grabbed his hand and twisted it behind his back, basic hold. He didn't know what was happening. I told him, I swear, I said, 'look, I'm a police captain. You touching me without my consent is assault. *Sexual* assault by the insinuation. So get the hell out of here before I arrest you, or better yet, break your arm and *then* arrest you'. He managed to call me a crazy bitch before running away".

Borst took a swig from her flask before continuing.

"All that, and he didn't even pay for my drinks. So, that was my night off. What a waste. I swear, men in this city . . . other than you, dad, they're all . . .

"Well, there is that Owen guy. Honestly, I think he's the only guy I've spoken to recently who could see me as a person. On the force, my squad puts me on a pedestal. And outside it, people are usually intimidated or angry that I have a badge. But he wasn't, he talked to me at my level. Hell, he even stood up to me. Don't get me wrong, I am disappointed he wasn't inclined to help me clean up this city. And I mean, obviously he's dealing with very serious mental health issues, I can see that. But I kinda . . . I don't know. There's something about him. It's not even about *that*, it's just . . . we could have done good together. And I clearly have no normal guys in my life outside of work".

Borst half-sighed, half-chuckled.

"At least work's going well. Chen's taking the exam. I'm glad, I think she'll be a great sergeant. And . . . oh, crap. Is that the time? I was going to stop by the store on my way in. I guess I can go at lunch, stretch my legs. Anyway, Dad, I better get going. I miss you".

Borst stretched, breathed in deep, replaced the flask in her inner jacket pocket, and left the cemetery feeling lighter.

. . .

It was a few weeks later. The weeks that went by weren't special or interesting by any means. They were boring, numbing, sad. But Owen didn't try to kill himself during that time. That wasn't unusual, sometimes whole months went by with no incident, and other times there'd be two attempts in a single week. It varied. He just went on, going through his usual routine of writing and staring at walls. At one point, he even went back to the bank to reactivate his debit card.

From time to time, Owen would think of Borst and her grand plan and all that. Being a hero. Whatever. Sometimes he'd feel guilty about turning her down. He'd think about calling her up to say, "You know what, maybe". But then he'd remember how he felt while going in after those girls, how they could have been hurt or worse just because of him. Well, not *because* of him, their captors were really at fault, but anyway . . . ugh. Fuck. The whole thing was confusing and upsetting, and whenever it popped into his mind, which was far more frequently than he'd have wanted, Owen got anxious and frustrated, and it'd take him hours to calm down.

As February became March, the weather got slightly warmer. Owen bought himself a new jacket because the old one was full of bullet holes, and he would still take walks around the neighbourhood, just because. What else was he going to do? Walks helped him clear his head when it was muddled by thoughts of Borst and what had happened there.

It was on one of those walks that he saw the girl. Just by chance, he was out on the street and happened to look up, maybe something caught his eye, or maybe he heard something, but he looked up, and there she was. Standing on the edge of a building. And somehow, he knew.

She was going to jump.

Owen sighed, and without consciously making the decision, he went into the building, fortunately finding the door unlocked, and started climbing the stairs up to the roof.

He didn't know the girl. He'd never seen her before. She was young and small, and she stood on the rooftop's ledge.

She heard Owen, or she heard *something* at least, and turned around. "Hey! Don't. Stay away!"

Owen walked steadily towards her. He didn't know if it was the right thing to do. He didn't know anything. But he moved forward.

"Stay away. I mean it. Stop it, or I'll—I'll jump!"

"Don't jump," he said. Not in a commanding tone, it was more of a polite request, really.

"Leave me alone. Go away. Don't come near me," she said, talking very fast.

But Owen did come near her. He walked right up to the edge, just next to her, and then he sat down, legs dangling. The girl was shaking, he noticed. "Do you want to sit with me?" he asked.

"No. I want you to go away. I'm . . . I'm going to jump. Just go away. Let me—"

"Okay. But just sit for a bit".

The girl hesitated a moment, then two. Owen wouldn't go away. He also didn't say anything else. He just sat there. Eventually, she realized she had little choice, and sat down next to him.

"Why did you come up here?" she asked miserably. She started to cry. Not full-on weeping, just tearing up.

"I don't know. I saw you. I guess I wanted to talk".

"Talk about what? Tell me not to kill myself? You don't even *know* me".

"Well, maybe I know more than you think".

"You don't know anything. Nobody does. You can't . . . you think you'll talk me out of it? I'm going to jump. I will. So—so you might as well just go and leave me alone. You can't change my mind, okay? Just go away".

"I'm not going to try and talk you out of it. I think . . . honestly, I believe it's your choice, everyone should have the right to kill themselves if that's what they want".

The girl wasn't expecting that. "You . . . really?"

Owen's words surprised even himself. "Yeah. I mean, I kind of *have* to believe that. I'd be a pretty big fucking hypocrite if I didn't. Look, it's your life. You should be allowed to do what you want with it. And if that's your choice, I think you should be allowed to end it. It's your right. Did you know suicide is illegal? Nobody ever gets arrested for it, but . . . well, in my opinion, that's just fucked up".

The girl didn't know what to think.

"So, what's your name?"

". . . Tess".

"Okay. I'm Owen".

That was awkward.

"Listen, you're right. I don't know who you are, or your circumstances, and I don't really understand you. But . . . I've been where you are. Literally. I know what it's like. I've jumped off a building before".

"Really? And you . . . you survived?"

"Yeah. See, that's what they don't tell you. When you try to kill yourself . . . I mean, I know what it takes. It's a huge thing. To get to that point, when you can bring yourself to do it . . . it's hard. It's the toughest journey a person can go through. The toughest, the darkest—yeah".

Tess was nodding.

"And when you do bring yourself to do it, sometimes you don't die. You just . . . don't. But even if it doesn't work out, a part of you still dies. And then you're left with . . . I don't know what. An empty shell? That's a cliché. So, I guess what I'm trying to say is, you have to be *sure*. You have to be absolutely certain because there's no going back".

"I know. I know what I'm doing. I didn't just come up here randomly. I've been planning this for weeks. I want to die, I just . . . I want the pain to stop, I want it to be over," Tess said, still half-crying.

"Okay. I believe you".

"Did you . . . did you really try to kill yourself?"

"Yeah".

"And did you . . . try again afterwards? After you—"

"Yes".

"But then, maybe you didn't really want to die. Maybe—"

"I promise you, I did. At the time, I truly and absolutely and completely and entirely intended to die".

Tess looked at him. "But, then . . . why aren't you dead?"

Owen almost smiled. "I don't know. I wish I knew. I have . . . I have this friend, who seems to think that . . . maybe I have a sort of purpose in life. At least, I think that's what she thinks. She says I have something in me, and . . . I don't know. I guess maybe she's right. I honestly don't know".

"Oh".

"It's like . . . I've been thinking about it recently, I guess some people would argue that God put me here for a reason, or if you're an atheist maybe it's fate, or whatever random forces hold the world together. You know what I mean?"

They were both looking out to the city's horizon. "I guess, but . . . that's bullshit", said Tess.

"Oh, yeah, I agree. It's total bullshit. But I guess lately I've been thinking . . . well, okay, the reason I wanted to die was because I was unhappy. I've got major depressive disorder. I haven't been happy a day in my life, not really. And I started to realize, slowly, that I'll probably *never* be happy. Ever. And when I got to that point . . . well, killing myself seemed like the only logical thing I could do. I mean, what's the point in living if you already know you're never going to be happy?"

Tess looked at him again. "I . . . feel that way too. Like I'll never be happy. Yeah. So that's why— might as well end it. It's just . . . it's hard. Like, *living* is hard, I mean".

"I get that. Maybe you also have a depressive disorder. Or maybe it's a different type of thing. You can go see a psychiatrist. They'll diagnose you. They can give you pills, or therapy. There's lots of different types of stuff they can try to do to help you get better. Or at least get to the point where you're a bit more okay".

"Did you try that?"

"Yeah".

"And . . . did it help?"

"Not really, no. Although . . . I guess I'm not trying to kill myself twenty-four-seven. Some days I guess I'm okay. I mean, some days are better and some days are worse. But I guess that's how it is for everybody. It's life".

"Yeah".

"Only difference is, when people like us are better, we still hate ourselves and feel miserable, and when we're worse, we're jumping off buildings. Right?"

For a split-second, he thought Tess would smile. She didn't. "But then . . . all you're telling me is that there *is* no point? There's no hope? I should just jump, and that's it?"

Owen looked Tess in the eye. Her eyes were sad, very sad. Almost as sad as his. "Not at all. I'm not here to tell you what to do. And there might be hope, I don't know. Those pills and therapy and group sessions, they could work for you. They *do* work for some people, I've seen it. Just . . . not everybody. And besides, the most important thing is—what I've realized lately is that maybe being unhappy for the rest of your life doesn't mean you have to kill yourself".

"So then . . . what?"

"Well, okay," Owen started explaining, struggling to find the words. "Say you're doomed to be unhappy. You'll never be even a little bit happy for a single day in your life. Never-ever. Even though, I guess we can't really know that for sure, right? But even if you really believe that you'll never be happy, you can still . . . it's like, there are still things you can do with your life. I mean, say you can use your life to help other people. Save lives, or just make someone else happy. Even if it's just one other person. Then . . . you know, even if it does hurt and it sucks and you live your life being miserable and depressed and you think about killing yourself every single day, maybe that's okay. Because you're still . . . you're doing something worth doing. Do you get what I'm saying at all?"

Tess thought about it for a minute. "So basically, you're talking about sacrificing your life to make other people happy? Suffering for the greater good? So, like a Jesus kind of thing?"

This time Owen did smile for a second. And when Tess saw that, she smiled a little too. "Yeah, exactly. I mean, look, we're about to sacrifice our lives anyway, right? Throw it all away, just jump. We're not going to be happy whether we live or die. Well, I mean, hey, you *could* still get happy, I don't know. No one ever knows for sure, like I said. But yeah, if it's a choice between just dying or living, maybe not a happy life but a meaningful one . . . well, I don't know, but it's a choice. Right? It's another option.

"And the thing about suicide," he added, "is that if it works, it's the *last* thing that ever does, right? So maybe try all the other options first. I don't know. I mean, it makes sense rationally, but I know it might not feel like it. I've been there".

Tess was looking down now, and suddenly she started weeping, breaking down, her whole body convulsing. Owen wasn't great at the human contact stuff, but he put a hand on her shoulder awkwardly. He was trying to comfort her, but also make sure she didn't just fall off the edge from the shaking.

It felt like she was crying forever. Then the sirens blared, and before a moment passed by, police cars and ambulances and a fire truck were screeching to a stop in front of the building, and someone started saying something incomprehensible through a megaphone.

Tess stood up again, still on the edge of the building. She wiped tears from her eyes.

"Fuck. Shit. I—I—"

"Are you gonna jump?" Owen asked. "I'm not going to stop you".

Tess looked him in the eye again. "Listen, thanks for . . . I know what you were trying to say earlier. And that may be okay for you, I don't know. But I was going to die today. And I need to—I *need* to do this. I have to. I don't have a choice. So . . . yeah. I'm sorry, I—"

Owen got to his feet too. "That's okay. If you jump, I jump," he said, taking hold of her hand.

"What? No—" Tess said, trying to pull her hand free, shaking her head violently, tears flying off her cheek. "Let me go".

"No. I'm not stopping you. You can jump. But if you jump, I jump too. We're both in the same place, same boat. We both want to die. Don't we?"

"I . . . let me go!" Tess yelled, trying to free her hand. Owen didn't pull her away from the ledge, but he didn't let go either. "They're coming up here! Let me go, please, I have to jump".

"Then jump. And I'm right with you".

"No! I can't . . . I can't jump if you jump".

"I want to die too, I'm telling you. You won't let me die?"

"N-no . . . I can't . . ."

"Yeah, well, see, neither can I".

Tess's body went limp. "Fuck you," she whispered. She got off the ledge, back to the surface of the roof, then fell to her knees and completely let herself go, weeping uncontrollably.

Owen got off the ledge too. He walked off the roof and down the stairs, just as the cops started to come up.

. . .

Borst was on a break, taking a stroll, taking in the streets of the 1-6. And looking for a corner store where she could get some dried apricots and maybe some vodka. She just finished the bottle she kept hidden in her desk drawer, and she didn't want to go without any in case she needed a drink. Sure, she had her flask, but it wasn't the same thing.

The brisk air was doing her good, especially after a few hours of sitting in her small, windowless office. Things were okay lately. Her squad was back on day shift, and with the days getting warmer, it wasn't so bad to be out in the sun in the middle of the day. D'Alfonso stopped getting on her case, probably because the big trafficking bust earned her some clout. Chen got most of the credit, and Borst was happy—it *was* Chen's operation in the first place, and she deserved the recognition. Borst had finally managed to convince her to register for the Sergeant's exam.

Like she told her dad's gravestone earlier that day, the whole Owen thing was a waste, and she was disappointed, but she tried not to think about it too much. Honestly, maybe it was a pipe dream anyway. It wasn't right, she was putting an untrained man at risk, and that, in turn, jeopardized others. Maybe D'Alfonso had a point about her being a bit too gung-ho about working in the line of duty.

Still. Crime was crime. Her dad knew that. He served, protected, saved lives. That's all Borst wanted to do, too. And it felt like it was getting harder every day because of politics, because of cops—racist or otherwise—abusing their power. There was inherent power, authority, in police work. And lately, there was more and more mistrust, abuse, and corruption. If only she had a way to bypass that, to do good without being bound by—

There were sirens ahead. Was she walking onto an active scene? Captain Borst cleared her mind and ran towards the flashing lights.

. . .

Owen waited in the hallway as the cops ran up, then walked back down casually. He was trying to pretend to be a random resident walking out. He didn't want to be subjected to a whole series of questionings like after the bank incident.

But of course, *of course*, as soon as he exited the building and started walking away, he heard his name being called.

"Owen!" she shouted. Of course she was there. It didn't make sense for a police captain to be on the scene of something as low-profile as a suicide attempt, and yet, there she was.

Captain Borst walked up to him. "Let's take a walk," she said, just like the last time. So they started walking.

"I saw what you did up there. Was lucky enough to stumble onto the scene just in time to recognize a stranger".

"Who called you? I didn't think—"

"Oh, no, it's not my scene. I just happened to be in the neighbourhood when—well. Fancy running into you being a hero again".

Owen didn't respond. He wasn't feeling up for this conversation.

"It's been a few weeks. How've you been?" she asked.

"I've been . . . you know. Same old".

"Still depressed and thinking of killing yourself?"

Dinah Borst was honest and to the point. Most people weren't. Most people were afraid of talking about suicide and mental health, and didn't know what to say, pussyfooting around the subject. Borst wasn't most people, and Owen appreciated that about her.

"Pretty much," he admitted.

"Well, I'm sorry to hear that. So, what made you go up there?"

"I don't know. I just saw that girl, and I went up. I didn't really think about it".

"Okay. Well, it looks to me like you saved another life".

Something snapped in him—the frustration of the last few weeks, the guilt. He found himself actually raising his voice a little. "Oh yeah, sure. I saved a life. Either that or I doomed a person to a lifetime of pain and misery. I *know* what she's going through. Maybe it looks to you like I did the right thing here, but I can tell you it's *not* that simple".

Borst looked at him. It was possibly the first time she's sensed any kind of genuine emotion in something he said, beyond hopelessness and resignation. "You're right, that's fair. It's not that simple. But still . . . you did it anyway".

"Yeah. I guess I did," he admitted.

"What *did* you do? Did you talk to her?"

"Yeah".

"What'd you say?"

"I said . . . I just told her about this idea I had lately".

"What's the idea?"

"It's just that . . . I've been thinking . . . well, *you* made me think of it. I mean, look—I've always lived under the assumption that I'm destined to be unhappy until I die. That's why I keep trying to kill myself. I want to stop being unhappy, being miserable. Just stop the pain. But now I'm thinking, maybe it's okay. Maybe I can be unhappy, depressed, and still have a life that's worth something. Maybe I could do something good with my life, something meaningful".

"I see, okay," Dinah smiled. "You mean . . . well, you told me you do some writing on the side, right? So, what, you're going to try and write some great, meaningful, inspiring story that'll touch people's hearts and then your life will have meaning even if you're depressed and unhappy?"

"Well . . . that wasn't really the idea".

"No. Because that's a *stupid* fucking idea," Dinah said. She took out her flask, and in the light of day, Owen could see it was one of those old-fashioned metallic ones, the type you never see anyone actually use. She made sure no one but Owen was watching, unscrewed the top, and took a gulp. The drink had a distinct and sharp odour.

"What are you drinking?"

Borst ignored the question. "So, from what you're telling me, you've been thinking about my offer some more".

Owen sighed. "Look . . . whatever you think I am, I'm *not* a hero. I mean, even with this girl . . . I took her hand, and I told her, 'If you jump, I jump'. And I'm thinking, I can't be sure . . . I don't know whether I said that because I really wanted to save her or whether I sort of just wanted us both to jump. Just jump and die. You know?"

"Yeah. Yeah, I get it. You're not sure. You're not sure whether you're a guy who just wants to die or whether you can spend your life trying to do the right thing. You're depressed, and you hate yourself, and you're completely incapable of admitting you might be a good person. I can see that much. But you know what? It doesn't matter what you say or think. You don't have to be sure. *I* am. *I* know. You're a good person. You are. You can argue about it all you want, you can argue about your intentions, whether you're doing good or trying to die, but the fact is, intentions don't matter. What matters are your actions. You've saved lives on multiple occasions now. You *are* a hero".

She took another swig and wiped her mouth with her sleeve.

"You're a fucking hero with a fucking superpower, and you can't die," she said, increasingly animated, waving her arm and pointing at him. "You're a superhero, and we're going to get you a cape and a dumbass superhero name. Immortal-man. And—"

"I was thinking Depresso, actually".

Dinah laughed, and Owen smiled a bit. "See? Okay. You're smiling. This is the first time I've seen you smile. Look, we're doing this. You and me. I'll get you . . . we'll work it out, let's meet on Monday. We'll talk it over, do it properly. I've been thinking up some ideas. We can find you a trainer—we'll do it privately—forget the police academy. I know just the person to help you out. And we'll get you checked out by some doctors who can tell us what's going on with your amazing ability to recover from deadly injuries, and then we'll put it all to use. We'll make sure you're trained, and equipped, and prepared. Get you ready to be a real hero who saves lives and does meaningful things, even if you're unhappy doing it. Okay? That sound good to you?"

The brief smile faded from his face, and for a few seconds that felt to Borst like hours, Owen didn't answer.

Then finally, he nodded. "Yeah, all right. Let's give it a shot".

"Yes!" Borst proclaimed, and then, smiling, she hugged him again. It was a brief hug, and the metal flask still in her hand was cold against his back, but still, it was nice. Hugs were nice.

"Okay. Perfect. Monday, right? Let's say 7:00 p.m., after day shift's over. I'll text you where to meet me. And you have my number, just in case. Yeah. You'll see, we'll do good, I promise".

"I hope so. But . . . well, if it doesn't work out—"

"If you don't like it, you walk away. At any point. Don't worry".

"Right. Okay, just as long as we're clear".

"Clear. I'm excited, Owen. I think we can . . . yeah. I've got ideas. Don't worry. We'll do it right this time around".

He nodded, looking unsure as to what to say.

"Okay. Monday. I better get back, I'm sure there's reports to write up. I am *so* glad . . . I was just walking down the street here. Serendipity. Trust me, it's the right thing".

Honestly, running into Owen really *was* serendipitous. She had just mentioned Owen to her dad's grave that morning, and now she was out on a random lunchtime walk. She never did expect to run into an active scene, let alone one where Owen was involved, but, lo and behold . . .

Borst was excited. She had lots of ideas on how to make it work. She knew exactly who to call, starting with Richardson, her old captain, who got promoted up to deputy chief. Sharon Richardson was now retired and, last Borst heard, occupying her time with offering private physical training sessions to wealthy clients. Richardson was an old champion of hers—she had fought for Borst's early promotions—and Borst knew her well. She was certain Richardson could be discreet and passionate about this project. Plus, she could physically and mentally train Owen to be ready to respond to emergencies and save lives, the way Borst was envisioning it. With any luck, they could also find a quiet doctor who might be willing to help evaluate Owen and figure out how he's able to . . . well, not die.

These were her rough plans, and she couldn't wait to set them in motion. Borst knew that with Owen by her side, she'd be able to step over the red tape, all those limitations of her position as a police captain, and get down to what she really wanted to do—what her father had done before her—good police work, serving and protecting the people. At the very least, maybe she could help Owen. She wanted to help him. Borst knew there was good inside this man, and he needed help to accept and let it out. Maybe she could offer that help.

Borst smiled and said, "Monday, then".

Owen nodded distractedly. He didn't answer for a minute. Finally, he asked, "Hey, Dinah . . . can I borrow your gun for a sec?"

"My gun?"

"Yeah".

Borst was confused. She knew she should have said no, but she was too excited, too distracted by the possibilities—she wasn't thinking straight. "Go ahead," she said, handing it over.

Owen grabbed her gun and inspected it. "Is the safety on?"

"Yeah, it's right there," Borst pointed out, mistaking his interest for enthusiasm. "I'm hoping that when we get you active, though, you wouldn't need a gun so much. I mean, you probably won't need it for protection, since you . . . well, you can't die. We'll figure it out".

"Right, yeah, no, I completely agree," Owen said, looking closely at the safety catch. "Okay, I see it. Thanks," Owen said, switching the safety off.

Then he put the gun to his temple and pulled the trigger.

Borst yelled, out of surprise more than anything. The loud *bang* of the shot was deafening. She did *not* expect the man to shoot himself when she handed him her gun. She was dumbfounded.

But Owen still stood there with her gun in his hand. The side of his head was bloodied, but other than that, he looked absolutely fine. He handed the gun back to Borst. "Sorry, just had to check," he said. "It's fine. I'll see you Monday".

Dinah couldn't believe what just happened. She took another swig from her flask and coughed. She suddenly realized this was going to be one hell of a journey—it wasn't going to be a smooth ride. She was dealing with a damaged human being, a depressed, possibly mentally unstable one at that. Sure, there were opportunities, but there would also be challenges, and potential costs.

Was she . . . what was she getting herself into?

At that moment, she wasn't sure if it felt right or wrong.

She looked up and stared into Owen's eyes. They were still the saddest eyes she'd ever seen.

Depresso II:
Rise of Unkillable

Anyone with half a heart would let me drown
Anyone with half a heart would pull me down
Anyone with half a heart would let me fall
Anyone with half a heart wouldn't care at all

— *Half a Heart*, S. Page & E. Robertson, 2006

1 – *The whole fucking thing collapsed*

"SO, what did the site supervisor say?" asked Neves. He'd taken his helmet off and was staring at the site, a factory near the docks.

On fire.

Fire Department Lieutenant Neves was just so damn tired of it all. It was this goddamn heatwave. Every day, something else in the city caught on fire—there was no respite. It's been that way the past three years, every damn summer, and nothing ever changed. You'd think City Hall would up the budget, learn from the shortcomings, but nope. Every summer they were short on personnel, short on equipment, and people died because fires were fires and heat was heat, and nothing ever got better. Neves wiped his sweaty brow. The factory was still on fire.

Mavrodin was walking towards him now, fighting his way through a crowd of onlookers. *Fucking idiots, they shouldn't be here*, Neves thought. He knew they'd have to move the crowds back, they were getting restless, swarming him to see if they could get any information. And of course, Mavrodin was taking his time, casually talking to some of these people, probably reassuring them.

Mavrodin was a good firefighter, and even better with people. He had a calming presence. The Lieutenant often sent him to deal with interviewing families, victims, or in this case, warehouse shift supervisors. Mavrodin spoke calmly, clearly, and he inevitably got the information out of them despite the nerve-wracking nature of the situation. Neves himself often got frustrated and would end up yelling. It was better to let Mav do it.

"Five personnel unaccounted for. They might be trapped in there, or they could've shuffled off in the confusion. Supervisor can't reach them by phone, though".

"So, they could be inside?"

"Could be".

"Well, shit".

"And we're not going in?"

"Can't. We don't have the equipment to deal with the chemicals that could be on-site. I radioed Central, but with the evening traffic, it'll take at least half an hour for them to drive it over here". Neves shook his head. He was angry, exasperated, helpless. "For now, the priority is to—"

"The fuck was that?" asked Mavrodin as a man ran past him *towards* the burning factory. He was there, and in a flash, he was gone.

"Go tackle him!" gestured Neves. Mav obeyed his command immediately. *What the hell was this idiot doing? Probably one of the floor workers who decided he needed to wipe the browser history off his laptop or something*, Neves reasoned. *Fucking idiot.*

The Lieutenant sighed, then assumed control. "Squad, let's go! Until the equipment gets in, we're on crowd control. We have to move these people back fifty feet. With me!"

. . .

Finally, he called.

Richardson picked up. She was waiting in her basement home-office, which she affectionately thought of as the Control Room.

"Finally! What happened?" she asked.

A raspy voice came through. "Got three out".

"That's fantastic".

"There might have been five," he started again, then paused to cough. "I heard some firefighter say there were five unaccounted for, but I could only find three of them. Then the whole fucking thing collapsed".

"I saw that. News picked up the story, they're broadcasting live. So you managed to get all three out to safety?"

"Yeah. Dragged them out one by one. They were heavy. I need to work on my upper body strength".

"You're doing fine, Owen. You got it done. You saved three people".

"Yeah".

"Anyone see you?"

"Couple of the firefighters. They didn't ask too many questions—they saw what I was doing. I passed the factory workers over to them, they picked them up and moved them off". Owen paused to cough again. "The firefighters hoisted them up properly. I had to literally drag them along the ground like sacks of potatoes, grabbing them by their feet. I'm too weak".

"Stop focusing on the negatives," Richardson said, shaking her head but also smiling.

There was a slight pause. "No word on the other two?" he asked. "There could have been two more in there".

"Nothing on the comms I'm tapped into. The fire squad hasn't even gone in yet".

"Seriously? Fuck".

"Union rules won't let them go in without the right equipment. There's danger of chemical contamination, explosions—"

"There already *was* an explosion. I got caught in it".

"Shit. Are you okay?"

"I'm fine. Going to be coughing soot for days, though".

"I can call Dr. Larner—"

"Don't, don't. It's fine. Look, I don't think there's anything more I can do here".

"Then you may as well come back in".

"It'll take about forty-five minutes".

"Call a cab".

"I did. Guy wouldn't let me in. I'm covered in explosion. I look like . . . I don't know. Anyway, it's fine. I'll just take the subway".

"Okay. Just a heads-up, we have a visitor".

"The Captain?"

"Yep".

Owen didn't react. He stayed on the line for another few seconds, then hung up.

Richardson smiled.

. . .

It took Owen about an hour to reach Richardson's place. Borst was already in the basement Control Room, beer in hand. She smiled as he walked in.

"You did good," she said, gesturing towards him.

"The other two—?"

"No other two," Richardson shook her head. "It's been confirmed on the comms. A couple of the workers just left the scene without telling anyone. You saved the only three trapped in that factory before it exploded. Zero casualties. The fire department has it under control now. You saved lives".

"Beer?" asked Borst.

"I need a shower," said Owen, walking off.

"I put out fresh clothes for you," said Richardson.

"Well, I need them. Thanks". He certainly did need them. His outfit was barely recognizable as clothes, half-torn and covered in soot and ash as it was.

The two women continued to converse while Owen showered. "He seems down," said Police Captain Dinah Borst.

"He was probably blaming himself for the two guys he couldn't find. He'll pick up now that he knows he saved everybody".

"Why *didn't* the fire force go in right away?"

"They didn't have the equipment to deal with the chemical stuff. Took the other squad forever to bring some over".

"Wow".

"And get this—the reason it took so long? The squad who had the equipment was stuck on another call up near Mount Pleasant. This heatwave is killing the city".

"They couldn't just drive the equipment over?" asked Borst.

"Not enough men or trucks, I'm guessing".

"Damn. So let me get this straight—blue-collared factory workers could have *died* while firefighters were busy saving some rich asshole's Mount Pleasant mansion?" she asked, thinking of the giant houses lining the city's famously affluent neighbourhood. "Capitalism at its best".

"You could say that," smiled Richardson. "Or, you could argue that the free-market system is the driving force of our economy, which allows us to have any capital for fire-fighting at all. Without capitalism, we'd *all* be dead".

"But how is it fair that people who are already rich are less likely to die in a fire? Fire should be the great leveller, but the fire departments around Mount

Pleasant are better equipped because they have money. It's the same with the police force".

"They pay higher taxes, Dinah".

"Oh please, some of them don't pay *any* taxes! The loopholes rich people exploit—"

"Okay, I'll give you that. But if we don't incentivize people to work and innovate, our economy would collapse".

Borst crossed her arms. "Are we seriously arguing about economics?"

"You started it, girl".

Borst rolled her eyes before changing the subject. "So . . . it seems to be working out well so far. With Owen, I mean".

"I'd say so," agreed the controller. Sharon Richardson was a retired deputy chief. Still in her early fifties, she lived off a respectable pension plus a comfortable after-tax cushion left to her by her late partner. She'd been looking for something to do when Borst contacted her about Owen.

"And you two get along".

"It's not so hard. He's a good guy. And he's getting better," Richardson started. "He's very hard on himself, but . . . look, he saved three more lives today. At the cost of a shirt and jeans".

Borst nodded.

"You just have to look the other way with some of his mental health issues. Sometimes he says things he doesn't mean".

"Well, that's the thing. I think he does mean them," said Borst. She knew exactly how deep Owen's depression ran after the time she lent him her gun, but that was months ago. He did seem better nowadays. She just couldn't tell exactly how much better he really was.

"Well, I'm no psychiatrist, but he seems better to me. Physically, too—I mean, when we first started out, he was so shrimpy. He looks more like a man now, don't you think?"

"I haven't noticed," Borst evaded, and Richardson smirked. If she was honest, Borst did notice, even though she tried not to. She reached for another beer before her face turned red.

"You sure you should be having another, Dinah?" asked her old mentor. "You're driving".

Borst twisted off the bottle cap in response. "And this thing with Owen, it's working for you, too?" she asked.

Richardson smiled. "Absolutely. I don't know where you found him, but if it weren't for being Owen's controller, or operator, or whatever we're calling it, I'd be . . . I don't know, offering personal training sessions to rich assholes, redecorating this ridiculous house, learning to play goddamn bridge, day-drinking . . . just generally feeling sorry for myself. You know. Retirement's boring. This is better".

Borst nodded.

"Honestly, it's not easy, but it's the best thing that could've happened. I feel like myself again. I'm glad you came to me, Dinah. This work, it keeps me . . . *me*. Owen and I, we're making a difference, we're doing good work. I'm happy".

"I'm really glad to hear that. Do you—do you think he's also happy?" asked the Captain, but before Richardson could answer, Owen walked back into the room, having showered and changed into a fresh outfit. There was still a bit of ashy gray soot in his black hair.

"Doesn't matter if I'm happy. So, those two other workers are fine? No casualties?"

"None. Tons of property damage, but the factory's insured, and I don't think we care about that," answered Richardson.

"We do not".

"What about the workers who lost their jobs?" asked Borst pointedly.

Richardson shook her head. "Well, they might get furloughed or laid off. Very sad. Not much we can do about that, though. I'd say, overall, a good afternoon. Good work. Right?"

"Yeah, maybe. I guess so," Owen nodded slowly.

"Why don't you get home?"

"I thought we're doing another workout tonight".

Richardson smiled at him. "I think, after today's operation, we'll take it easy".

"But I told you, I'm too weak, I need to—"

"Owen, stop. Remember what we talked about? Celebrate small wins. You need to work on that. Go get yourself a nice dinner. Watch a movie. Relax. Come back tomorrow. We'll train and see if there's anyone else you can save".

He sighed. "Okay".

"I'll drive you home," Borst volunteered, taking her car keys out of her pocket and twirling them around her finger.

"You don't have to, it's okay, I'll—"

"Come on," she sighed. Everything was always an argument with this guy. "It's not like I get down here too often. We could catch up. It's just a ride, don't be difficult".

"Okay, sure. Thanks".

"Thanks for the beer, Chief," waved Borst.

"Visit again soon now," said Richardson. "I'll see you tomorrow, Owen".

Owen nodded and followed the Captain upstairs.

. . .

"So, what's wrong?" asked Borst, turning on the ignition.

"Nothing. Lungs are a bit clogged up, but they'll probably clear by tomorrow".

"That's not what I meant. Come on. I know you better than that".

"Dinah—"

"You're unhappy. Something happened out there today. Tell me".

Owen sighed. But then, to her surprise, instead of arguing or deflecting, he just told her.

"After I dragged those three guys out of the building, I went back in. I thought there could be more people inside . . . then the whole place fucking exploded. It was crazy. I haven't been in an explosion before, it's just fire and burning, and . . . I think I passed out for a bit. Then, when I woke up, I realized I got . . . my leg got trapped under some debris. There was just heat and smoke—I couldn't see anything, I couldn't breathe, I couldn't . . . I thought I was gonna die".

Shit, thought Borst, but she didn't say anything. Owen continued after a moment.

"I thought . . . yeah. Anyway, a couple of minutes passed, and my eyes cleared. I could see again, and I . . . I wasn't dead. Obviously. Took me a while to un-trap myself, get my leg free, let it recover, and then get out of the collapsed building. Yeah. So, that's what happened".

"How did you feel? It's been a while since you've . . . you know. Been close to death".

"Since I tried to kill myself, you mean? Yeah. It has been a while, and I've been better, *much* better. I was starting to think maybe I didn't want to try killing myself anymore. Maybe this new life, where I save people, maybe I was overcoming my depression. Maybe I didn't want to die so badly".

"And?"

"That's the thing . . . When I thought I was dying, in the burning building, I felt . . . relief. I felt, uh—I guess it made me realize I still do want to die. Nothing's really changed".

Shit, she thought once more. "But . . . well, I mean, you said you still want to help people even if you're unhappy. So—"

"Nothing's changed," Owen interrupted. "I'll still try to save people. Everything stays the same. I was just . . . I guess I was hoping things might improve. You know, that doing good would help my mental health. I guess it hasn't. So, now I know. And that's okay. I'm okay".

"But *are* you? I mean . . . what about trying therapy again? We said—"

"Maybe. I'll think about it".

"I can speak to Dr. Larner," said Borst. He was the same doctor who investigated Owen's miraculous inability to die. The doctor ran multiple tests but found no reason for the unnatural healing factor, or whatever it was, that prevented Owen from dying no matter what peril his body was under—fires, explosions, gunshot wounds, suffocation—nothing fazed him, and hours later, his body was inevitably fine.

"Larner's not a psychiatrist".

"No, but he had some theories. He thinks we can test your hormone levels, brain activity".

"That's not really therapy. But, you know, sure, whatever he wants," Owen said dismissively.

They were quiet for a bit. Borst didn't know what to say. She felt worried. She'd been busy the past few weeks, but before that, the more she and Owen worked together, the more they interacted, the more she saw how dedicated Owen was to helping people, doing good. He cared so much, *too* much, and was always so hard on himself. He was a good man inside, but he was troubled. And Borst realized she cared about him. She wanted him to be okay, to be happy. Whether that was because he was a kind person trying to save people or because they were friends now, or because of something more . . . she couldn't tell.

"Owen . . . I'm really happy you're doing this. With Richardson, you know, you're doing good. Really. I think it's important. I just . . . I want *you* to be happy too, eventually," she said, feeling the weight of the truth in those words.

"I know you want that. And I appreciate it. I just don't know if I'll ever get there".

Borst felt her eyes grow moist. This guy . . . it was so sad. What could she do?

"Why don't we drive over to my place? Let's do dinner. I don't think you should be alone tonight".

"I *need* to be alone tonight. I need to process".

"But—"

"Dinah—"

"Please. Just come over. It's just dinner, time together. I'll drive you home right after".

"Tomorrow. Okay? I'll come over for dinner tomorrow".

"Tomorrow. You promise? That means you're not allowed to try to kill yourself tonight because we're doing dinner tomorrow. Okay?"

"I . . . don't worry, I won't. Not going to try and kill myself tonight. I already had a building collapse on top of me anyway—that's probably enough for one day. Don't worry, Dinah, it's not that I want to kill myself right now. I just don't want to be alive. It's hard to explain, but they're different things. It's just . . . look, I just need time to sort my thoughts out tonight. Seriously, don't worry. I told you, I want to die, but I'm not going to do anything. I'm okay".

"Okay. If you say so, I trust you". Dinah made a turn onto Owen's street. "And you'll come over tomorrow for dinner. It'll be nice, just a nice, normal night, we'll chat, catch up".

"Yeah. Sure. Thanks for the ride, Dinah," he said as he opened her car door.

She wasn't really sure what else to say, so she just watched him get out and wave. She waved back, still feeling like she had left too much unsaid.

2 – *You're just not*

THE first thing Owen did when he got back home was take another shower. He couldn't explain it, but he never felt completely clean until he could shower in his own apartment. Besides, in this heatwave, by the time he finished climbing the stairs up to his apartment, he was drenched in sweat.

He had one hell of a day. Fuck. Dinah was . . . she wanted to have dinner tomorrow. She was really . . .

She cared. And that scared the fuck out of him.

Because Owen just wanted to die.

He *still* just wanted to die.

An old therapist, one of the better ones he'd had over the years, once told him that everything we experience as humans is the result of thousands of years of evolutionary biology, and that included human emotions. Every emotion had a purpose. Feeling happy was a signal that you're experiencing something positive, something physically or psychologically beneficial, which meant you should keep going. Feeling sad meant the opposite—something is wrong, and your body or mind was signalling that you should slow down, figure out what was happening that wasn't right, and fix it. Even guilt had a purpose—guilt meant you had done something you regret, and you needed to stop, analyze, learn from it, and make sure you don't do the same thing again.

So, what evolutionary purpose did suicidal ideation have?

Well, evolution is based on random mutations. Those random mutations that happen to be beneficial for the purpose of surviving and reproducing get passed on—a fish that randomly mutates himself some legs can start walking on the ground, thereby escaping bigger, predatory fish. That means the fish is more likely to live on, reproduce, and pass on the random leg mutation. But that *didn't* mean every trait was good. Plenty of fish randomly developed bad traits, smaller fins, poor vision, bright colours that attracted predators, whatever. And if those mutations made it harder for them to thrive, they died off—they couldn't survive, so their traits never passed on.

Evo-fucking-lution.

Maybe his depression, his suicidal tendencies, were just that. A defective trait, a hindering mutation. Bad luck.

This was what Owen thought to himself while he was showering for the second time that evening.

The thing was, he was doing better, actually. Much better.

These past few months were a marked improvement. These negative thoughts about suicide, evolution and life were getting less and less frequent. That might have been because he had other things to focus on, Owen reckoned, as he got out of the shower and started his nightly workout routine of floor and standing exercises that mostly targeted his abs, upper back, and shoulders.

The first time Dinah called him out on a mission—the human trafficking fiasco—was a disaster. People got shot. He got shot, a multitude of times. It freaked him out. But once he made the decision to try doing good, to actually work at it, things changed. Dinah realized that he wasn't ready to be sent out into volatile situations. He wasn't a trained officer—he was barely passable as a functional human being. He was slight, weak. So, instead of throwing him into the deep-end again, Borst was smart enough to hook him up with Richardson.

Sharon Richardson was a retired cop, Dinah's old boss, and she was great. It was a perfect partnership. For one thing, Richardson was a certified physical trainer who, in the span of a few short months, turned him from a skinny weakling into a serviceable semi-weakling, with just enough noticeable muscle to contend with some real-world obstacles. More importantly, though, her decades on the force made her a perfect mentor who could help Owen mentally prepare to face dangerous situations.

Richardson seemed to savour having something to do—she kept complaining about retirement rotting her mind—and she was passionate about teaching and training, sharing her experiences. She was very patient with him. She came up with a plan and executed it with relish, and even though Owen couldn't share her enthusiasm—he couldn't feel enthusiasm for anything as a result of years of severe depression—he found it easy to follow the plan, and seeing results encouraged him to keep going. During the first month of training with Richardson, he didn't see any action. He just prepared.

Meanwhile, Dinah found Dr. Larner, a discreet professor at one of the university hospitals with impressive academic, research, and practical expertise. Larner conducted a whole series of tests on Owen—bloodwork, x-rays, stress tests, the whole shebang. After a month, the doctor still couldn't explain anything of what he was seeing. Owen's cells, his body, just . . . couldn't be harmed. Owen had an unnatural, innate repair mechanism at every level, cellular to physiological. Whether it was magic or an actual freak biological mutation, the doctor couldn't tell. But he *could* demonstrate that wounds closed far faster than they had any right to, different types of cells and tissue samples could regenerate with no adverse effects, and a wide variety of fatal injuries were, well, anything but fatal.

The doctor was utterly stumped. At one point, he had Owen cut the tip of his own little finger off. It just grew back. It defied science.

Of course, Owen had known all of this *before* meeting Dr. Larner. That was how Dinah found him in the first place, she found his multiple records of suicide attempts. Owen had tried everything over the years—shooting himself, jumping off buildings, drowning, stab wounds, asphyxiation. Nothing ever worked. He never died. No injury left any permanent markings, including the bullet wounds from the bank robbery that led to Dinah and Owen's first meeting.

It was this unnatural physiological trait, this super-healing ability that what made him suitable for Dinah's superhero plan.

While he was busy following the training regimen, Richardson and Dinah procured some equipment and built the control room in Richardson's basement. As Owen was building strength and speed and learning the basics of self-defence, the policewomen "borrowed" radios and other devices for monitoring official emergency communications.

With everything in place, Richardson spent her time listening to police broadcasts, trying to identify appropriate cases for him to tackle. Small stuff at first—fires, accidents, crashes—situations where there was no risk of violence, but he could still contribute. Later on, when she thought he might be ready, Richardson sent him to tackle robberies and domestic abuse cases when the police were too stretched and couldn't get to the scene quickly enough.

Day after day, call after call, his confidence started building. He was helping people, saving lives. And eventually, Dinah called on him again, requesting his help. It was a situation eerily similar to his very first op—her squad had identified a weapon-smuggling organization but couldn't bust it because a lack of evidence meant they couldn't get a warrant. Borst sent Owen in. Unlike the first case, the human trafficking ring, he managed to get the evidence and get out no problem. No shots, no one got hurt. The police got their warrant, got in, and arrested the whole gang.

For the first time in years, Owen felt . . . proud? Satisfied? Happy? No, not happy. But he did well. He made a difference. And that was a positive feeling of sorts.

He still wanted to die. Anytime he took a bullet, or any injury really, a part of him hoped that maybe this time it would stick. This time he'd die.

He never did.

So, he wanted to do more. He knew he *could*, and maybe it would get him closer to . . .

Closer to what? To saving more people . . . or to dying? Either way, he wanted, *needed*, to do more.

Richardson kept warning him about it. He couldn't get carried away, couldn't get addicted to it. He was contributing, doing good, but he had to pace it, grow into it. If he rushed things, he'd end up dead. Richardson knew he was very much okay with ending up dead himself, but, she pointed out, he might end up killing others in the process. And neither of them was okay with *that*. So, no recklessness.

He knew she was right.

But still. There was more he could do.

Lately, the level of violence in the city was growing out of control. Escalating. It was in all the papers, all the news sites. The heatwave was sparking more than just fires. There were so many violent incidents on a daily basis—shootings, muggings, random assaults, gang violence, dead bodies found all over the place—something was brewing in this city.

And Dinah was probably caught up in it. He knew she'd been busy at work, being a real cop, investigating, fighting crime. He hadn't seen her in weeks, not until today. They barely spoke.

And now, all of a sudden, she wanted to have dinner tomorrow.

Was it just dinner to catch up, as . . . sort-of colleagues, friends? Or . . .

No. Don't even think about it. It's her, it's Dinah. She cares, sure, she cares too much, and that scares you, but she doesn't . . . you're not . . . you're just not.

That's what Owen thought as he wrapped up his exercises.

He then stared at the wall for a few minutes. Clearing his head. Trying not to dwell on any thoughts, especially not negative ones. The thoughts passed in and out. No judgement. It was basically meditation. He didn't like the word—a couple of past therapists, bad ones, tried to get him to take up "meditation", guided crap that felt fluffy and meaningless. "Picture yourself in a meadow" or some shit. He hated that. But this, just sitting and clearing his head, registering emotions and getting in touch with his own mind, this wasn't bad. It wasn't always helpful, but it usually wasn't harmful, either. And it did help him keep track of how he was feeling.

Owen was still depressed. He still struggled with his mental health.

But at least he was putting his time, his life, to good use. He believed karma was a made-up concept. Being a good person didn't mean good things would happen to him or that he'd start feeling any better.

It couldn't hurt, though. Or, well, it could. But it couldn't kill him, so . . . whatever.

It was getting late. But as usual, sleep wouldn't come.

Maybe he'd go out for a night walk. The weather was bearable at night, cooler. He'd been going out at night pretty often these days. Owen grabbed his stuff, put on his headphones, and took off.

. . .

Dinah took a big swallow from the bottle of whiskey she kept by her bed. It helped her sleep.

She needed it tonight. What a hell of a day.

What a hell of a summer.

It's been non-stop, and today was just more of the same. The morning started with an emergency captains' meeting at Central. D'Alfonso, her division inspector, called in all the captains of the downtown precincts to discuss recent developments. "I've never seen anything like it," he said before sharing the stats and diving into a few specific cases.

It painted a worse picture than Captain Dinah Borst of the 16th precinct realized.

Grisly murders, all presumably gang-related. One particularly gruesome scene had seven bodies, and four were identified as known criminals. Just ten days ago, three high-ranking individuals of the Chinese syndicate had been found dead in their homes, all on the same morning. And then, right before the weekend, the scene at that restaurant . . .

"This is gang warfare at a whole new level. I can't make any sense of it," said D'Alfonso. He sounded wearier than she'd ever heard him. "We've had a few years of relative peace, and now . . . something's snapped. Every known gang is taking casualties, and we don't know why, whether it's a play for territory, or just an escalation getting out of hand. We don't know who's instigating it, who's winning, who's losing. The one thing we do know," he emphasized, "is that we've got eight informants and three undercover operatives dead".

That made everyone pause. Three operatives, *officers* . . . dead?

"The decision's been made. We're pulling all undercover operatives out of active operations. We've got no choice". That led to a long and entirely pointless debate, which Dinah stayed out of. Part of her agreed that sacrificing operations limited their ability to investigate and respond to the escalating levels of violence, while a bigger part supported D'Alfonso's argument that the risks were too great. Both parts of her heard that the decision had already been made upstairs—captains arguing wasn't going to change the Commissioner's mind.

"So, what *are* we doing? How we do respond?" she asked when the room finally got quiet, addressing D'Alfonso directly.

He sighed. "I wish I knew. Keep investigating each scene. See if you can piece things together. Somebody started this war, and there's a reason it keeps going and peace hasn't been brokered yet, despite all the bloodshed. Let's see if we can sniff anything out. I'll be asking you to meet more regularly, keep the channels of communication open. And another thing, which doesn't leave this room—Major Crime is under a new directive to take over gang-related investigations. Ever since the change in personnel over at the Major Crimes Unit . . ." D'Alfonso trailed off with another sigh. "Look, you all know I'm not the biggest fan of MC. I recommend you keep charge of all scenes in your own precincts. If the MCU starts to badger you, feel free to escalate to me".

Those were the latest instructions. People are dying. Do your job, and don't let political red tape get in the way.

Well, Borst could get behind that. But it did leave her exhausted and dispirited. As far as she could remember, the city has never been this bad. And she's lived here her entire life. Was it the heatwave, or was something else going on?

The overtime also meant she had less and less time for Owen. He and Richardson made a good team, they didn't rely on her for anything, but Borst still felt frustrated. She wanted to get closer to Owen, because . . .

Well, because the work they were doing was important. Maybe he could even help with the gang crime spree at some point. And also because . . . she worried about him, and . . . she liked his honesty, openness. He was very genuine. There was just something about him, something real and raw that touched her. She was glad she got to see him today. He seemed well.

Was he, though? She asked herself. It was nearly impossible to tell. Her goal was to turn him into an operative who was mentally stable enough to protect and save lives outside of the narrow, politically drawn confines of official police work. She honestly believed he could make a difference. On top of which, having a positive purpose might help Owen grow mentally healthier. She really wanted him to find happiness, and she wanted to be a part of that. But what if his psyche was more fragile than she realized? He still wanted to die. Was she doing right by him?

Dinner tomorrow. She had an evening off, and she hoped he would show up. Maybe they could talk, get closer, and figure things out. She wanted to understand him better, to help. To . . . well. She wasn't sure what she wanted. If nothing else, it would be good to just have one night off without having to worry about yet another murder scene. The photos from that restaurant . . .

Dinah had another swig of the whiskey, then flicked the bedside lamp off. It was late. Time to call it a night.

. . .

The night air was pleasant. The world pressed pause on the oppressive daytime heat. You could finally breathe out there. And if you happened to walk by the water, you might even catch a breeze.

The unkillable man found himself sitting on a bench, out in front of the bay.

He took the phones out of pocket one-by-one, nodding to himself. He checked the messages on each of the disposable cheap burner phones, responded to a couple just to make sure things kept moving along. He threw one of the phones into the waters of the bay.

Gathering intelligence. Information. That's how you got ahead.

He then looked around to make sure he wasn't being watched, took the gun out, and threw it into the water too. The splash was barely audible. This city was loud, even at night.

Everything was going according to plan. People were dead, but that just meant he was consolidating. Taking out the trash.

He was getting closer to the top. He already had his foot in the door, having taken out the top leadership of nearly every major gang and crime organization in the city. He was going to single-handedly clean this city up, remake it the way he wanted. Which was . . . what was it again? What was he working towards? Taking out crime. Or . . . taking over?

Did it really matter?

All he knew was that killing bad guys was the closest he could get to feeling good. To feeling anything, really. That power was intoxicating. And they couldn't kill him. They couldn't do anything.

The plan was to get to the top. What happened after, he'd figure out later. It didn't really matter. He was just trying to do what felt right. He knew that if he stopped to think about it, he'd be forced to recognize the abyss inside, and he might never surface again. So, ignore the question of morality. *You're killing bad guys. It's a good thing. Keep going. Clean up the city. Take over. Do what it takes to feel a teeny-tiny bit less like crap.*

He was getting there. It's taken a lot of work, a lot of murders, a lot of sleepless nights, but it would soon pay off.

Besides, sleepless nights were easy—it wasn't like he slept much anyway. He didn't need to. He didn't need much food, either, but he decided to grab a quick falafel on the way back. He passed a place that looked like it would still be open, and it's been about a day since the last time he ate.

When you can't be killed, it's easy to lose track, to stop paying attention to things that weren't important, like food. What could he say? Life was busy these days. Taking over organized crime in this city bit-by-bit, all by himself, while keeping it relatively quiet—especially from the cops—it wasn't an easy job. But he was getting there.

Being unkillable helped.

He rolled up his pant leg, looking at the spot where he got hurt earlier that day. He nearly died. But he didn't. By now, there wasn't even a mark. Well, as long as he wasn't dead, he might as well keep going. It seemed to be working so far. He felt good.

No, correction. He felt fine. Neutral. Not good. He *never* felt good. He never felt happy. There were things that got him close, maybe for a second or two, but they always faded very, *very* quickly.

Maybe this'll do it. He was close. Part of him wanted to stop, tie some rocks to his legs, and throw himself into the damn bay. See if he could die that way. He knew he couldn't. Instead, he might as well try the other way. Take out the next gang. If he succeeded, he'd be a step closer to the top. If he failed . . . well, whatever.

It couldn't hurt, anyway.

Or, it *could*. He could get shot, drowned again, shot some more. It could *hurt*.

But it couldn't fucking kill him.

3 – *That's the story*

"I'M glad you came," said Borst. "I wasn't sure you would".

Owen nodded. "Thanks for having me".

"I've been meaning to do this for a while. Catch-up, I mean. It's been too long. I haven't even managed to stop by Richardson's these past few weeks. Haven't had a chance till yesterday".

"You've been busy".

"Yeah, very. Plus, my squad was on night shift for a few weeks. We just swapped back. And then this heatwave . . . it's turning the whole damn city upside-down".

"What's been going on?"

"Wait, let's sit down first. Wine?" asked Borst.

"Thanks, no, I'm good".

"You sure? I've got something stronger if—"

"I don't drink".

That gave Borst pause. "You don't drink?"

"I stopped. Alcohol and depression don't mix well".

"Ah, right. Shit, I'm sorry, I didn't think—I'm sorry".

"It's okay, you didn't know".

Borst nodded. She felt awkward. "Well, umm . . . do you mind if I have some? Or, I mean, I don't have to," she asked, having already poured herself a glass.

"Not at all, it doesn't bother me. Really, it's fine".

"Good. And I hope you don't mind, I know I invited you for dinner, but I didn't actually cook anything. I figured we'll just order in. I, uh . . . I don't really cook".

"That's fine".

"I figured this is more . . . you know, for the company. Spend some time together, catch-up".

"Yeah. So, you were saying, what's been going on at work?"

Borst sighed and took a sip of wine. She wasn't sure what she was allowed to say. "Well, it's . . . we're hoping it's not a full-out gang war, but it's starting to look like it might be. Deaths left-and-right".

"I've seen it on the news," Owen nodded. "Dead criminals, though?"

"Yeah".

"Isn't that a good thing, in a way?"

"It's still murder, Owen. And if it keeps escalating . . . just today we found the body of another of our UCOs".

"UCO?"

"Sorry, I forgot, I'm using the acronym. Undercover officer. Killed along with six gang members. They were all shot in a restaurant, broad daylight. So we lost an asset, a good cop, we lost lives. No, it's not a good thing. Not to mention, if it keeps escalating, we're going to see innocents getting hurt. There'll be blood on the streets. *More* blood, I mean".

"Is there anything I can do?" Owen asked after a moment. It was a sincere question. He wanted to help, Borst could tell.

She sighed. "No, unfortunately. Not at this point. It's not a question of getting in and surviving shoot-outs, or . . . no, right now it's still a question of gathering information, infiltration, detective work".

"Oh. Right".

"We're completely blind. No clue who started this war, why it intensified so quickly. We need to know what we're up against here, ideally before it gets completely out of hand. That's proper police work, and . . . I don't know how you could help, honestly. But you know I'll use you when I can. If you're okay with that".

"Of course".

There followed a short awkward silence.

"How was today?" Borst asked.

"Quiet. No action today," said Owen. He sounded disappointed.

"Well, maybe after yesterday, that's a good thing".

"Yeah. I was still coughing up black stuff until a couple of hours ago," he admitted.

"Are you still . . . you know, what we talked about yesterday, in the car. Are you still thinking about that?"

"I'm okay," he said. Borst couldn't tell if he was being honest or evasive. When he spoke, Owen tended to be monotonic, his voice was always very soft and expressionless. She could never quite read him.

"Good," she responded tentatively. "Hopefully we won't have to send you into too many fires . . . although with this heatwave, we might. Did Sharon tell you? There was another fire yesterday at the same time, up at Mount Pleasant. That's why it took so long for the firefighters to get the equipment they needed to get into that factory".

"Mount Pleasant?" Owen asked, suddenly looking a tiny bit more alert.

"Yeah, one of the big houses there".

"Do you remember the address?"

"I can look it up," Borst said, pulling out her phone. Why was Owen so interested? He looked tense. She gave him the address.

"Oh. Good".

"Why is that a relief?"

"I grew up on that street, couple of houses over".

Borst was surprised. Owen grew up in the richest section of the city? Every house on that street, unofficially known as Millionaire Row, was essentially a mansion. Celebrities owned a few of them, rich businessmen the rest. *That's* where Owen grew up?

It struck her that there was a lot she didn't know about him. "You never told me that," she said.

"You never asked".

"Can I ask now?"

"What do you want to know?"

"About . . . you. Your childhood".

"Maybe let's order food, first".

A half-hour or so later, they were seated across from each other at Borst's small dining table, sharing a couple of Thai dishes.

"So, go on. Tell me your story. Did you really grow up on Millionaire Row?"

Borst had never seen Owen fully smile. But sometimes he would have an expression on, something to do with his eyebrows, which was as close to a smile as he'd get.

"I never told you my real name, did I?"

"It's . . . I know your name. Owen Kale. I've got your files, social security—"

"I had it legally changed. It was a dumb joke . . . Kale stands for Kay-Ell. I was born Owen Kline-Laurie".

"Kline . . . as in Kline-Laurie Media? Your father's—"

"Jeremy Kline-Laurie. Yeah".

Borst could feel her eyes grow wide. This was . . . new information.

Kline-Laurie Media was a huge media and telecommunications conglomerate, one of the nation's largest corporations. They had a goddamn downtown building with their logo on it.

And Owen was *heir* to that empire?

Shit. This was crazy.

"I—wow. I had no idea".

"I realize that. I maybe should have mentioned it, but I normally try to keep it quiet. For obvious reasons".

Borst nodded.

"You probably know some of the story. My dad was one of the biggest high-profile CEOs in the country. But he wasn't a very . . . *present* father, as you can imagine. My mom died when I was ten. Car crash. My sister was six. I didn't know it at the time, but my mom was . . . deeply unhappy. An alcoholic and a drug addict, too. I don't know if that contributed to the accident, but if it did, my dad must have kept it quiet. He had the power to do that.

"My sister and I were mostly raised by nannies, tutors. I don't think I had an actual conversation with my father until . . . probably the time I graduated high-school. When we did speak, he'd comment on my grades, or school. I had straight A's, not that he cared, but I wasn't on any sports teams. He'd always ask whether I was number one in my class. I was, mostly. If I wasn't, he'd ask why. Why didn't I work harder? Why wasn't I on the hockey team?

"Anyway, I always felt like a disappointment. It was mostly the sports thing. My dad was kind of a jock, and I . . . well, you get the idea. I don't know whether depression is genetic or a combination of nature and nurture, but in that environment, I don't think it's a surprise. My sister and I both had the symptoms from pretty early on.

"My dad wanted me to go into journalism, manage the business after him. I always liked writing, but I hated the idea of writing with a deadline and a word count. I was more into creative writing, fiction. Journalism bugged me, but I wanted my dad to be proud, I guess, so I went into a journalism program, one of the top ones. I went away for school. And I think being away from home, no family, no friends—just feeling stuck in something I didn't really want to do with no way out—that's what led to my first attempt".

"The first time you tried to . . . kill yourself?" asked Borst, trying to be gentle.

"Yeah. One of many. It didn't take, obviously. My dad never even visited when I was in the hospital. My sister called, but she was still home, and she wasn't going to fly out on her own, she was just fourteen or fifteen, and . . . anyway, I was dismissed after a couple of weeks, and then just went back to school like it was nothing".

"That's when you figured out your . . . you know, your powers?"

"Slowly. I tried cutting myself, and I healed almost immediately. I was on medication, therapy. For a couple of years, I was kind of out of it . . . mostly drowsy from the medication, constantly exhausted and kind of just . . . I can't describe it. I just didn't feel awake. For *two years*. I was almost done with school when my father's plane went down".

Borst remembered the story. Jeremy Kline-Laurie's private jet crash. It was on all the news channels for almost a week back then.

"I flew home for the funeral. I had enough credits to graduate with an undeclared major, so I never went back to school after that. It was a big shock, and I was still so numb from the pills and everything else . . . I don't even remember the funeral. I don't remember much of that time".

"Well, of course, it was—it must have been traumatic".

"It was, but the bigger shock was my sister. And I'll never forgive myself. I let them drug me up, numb me, and I should've . . . I should have realized, if I was going through shit, my sister was going through the same stuff, probably worse. She was younger. I should have . . . should have been there. Should have saved her".

"What happened?"

"She overdosed on heroin".

"Shit. I didn't . . . I'm so—"

Owen's face was devoid of any expression. Impassive. Borst couldn't imagine what was going through his head, reliving everything he was telling her. She wanted to hold him, to help. But she knew there was no way to help through that sort of grief.

"It's okay, I know. You don't have to . . . look, I've had years and years of therapy, I've processed most it. You don't have to feel sorry or anything".

"I understand, but . . . still. I didn't know".

"Well, how would you? I never told you. It's okay, really. Don't worry about it".

"What happened after that?"

"Not a lot. I was the only one left, but I had no interest in taking over the business or anything like that. I changed my name, sold the house, bought a small apartment. I still have a seat on the board technically, but I rarely go in for meetings. They only keep me on out of some sort of moral obligation, I figure. Or maybe because I own a lot of stock.

"And the depression . . . I mean, that part you know. I've been struggling ever since. Don't get me wrong, Dinah, I—look, I know I've got a shit-ton of privilege. That's the thing, it's actually a source of guilt, too, but I know, with my money, with . . . being a man, being white . . . I *get* to deal with my depression. It's my demon. I've been in therapy, I've tried the medication—I could afford it —I know so many people can't. But it doesn't . . . doesn't change the fact that I'm depressed, and some . . . some periods are worse, and I . . ."

"I know. You've tried to kill yourself. A lot".

"Yeah. It just never works, because . . . well, you know. I can't die".

"Yeah".

"And that's been my life. I . . . there's been some months, some years, when I've been better. That's when I tried to use my money, and company resources, to set up charity stuff, supporting mental health initiatives. I was pretty involved at first, but I couldn't . . . I don't know. I couldn't run a business, a charity, when every time, after a while, I started getting seriously suicidal again. So I ended up finding some people, good people, to run it. And every time, I end up back in my apartment, in my room. Alone. Me and the depression, I guess. That's the story".

Borst got up to clear the table. She needed a minute to digest.

"Owen, I . . . I'm glad you shared that with me".

He nodded. "Thanks for listening. It's, uh . . . I guess I'm glad you know".

She smiled. He was okay. That was a relief.

"What about you? Your story?" he asked.

"Oh, umm . . . hold up," said Borst. She needed a drink for this—scotch, she decided. She poured two fingers, two ice cubes. "You sure you don't want a drink? Juice?"

"More water would be nice".

She moved to the couch, handing Owen a glass as he joined her. "So, my story. Well, I didn't grow up near Mount Pleasant, that's for sure. I grew up right here, actually. Across the street".

"Really?"

"Yep. My dad used to live across the street, and when I moved out, I rented this place here. Didn't want to move too far. He raised me . . . well, my grandparents more so. My mother left us when I was too young to remember. I looked her up after I graduated. She remarried, has a new family now. For a while I thought I'd reach out, but I decided . . . what's the point?

"Anyway, yeah. Pretty normal life. I was really close to my grandparents. My dad was a cop".

"Oh".

"Yeah," Borst smiled. "He did *not* want me following in his footsteps. He was also pretty strict on me getting good grades, doing well at school, no boys allowed until I was eighteen, that sort of thing. He wanted me to be a lawyer. I actually did get my law degree. Bet you wouldn't have guessed that".

"You're smart. It's not so far-fetched".

Borst laughed. "Thanks".

"So, why did you become a cop after all?"

"Well, my dad died. Cancer. Right after I finished my degree. I was supposed to take the bar exam, but . . . I deferred. At that point, my grandparents were gone, so it was the two of us, and I didn't . . . uh, I didn't want to sacrifice time with my dad to study. I took care of him, and those few months . . . I mean, it was hell, but I'm so glad I did that. We got closer, I learned so much from him, about his life, and about . . . myself, I guess. You know?"

"It's great you had the chance to spend that time with him".

"Yeah, absolutely. I'm super grateful for that," Borst said, trying to be tactful. "Anyway, after he passed, I realized, as much as law was interesting, my heart was set on joining the force. I just wanted to be like my dad. He was my hero, you know? Plus, well, I didn't love being a lawyer. So I enrolled in the academy. And one thing my dad taught me, *instilled* in me, I guess, is the desire to always excel. I could never stand the idea of failing, I sort of have this fear of failure. So I pushed myself as hard as I could, and I got ahead. I did well. Made detective first- and second-grade in record time. Richardson helped with that, actually. And I kept working hard, distinguishing myself. It didn't leave me much time to do anything more with my life . . . a few relationships here and there. You know, the normal life of a busy working person, more or less".

Owen nodded. They were silent for a minute before Borst laughed. "I don't know what else to tell you".

"I'm glad we shared, though," he said. "I feel like maybe we'll understand each other better from now on".

"Yeah. Yeah, exactly".

"I didn't realize how much being a cop meant to you".

"It does. It's not just about my dad. I mean, yes, a lot of it is, sure, but . . . it just feels like that's my purpose in life. To prevent crime, make the city safer. And I'm good at it".

"You really are".

"You are, too!" said Borst as she got up to pour herself another glass. She could sense she was probably having a bit too much, but . . . it was a rare a night off, a social night. She was allowed.

"I'm . . . well, I'm trying," said Owen. "I hope I'm getting there".

"But does it *feel* right? Are you—do you find it meaningful, enjoyable?"

"Well—"

"I mean, okay, enjoyable isn't the right word, but—"

"No, I got what you were trying to ask. I don't know. Yes and no. I think . . . on the one hand, I know I'm making a difference, and that's good. I *am* helping, saving lives, all of that. But on the other hand . . . it doesn't really feel like I'm getting anything done, like I'm solving anything. Do you know what I mean? There's always *more*. More people I could help, more I could do. It's like, as much as I'm doing right, I never get to the end of it. It's frustrating".

Borst nodded. "I understand. It took me years to make peace with that. Maybe it was easier because I saw my dad struggle with it too. It does get better—you get a clearer perspective after a while. But there's always ups and downs. I mean, fuck, these few weeks have been a shitshow. I definitely don't feel good about the work right now. But in the grand scheme of things . . . you know. It's still meaningful".

"I hope so".

Borst fiddled with her glass for a minute. "I still can't get over the fact that you're a Kline-Laurie. I mean, you're fucking rich! And now you're doing this hero thing. I mean, this is going to sound totally insensitive and is entirely the result of me drinking a bit much, but . . . come on, Owen, you're basically goddamn Batman".

A second after saying that she remembered that Owen's parents were dead. "Shit, I didn't mean—"

"It's okay, Dinah. Maybe I am like Batman, sort of. I guess that's cool, if you look at it that way," he said, but he sounded sort of detached.

"You know, I'm sorry it's taken so long for us to get together and talk. We should have done this long ago—get to know each other. But we were so focused on setting you up with Sharon and Dr. Larner, and then this wave of gang crime started and . . ."

"I know. You don't have to apologize for it".

"No, I know. Just . . . I'm glad. It's nice to spend time, you know, not at a crime scene, for once. Just . . . talking to a person".

"Sure. It's been good. Dinah, I'm . . . I'm glad we met, and . . . you know, everything that's happened since. Everything you've done for me, pushing me . . . without you, it wouldn't have happened. I mean, we both know how hard I tried to get out of it, tried to . . . just give up. But these have been some of my best months, honestly".

"I'm really happy to hear that," smiled Borst.

"Yeah. So, thank you. Seriously. Anyway," Owen continued, "it's getting late. I should maybe go, I'm training with Richardson first thing tomorrow morning and—"

"You don't have to".

"Huh?"

"You don't have to go," she said. Well, it was probably more the scotch that said it. It was definitely the scotch that put her hand on his thigh.

She looked into his eyes. They used to be the saddest eyes she had ever seen. They still were, but she thought maybe now there was something else she could see in them, too. Some . . . *light*.

She sank into it, and he sank too, and one thing led to another, and they lost themselves in each other as night fell.

4 – *I'm Unkillable*

"A.J.? What the fuck are *you* doing here?"

"Sturgess called me in. You too?"

"Shit. I don't like this".

Linc started pacing. There were too many of them there. They were on the third floor of an abandoned, condemned parking garage out by the docks. A classic spot for a meet. It was almost three in the morning, and the garage was empty other than his boys, Tony's, and now A.J.'s crew. Why the hell would Sturgess call them all in at the same time in the middle of the night?

"You think it's a sting or something?" asked Tony. Tony's always been a small, cowardly shit, but today he might have had a point.

"I don't fucking know. Just stay alert".

"He called you guys in too?" A.J. asked, looking confused. "Fuck, you think the rumours are true?"

"What rumours you talking about, man?" asked Craig, one of Linc's boys. Craig was getting mouthy, starting to feel like he could voice an opinion. Linc would have to deal with him later, knock him down a peg.

"Big bosses are clearing house. I heard whole crews are getting mowed down".

"I heard that too, man," Tony contributed. "You know Big Singh? Crazy tall Indian guy operating out near Midtown? Him and his whole crew, dead. They found them a week, week-and-a-half ago".

"Who told you that?" asked Linc. This rumour sounded pretty dubious to him.

"Cop. Got a couple of my regular buyers wearing the uniform. Intel's legit, man. They kept it out of the papers, but it's true. I think we should bail. I'm giving Sturgess five more minutes before I'm out of here".

Linc resumed his pacing. Everybody was on edge. The tension was so high you could feel it on your skin, mixed in with the grease and sweat. This fucking heatwave. Five minutes passed, then ten. Tony walked over to the edge of the lot, looking out up and down the street. "No cars coming, man. Sturgess ain't coming, this smells like a set-up. I don't like it".

"Then go," said Craig.

"Yeah. Fuck it. Yeah, look, if Sturgess shows up, just tell him—"

"Tony, we ain't telling him nothing. Fuck you. If you're too scared to wait it out, you tell him that," said Linc. He was feeling anxious too, but Tony was being a goddamn coward, and that just pissed him off.

For a minute, Tony teetered. "Fine, yeah. I'll text him. Whatever, man. It's your funeral. Come on, boys".

Tony gestured to his crew and was just about to open the door to his car when a voice called out from the other, unlit side of the parking garage.

"Nobody's going anywhere". It was a calm, stoic voice. The owner of the voice slowly walked towards the assembled crews. They could hear his footsteps before he stepped into the light of the few ceiling fixtures that weren't smashed. Once he was finally visible, he turned out to be some pale, short, skinny guy, wearing a polo shirt and a backpack. Completely unintimidating. Linc almost snorted.

"Who the fuck are you? And where's Sturgess?"

The guy took off his backpack and tossed it in the direction of Tony, who took a step away from his car to pick it up. He unzipped the backpack only to drop it immediately, shouting, "Shit! What the *fuck*?!"

Linc couldn't see what it was. "What's in the bag, Tony?" he asked. He hated that he was the one who had to take command of this situation. Tony and A.J. were both too stupid, so it had to be him. But Linc felt uneasy. He wanted to get out of there.

"Pull it out," the stranger instructed Tony. "Go on. Show everybody—your friends wanna see".

Tony just shook his head. His face was pale as fuck. He looked like he was about to puke.

"*Somebody* tell me what's in the fucking bag!" Linc shouted. He was about to lose it. "Fuck it". He walked over, picked the backpack up himself, and reached inside.

Whatever was inside was . . . furry? That couldn't be right. It felt gross. Linc grabbed at whatever the strands were that tickled his fingers and pulled the object out of the bag.

It turned out to be a severed head.

Linc dropped it on the ground and puked, having the mind to at least turn his own head so he didn't hit the severed one. Then a couple of the other guys vomited, too. The head rolled on the floor. It was sort of staring at Linc with its dead eyes.

Linc turned to look at the guy who brought the head with him, in a fucking backpack. This small, puny asshole. He was just standing there, scratching his neck.

"Is that . . . *Sturgess*?" asked A.J., incredulous. Linc couldn't bring himself to answer without heaving again.

"Well, obviously," muttered the stranger, finally speaking again. He sounded impatient. "Of course it's Sturgess. Who did you *think*? Look, can we all move past the severed head, stop with the puking, and just—"

"Somebody shoot this motherfucker," coughed Linc.

For a moment, nobody moved.

Then his boys, starting with Craig, finally responded, followed by Tony and A.J.'s guys. They all pulled out their weapons and pointed them at the stranger.

The guy just stood there. Linc expected him to cower, or at the very least put his hands up. Instead, he spoke.

"Wow, you people are bad at following directions. The guy over there said shoot me. So go on".

Craig looked at his leader, confused. "*Shoot* him already," ordered Linc, perfectly infuriated now.

Finally, they shot him. Linc saw it. At least five boys all shooting once, twice, ten times. Bullets flying, flesh hit, blood splattering, body falling. He saw it all.

The shooting part made sense. What came next didn't.

Because next, Linc saw the guy get back up.

"Shit, that hurt. All right, fine. Get that out of your system? Good, now—"

"Fuck, are you—*shoot this asshole down*!" Linc interrupted. Behind him, he heard A.J. issue a similar command. He grabbed Craig's gun out of his hand, stepped forward, and emptied the entire cartridge into the body of this clown.

He was dead. He had to be dead. This guy, who had brought them Sturgess's head in a backpack, was dead. Linc shot him, *many* fucking times. He was riddled with bullets, literally. He was dead.

Except he got back the fuck up, and Linc backed off. He didn't know what the fuck was going on, this guy, this dead guy wasn't dead, and what the fuck.

No one said anything for a second while the guy coughed up two bullets and spat them onto the dusty floor of the garage like two batches of metallic mucus. "Okay, we done?" he asked, sounding gravelly now.

"Who . . . w-what are you?" Linc asked. He was shocked, disgusted, confused, angry, and mostly in utter disbelief at what he was witnessing.

"I'm Unkillable. Anyway, can we please focus?"

The unkillable guy started walking now. He came up to Tony. Tony, the coward, physically recoiled away from him.

"Can I have this?" asked Unkillable, grabbing Tony's gun. The asshole let him have it.

Tony was shot first. In the chest. He dropped. Then his two boys. Unkillable proceeded to shoot one of A.J.'s guys, then he aimed at Craig.

There was a split-second where Linc had to react. No one else was reacting. Craig was an asshole, but fuck, they were dropping like flies, and Craig was one of *his* guys. Linc had a duty to his boys. He raised the gun in his hand, pointing it at that freak-of-nature unkillable person, then squeezed the trigger again, before he remembered.

He was out of bullets.

Unkillable pulled his trigger next.

He was out of bullets, too.

"Looks like you lucked out," he said to Craig, tapping him on the shoulder.

"Now then," he continued, facing the crew boys. Well, the remainder of the crews, anyway. "Fuck, you know how much work it took me to get you all in one place? Shit, the Asians, the Italians, that was easy. They just love getting in the same room to discuss shit. I got them both in restaurants. Had myself a nice meal after. But you shitheads? With the burner phones, and with nobody knowing anyone's names, it's so fucking decentralized. Flat corporate structure shit. It's a damn pain".

All Linc could do was shake his head. *What was happening?*

"You guys look confused. Right, let me spell it out for you—I'm taking down *all* crime in this city. I'm taking over, it's all mine. Give me . . . I don't know, two weeks? Yeah, probably about two weeks, and I'll get to the top. I'm already most of the way there. Been taking out all the trash. So anyway, now you work for *me*. Got it? Good. Hey, you!"

He pointed a finger at one of A.J.'s boys, who immediately put his hands up as if Unkillable was pointing an Uzi at him. "Go through pockets. All these guys, on the floor," he said, motioning to the boys he just murdered. "You know, the dead ones. I want their wallets, phones, and car keys. Good. You can put them in this backpack, here. Don't worry, it's empty". He picked up the backpack from the floor, still dripping with the blood from Sturgess's head, which was lying ignored on the dusty ground staring up. Everything smelled awful, Linc realized, of vomit and gunpowder and rotting flesh. He felt nauseated. Meanwhile, Unkillable was pointing at him.

"You. You're clearly the grown-up here. Taking charge, emptying a fucking clip at me. I respect that. I mean, you shoot me again and you're dead, but dead and respected. For now, I'm gonna use you. I'm sure you know names, numbers, places, all the little things, little details I need to know".

"Why would I fucking help you?" asked Linc, spitting at the ground in front of this asshole.

The two men stared at each other. Linc hadn't noticed this guy's eyes before. They were like two black, blank holes. He's had no visible expression on his face since he showed up. There was something unsettlingly inhuman about him. Suddenly, Linc felt terrified.

"Why would you help me? Is that not clear? That's confusing to you? Buddy, you have no choice. You do what I say, or you die. I will shoot you. There is *nothing* you can do to me, understand? You could try. I'd love to see you try. Shoot me some more, if you want. But then I will kill you. Or, you do what I say, and maybe then you don't end up dead like your—"

The speech was broken by the loud sound of a gunshot.

It was Craig. Craig found the balls to try and shoot the guy again.

This time, Unkillable didn't even fall down. He looked at the wound on his chest, which bled for a moment. Then he looked at Craig.

"Oh, you really like to push your luck, don't you?"

"Sorry," muttered Craig.

"Yeah, you better be," Unkillable sighed. "Boys, this is a good thing here. Trust me. World's about to change. And now, you're on *my* side. Let's go".

5 – *Outer space shit*

WHEN she woke up, he wasn't there.

The other side of the bed was cold. Shower wasn't running. No sound from the kitchen. You didn't have to be a detective—which she was—to realize Owen was gone.

She rolled over and checked her phone. No text, nothing.

Borst wasn't going to pretend she wasn't hurt.

Okay, she probably shouldn't have had *that* much to drink last night. Did she pressure him into it? No, no, she wouldn't have. Besides, he could have said no, he was a grown-up. And they had a nice evening, a good talk. *Really* good talk. And then good . . . Well, it was a mutually . . . it was a good thing. As far as she could remember.

He was probably just processing. It wasn't—she wasn't going to take it personally.

They'd talk about it. Later. She'd give him some time to process. And if he didn't call, she would call him. Or . . . well, she might just check in with Richardson. Yeah, that was . . . that's a better idea. She wouldn't *tell* her anything, just check in, ask how he's doing. He was fine, just confused, probably. If he wasn't happy with what had happened, she could say it was a one-time thing, a mistake, it wouldn't happen again.

But what if she *wanted* it to happen again? What if they *both* wanted it to happen again?

Okay, that's dumb. You're getting ahead of yourself, Borst thought. *Stop thinking about that, just focus. Get up, Dinah. Work time. Let's go.*

She got up. She didn't think about it. She showered. She didn't think about it. She got into her car and drove to the precinct. And she absolutely, definitely didn't think about it.

. . .

They drove in silence. Linc wasn't sure how he became Unkillable's personal chauffeur, but he was still alive. That probably should have counted for something. Considering everything he's seen over the past—has it really only been a few hours?—Linc was more aware than ever that his life could be cut short at any fucking moment.

Between the garage carnage and now, the guy hardly spoke. On the other hand, he had killed more than half a dozen people personally, and ordered two more executions. He also snorted a full bag of cocaine, *quality* cocaine, and seemed completely unaffected by it. He then interrogated Linc and A.J., let A.J. go, and then ordered Linc to drive him over to the biggest boss Linc knew.

Linc just wanted sleep. It was early morning now, almost eight, and he hadn't been to bed yet. He was running on fumes, just following orders at this point, trying not to get shot by this crazy person, this *freak*. So he drove him. Neither man spoke, and Linc was all right with that. He stopped in front of the building in question, a luxury residential building right downtown.

"This is it?" asked his passenger.

Linc grunted in response. He wanted nothing to do with this, but he had no choice.

"Fuck, that's fancy," Unkillable commented on the building. "Nice. Well, go on, drive us in. I'm sure they have guest parking spots. You're coming with. We're both going up".

Shit. Linc was hoping he'd be let off the hook once they've arrived, or have an opportunity to escape somehow. Looks like there would be no such luck. He was stuck with the unlikable monster.

Linc trembled as he got out of his now-parked car and followed Unkillable into the lobby.

"See, I like this. It's fancy, but it's not tacky," Unkillable remarked. He wasn't wrong. This downtown building certainly was a hallmark of affluence and good taste. It also happened to house the big boss, the guy who put up the capital for the various smaller gangs he controlled running drugs and girls around the city, the strategist who had the full picture, the crime-lord who negotiated for territory with the Asians, the Russians, the Italians, and everyone else, the genius who had the cops in his pocket, the man whose word was law.

Most of the boys Linc had to deal with had a vague notion the boss existed, but that was about it. A handful of the crew heads, like A.J., even knew what name he went by—the Accountant. Linc was the only guy he knew at his level who had *seen* the Accountant, real name Rowan Nelson. Linc googled him once—Mr. Nelson was a high-ranking partner in a mid-sized accounting firm. No wonder he was good at making lists, allocating funds, and coordinating shit.

It was maybe six months ago, on a Tuesday, when Linc got a call from Sturgess, his supplier, one guy up the chain. Sturgess called once a week, always on Sunday. They'd coordinate a meet-up, or Linc would send Craig or one of his other boys over. They'd pick up the merch for the week, and Linc would pay the 70% cut from the previous week. The other 30% he kept, to distribute among himself and his crew. Simple and very consistent. So when Sturgess called on a Tuesday rather than a Sunday, Linc was a little alarmed, but he picked up anyway.

The instructions were simple. Someone high-up needed "party supplies". Sturgess knew Linc had quality material left over from Sunday, so he was to deliver it, personally. The address was the same as now, same downtown building. He was buzzed up to the penthouse, and the door was opened by some old nerd, maybe in his 50s, bald, glasses, wearing a suit. Linc figured he was an assistant or something.

"Umm . . . I'm delivering a package," Linc said.

"Come in," said the nondescript man, leading him into some sort of fancy, extravagantly decorated room, maybe a study, where he sat on a very plush sofa, very comfortable. "You know who I am?"

Linc shook his head.

"They call me the Accountant".

Shit. Linc had heard the rumours. He never figured he'd get to meet the guy in person.

"My real name is Rowan, Rowan Nelson. Few people know that name. Those who have attempted to abuse the knowledge are dead. But I believe that, since we're doing honest business, we should be on equal grounds. And I *do* know your name. I know your name, your cousins' names, the name of the aunt who raised you, the diabetic one you're looking after these days. I know plenty of names".

Lincoln nodded. It was a threat, but him being here was an opportunity too.

"I've heard good things about you, Mr. Lincoln Fredericks. Our mutual friend, Mr. Dillon Sturgess, reports that you've shown the most potential out of all the folks in his line of direct management. So I wanted to get a look at you. I like what I'm seeing. May I see the goods?"

Linc retrieved the package. The Accountant inspected it visually but didn't partake. He instead took a scale off a shelf in the room and tested the package. Finally, he nodded.

"Yes. Good. I do appreciate honesty. Mr. Fredericks, do you like the life you're leading?"

"Yes, sir".

"Hmm . . . it's good to appreciate what you have. But ambition is important, too. Given a choice, would you want to move into a bigger role in my operation?"

"Absolutely, sir".

"Do you think you're ready?"

Linc considered the question. "I won't know until I try, sir".

"Good answer. You're young, but not inexperienced. I'll talk to Sturgess. We'll up your volume, I recommend you recruit some additional headcount. I'd give it another few months, but I project there'll be an appropriate opening and that you'd be a good fit". Rowan stood up. "Glad to have had the chance to meet you in person, and I appreciate that you didn't try to skimp the product or cheat me," he said, holding out a hand. Linc shook it and took the hint, seeing himself out.

That was it. Afterwards, Linc felt confused. He had met the Accountant, but . . . they barely spoke about anything at all. It seemed like the Accountant was pleased with him, but Linc hadn't done anything more than courier some product and give a couple of good answers. He wasn't sure whether to feel proud or disappointed, or both. He hoped that next time he got a chance like this, he'd be able to impress the Accountant, to do well.

And now, about six months later, Linc *was* back. But under very different circumstances.

He hadn't wanted to drive the psychotic lunatic here, he wasn't *going* to, but somehow Unkillable already knew all about the Accountant. Once he figured—based on the description Linc was forced to divulge—that Linc knew the Accountant's address, he gave Linc a simple choice—drive or die.

Wasn't much of a choice, really. Linc drove.

"You said you've been here?" asked the psycho as they crossed a tasteful lobby towards the elevators. Linc nodded. "I'd ask if there's anything I should watch out for, but I don't trust you anyway".

"Excuse me—" started one of the security guards behind the lobby desk. He was promptly ignored. Unkillable tried to open a glass door leading to the elevator hall, but Linc knew you had to be buzzed in. The Accountant lived in a fancy and *secure* building.

"Hey, open the door for me?" Unkillable asked the guard.

"Are you visiting one of the residents?"

"Yes, we are".

"Which unit? I'll have to ring them up".

"I'd really rather you didn't".

"I can't just let you up. Building policy. I have to check with the resident you're here to see".

Unkillable rubbed his chin. "Mr. Lincoln! What do you think we should do here?"

"I don't want to shoot this guy," Linc answered, expecting Unkillable to order him to get violent.

"No, no, we don't need to do that. You know what? Ring up apartment . . . what was the number?"

"It's the penthouse," mumbled Linc.

"Yes, ring them up, and ask for Rowan. And say there's a Lincoln . . . what's your last name, buddy?"

"Fredericks".

"A Lincoln Fredericks here to see him. Let's see. You think he'd let you up?"

"I have no idea," answered Linc honestly while the guard rang up the suite.

A minute later, they were in the elevator. Linc did *not* expect the secretive head of a crime organization to just let him into his home uninvited. In fact, he was hoping the Accountant wouldn't buzz them up. Linc figured if Unkillable was forced to shoot his way up, somebody would hear something, maybe call the police. *Something* would have to give. And maybe he'd manage to make a run for it in the chaos.

He *really* wanted to make a run for it. But he saw what happened when Craig tried to make a run for it.

Craig was now dead.

So there he was, riding up the elevator early in the morning.

Fucking hell.

. . .

The shit hit the fan as soon as she walked into the precinct station.

"Ma'am! Chen just called in, she's looking for you".

"Don't call me ma'am", Borst said, taking the call. Sergeant Chen was a good cop, one of her best. Borst fought hard for her recent promotion. She wanted to see her good, hard-working cops get the recognition they deserved. Especially if they were female. Women cops were still passed over far too often in the force.

"Chen?"

"Captain Borst, I'm on a scene. Major Crime's here too, they're insisting it's their scene. But I have a strong suspicion it's got something to do with the gang crimes we've been investigating, and—"

"Text me the location. I'm on my way. Cordon the area, let the police photographers through, but no forensics, and don't let the MCU take charge yet. Where are you?"

It took her too long to drive over. Fucking traffic. By the time she got to the parking garage out by the docks, Landau and Prakash from Major Crime were already strutting around, acting like the scene was theirs.

"Fellows, what's going on here?" she asked, assuming a commanding tone.

"Borst, this is clearly MC. We've got multiple homicides. Tell your people to back off".

"The way I see it, Prakash, this shoot-out happened in *my* precinct. My officers were first responders. Plus, we've been investigating a series of clearly gang-related shoot-outs. We get charge of the scene".

"Bullshit. Dead people means Major Crime. That's how it's done, you know that".

Borst felt her blood start to boil against the condescending prick. “Prakash, you want a fucking gang war on our hands? Because that’s what this leads to. And if that’s what we get, my precinct’s going to see a hell of a lot more dead people, and somehow I don’t see your lot volunteering to pick up the fucking slack. So calm down and get the hell out of my crime scene”.

She ducked under the yellow police tape. She knew that dick Prakash was right behind her, but who gave a shit, let him follow. Borst marched on, trying her best to keep herself from wincing at the pure stench of the scene. Blood, and . . . vomit? Ugh. Borst was tempted to take a swig from her flask, let the alcohol take the smell out of her nose, but she couldn’t do that with the MCU dicks tailing her.

“What do we got?” she finally asked Chen.

“Four bodies, and one . . . uhm, one decapitated head”.

“One *what*?”

Chen pointed. On the ground, staring upwards, laid a head. “Fucking hell,” Borst said. There wasn’t much else to be said to that.

“Med expert put the time of death for the bodies between two and four a.m. last night. Cause of death would be gunshot wounds in each case. Not sure about the head. We’re trying to identify the bodies”.

“We think it’s gang-related?”

Chen pulled Borst closer, whispering. “Based on the outfits, the scene, it’s a maybe. We found nothing on the bodies—no I.D.’s, phones, weapons, nothing. Given the number of shooting sprees we’ve had lately with a similar M-O, it’s *got* to be related, but . . . I don’t think I have enough to keep Major Crime away”.

Borst nodded. “What else?”

“Well, there’s definitely . . . something doesn’t make sense here. Look over there,” Chen pointed to a spot a few feet away from one of the bodies. It was covered in bloodstains. There were bullet casings, multiple gunshot marks all over the concrete. “I’ve been trying to reconstruct the scene. We think this was an execution. The bullets are different sizes, so it must have been a bunch of these guys all shooting at one person. But there wasn’t a body there. The bodies we *did* find were all shot exactly once each, as far as I can tell”.

“They must have dragged the body off,” said Landau. He and Prakash were still hanging around, trying to participate.

Borst ignored him. "Can we tell where the cars stood? I'm assuming they drove off. We'll need analysis of any track marks and footprints. I see some in that blood puddle over there. Could be an execution and a retaliation. They executed this one vic, another gang sprang in, shot back, hit a few of their rivals, and removed their friend, or friends. *Or*, it could have been the other way around. This guy got lucky somehow, killed four and then was mowed down by the survivors. Either way, this strongly suggests an inter-gang conflict".

"Where does the severed head fit in, with no matching body on the scene?"

"It *could* explain the vomit. I don't want to speculate too much yet. Chen, work with those theories, there could be something there".

"Give it up, Borst. You don't have enough to base anything on. It may or may *not* be gang-related. It's an MCU scene. Major. Crime. Got it?" Prakash argued again.

Borst took a deep breath. Fuck it. He wasn't wrong.

"Look, I know we have four bodies, which is major. But we *do* have stakes in this investigation. So we investigate in parallel. Chen's still first on the scene, so she leads. That's the best you're going to get".

Prakash nodded. "I'll have to check with my captain, but we could probably use the extra resources. Fine, have it your way. Can we get forensics in here now?"

"Go for it, but tell them to watch their step".

Prakash and Landau turned away, and Borst could have sworn she heard one of them mutter "bitch". She was glad she got to them. Pricks.

"Chen, I want you on this one. Follow it close. Take Santiago and Brewster. See if there's any security cameras, witnesses. I doubt you'll find much, but maybe we'll get lucky. Chase any links to the other scenes we're looking at. Trace every single bullet".

"Already on it, Captain. I also have one of our men at the hospital".

Borst looked back at Chen questioningly. "Hospital?"

"One of the victims is still alive".

. . .

"Hi! You know this guy, right?" asked Unkillable as the door was opened by Rowan Nelson, the Accountant.

The secretive crime mogul surveyed the two men in front of him. "Mr. Lincoln Fredericks. He's a loyal associate, yes. And you are?"

"I'm the guy waiting for you to invite me in. Not very polite so far".

"My apologies. Do come in. Can I offer you some coffee?" asked Rowan. It *was* morning, after all.

Linc was confused. He felt like he should say something, warn Rowan off, but . . . well, he might get shot for it. Shit was complex. He'd just wait it out and see where things went.

The three men found themselves in the same study Linc visited previously, sitting on the same sofa with Unkillable next to him. It was still plush, but nothing about the situation was comfortable. Unkillable accepted a cup of coffee, and downed it in one go. His face went pale very suddenly, but then recovered its usual colour.

"Oof! That was *not* at all subtle. I did *not* expect poison. You must have heard about me".

Rowan frowned. "I have".

"I'm Unkillable".

"So I've heard".

"Who told you?"

"Well, I have a few police officers in my employ who first alerted me to a few of your . . . sprees".

"Corrupt cops? That is smart. But they wouldn't have told you much".

"No, I heard the details from the Italians, and I put two and two together".

"The Italians, huh?"

"Do you know Grossi?"

"I killed Grossi".

"Yes. His son's not very happy about that".

"Ah. Excuse me a second, I've got to send a text," said Unkillable. He dug into his pocket, threw five cell phones onto the Accountant's coffee table, identified a particular one, and sent out a text. Linc caught a glimpse of it. It was an execution order on Grossi Jr.

"Sorry about that. Where were we?"

"Just making introductions".

"Right, yes. After you tried to poison me. Not very manly. Well, what have you heard?"

"You're unkillable. Or so you claim. Bullets don't work. Does drowning work?"

"The Chinese tried that. Weighed me down with rocks, the whole thing. Took me two fucking days to get out of the fucking river, and let me tell you, I was not happy when I made it back to their warehouse".

"Has anyone tried snapping your neck?"

"Actually, no, not yet".

"Let's give it a shot, shall we?"

At the Accountant's command, two burly men burst into the room, walking around the couch. One of them positioned himself behind Unkillable, who was probably less than half his size. The henchman grabbed Unkillable's head in his gigantic hands, and twisted.

Linc heard a very audible *crack*. The psycho's body slumped into the sofa cushions. For a moment, nobody moved.

"Well, that's that," said Rowan, dusting his knees off and starting to get up.

He stopped halfway to upright as Unkillable spoke. "Woah. That is . . . going to leave me with a stiff neck for hours," he said, twisting his head this way and that. "Shit".

"Hmm. That didn't work," summarized the Accountant.

"It did not. Are we done, or what else you got?" asked Unkillable.

"Cut off his head," ordered Rowan.

His two giant subordinates stepped over. Each one grabbed hold of one of Unkillable's arms, lifting him off the couch. One of the two held out what looked like a ninja sword. "In the bathroom, please. I don't want blood splatter here".

"No, we wouldn't want that. Linc, please shoot this guy," said Unkillable, gesturing at the henchman to his left.

Linc didn't even think about it. At Unkillable's command, he shot at the guy holding the sword. The guy fell back. There was going to be a bloodstain on the carpet after all.

The other big fellow let go of Unkillable and went for his gun, but the small psychopath was quick—he disarmed Rowan's bodyguard and shot him in the neck.

"I expected loyalty, Lincoln," commented the Accountant. "I'm deeply disappointed".

"Actually, I didn't expect that either," Unkillable chimed in. "Stockholm syndrome? Or just backing the better horse?"

Linc didn't know what to say.

"Did we get blood on the carpet? Damn. You must have cleaner crews, right? Body removal?"

Rowan nodded. "Don't worry about that—I know people".

"Good. Since I'm taking over your place, I'll want it relatively clean".

"And what if I said I'd rather burn this place down than let you have it?"

"Funny you should suggest that! That's exactly what the Italian did, Grossi, just a couple of days ago. He set his own house on fire. Nice big mansion near Mount Pleasant. Shame, really. Hey, Linc," Unkillable turned to his now seemingly-loyal associate, "Go through the apartment. See if there are any more assholes lurking around. Also, grab any drugs, phones, laptops . . . anything interesting you can find".

Linc obeyed. While he was out of the room, the two bosses conferred.

"So, what are you really?"

"Alien. Outer space shit".

Rowan did not respond.

"Okay, I'm lying. I don't know, actually. I'm just Unkillable".

"And now you're going to kill me?"

"Oh, not until I get information out of you. Names and contact information of those cops on your payroll, for example. I mean, there's a lot of information I need, and I'm willing to bet you've got all of it. Everybody knows *about* you, but few men know your name, Mr. Accountant. That says a lot".

Rowan poured them both some more coffee. Proper coffee, this time. "You're a smart man," he said.

"You were expecting otherwise?"

"Let's say, I *hoped* otherwise. In my head, there's a thousand calculations running, different contingency plans, trying to think of a way out of it. But I think this might be it for me," admitted the Accountant. "I haven't managed to come up with anything useful yet".

"You're struggling with factoring in a variable you don't understand. I sympathize".

"We could work together".

"We could try. Eventually, you'd try to kill me. You'll fail. Then I'd *have* to kill you".

"Why?"

"How'd you get to where you are? This fancy fucking penthouse. The ledgers you've got, which I bet cover dozens of *associates*, millions—billions?—of dollars tied up in drugs and whores. Look, the Italians do the organized crime bullshit, racketeering, protection money, union squeezing. The Asians do the smuggling. The other folks, Russians and, I don't know, Latinos, whoever, they run around shooting everybody's heads off—"

"That's incredibly racist, you know".

"Sure. Fuck you. I kill people indiscriminately, and you're gonna complain about racism? My point is, you're the only one in the city with visibility to all of it. People respect you. *Everyone* respects you. Respect you enough not to give up your name. So, how'd you get here? You ever shot a guy in your life?"

Rowan shook his head.

"See, I figured you hadn't. Because you never tried to shoot me. *Everybody* tries to shoot me. It's the first thing they do. Even if they know it doesn't work, there's an instinct in people who've shot, who've killed in the past . . . shooting becomes a *thing* with them. Just a response. You don't have that, so I figured you've never shot anyone. But then, how'd you end up the biggest crime lord in the whole fucking city?"

"State, actually".

"Fuck! Seriously?"

Linc got back to the room. He had a whole bunch of electronics and plastic bags with him. "No one else in the apartment," he said. Unkillable nodded.

"You knew about me and figured two guards were enough?"

"If the stories I heard were false, two would be enough. If they were true, it wouldn't make a difference, two or twenty".

"You're fucking smart, too. So answer my question already".

"You wanted to hear how I worked my way up here. Sure, I'll tell you. When I got started, this whole thing was a nickels-and-dimes operation, small-time crooks. The city had gangs, mobs, a whole lot of teenagers running around like life was *West Side Story*. All it took was a bit of vision. Instead of gangs just shooting one another, have them be productive, give them something to do, a purpose. It required foresight and organization. That's where I came in. They call me the Accountant because I *am* an accountant. I know how to organize process flows, how to implement controls so that the people who get paid get paid what they deserve, no more and no less. When the credits and debits all balance, everybody gets their fair share of the profit, and you can keep growing at a reasonable rate. See? That's why we should work together. I have value. I know what—"

"Ah, fuck it. Forget I asked," said Unkillable, getting up. "I think maybe they just call you the Accountant because you're fucking *boring*".

"You're going to shoot me now?"

"Already told you. I'm going to pick your brain first. I'm usurping your position. Like one of those . . . you know, there's an animal that digs under its prey's skin, lays eggs, and then it bursts out. Or am I making that up? Like a spider or something. Or wait, no, I'm thinking of *Alien.* The movie. Anyway, I'm the new Accountant. Except it's a fucking dumb name, so I'll keep Unkillable. But first, you'll tell me everything".

"You're going to torture me".

"Am I? I don't know. You're a smart guy. You feel like starting by going over some files on that laptop there, getting me up to speed? I can torture you if you want. I can get Linc to do it, too, now that he's so loyal all of a sudden. What do you think, Linc? But I think we'll all feel better if we just . . . you know, pretend it's just you training up your successor before your retirement. We'll even get a cake in. Celebrate".

"But then you'll shoot me. You won't let me live".

"You have a family, Accountant?"

"Yes. Three daughters".

"Linc, is he lying to me?"

"I-I don't know".

"Did you see any photos in his bedroom?"

"I . . . didn't notice".

"Check if there's anything on the fridge, too. We'll wait".

This is . . . fucked up. Right? Linc asked himself. A minute later, he was back in the study. "Nothing. No family photos, nothing on the fridge".

"Did you lie to me, Accountant?"

"Fine, I'll admit it. Yes, I lied".

"You're scared of me?"

"I guess I am".

"Good. Then you'll stop giving me bullshit. Now, let's get to work. I have a fucking criminal empire to learn about and take control of before I get rid of you," said Unkillable.

Linc wondered whether he backed the right horse after all.

. . .

He called that night after her shift ended. She was just about to leave when her cell rang.

"Hi".

"Hi".

"Uhm . . . look, I'm sorry".

"Yeah. You should be," Borst said. She spent the whole damn day thinking about what she would say to him. This was one of the kinder, calmer options.

"I know. I shouldn't have just left like that—that was shitty. I just needed to think. It's been a really long time, and I've been stuck inside my head for so long that things . . . get complicated. I started to overthink, and . . . well, I shouldn't have left without saying anything," Owen tried to explain.

"Okay".

"How are you feeling?"

Borst sighed. "Annoyed. At you, at . . . work stuff".

"That's fair".

"Do you regret it? Last night?" she asked.

"What do you mean? I just told you, I shouldn't have left like—"

"No, I meant . . . do you regret coming over? Doing . . . what we ended up doing".

"No. I don't . . . I don't regret that. Do you?"

"I guess not. I was just worried *you* did. That you'd freak out and . . . things between us would change. Or that I'd hurt you . . . I'm really scared of hurting you".

"Dinah, look . . . it's me. My whole thing is you can hurt me, and I get better. I heal. You know?

Borst chuckled despite herself. “Okay, I guess that’s true. I didn’t think about it that way”.

“You don’t have to feel like you have to walk on eggshells around me. I’m an adult, you know. Sure, I have depression, but that doesn’t mean I can’t have normal human relationships. Unfortunately, it also doesn’t guarantee that I won’t be a jerk on occasion. And I apologize for that. You deserve better”.

Borst nodded to herself. “Yeah, I do. Anyway, how was your day?”

“It was fine. Training with Richardson. Booked a board meeting, first one in months I’m actually thinking of attending”.

“That’s good”.

“Yeah. How about you? You said some annoying stuff happened at work?”

“Just . . . politics. Major Crime's fighting us over a crime scene. The gang stuff I told you about yesterday seems to just keep escalating”.

“And there’s still nothing I can help with?”

“Nothing yet”.

“I’ll be on standby anytime you need me”.

“I know. And maybe we can do another dinner some evening?” she suggested, hoping it wasn’t a mistake.

“Yeah. Let’s do that. Let me know what works for you”.

She was very tempted to suggest that very night. But *he* didn’t suggest it, and she didn’t want to push it. Like her grandma always said, if it’s meant to happen, it’ll happen. No need to rush things.

“I better drive home,” she ended up saying. It was the mature thing to say. Right?

“Okay. Talk tomorrow?”

“Night, Owen”.

“Goodnight Dinah”.

6 — *Wasn't human*

TRAFFIC was awful the next morning. Several lights were out—the city was experiencing rolling blackouts due to the heatwave. Borst was tempted to blare the siren just to be able to move and make it into the station. Would that have been so immoral?

And, of course, for the second day in a row, she barely made it into the building before she was called out again. This time it was Santiago with an urgent message.

"Captain! Just got a call. The vic from that garage shooting yesterday woke up. Doctors okayed him for questioning".

"Which hospital? City University?"

"Yeah. Chen is already en-route".

"Does the MCU know about this?"

"I don't think so".

Without even stepping into her office, her car keys still in hand, Borst turned right back around. "Good. Tell Chen to wait, don't tell anyone else. I'll be right there".

This time Borst *did* put the siren on. Chen only had to wait fifteen minutes for her.

"What do we know?" asked the captain as soon as she found her sergeant.

"Anthony DeMatteo. Couple of arrests, petty stuff, possession. Nothing major".

Borst nodded. "Are you his doctor?" she asked the white-coated woman who had just left the victim's room.

"Dr. Fulson. Yes".

"And you cleared him for an interview?"

"He's fine. Bullet went clean through muscle. He's just being a little bitch about it. Go on ahead".

Borst smiled, thanked the doctor, and walked in. Chen was right on her heels with a notebook ready.

"Mr. DeMatteo?"

"Who're you?" asked the nervous-looking guy on the hospital bed. He was young and heavily tattooed.

"Captain Borst. This is Sergeant Chen. We're here to ask you some questions. You've already been informed of your rights, you have the right to a lawyer, everything you say can and will be used against you, you may—"

"I'll talk," Tony interrupted. "You *have* to get this guy".

"What guy?"

"The guy from the shoot-out! It was a fucking genocide".

Borst blinked, but decided not to correct her witness's misuse of the term. "Why don't you tell us what happened, from the start".

"Right. Well, there were a bunch of us out in that garage—"

"What were you doing? Drug deal?"

"No," Tony shook his head. "No, no, just, uh, just chilling. You know".

Borst doubted that very much, but no drugs were found at the scene.

"Sure. Guys just randomly chilling at an abandoned garage in the middle of the night. So, what happened?"

"Well, this guy showed up. He had a bag with a fucking head in it, and—"

Borst remembered the decapitated head. Frankly, she'd been trying to forget about it. For one thing, it didn't quite fit any of her theories so far, which bothered her to no end. For another thing, it was a decapitated head. Fucking gruesome.

"Slow down. A guy?"

"Yes".

"Ever seen this guy before?"

"Never".

"Right. And he had a *head* in a *bag*?"

"Yes, in a backpack".

"Whose head?"

The guy froze for a second. "I don't know. Just some head".

"You don't know the head?"

Tony shook his head. Borst could tell he was lying, but she let it slide for the moment. "What happened to the head? And how did you know it was in the bag in the first place?"

"Well, we didn't know at first, but we took it out—someone took the head out of the bag".

"Who took it out? Was it the same guy who brought the bag?"

"I don't . . . I don't remember. I think . . . no. No, he, the guy, he threw the bag at me, and I looked inside, and . . . I saw the head. Then someone else grabbed the bag and took . . . took the . . ."

Tony looked like he was about to vomit. Borst decided to change tracks. "Okay. So, the head's out. You all see the head. Then what happens?"

"Some of the guys, well, we all kind of freaked over the head, so then . . . some of the guys shot at the guy. The guy with the bag".

"You shot at the guy? You all had unregistered weapons?"

"No-no-no, *I* didn't—I don't—I mean . . ."

"It's fine, we already know there were multiple weapons at the scene. We're not after you, Tony. We're after this guy. You and us, we're working together here. Looks, let's take a step back. What'd he look like, the guy?"

"Short, skinny, messy dark hair . . . I don't know".

"Would you recognize him from a line-up?"

"I don't know. The light was bad in that garage, and he shot me pretty early on. I guess I passed out".

"So, you don't know anything useful," Borst said, exasperated. "Well, shit. In that case, once you're released, we'll probably want to move you to police custody. You'll be charged with—"

"Wait! Wait, I didn't even get to the main part! I didn't get a good look, but . . . okay, so we shot at him, right? I mean, I mean the other guys shot at him. He got—he got shot. Like, a whole bunch of times, and . . . and then he—he got back up".

Borst was silent for a moment. That *couldn't* be right.

"What do you mean?" Chen asked. "Shot and got back up?"

"I'm talking like . . . ten, twenty bullets, at least. Head shots, chest shots, everywhere. Tons of fucking blood. We shot the guy. And he . . . I think he like, fell down. Like, we *hit* him, and he fell. He definitely got shot. Shit, I was sure he was dead. But then he got *back up*—right back up—like it was nothing, like he wasn't ever shot. Like the bullets didn't touch him. It didn't make no sense, it just . . . I can't describe it".

"The bullets passed through him? Like he was incorporeal?"

"In-what?"

"A ghost. The bullets shot *through* him, you said," Borst tried to clarify.

"No, no. They *hit* him, he . . . I'm pretty sure he bled. But he just kind of, he just shook it off".

Shit, thought Borst. *It . . . it* can't *be.*

But she knew it could. The bullet patterns, the blood spray patterns. It made sense. She remembered the garage scene. There was that *one spot* where somebody clearly got shot by a barrage of bullets—the marks and shells were there, not to mention the bloodstains. But no *body*. The stray bullets came from multiple weapons, but those found in the victims all came from the same gun.

It made little sense at the time. Unless . . .

If this guy, Tony, was telling the truth, everything seemed to fall into place.

"Did he give a name? Anything we can use to identify him?"

Tony shook his head. "No name. He's Unkillable, that's all he said. And he *was*, I swear. He wasn't human. We shot him, and nothing. It was freaky as fuck. He must be some kind of . . . I don't know. I don't know what he is. But you *have* to get him. He's fucking dangerous".

Borst nodded. "Don't worry. We'll… take care of it. Thanks for the cooperation," she managed, her head swimming.

"Captain?" asked Chen as they left the room. "What are you thinking?"

"I need to make a couple of calls," said Borst. "Give me a minute".

Could it be him? Unkillable . . . it fit the evidence. It fit everything. But it couldn't . . .

That morning. She woke up, and he was gone.

Even the timeline worked.

Or did it?

Borst made sure Chen wasn't looking and pulled out her flask, taking a good swig just to steady herself. Then she pulled out her phone. She called Everett. He was a police technical analyst and a friend.

"Borst? How you doing?"

"Good, good, just out on a big case. Listen, if I give you a phone number and a time horizon, can you triangulate locations for me?"

"You know I need a warrant for that, Borst".

"Fuck, you're right. Okay, I'll get the warrant. What if I send the information now? Would you pull up the data and just sit on it until I get the warrant? It'll speed things up massively".

Everett sighed. "For you, sure. What's it for?"

"It's a multiple homicide case. You know I wouldn't ask if it wasn't important".

"Okay, text the details over, I'll get to it. But I'm not sending the data until you get that warrant".

"I'm on it".

Borst hung up. She was just about to make a second call, this time to Richardson.

Because she was thinking . . . *Unkillable. What if it was Owen? Could it have been?*

Because in that case, she had to follow the train of thought, consider the possibilities.

What if it wasn't *just* Owen—what if Richardson was in on it too? What if she put him up to it?

Shit.

Okay, warrant first. She knew where Owen was until she fell asleep. That must have been . . . midnight, 1:00 a.m. If she could verify his movements afterwards . . . he must have gone home. So, get the warrant, get his location for the night, and rule him out. Simple.

As long as you can rule him out, there's no need to alert Richardson, no need to cast suspicion on anyone. Just rule him out. He couldn't have done it.

He couldn't have . . .

"Chen, I have to—" Borst started, but Chen was on another call. Borst waited.

"Captain, that was Prakash. Major Crime is onto something, they're commencing an armed operation, something heavy. They think it's related to the garage shoot-out".

"Armed op? Okay. I want you to head on over—you'll support the op on my authority. I want you over their shoulder the whole way through. Share our notes from the interview with that clown as a show of good faith. And Chen, be safe. I've got to chase down a warrant and follow a lead. I'll meet you back at the precinct after the op".

Chen nodded, and the two cops headed out of the hospital.

. . .

Linc was trembling. He couldn't control it.

The past—one day? Two? It felt like a decade—had been endlessly stressful. The psychopathic monster has been in and out of the penthouse, making sure to always leave Linc with no phone, laptop, wallet, gun, or any means of communication. Not that Linc was tempted to risk it. He was scared. Terrified.

Rowan the Accountant was dead now.

Unkillable forced Linc himself to pull the trigger. He shot Rowan in the back of the head, merely grateful that he didn't have to look him in the eye.

Everything was a blur after that.

Random people would come up to the apartment—Linc assumed most were members of different criminal organizations—and leave, or die. Linc was ordered to summon cleaning crews from the Accountant's list every three or four hours.

Based on what he'd heard, Unkillable was consolidating, building up a central empire in control of the whole city, placed firmly under his scrawny thumb. A good number of associates appeared to be excited by the proposition. Another good number had been shot. Some by Linc, on command.

At this point, he was half numb, half revolted. All he wanted was to be out of that penthouse, back to his old life. But that old life was gone, forever—the psychopath made him a promise.

"Look, I'm going out, but I'll be back. You'll be here, or you'll be dead. I have your phone with your contacts, photos. Thanks to the late Mr. Accounting, I know everything there is to know about your life. I know where you live, I know about your aunt, your vulnerabilities. You know me. I don't care who I hurt. I'll hunt you and yours down if I have to. Don't make me have to".

Fuck.

He said it all so casually, too. Like it was barely a threat. Like he was *bored*. It was only a few hours ago that Linc finally put it together, what was so unsettling about this freak. It wasn't just that he couldn't be killed—it was his callousness. He would kill, he'd get shot, and he didn't give a shit. He wasn't some sort of supervillain, laughing maniacally and mocking people who opposed him. He just had them shot, coldly and calmly. He didn't seem to regret killing but didn't celebrate it either. To him, shooting a guy in the head was akin to stepping on an ant. Half the time, it honestly seemed like he didn't even want to be there, didn't want to be doing any of it. He didn't appear to take any joy in it.

Why was he even doing this?

Over a couple of days, Unkillable had consumed copious amounts of drugs—enough to supply a whole neighbourhood for at least a week. Insane. He also summoned multiple girls into the Accountant's luxurious bedroom. He shot many, many people. He was living like a movie gangster, fucking, snorting, and killing indiscriminately.

Yet, Linc hadn't seen him crack a single smile. In fact, he hadn't seen the blank expression on his face change much at all. Was he some sort of alien? Killer robot? Anything was possible at this point. He was fucking Unkillable—how did that make any sense?

At times, it felt like he was *trying* to be human because he knew he wasn't. At one point, he asked Linc if he wanted anything—drugs, or one of the ladies. "I don't mean to be selfish, I just wasn't thinking about it. Help yourself if you'd like," he said. Linc politely declined.

Earlier, the monster was conferring with some associates, and Linc had a chance to take a nap for the first time in literally days. It was no wonder he was so dazed, it wasn't just the shock and the murders, he'd been awake for ages. He needed sleep, badly.

Linc woke up with a clearer head and a new resolve.

It was simple, actually. Even if he kept obeying this asshole, there was a good chance Unkillable would eventually kill him anyway. If he escaped, Unkillable would kill him and come after his aunt, his crew . . . everyone. And he knew he couldn't stop the monster by himself. No criminal in the city could stop him.

Which left only one option. Sic the pigs on him. Let the police figure it out.

Of course, he had to make sure Unkillable didn't find out, or Linc was as good as dead anyway. He'd have to wait for the right moment. He had no access to a phone, barely a moment alone in the apartment. Even when Unkillable was out, there was usually someone else there. He could try to conspire with another associate, but if they snitched, he was dead. Better to wait and go it alone.

It finally happened, fifteen minutes ago. The small creep stuck his head out of the study, calling out to Linc who was in the kitchen. It was just the two of them in the apartment.

"Hey, I ordered food! Forgot all about food, when's the last time we ate? Sorry about that, I don't really need to eat, so I sometimes forget other people do. Anyway, food's downstairs. Would you go down and grab it?"

And there it was. The opportunity.

Linc was shaking during the elevator ride.

The delivery girl was outside the lobby. "Hey, this is going to sound weird, but can I borrow your phone?" he asked her.

"Huh? Look, I've got three more deliveries to make, I've got to—"

"*Please*. I'd pay you, but I got nothing on me. I . . . I'm fucking desperate, it's life or death, seriously. Please".

The delivery girl looked flustered, undecided. But finally, she lent Linc her phone.

"Just make it quick".

He dialled.

"Nine-one-one, what's your emergency?"

Explaining the situation was difficult. "Yes. I . . . there's a guy here, he's . . . look, there was a shoot-out, big gang shoot-out, in a garage by the docks, two days ago," he said, giving a rough address. "The guy who did it, he's here, you have to come get him. He's very, *very* dangerous, armed—"

"Sir, please slow down. I'm transferring you to—"

"There's no time. He'll suspect me. I have to go back. Look, it's . . . organized crime, he's a killer. You have to bring in a whole team, everything you've got".

"Sir, if this is a prank, the police doesn't take it lightly. This line is for emergencies only".

"This *is* an emergency, damn it! There's a killer".

"Hold on please".

The delivery girl wasn't happy. "Will it take much longer? I really have to go!"

Hell only knew what Unkillable was thinking upstairs.

Linc was agitated.

Another voice came on now. "Hi, this is Detective third-grade Prakash of Major Crime. You said you have information about a shoot-out?"

"Yes. At a garage, by the docks, an abandoned parking garage, two or three nights ago".

"Can you identify the perp? We'll need you to come down—"

"Stop! Listen to me, just fucking *listen*. It's a hostage situation. The same guy, the guy who shot all those people out at the garage, he's *here*, and he's got me . . . I have to get back. It's a fucking emergency, get a whole hit squad, a SWAT team, the place is full of guys and weapons. Just please, come in and get him. He's un—he's a fucking monster," said Linc. He was about to say Unkillable, but he didn't think he'd be able to explain.

All he could do was hope the police would believe him and come ready to nab the freak somehow.

"What's your location?" asked the cop on the line.

If he was shaking in the elevator on the way down, on the way back up he was convulsing so badly it was like his legs were made of jelly in an earthquake. He was worried about dropping the food.

He entered the penthouse, placed the food on the kitchen counter, and sat back down. His biggest fear for the moment was four words—*what took so long?*

Luckily, Unkillable didn't ask that.

That was fifteen minutes ago. It felt like an eternity had passed.

It was all Linc could do not to shake anymore. He couldn't have Unkillable getting suspicious.

Would they come?

Then, suddenly, finally, it happened.

All he heard was a shout of "Armed Police!" and then the penthouse door burst open. Without thinking, Linc jumped and ran off to hide out on the balcony.

He couldn't quite see what was happening, but he heard it. Cops, a good lot of them, swarming the apartment. The study door opened. Then more shouting.

"On the ground! Now!"

"Hands above your head!"

There were footsteps, then some soft mumbling. That must have been *him*.

"Ground, now!"

Finally, a gunshot and a sound that might have been a body falling down.

Some sort of physical struggle.

"Drop the weapon!"

"Don't shoot!"

Then more gunshots.

Linc lost track of what was happening. He was trembling, crouching on the balcony, head between his knees.

It felt like ages. Finally, the balcony door slid open.

"Come inside. Don't be such a fucking coward".

Shit.

He recognized the voice. It wasn't a cop. It was Unkillable.

Linc followed him in. There were at least six cops, dead cops, strewn around the apartment. One Asian woman, out of uniform but wearing a bulletproof vest, was on the floor, leaning against a wall and cradling a wounded, severely bleeding arm.

The monster picked up a gun and handed it to Linc. "Cover her, so she doesn't try to make a run for it".

While Linc pointed the weapon at the cop, Unkillable picked up a container of chow-mein and started stuffing his face. "Excuse my manners, but it's getting cold. Either of you want any?"

Neither Linc nor the cop responded.

"Well, you'll want some after the shock's over. So, Linc, what do you think? How'd the cops find us?"

"I . . . I don't know".

"Hmm. You have to get more creative. Really *think* about problems and possibilities. What I figure is one of the Accountant's cops, his inside men, didn't like what they heard. I contacted a bunch of them yesterday to inform them of the change in management. I guess this was the response".

"Oh".

"What do you think? What's your name, officer?"

"Chen," said the officer still on the floor.

"Detective?"

"Sergeant".

"Ah. Impressive. What's your . . . unit? Whatever you call it".

"Fuck off".

Unkillable walked over and rummaged through her jacket pocket. She spat at him. "Hey, relax. That's not very nice". He grabbed her badge. "16th Precinct. Right".

He washed the spit off his face in the kitchen sink and got back to his Chinese food. While he ate, Linc just stood there, gun still pointed at the cop who sat there bleeding. It was all so surreal, so unnerving.

"Fine. Lincoln, buddy, I'm off. I have a few things to take care of. We've got this to deal with now, too. Such a shame, we were so close. But . . . maybe . . . hmm. Getting an idea. Anyway, while I'm gone, here's what's going to happen". He was inspecting one of the bodies on the floor, grabbing something. "Come here," he said to Lincoln, pulling him by the arm.

His hand was so skinny, the pull so feeble, that Unkillable felt weak. For a split second, Linc was tempted to just break the guy, snap him in half. Then he remembered. Unkillable. Right.

He snapped out of his thoughts at a metallic sound.

The psycho had just handcuffed him to the door of the fridge.

"Like I said, I'm going out. Here's a phone," he said, handing it to Linc. "I need you to first call up another cleaning crew for this new mess. Then, assemble me an army. The contacts are stored on the phone, the Accountant had a system. I need weapons, I need twenty, thirty guys. Maybe more. See what you can do. Let's say . . . four hours. No, make it five, let's do that. Get the guys here, the weapons, order more food so that they're happy. Pizza or something. Get the guard downstairs to buzz everyone up. You got it?"

"Uh, yeah. Yeah".

"Good. And the handcuffs . . . look, it's an insurance policy. I'm sure you get it".

Linc didn't say anything.

Unkillable surveyed the room. "This is kind of fucked up, right?"

"How'd you . . . kill them all?"

"Oh, that's easy. You drop down, shoot for the legs. The legs are never protected. Then they fall down, and you aim for the heads. I took the gun off the guy trying to cuff me. Piece of cake. Oh, the shoot-at-the-legs thing only works if you're unkillable, like me. You probably shouldn't try it yourself. They hit me about five or six times".

"Right".

"Anything else?"

Linc shook his head.

"Good. I'll see you a few hours. Get me my army. Don't fuck it up".

Unkillable moved towards the door where Sergeant Chen was perched.

"Let me guess, I'm coming with?" she asked with a sneer.

"Nope," said Unkillable, and shot her in the head.

As he walked out of the apartment without even looking back, Linc started puking his guts out.

7 – *Were you there?*

HOURS.

It took fucking *hours* to get the damn warrant. Unbelievable. But finally, she managed to convince a judge and get it approved.

She called Everett.

“Hey! I have the warrant. I’ll email it over—would you mind sending the tracking data right away?”

“You got the warrant?”

“Yeah”.

“Then I can just tell you, no need to send anything. There’s nothing to send, there’s no data”.

“Huh?”

“The phone number you gave me shows no records between 1:00 a.m. and 8:00 a.m. on the morning you asked for. You sure you gave me the right date?”

Borst double-checked her earlier text. “Yeah, it’s right”.

“I expanded the search window, so I can send you where the phone was before and since”.

“Why wouldn’t there be any data for that morning?”

“Phone must have been off. That’s the only way to explain it”.

Fuck.

“Thanks, Everett”.

“You still want the data with the expanded window?”

“Yeah, sure. Email it to me. I’ll check it out later. Thanks”.

Fuck.

Okay, so . . . run-down. Witness testimony suggests that the garage shoot-out involved a person who got shot multiple times by multiple weapons, then got back up like nothing happened. Evidence on the scene corroborates this testimony, impossible as it sounds. Except Borst knew there was a way it was possible.

She knew one person who could get shot dozens of times and get right back up.

And his phone was *off* during the hours the shoot-out took place, so she couldn't rule him out.

She had to bring Owen in for questioning. She had no choice.

Okay. So . . . call Richardson. Find out where he was.

Before she did, though, she needed a drink. Her flask was starting to get too light for this time of day. Didn't she have a bottle of something in her glove compartment? Ah, fuck it. Call first.

Richardson picked up after just a couple of rings. "Dinah?"

"Hi Sharon. I need to check on a couple of things with you".

"Sure. What's going on?"

"Did you and Owen conduct any operation two nights ago? This would be the night after the factory fire at the docks".

"No, things have been pretty quiet after that fire. I thought you two had dinner that night?"

"Yes, I'm asking about afterwards. Early morning hours, 2:00 a.m., 3:00 a.m.?"

"I was in bed, Dinah. What's—"

"Sharon, where's Owen now?"

Richardson paused for a second. When she answered, she spoke slowly. She sounded suspicious. This wasn't good.

"Owen's out on an op right now. Dinah, what's going on?"

"What's the op? Where?"

"High Pits".

Shit. High Pits was a known hotspot for all kinds of violence. The area, which encompassed a few blocks, was named after its location on High Street and the nearby park, which used to be a giant sandpit. The name stuck because the neighbourhood was still a fucking pit. It had one of the highest weapons-per-capita figures in the country. The territory was always in dispute—Latin gangs, the Italians, everyone trying to make a claim for it. On hot summers like this, there were shootings in High Pits every other week.

"Why did you send Owen into High Pits?"

"Well, the police don't go in there," Richardson said, and Borst knew this to be true. Sadly, the local precinct tended to look the other way when it came to any crime out of High Pits. They didn't have the resources to deal with it, not to mention that annual police casualties didn't encourage them to put themselves in danger by getting any more active.

"I still have some informants down there," Richardson continued. "One of the local gangs, the Pit Serpents or something like that, they got their hands on some weapons. I asked Owen to nab them".

So . . . Owen was fighting gang crime. That wasn't what Borst wanted to hear.

But maybe this was a good thing. If Richardson's been sending Owen out to murder gang members, she wouldn't be dumb enough to tell Borst about sending him out on an op in High Pits. Or . . . was Richardson smart enough to give Borst *just* enough information to throw her off the scent? Was it a double bluff?

Maybe Richardson wasn't even in on it. What if Owen was on his own personal crusade to take out crime in this city? There was reason to believe he *may* have gunned down several members of an armed gang. And now he was heading into High Pits. Was he becoming a vigilante? Borst had to admit, he wasn't mentally stable. She thought it was just the depression, but what if there was more to it than that? Was it possible?

"Was he . . . did Owen seem eager to go?" she asked, fishing for clues, anything.

"Yeah. It's been a few days without action. And ever since your dinner he seems . . . extra motivated. Sort of on-edge. Dinah, what happened that night?"

"That's what I'm trying to find out," said Borst. "I'm heading over to High Pits. Text me the address".

"It's the high-school, Jefferson High. Are you sure that's a good idea? Cops walking into High Pits—"

"I'm in an unmarked vehicle, out of uniform. You know that, Sharon. I'll be fine".

"Well, just be careful. Do you want me to call Owen and give him a heads up?"

"Don't. In fact, stay off-coms with Owen for the time being".

Again, Richardson took a moment to respond.

"Dinah, I think you better tell me what's going on".

"Not until I know who to trust. Sorry, Sharon. I'll call you when this is all cleared up. We'll laugh about it later". Borst wished to all hell that'd be the case. Just a dumb mistake is all, a misunderstanding. It *had* to be.

Because even though all the evidence she had suggested that Owen was out there killing people, she knew it couldn't have been him.

It just couldn't.

Right?

Borst drove off, siren on.

. . .

She turned the siren off as she got close. Don't want to attract attention in High Pits. She turned onto High Street and parked in front of Jefferson High. Richardson explained that the asshole Serpents, a local wannabe gang, operated out of the decrepit gym and paid the janitors off to store stuff on school premises.

Guns, this close to kids. Not to mention drugs, and recruitment opportunities. It was sickening.

Borst walked around the school building, looking for any sign of trouble. Approaching the gym building out back, she heard two gunshots. She was just about to draw her weapon and walk in when she paused, listening.

"—stop shooting. I'm taking these. Got it?"

She recognized Owen's voice.

"The fuck are you? You police?"

"Yes. But I'm letting you off with a warning. No more guns in schools. If I hear of you Serpent clowns on school grounds again, I will personally—"

There was another gunshot. Borst held her breath.

"What did I *just* say? You can't shoot me. Doesn't work. Spread the word, get out of this school. Now get the fuck out of here".

He sounded . . . different. Commanding. Almost . . . confident. Borst was used to him talking in a flat, dispassionate voice. This was a different Owen.

Who shot whom? What was happening in there?

The gymnasium's door opened and two kids, teenagers, ran out. A minute later, Owen walked out, holding a plastic crate, the kind gym teachers use to hold basketballs or dodgeballs. It contained guns instead. Automatics.

"Dinah?" he noticed her, looking confused. "What are you doing here?"

Shit. She wasn't ready for him. She walked past him into the gym. She had to make sure.

No one inside. No one hurt.

"You let them go?"

"They're just kids. I don't know. What was I going to do? I can't actually arrest them, I'm not a cop. I just hope I scared them off enough. And I'm confiscating these".

Borst nodded. "You can't tell them you're a cop, you know. That's impersonating an officer. It's a crime".

"You want to arrest me?" he asked. He was joking, she knew, but . . . fuck. "Anyway," he continued, "why *are* you here?"

"I . . . have to ask you some questions. What happened here?"

"Richardson sent me out. Did she tell you where I was? She said High Pits is full of these gangs, kids really, sometimes they get their hands on guns. I just dropped by to take them out of their hands. They shot me a couple of times, but yeah, I scared them off. Hopefully, they do spread the word about the guy who can't die. Maybe it'll help lower crime in this neighbourhood".

"This neighbourhood's a hellhole," Borst sighed.

Owen nodded.

"Are you . . . Owen, are you trying to fight gang crime in this city?"

"Sure. I mean, wherever I can help. You said it yourself—it's all over the papers, the gang war, the violence this summer. It's out of control, and Richardson and I have been trying to think of some ways we can help".

Borst shook her head. "No, that's—that's not what I meant. Owen, where were you the night after . . . after our dinner?"

Owen eyed her, seemingly confused. "I already apologized for that, Dinah. I thought we were past it".

"Where did you go? What time?"

"I don't know. I waited until you fell asleep. I couldn't sleep, and I . . . I left, I just—I took a walk. I walked home".

"All the way home? From my place? It's over an hour. In the middle of the night?"

"Yeah. I needed to sort things out in my head. Walking helps".

"Your phone was off".

"My battery died. It's a shitty old phone, I need to get a new one. Wait . . . how did you know it was off?"

Borst bit her lip. "Owen . . . look, I need to bring you in".

"In where? What's going on?"

"In for questioning. Come with me".

"I don't—"

"Owen. Let's go".

She led him to her car parked across the street. He tossed the confiscated guns in her back seat, and they drove to her precinct station. She'd have to figure out what to do with the guns. There'll be a report to write. Well, that's a small headache for later. She had bigger headaches to worry about first.

It was a tense car ride. Neither of them said anything. She figured Owen could sense something was wrong, but he didn't ask anything, he didn't protest, he didn't . . .

Was it him? It couldn't be, could it?

All the evidence pointed to it. He had an opportunity, no alibi. Was there a motive? Possibly. He goes out on ops, busts gangs. He wants to save people. That's kind of a motive.

Worse . . . what if *she* was the motive? She turned him on to . . . to fighting crime. Being a hero.

What if it was all her fault?

She kept quiet. It was a short ride. She led him into an interrogation room.

"I'll be back in a minute".

He just nodded. He looked sad. He didn't look this miserable at High Pits minutes ago.

Wait, no, she told herself. *He could be . . . Owen might be a murderer. Clear your fucking head. You're about to interview him. You have to be impartial.*

But how could she be?

She stepped into her office. There was a bottle of scotch in her desk. Half full. Wait, no, there was barely a quarter left. When did it get so low? It didn't matter. With her back to the squad room so no one could see, she swallowed a mouthful straight from the bottle then left her office to find Santiago.

"Where's Chen?" she asked him.

"She's not with you?"

"She got pulled into an armed op with Major Crime, but that was hours ago. She didn't report back?" Borst asked. This was concerning, but she'd have to deal with it later.

"I didn't hear anything. Should I contact the MCU?"

"Yeah, give them a call. I'm surprised she hasn't reported back . . . okay. I'm about to interview a suspect, and I can't be disturbed. It's critical. If you find Chen, tell her to come in immediately. I'll talk to her after this interview".

"Do you want anyone else in on it? I can—"

"It's okay, I got it".

Outside the door to the interrogation room, Borst took a deep breath.

She knew what she was doing, what it meant. She just wished to all hell that she was wrong.

Fuck.

Okay, in we go.

. . .

"I'm going to ask you some questions".

"Is this an official police interview? What's going on?"

"I'm going to ask you some questions. It's an official, voluntary police interview, yes, but we're not charging you with anything yet. You can stop talking and walk out anytime you like. For now. You can ask for a lawyer at any point, that's your right. Whatever you want".

"Okay".

"It's important you understand your rights".

"Yes".

"Look, cameras are off, but I've got the tape running. That's just for my benefit. I'm not going to pull any good-cop, bad-cop bullshit with you. It's just you and me in a room. I'm going to ask you questions, and I need you to answer them honestly".

"I've always been honest with you. You know that".

"I hope so. Where were you the night between July 13 and 14?"

"I already told you. I was walking around the city".

"With your phone off?"

"My phone was dead".

"Were you by the docks, by any chance?"

"The docks? No, I wasn't even close to the East Side".

"How about here? For the tape, I'm presenting photos of the scene of the shoot-out that took place early morning, July 14".

"That looks like a parking garage".

"Were you there?"

"No".

"You claim that you did not take part in a violent confrontation between known gang members in the early hours of July 14, at the pictured location?"

"I did not".

"Did you take part in a violent confrontation today?"

"I . . . yes, you just saw me. I was trying to take the guns away from those kids. I got shot. I didn't—"

"On the night between the 13th and the 14th, did you have a weapon on you?"

"No, of course not. I was coming back from *your* place, you know I didn't have a weapon".

"Did you have a backpack on you?"

"No, I had nothing on me".

"Do you know anything about this? For the tape, it's a photo of the severed head found on the scene of the garage shoot-out".

"Severed head? What the fuck? What is this photo? You think I could have had anything to do with *that*?"

"Do you know whose head that is?"

"I have no idea".

"You've never seen this person before? Alive or dead?"

"Never".

"Look, we have a witness. One of the gang members who got shot that night survived. If I bring him here, will he be able to identify you as the perpetrator of the shooting?"

"I wasn't there. So, no".

"Said witness claims the perpetrator of the shooting on July 14 was shot multiple times in the head and chest, and got back up like he, and I quote, 'Wasn't ever shot'. He describes the perpetrator as being hit by at least ten or twenty bullets and just walking it off".

Silence.

"Nothing to say?"

"I don't understand".

"Our examination of the scene seems to support the testimony. On July 14, around 3:00 a.m., a man was shot multiple times, leaving bloodstains and bullet marks but no body. The witness says he got back up without a scratch. Does the description of this perpetrator and his . . . his special abilities, does it remind you of anyone?"

"It wasn't me".

"Would you describe, for the tape, your own special abilities?"

"I—you *know* what I can do. I can't die".

"Has this been verified by witnesses?"

"Yes, of course. *You've* seen it. You had a doctor check me out. You *know* I can't die".

"Have you ever been shot multiple times in the head and chest only to get back up as if nothing happened?"

"Yes. A bunch of times. You already know this".

"Describe your activities with Sharon Richardson".

"That was *your* idea! You introduced us!"

"What have you two been doing?"

"We've been saving lives. She sends me out on ops where I could be useful. Where my abilities could be useful".

"Your ability to survive grievous injuries?"

"Yes".

"Have you been tackling crime? Gang violence?"

"I . . . some of the ops, yeah. They've involved me going up against gangs. We broke down weapon rings, drug busts. Sure".

"Would you describe your, or Sharon Richardson's, mission as a vendetta against organized crime factions in this city?"

"No. That's ridiculous. Most of the time we tackle accidents, fires, we don't . . . you *know* what we're about, *you* put us together!"

"This is the last chance to tell me the truth".

"I *have* been telling the truth! You know me, you know—"

"I'm sorry. Owen, you're under arrest on suspicion of murder as per your suspected involvement in the shoot-out on July 14. We'll be moving you to a cell. You have a right to call a lawyer, anything you say from this point on can and will be used against you".

. . .

She expected him to protest. To yell, to argue, to say something, anything.

He just sat there. He looked at her, not glaring, not angry, just . . . he looked disappointed. *Betrayed.* And she felt like utter shit. But she had to do her job. She had to.

Santiago was there as soon as she exited the room.

"I need you to process and move—"

"Captain, it's urgent. I spoke with Major Crime, they—"

"Santiago, focus. I just arrested the man in that interrogation room, would you *please* just process and put him in a cell. I'm going out because it's been a *very* difficult day and I have to clear my head. Now—"

"But Captain, Chen—"

"I'll deal with Chen in an hour. I just need *one hour*, okay? Process him. Book him. Move him to a cell. Alone, just him, don't put him in with anyone else. Just . . . look, I'm leaving my phone at my desk," Borst said as she walked through the squad room and into her office. "That means no calls. For one hour. You're in charge". She walked away before he could say anything more.

She just needed an hour away from this bullshit. From this messed up, *fucked up* day.

8 – *He killed everyone*

OWEN couldn't believe what had happened.

He couldn't believe *her*. Borst. Dinah. She . . . what was she playing at?

Did she really think . . .

Yes. She must be thinking that. She must genuinely believe that he could have shot people, been involved in what was basically murder. She must believe it, because he was now in a cell, his fingers stained with ink, his head dully pounding. And, most of all, his soul just . . . withering. That's what it felt like.

He hadn't felt so lost in weeks. *Months.* Not since . . . not since before Dinah entered his life. And now she went and twisted it all around him, and he was in freefall. Literally alone and shut in a cell, metaphorically plunging through an endless, pitch-black abyss that went on forever and ever and ever.

Okay, stop that. First, you go over what you know. Don't start speculating about what she might be feeling or thinking. Owen knew that. S*tart with you.*

So, what did *he* know?

He knew he was miserable. Okay. He . . . okay, start at the beginning. Dinah recruited him to this hero crusade of hers. She connected him with Richardson. He'd been training, physically and mentally. He was saving lives, doing good.

And it felt good. He's been feeling better mentally, stronger. He could recognize that—he'd had periods in his life when he felt better, and this had been one of those. He was better. It didn't mean he was happy, it didn't mean he was cured of his depression, it didn't even mean he didn't still want to die—the incident at the burning factory proved that—but he *had* gotten better.

And things with Dinah . . . that one night they had, it was good. Yes, he freaked out. He shouldn't have, and he wasn't proud of sneaking out, but he couldn't change that now. He genuinely did spend the night walking the streets and trying to figure out what he felt . . . guilty, sad, excited, content, disgusted . . . so many conflicting emotions.

Just the usual, then.

But there was hope, that's for sure. And hope can be a beautiful thing.

Except now, for reasons he didn't understand and wasn't ready to speculate about yet, it seemed Dinah suspected him of being involved in that shoot-out she mentioned. Officially. She threw him in a cell, no less.

Hope turned into a suffocating cloud of disappointment dust.

Owen tried to clear his head from all thought for a few minutes. It wasn't working.

Fine, now was the time to speculate.

She thought he'd done it. She must be thinking that, or he wouldn't be locked up. This seemed to be based on a witness's testimony—she said someone had gotten shot and got back up.

That did sound like him. And the evidence corroborated it, whatever that meant. Plus, his phone did die, so there was no proof he *wasn't* there.

When he looked at it that way, he couldn't blame her for thinking he might be responsible.

He *had* been taking down criminals, too, with Richardson. Gangs. That might seem like part of a pattern.

This didn't look good for him.

Now, yes, he could have reasonably expected better from Dinah. She *knew* him. She was the one who recruited him to fight crime. Maybe that's why she might feel more conflicted, or responsible, but . . . she should have given him the benefit of the doubt. She knew he's a good person. She knew what he's been doing for the city.

So, it was disappointing she arrested him. He felt hurt. Even if he could understand her point of view, it was still reasonable and justifiable for him to feel hurt.

Okay. Owen felt that he'd processed his emotions. He was no longer plunging in freefall. It was more of a slow, sinking feeling. He was very familiar with that one. He could deal with it.

Right. That left a couple of questions.

Who *was* the person at the shoot-out who supposedly got back up after getting shot multiple times?

Was it *him*, somehow? Was he sleep-walking, or . . . maybe his powers had some dark side he wasn't aware of? Or, maybe just as disturbingly . . . was there someone else out there, someone else like him? With the same crazy powers, but ready to use them for killing people?

And if that was the case, how was he going to take this person down?

The other question was . . . what was he going to do next? Richardson. She'd be able to talk sense into Borst. Dinah was probably just conflicted, caught between her duty as a cop and whatever she was feeling towards him. Not just in the potentially romantic sense, but in terms of responsibility. After all, Dinah created this new version of him. If there was a chance Owen killed people, she'd feel like the blood was on her hands. Of course she was reeling. But Richardson could set her straight, surely.

Owen's been through so many years of therapy, he was pretty adept at going through that sort of emotional-logic exercise. Things made a bit more sense now.

Richardson.

He had the right to a phone call, didn't he? He'd just ask a cop for his call, and—

Wait, what . . . what was happening?

There was some sort of commotion outside his cell. Owen strained to see, to hear.

Seconds later, once he did manage to see and hear, he wished to hell he didn't.

. . .

Borst needed . . . she just needed . . .

Oh.

Without thinking, she came *here*. Got into her car and drove here.

Borst found herself parked outside the cemetery. She turned the ignition off and rummaged in the glove compartment. Slowly, she refilled her flask and drank, just a small swig. Then a larger swig. Then she got out of her car and walked, still not thinking. She just let her feet carry her along. She hadn't been here in . . . wow. It's been *months*. She used to come here weekly, at least.

Her father's grave.

It was quiet. It made for a good thinking spot.

And that's what she needed. Just a bit of quiet, to think. To process. To fix it.

So . . . *calm down. Think.*

Could it have been Owen?

It fit the evidence. He had motive. No alibi.

So, logic says yes.

What about instinct? Good cops learned to trust instinct, too. Go with the gut. Her dad taught her to be a good cop. So, instinct . . .

Well, instinct said no.

Borst was sweating. This heatwave . . .

For months, there have been gang shoot-outs. But there's been a pattern to them. That's what she's been wrestling with for the past few days. She was so focused on individual cases, isolated incidents of violence, that she hadn't had a moment to properly think. The only time off she's had was that one night, that one dinner.

If it really *was* Owen, he'd been active for weeks. Well before that one dinner.

The evidence at each scene had been similar. More bullets, more bloodstains, than could be explained by the number of bodies. Violence, hacked limbs. The severed head was new, but it didn't break the pattern.

That was the thing to isolate. Patterns.

Captain Borst was a damn good detective. She followed in her father's footsteps, so she knew how to find patterns that would crack a case wide open. And she knew how to check whether the theories fit or not.

This one fit.

There was someone out there, someone who could get up after getting shot and stabbed and . . . well, someone who could heal, who couldn't be killed. And that person was targeting the city's major gangs. Taking them out one-by-one, methodically. This person was smart. Or he was working *with* someone smart, someone who knew the players, who understood how crime organizations worked in this city.

Owen. And Richardson. It fit too damn well.

Her eyes suddenly focused on the gravestone, as if only just noticing it was there.

"Hi, Dad," she mumbled. "Dad, I . . ."

She sighed. "What would you have done, Dad? I don't . . . I don't know what's right. Owen's . . . I wish you were here, Dad. I wish . . . you'd know what to do. You'd tell me. You were a cop first. Always. Before you were a husband, a father . . . you were a cop. Best damn officer in the city. Always confident, always . . .

"What's the right thing here? I feel like I'm either betraying a person I care about or betraying my own values. It's like . . . it's just like back when you were sick. I had to choose between what you wanted me to do—keep studying for the bar exam—and what felt like the right thing, which was being by your side. You were barely there, barely awake, and I had no one, no one to ask for guidance, no . . ."

She choked up. The tears started to flow. She sat on the ground in front of the grave.

"I was so fucking alone then. And now, same thing. You're not here. I know I made the right choice back then. Even if, when you were awake, you'd always tell me, 'Go study, kid'. I loved you, but I hated you for saying that. You made me feel guilty for being with you. You were dying, and . . ." she swallowed hard. "I did the right thing then. And afterwards, too. Deciding that law wasn't for me, going into the police academy. I wanted to be with you, and then I wanted to be like you. What was wrong with that? Why did you have to make it so difficult?

"And now, look at me. As soon as it's difficult again, I break down. Fine, I know what you'd say. 'Get yourself together'. I'm just . . . tired of being alone. With Owen, I thought maybe I don't have to be. And look where that got me. If he's the culprit . . . I was so blind. A bad cop. And if he's innocent, then I just arrested an innocent person, scarred someone who's trying to recover from depression. Someone I might have . . . cared about. So, either way, I'm the shittiest person in the world.

Crying harder now, Borst just let herself go.

Then it slowed down, until finally, the crying stopped.

"Fine. Fuck. Sorry, Dad. You're right. Enough self-pity, I'm not a shitty person. I'm a good cop, just doing the job. If it was Owen, I arrested him, and saved the city from probably the worst criminal in history. If it wasn't him, I still acted on the evidence. It was the right call.

"'So, kid, get up already'. That's what you'd say, Dad. 'Stop feeling sorry for yourself and get back to work,' right? Fine. So, what's next? How do I solve this, what do I have to work with . . . oh!"

Borst just realized. She had a witness. Right.

This was easy. It's so simple. Why hadn't she thought of it earlier?

"I just have to show Owen to the witness—that Tony kid. See if he makes a positive ID. Or . . . hell, I don't even need to bring Owen to the hospital. Just a photo. I don't have any photos of Owen on my phone, but I guess I'd be able to look some up. His father was a celebrity businessman. A quick image search—"

Oh, right. Her phone. She left it at her desk.

She took a deep breath, got up, and shook the dirt off.

"Sorry, Dad. I've got to go. Got a plan now. Thanks for . . . listening. And sorry about the things I said earlier. It was a difficult time, but it wasn't your fault. Love you. I'll be back soon," she promised.

Dinah Borst got back in her car and drove back to the precinct. Some minutes later, once she got there, she wished she hadn't.

. . .

It was a massacre.

At least that's what the media outlets called it much later. But, experiencing it first-hand, there was really only one word that could do it justice—hell.

"Simple plan, guys. Get in there and shoot everyone. No one walks away. No tactics, no battle plan. Just walk in and start killing. Any questions?" asked Unkillable, rhetorically. He didn't even pause. "No questions. Go!"

About half the army assembled—and it *was* a fucking army, at least thirty people and armed to the teeth—charged in, shouting, cheering. The other half didn't, not right away, so the freak shot at them, killing a couple, yelling at them to go, to kill, and *then* they ran in.

Linc was the only one left behind. Him and Unkillable.

"Go on".

Linc shook his head.

"Oh, Lincoln. You do realize I *know* it was you, right? You called the cops on me, in the penthouse. I know".

"N-no—"

"I know, Lincoln. I've got cops on the payroll. Well, the Accountant does. *Did*. And now I do. Although I suppose, if the crooked cops work in there, they might already be dead. Like those cops you called in to arrest me. Remember? Yeah. You know, I wanted to trust you. I'm genuinely disappointed".

Lincoln didn't say anything. He couldn't even look the monster in the face.

"Go on. Run in, shoot some cops for me".

"I'm not going in there".

"If you don't, I'll just shoot you".

"You'll shoot me anyway".

"I wouldn't do that, now would I? Actually, no, that's exactly what I'd do," said Unkillable. The words were sarcastic, but the voice was so flat it was hard to tell if he was joking. "I see your point. Tell you what, I'll either shoot you right now, or else you go in there, you *participate*, and if you make it out alive, who knows. Either way, you'll get to live at least a couple more seconds. What do you say?"

Finally, Linc found it within himself to look Unkillable in the eye.

He looked like a man, but his eyes were dead. Linc gave him the angriest glare he could muster, but Unkillable wasn't moved in the slightest. Linc wasn't sure if he was terrifying or pathetic.

But he did walk. With Unkillable right behind him, they entered the precinct station building.

Inside, the carnage had already begun. There was red splattered everywhere, and the smell of smoke and metal. The cops were firing back, but Unkillable's men were equipped with more than just standard-issue handguns, they had semi-automatics, real fucking weapons. Plus, at least half of them had a *lot* of enthusiasm. The other half had a lot of fear. Within seconds, Linc saw men die, fall. He was going to puke again.

Then he slipped.

It was probably the puddled blood. He slipped and fell to the ground, and Unkillable circled around him, shooting.

"Dead already?" Linc heard him mutter. "Ugh, I *really* wanted to be the one to shoot you. Ah, fuck it". Then the psychopathic killer moved on.

He must have thought Linc was dead, shot.

Linc almost breathed a sigh of relief, but he knew there was now only one way out of this. All he had to do was lie there, as still as possible, and hope for the best.

So Linc didn't see much of it.

But he heard it. He heard the massacre. He heard hell.

It was all he could do not to puke, not to cry, not to tremble, not to open his eyes. Someone stomped on him at one point, running for the door. Their body fell before they could reach it. Linc didn't react. He just kept repeating three words in his head, like some sort of maniacal religious mantra. The only phrase that could end up saving him.

I'm already dead. I'm already dead. I'm already dead.

. . .

Owen didn't see much of it, either. He heard it before he could see it. In fact, he *smelled* it before he could see it.

First came a familiar, harsh scent. Then gunshots.

In a police station? He wondered.

Too loud, and too many.

The scent got stronger. Smoke, metal, something acrid . . . was it blood? Or just . . . death?

The odours, the sounds, they took him back to a basement, months ago, when he released those girls, and they ran as their traffickers fired after them before the police moved in, and he . . . he was there. He'd gotten shot several times. But he got up, shook it off, and made it out. None of the girls died. A couple got hit, but he managed to save them all, despite himself.

It was still traumatizing as fuck. He'd had nightmares that put him back there.

Now this . . . what *was* this? What was happening?

The sounds moved, people moved, and suddenly he could see.

Men, armed with fucking rifles and wearing army gear, moved through the squad-room. From his cell he could see cops getting up, reaching for their weapons, and getting blown apart before they could make a move.

The guys moving through the station didn't appear to be after anyone or anything specific. They were just out to slaughter everyone.

What the fuck was happening?

"Hey! Let me out! I can help!" he shouted.

There was a cop nearby. He ignored Owen.

Owen was locked in a cell. He was just a prisoner. Why would anyone let him out? Still, he had to try.

"Please, come on. I can—"

The cop drew his gun and stood adjacent to a wall. "Shut up," he grunted towards Owen. In the next cell over, a couple of other guys were locked up, actual criminals. They started making noise. "Over here! Hey, let us out!" they shouted as the cops tried to hush them.

At the end of the corridor in front of him, Owen could see an armed man approaching. He was visible from Owen's position, but not the cop's. Owen tried to catch the cop's eye.

"Hey! Someone's coming from that direction," he said.

The cop was too slow to react, though. Within a second he was on the floor and bleeding, a bullet through his head. The blood splattered at Owen's feet, hitting his shoes.

The other prisoners were still shouting as the armed infiltrator advanced towards the locked cells. They probably assumed this criminal was on their side, that he'd release them. The guy was tall, muscular, and sporting an impressive number of very visible, violent tattoos. He reached the holding cells, pointed his semi-automatic weapon, and sprayed the inmates with bullets.

The other prisoners stopped shouting.

Owen was hit three or four times. This executioner knew what he was doing. Owen felt a now somewhat-familiar sensation, the hot stinging pain of the bullets, sharp and radiating. It hurt like hell.

But it didn't kill him. It didn't even knock him out. Owen was fully awake, eyes open, and he was watching as his assailant fell, shot by a cop. Three uniformed men ran past his cell, not even sparing him a look. They were probably focused on getting away, making it out alive.

Owen sat down. He didn't have a good view—the cells opened to a corridor, so he had an obstructed view of the detective squad room, and that's about it. By that point, the sights, sounds, and smells all blended together—men running, cops and invaders, all with weapons out, gunshots ringing out, screams, groans, blood, guts.

He didn't know how to process it, so he didn't. He just sat there. At one point, he was shot again by some guy. It barely phased him.

Eventually, it faded. Things stopped moving, and he couldn't see anyone or anything. Then the sounds stopped, no more voices, no more shots.

It was just the lingering odour of death that was left.

He waited forever. Someone would surely get up, walk by. Someone would scream for help. Someone would . . . would do something. Be alive. He couldn't be the only one left, could he?

But no, nothing. For a long, long time, seemingly an eternity, there was nothing.

Owen was stuck in a cell, and everyone else was dead.

. . .

As soon as she drove into the parking lot, Captain Borst could tell something was wrong.

At least that's what she told herself afterwards. If she was honest, maybe she was still focused on her investigation, on the fact that she'd arrested Owen, on trying to convince herself she was doing the right thing, doing her job. Maybe she wasn't paying much attention. Maybe she didn't actually realize something was wrong until she was out of her car, about to walk in, when she finally registered the lack of movement or noise.

And the bloodstains.

Those were certainly a clue.

She walked in through the precinct station's main entrance off the parking lot, leaving the normal world she had always known behind, and stepping into a fucking nightmare.

Blood and dead bodies everywhere.

"Hello?" she said, her voice betraying her, not sounding like herself. "Anyone? What . . . what the fuck happened?"

Reflexively, she reached down for something. She realized there was an object in her hand. She expected it to be her gun or maybe her phone. It was her flask. She took a sip. It didn't help. She was still in hell. She replaced the flask in her jacket, drew her weapon, and took a step forward.

There was a body in a pool of blood, almost adjacent to the door. She didn't know him. Not a cop. Young. A kid, practically. Gang?

He was breathing. She tapped him with her foot.

"Is it over?" he asked, opening his eyes. They were bloodshot. But he was alive.

"I don't know. What happened here?" she asked.

"He killed everyone. He . . . I got him an army. He just . . . it was . . ."

The kid tried sitting up, then puked on her shoes. It would have been more upsetting had she not already stepped in puddles of blood.

"Can you stand?"

Slowly, he got up.

"What's your name?"

"Lincoln".

"Lincoln, are you injured?"

"I'm okay".

"Good. I want you by my side. I'm going to survey the station. We're going to find any survivors. Then I'm going to take you to another station, and you're going to tell me everything that happened here. Okay?"

"Yeah. Okay".

"Are there any other armed personnel in here?"

"I don't know. I think they all left. Or maybe he shot them all".

This wasn't the time to inquire about who this *he* was. Borst held her gun level. She had to secure the scene, work out what she was looking at, before she called for medics and reinforcements.

"With me, kid".

They started walking, slowly, one corridor after another. Borst stopped counting the bodies, stopped looking at their faces after she saw Santiago, Ransom, Horne, Nazim. Her whole squad was here. Dead. *All* of them.

This was . . . this was a failure. It was on her. She failed them all, she has failed as a captain.

What the fuck? What the *fuck*???

No one alive. Nothing but bodies. So many bodies.

Then she remembered and started heading towards the cells.

. . .

He sat there forever, and everyone was dead.

Then she was there.

"What happened here?" Borst asked.

"I don't know. Some sort of attack. Just an endless barrage of guys coming in with guns and shooting up anyone they could see. I don't fucking know," Owen said in a flat, tired voice.

Borst found the keys on the floor. She unlocked the cell.

"Who's this?" Owen gestured at the bloodstained kid besides her.

"Lone survivor. Lincoln. I need to question him. Watch him a minute, I have to call . . . everybody".

It suddenly hit her. All the calls she'd have to make. All the families, loved ones.

So many dead.

How? How could this have happened?

While she started making calls to dispatch, getting reinforcements onto the scene, Owen was left with Lincoln.

"So, who are you? You're with the . . . the bad guys? I don't know what to call them".

"Yeah. I was pretending to be dead".

"Who did this?"

"He's . . . I don't know his name, actually. He's Unkillable".

"Unkillable," repeated Owen. He was beginning to understand. "This guy, he gets shot and gets up like nothing happened?"

"Yeah. How'd you know? You met him?"

It all clicked together.

He waited for Borst to hang up.

"Okay, officers are on the way. This is a fucking nightmare".

"I know. We need to move this guy somewhere safe where we can talk. Dinah, there's someone else out there who can't die".

And suddenly, it all clicked together for her, too.

"He calls himself Unkillable," Lincoln volunteered. "He's been taking out gangs, taking over. I think he's killed half the organized crime in this city".

"And now he's moved on to the police. Fuck. We're gonna get him," said Borst, full of fury.

"You can't. He . . . he's untouchable. I tried, the police, everyone tried. You can't get him".

"*I* can," said Owen. "I just need to know where he is".

"Wait," said Borst. "What we need is proper witness testimony, and we need to come up with a plan. Police reinforcements are on their way here to secure the scene and investigate. I'm going to take Lincoln to another precinct. I'll interview him. We have to do this right. We get what we need, get a warrant—"

"They sent a whole fucking SWAT team after him, and he shook them off like nothing," Lincoln interrupted. "Just shot them all. Look at what he did here! I'm telling you, you can't just . . . just arrest him, or . . . you can't do anything, he's—"

"Dinah. He's right. This is beyond warrants. You need me for this. This is *exactly* what you recruited me for".

She took a second to think it through.

Owen was right.

She wanted to trust him.

So, she did.

"Fine. We'll take this kid to Richardson. We'll talk there and come up with a plan".

"I'll let her know we're coming while you're dealing with the cops. Where's my phone?"

"In that drawer, here, here's the key. Grab it quick, and let's get you two out of here before anyone else comes in and you get arrested all over again".

Soon the two of them were waiting in Borst's car as she was dealing with protocols. Not that there *was* a protocol for a fucking militant attack executing an entire station's worth of officers. What a nightmare.

Owen checked his phone. He only had 13% battery left and ten missed calls from Richardson, not to mention dozens of texts.

"You really think you can get him?" Lincoln asked from the back seat.

"He calls himself Unkillable? Well, he's about to come up against Depresso".

9 – *What I'm for*

"DO you know how many times I tried to call you? You should've—"

"Sharon, we have bigger things to focus on at the moment," said Borst. The four of them were huddled in the Control Room in Richardson's basement. "Lincoln, we need you to tell us everything".

It took twenty minutes, half an hour, for Linc to recount the full story from his perspective.

"So . . . we're dealing with someone who's got Owen's powers. He's unkillable, and he's . . . what's he after?" asked Richardson.

"He said he's taking over organized crime in the city. Or taking them down—I'm not really sure".

"Does it look like he's actually trying to take over, or is he just randomly killing people?"

Linc grimaced. "I don't know. He went after the Accountant intentionally, he spent a lot of time going over his files. I think he has a plan, but then, other times it looks like he's just randomly doing whatever he feels like".

"That makes him dangerous," Borst thought aloud.

"You're going to need this kid to testify," Richardson told Borst. "You've got to keep him safe".

"I know. But first we have to focus on taking Unkillable down".

"You need a carefully coordinated attack. With a full squad of—"

"He's already killed a full squad, a whole team. Then, when there was just the one cop left, he checked her badge. I think that's how he decided to hit your station. After that, he shot her in the face. He has no problem killing, and it doesn't matter how many officers you send after him".

An officer from her precinct? Borst suddenly remembered. *Oh no.*

"This officer he shot, was she . . . an Asian female?"

"Yes," Linc confirmed.

"One of yours?" Richardson asked.

Borst nodded. Chen.

Shit.

Her Chen. Yes. One of hers. Even after seeing her whole squad mowed down, news of Chen's death hit her like a gut punch. She liked Chen.

Borst swallowed. There was nothing she could do but take the bastard down hard. She tuned back into the conversation.

Richardson spoke. "Look, I know he took out the hit squad, but they didn't know what they were stepping into. We do. If the squad's prepared, protected, coming into the apartment with a careful plan, with sniper support—"

"Snipers won't do anything," Linc interjected. "I've seen him get shot and just bounce back. It's pointless".

"What if we wait until he goes out?" continued Richardson. "He has to leave the penthouse at some point. We surround him, overwhelm him. He won't be able to put up a resistance if we plan it out, use an open space, fifty armed cops. He'll have to surrender".

"He won't. He'll keep shooting, and your guys won't be able to hurt him. He's untouchable, I'm telling you," Linc kept arguing.

"Look, we don't need a fucking assault on the guy," contended Borst, her mind starting to clear. "What we need is to incapacitate him. If we have him in handcuffs, in shackles, immobilized, then we're good. We arrest him, drag him to a cell, put him on trial. He's just a man, he's not super-strong or anything. We just need him in cuffs, that's it".

"That makes sense," Linc admitted.

"But how do you cuff him if you can't get near him?" argued Richardson. "He'll just shoot anyone who comes near, you said. I still think, if we surround him in the open, someone is going to manage to get in there and grab him. It's got to be a numbers game. We can overwhelm him".

"He'll just wiggle away. You don't know him", Linc shook his head.

"I tend to agree. He seems to have walked away from multiple shoot-outs with massive casualties. It's not about overwhelming him. I'm thinking we're better off trying to catch him off guard. You said he's had drugs and prostitutes brought up?" Borst asked Linc.

"Lots of them".

"Ah, you're thinking an undercover op?" Richardson suggested.

Borst nodded. "We send a cop disguised as a call girl. She gets his guard down, slaps the cuffs on him. I could do it. If we need to, we can inject him with a tranquillizer. Once he's cuffed, we've got him".

"I think that works".

Owen, who hasn't said much thus far, stood up.

"What is it?" asked Richardson.

"Your plans are all too risky. Undercover cops, outdoors ambush . . . Look, Dinah's right, all we need is for someone to get close and shackle him. Tranquillizers wouldn't work on him. They don't work on me, Dr. Larner tested it. So, it has to be physical restraints. The problem is, it doesn't matter if it's a full assault or a bluff with hookers and drug dealers—anyone getting close to him is at high risk. The guy is volatile, violent, he'd shoot anybody without thinking twice. There's nobody you can send in without risking lives. So, send me".

"Owen—"

"No. This is why I'm here, this is what I'm *for*—situations where anyone else risks getting *dead*. Well, I can't die. I'm the same as him. He can't do anything to me. So, get me some handcuffs or whatever, and let's do it already".

Borst and Richardson looked at one another.

"Are you sure?" Borst asked.

"Yes".

"Sharon?"

"It makes sense on paper, but . . . I haven't trained him for this".

"You can't train for something like this. But I get the unkillable thing better than anyone. Nobody's better equipped than me".

"That's . . . fair," concurred Sharon. "But I still—"

"Sharon. Come on", said Owen. They stared each other down for a minute, an unspoken conversation taking place between them.

Finally, Richardson sighed. "Okay. Send him in. Let me get some equipment".

"He'll kill you," Linc said, directed at Owen.

"I'm like him. I can't die".

Borst nodded. "Lincoln, you're staying here. When this is done, I'm putting security on you, and we'll talk to the District Attorney to get you a plea deal. You'll be a key witness in bringing Unkillable to justice. He'll rot in jail, don't you fucking doubt it".

"You better call the MCU for backup," Richardson pointed out.

"How are we actually doing it? We should plan—"

"I'm going in. That's it," said Owen.

"You'll enter the apartment alone. But I'm stationing cops outside the apartment, in the hallway, in the lobby, in front of the damn building".

"Fine. Just make sure he can't see them".

"I'm giving you one hour in the apartment. Then we're moving in".

"You can't take the risk. I don't know how long it'll take. Do *not* go in," said Owen.

"Well, I am not just . . . leaving you there," argued Borst.

"You still don't trust me?"

"Owen, it's not about that".

"Six".

"Huh?"

"Six hours. I don't know how long I'll need or what it'll take. Give me six hours".

Borst paused. "You get three".

"Fine. Three hours".

"Let's go".

. . .

They didn't speak on the drive over.

It was a heavy, overbearing silence.

Finally, she couldn't take it anymore.

"Look . . . Owen, I just, I wanted to say . . . I'm sorry. I'm sorry for arresting you, for not . . . not trusting you. I'm really . . . I just couldn't *know*—"

"Dinah, I get it. You did the right thing, given what you knew. I thought it over—I had time to think it over, stuck in that cell. And I understand".

"Okay. Good. I just . . . I didn't want to send you up there without . . . well, you know".

"Let's just get this done".

"You've got your equipment? Everything you need?"

Owen patted the gym bag on his lap. "Wide variety of cuffs and shackles".

"Vest on? Gun?"

"No weapons. No vest".

"You can't—"

"It'll be fine. I've got some ideas".

"What ideas? Owen, I really think—"

"Dinah, trust me. This guy—if he's really the same as me, if he's unkillable—then this is what you found me for. This is what it all comes down to. It's . . . it's my purpose. I can do this".

"Look, I know you think that, but you can't know—"

"I don't *know*. But I trust myself. Which, honestly, isn't something I'm used to. You know how much I hate and doubt myself, so let me have this one. Besides, I'm the best shot you've got".

Borst had to admit he was right.

"Okay. Yeah. Sorry".

"It's fine. We'll have a proper conversation after it's done".

"Yeah. I think . . . we really should".

They fell into another silence. Two minutes later, they arrived at the front of the luxury high-rise apartment building. The streets had been cordoned off, discreetly, and armed officers were already on the scene.

Owen was looking up.

"Right. This is it," he said.

"I'll see you after," Borst said. It suddenly hit her—she could lose him. She had already lost so much that day. She felt the sudden desire to squeeze his shoulder, hug him. She felt the tears well up, and she braced herself.

"Owen—" she started.

But he was already out of the car, walking off to face the crazy killer.

She was too late.

10 – *Symbolism*

OWEN knocked.

"Who fucking is it?" asked a voice from within the penthouse apartment after a minute.

"Open up," Owen answered. It wasn't a command. More of a suggestion, really.

"You the police?"

"No. I'm a fucking superhero who's here to take you down, Unkillable".

Nothing happened for a bit.

Then the door opened.

Owen got his first glimpse of his supervillain archnemesis.

He does kind of looks like me, he thought. Skinny, short, wild dark hair.

Dead eyes.

Owen wasn't sure what he expected. This guy wasn't intimidating—he just looked sad and sort of detached. Maybe that's what made him terrifying to most people. But Owen's first impression wasn't one of fear. He felt . . . pity.

"You? Superhero? Are you fucking kidding me?" asked Unkillable.

"Let me in. We'll talk".

"What's in the bag?"

"Stuff".

"Are you armed?"

"If I was, I'd have shot you already".

"Fair. What if I shoot you?"

"Go for it".

The two men stared each other down.

"Okay, come in," said Unkillable.

And then Owen was in. He was led to a remarkably comfortable sofa in a heavily decorated study that smelled of disinfectant.

Unkillable pointed a gun at Owen as he sat.

"So, I can shoot you?"

"Sure".

"You're not scared? I might shoot you in the head—a vest won't save you," he said, walking up to Owen and holding the gun directly at his forehead.

"I'm not wearing a vest," Owen shook his head.

"Okay, you're weird. I'm gonna shoot you now," said Unkillable.

And then he shot Owen.

Owen grimaced, coughed, and rubbed his temples.

Unkillable stepped back. His dead eyes went wide.

"Ohhh!" he exclaimed. "You're like *me*?"

Owen nodded.

"Hey, do you also get . . . with a headshot, there's this really bad, high-pitched ringing in your ears. You got that now?"

"Yeah. Shit, it's bad," complained Owen.

"I know! I've gotten used to body shots, they barely sting now. But the head, your jaw always gets stiff, I fucking hate it".

Unkillable stood there for a few seconds, just watching Owen recover.

"So. You're *also* unkillable. Who the fuck are you, and why are you here?" he asked.

"Sit down, let's talk about it".

Unkillable gave Owen a flat, expressionless look. Then he sat down, cross-legged, on a recliner chair by the sofa. "All right. Well?"

"I'm Owen. I'm . . . yeah, like you".

"Unkillable, huh?"

"As far as I can tell".

"What have you tried?"

"All of it".

"Go on. List it out. We can make it into a bingo card," Unkillable said, and Owen understood why Linc had found him so disconcerting. The joke, combined with his deadpan face, was unsettling.

"I've been shot. Lots of times. Stabbed. I tried jumping".

"Jumping?"

"Off a building".

"Right, yeah. Of course".

"Drowned myself, carbon monoxide—"

"Oh, I haven't tried that one!"

Owen stopped. "Did you—in what context did you . . . try to die?"

"What do you mean?"

"Well . . . most of my near-deaths came from . . . you know, suicide attempts".

"Right. Sure".

"You too?" Owen asked Unkillable. It was the question he's been wanting to ask, really.

Were they the same? And if so—where did the paths diverge? Where did this guy go wrong, becoming a killing machine, whereas Owen managed to have a life that recently graduated from purely meaningless to one where he *saved* lives?

Could Owen have gone the other path? Turn bad? And could Unkillable be saved the same way he was?

The man answered. "Initially, sure. I tried to kill myself a whole bunch of times. But that was a long time ago, and in a whole other city. Another life, really".

"Tell me".

"What is this, group therapy session?" mocked the villain.

"I'm just trying to understand".

Unkillable scratched his head. "I don't know why you want to know, but I guess if anyone can understand . . ." he started. Then he coughed. "Man, this is dumb. It . . . seriously, it feels like that scene in the movie where the bad guy reveals his origin story, or his secret evil plan, or whatever. Meanwhile, your friends, or the cops, or whoever, would be coming up with a plan to stop me. Is that it?"

"*I'm* the plan. I'll be stopping you, whatever happens".

"Will you, now? And how are you going to do that?"

"Tell me what I want to know, how you got to be . . . *you*, and then I'll tell you how I'm going to stop you," offered Owen.

"Or I could just shoot you again".

"You could. Shoot me a hundred times. Won't change anything".

"I believe that, but I'm going to test it out one more time anyway. It'll make me feel better".

Unkillable shot Owen again. Nothing happened.

"Ah! Fucking . . . okay, you tried that. Now, will you tell me your story?" Owen asked.

"What fucking story? What are you talking about? You seriously just want to talk? What are you *really* after here?"

Owen took a breath. "Look, honestly? I want to understand, for purely selfish reasons, why you are the way that you are. I just want to know how far off I was from becoming you".

"So . . . you're honestly not just stalling for time? Huh. I don't believe you at all, but okay, I guess I get it. You want to see whether I'm redeemable? Whether you can add me to whatever fucking . . . whatever your mission is, your dumb *superhero* bullshit, whatever you were talking about earlier? What is it, anyway?"

"I save lives".

"Do you seriously think you're a superhero?"

"No, not really. It's not like I'm Batman. But—well, sort of. Basically, if there's a fire, any kind of deadly situation that's too dangerous for the police or other emergency responders, I go in. I can't die anyway, so I go in, and I save people".

"Wow, that is . . . dumb. *So* dumb. And what, you want me to join you? Is that it?"

"Oh, no. I don't think you're redeemable. Even if you were, man, you killed hundreds of people. We have witness testimonies. You're not joining me, you're going to jail".

"Am I?"

"Oh yeah".

"And you're the one who's going to put me there? In jail?"

"Yeah".

"How are you going to do that?" asked Unkillable, increasingly agitated. "And what's in that fucking bag? Don't move," he said, grabbing hold of the gym bag by Owen's feet.

Owen didn't make a move to stop him.

"Oh, I see. Handcuffs. You figure you can cuff me up, and then I'll be rendered helpless, and you'll just hand me over to the police".

"Maybe".

Unkillable shook his head and tossed the bag to the other side of the room. "It *would* work . . . except I'm not going to let you get anywhere near me with any cuffs. So . . . you wanna give up and go home? Or what *are* we doing here?"

Owen paused, thinking. What was he doing? What *was* the plan?

He needed to get the cuffs on the psychopath. He could instigate a physical confrontation. With his recent training with Richardson, maybe he'd be able to take this guy on, but . . . there had to be a better way. A smarter way. He had a little under three hours. For now, maybe the thing to do was to take his time. Stall. Figure it out when he had the full picture.

"I guess I still want to understand".

"Understand what?"

"You".

"I swear, I'm going to kick you out of here—"

"How?"

"What?" asked Unkillable.

"How would you kick me out of here? We have the same problem. You're not going to just let me put handcuffs on you, but I'm not going to let you throw me out now that I'm here".

"I . . . huh. I can't shoot you . . . shit, good point".

"We're at a stalemate," Owen pointed out.

"Right. So . . . what do we do? Rock-paper-scissors?"

Owen's eyes narrowed at the suggestion. Another joke? "Are you genuinely a psychopath, or are you just acting like one?"

"You know, at some point, I lost track. I don't even know who I am anymore. I'm this . . . caricature of what I think I'm supposed to be. It's confusing. But it works".

"Works for what?"

Unkillable sighed. "Okay, fine. You want to psychoanalyze me so bad? You go first".

"Sure. What do you want to know?"

"What made you *you*? How does a guy become so deranged he fashions himself as a fucking superhero?"

Owen nodded.

"It wasn't my idea, trust me. I used to be just this depressed, suicidal person who didn't do anything. I kept trying to kill myself, but it never worked, so I realized I was . . . you know, unkillable. Like you. Then one day I stumbled into this, uh, bank robbery situation. Just randomly. And I guess I stood up to the guy who was robbing the place".

"Like what, you grabbed the gun away, knocked him out, and saved the day?"

"No, no, I just told him . . . I just said I wasn't going to lie down on the ground. So, he shot me, and that didn't do anything, and he freaked out. And then the police came".

"That's it?"

"Yeah. It sounds stupid when you say it out loud . . . then this captain at the police station interviewed me, and she came up with the idea to use my powers for good, and . . . at first, I said no, hell no. I didn't give a shit about other people, I just wanted to die. But she talked me into it, and . . . other stuff happened. So yeah, we set it up. That's basically it".

"That is a really dumb backstory".

"Thanks".

Unkillable crossed his arms. He looked pensive for a minute.

"What's it like?"

"What?"

"Saving people. You feel good?"

"It doesn't . . . I don't feel bad, I guess. I used to. I used to feel bad. All the time. *All* the time. I mean, I was depressed, but it was more than that—I chose to be miserable. Didn't do anything about it. So . . . in comparison, choosing to do things, anything, especially this stuff that helps other people . . . it's not as bad".

"Huh".

They sat in silence for a minute.

"Well, I'll admit, it's a good pitch. But I'm not sold".

"Wasn't trying to sell you on anything," said Owen.

"Sure. Fuck off".

"So what about you? How'd you get to be a supervillain?"

"I'm not a fucking supervillain".

"No? You killed . . . how many people *have* you killed?"

"I stopped counting ages ago".

"You've been taking out gangs across the city. You're an unkillable crime lord. How is that not a supervillain?"

Unkillable bolted up. "Because life's not a fucking comic-book!" he shouted. "You think I'm doing this for *fun*? Because it makes me feel *happy*? Trying to take over the fucking world like *Pinky and the Brain*? Fuck you!"

"Then what are you doing?"

"I don't . . . fuck—I don't *know*. Okay? That's the truth. I don't fucking know what I'm doing".

"You've taken over the mob and you don't know what you're doing? No masterplan?"

"I don't . . . maybe. Not really. I don't know".

"You're not making any sense. Do you want to just tell me about it? Look, I'm not going anywhere anytime soon. You're not going to let me arrest you or anything. We're kind of stuck. Might as well, you know, try to make some sense of the bullshit".

Unkillable sat back down and was silent for a good long minute.

"This is stupid. Ugh, fine. Fuck you. You want to know my story?" asked Unkillable. Then he started narrating.

"I was . . . I guess I'm sort of like you in some ways. I was depressed, suicidal. That whole thing. To be honest though, everyone was, where I came from. It was a shithole. The city I grew up in was already the butt of every fucking joke, and then the financial crisis kind of . . . left it for dead. I was as poor as the next kid, and none of us had any prospects. Death was preferable, honestly. We left school, some of us graduating and some of us just sick of it, dropping out. We found menial service or manufacturing jobs like our parents, and just hoped to hell we'd get to keep them week-in, week-out. The money we made went to rent, food, and drugs. And that was life—that was it".

"Did you ever feel happy?"

"No. That's the thing, everyone else, every once in a while, they'd be happy. Drinking or getting high, they'd party, fuck, or just zone out in front of the TV. Some had kids. And they were *content.* They were fine with that life. But me . . . drugs took the edge off, for about a minute, but . . . I was just so unhappy, so *angry*, every fucking minute of every fucking day. I kind of felt like there was something wrong with me. So, one day, I had enough. I got a gun and shot myself in the head. Then I got back up. There was blood and bits of brain all over the place, but I was alive, so I figured I messed it up. I shot myself in the head again. Same thing.

"I tried a couple of other things—overdosing, jumping—like you did. Nothing worked. I figured with the overdose, maybe I just needed more drugs. So I chased up my dealer, and he pointed me to another guy, and it was me and Jenny—she was a friend of mine—we were together. And we walked up to this dealer who was more of a pro, I guess, more connected. We got into a fight, just an argument, and he was—he must've been high—and he shot Jenny, and she died, and then he shot me, and I didn't die, so I took his gun off of him.

"And it was *that*. Pointing the gun at the guy, just then, I felt this . . . *power*, for the first time in my whole life. And it didn't suck so fucking bad. At that moment, I felt slightly, ever-so-slightly less in pain. Or less focused on the pain. I guess that's how I started. Does that answer anything?"

Maybe it did, thought Owen.

"I shot the guy. And it didn't suck. It didn't feel bad. It felt all right, good, almost. The guy's boss, his contact, whatever you want to call it, the guy one-level-up in the organization, he somehow found me. I figured he'd try to kill me, which honestly I was okay with, I was still suicidal and had zero desire to live. But instead, he offered me a job. I took it. I had to shoot people, and I got more money and drugs than ever before. Girls, too. All these things—drugs, fucking—they don't solve the issue, but sometimes, if you're lucky, for about half a second, they make you forget the shit. They mask it. And that's better than nothing.

"But it's nowhere near power. The power that comes with a gun. It was new, and it was . . . good. At first. But then it . . . kind of faded. And one thing led to another, and I thought, maybe all I needed was *more* of that. To move up. So the guy who recruited me, I shot him, killed him, and I got to take his place. I moved up, and I kept on doing that. Eventually, they got wise to me, tried to kill me. But that didn't work, it never worked, so . . . so, I got them. In three months—can't fucking believe that's all it took—but yeah, three months and I was basically at the top, ruling the entire local crime empire. Not that it was much of an empire. Small city, you know. But I was now top of it.

"And for another couple of months, yeah, that was okay. I didn't think about killing myself all the time, life wasn't completely unbearable. But then, little by little, it got shit again.

"So, I bailed. I shot a few more people, packed up my shit, grabbed some guns and drugs, and took an overnight bus here. *This* city. Biggest and brightest city in the country, right? I figured I'd make my way up here, take over organized crime again. It'll kill a few more months, at least, and I won't be so miserable while I was doing it. And afterwards . . . I don't know. I didn't exactly have a plan. But that was the idea, one step at a time, you know?"

"And that's what you did".

"That's what I did. Took over, one gang at a time. This was a bigger endeavour, let me tell you. It's taken ages, planning. Must have taken over a thousand bullets, mostly shot in my direction. I've killed at least a hundred men. At *least*. Not even counting the police station I hit up. I assume you're here because of that?"

"Pretty much".

"Yeah. So, well, there you have it. That's the whole fucking story. Happy?" asked Unkillable. There was a tiny bit of anger, of poison, in his voice.

"Not really, no," Owen answered honestly.

Unkillable shot him a couple of times, but Owen shook it off. Maybe he was getting used to bullets.

"Sorry, you just pissed me off a bit. I don't like to think about the past. It reminds me of the future".

"What's in the future?"

"More pain. More bullshit".

"Yeah," nodded Owen.

"Fuck. So . . . does that answer your fucking question? Are we the same, or what?"

"I don't know. Maybe. Maybe we could have been. I definitely used to . . . I used to feel angry. Hopeless. When I thought about the future I . . . I saw nothing but pain".

"Right, yeah, so you know. Life is bullshit, everything's bullshit, it doesn't matter. All you can do is chase the moment, try for a second, for *one* damn second, to stop the pain. Even though you know, after that second, there'll be pain again. And there's no end, no *fucking* end, because I can't die. So . . . so . . . what else is there?"

"I don't know. But I'll tell you, now, when I look at the future, I think . . . maybe tomorrow I'll get to save somebody. Make a difference in their life".

"Oh, fuck that".

"No, seriously. It's not . . . it doesn't feel me with joy or anything, but . . . it's something to do," Owen argued.

"So, the difference between you and me is that you have something to do? Or maybe you believe in the sanctity of life and being a fucking goody-two-shoes and saving kittens off trees and—"

"No, I don't. I . . . I don't know. Maybe. Or maybe it's about our backgrounds. I didn't grow up poor. Maybe that's . . . I mean, there are different stressors, obviously, but, well, I've had privileges I'm sure you didn't".

"Oh, I could fucking puke! You think that because I was poor and you weren't, I started killing people, and you became, what, a saviour? Shit, that is . . . I don't even know. Conceited, but like, on a whole other level".

"No, no, that's not what I'm saying. And, I mean, there are other . . . other differences. It's just maybe your circumstances brought you closer to drugs, crime, that sort of thing. I've never held a gun, never even saw one until I bought one with the sole purpose of shooting myself in the head, you know?"

"Fine. That *is* different. And you've never tried drugs, either?"

"No, I did, but . . . they just never *did* anything. At all".

"Ah".

"But maybe the difference is the people around us. That policewoman I was telling you about. Without her, I wouldn't be saving anyone".

"I don't know, man. And I don't fucking care. This is a seriously dumb bullshit therapy session, and I have *lost* my interest. How about you just get the fuck out?" asked Unkillable, exasperated.

"You know I'm not going to," Owen responded.

Unkillable shot him again.

"You're really not bored of this? I am getting a *lot* of bloodstains on my couch, asshole".

"I'm taking you down".

"How? How the *fuck* are you going to take me down?"

"Honestly, I don't know".

"What the *fuck*! Get the fuck out of here—" Unkillable shouted again as he pounced at Owen.

That's when the physical struggle started.

In many ways, it was comical. In others, merely pathetic. Two grown, skinny men, wrestling ineffectually. Unkillable was first to strike, jumping on top of Owen and trying to grab his neck. Owen wriggled away and threw Unkillable to the ground, kicking at him, but the villain clambered back up. The two exchanged punches briefly—Owen landing the bulk of the hits, likely thanks to Richardson's training—before Unkillable attempted to tackle Owen, which resulted in both of them slamming into the Accountant's coffee table.

Owen got up first. He was clearly in better shape. "You done?"

Unkillable rose, then tackled Owen again, sending him flying backwards over the sofa. When he got back up, Unkillable was holding a fucking sword, the same sword the Accountant's henchman nearly used to slice his head off.

"A sword? Seriously?!"

"Fuck off," said the psychopath, hacking at Owen, who kept backing away out of the sword's reach. Finally, Unkillable connected with his arm, producing a bloody gash and making Owen wince. "Shit, that really hurts".

"I'm gonna fucking *kill* you," roared Unkillable, having gotten pretty unhinged at that point. He stabbed Owen with the sword, which then became lodged in Owen's chest. Unkillable tried to pull it out, but couldn't. Owen backed away a step and removed the sword himself.

"Shit!" yelled Unkillable, who was now disarmed. Owen dripped blood onto the carpet.

"This is fucking stupid".

"I hate you!"

"I don't give a shit". Owen threw the sword down away from Unkillable.

They were both breathing hard.

"Fuck," said Unkillable, calmer now. "Fine. Okay. This *is* pointless, you're right". He sat back down. Owen pushed the sofa back upright and joined him.

"Sorry," mumbled Unkillable.

"Are you actually *apologizing*? You fucking kill people for the fun of it," said Owen, incredulous.

"Well . . . usually when I hurt people, they don't get back up, so this is kind of new to me, I guess".

"That's bullshit. Do you even realize how many people you've hurt? For every person you kill, there's a family behind them, they have friends, they—"

"I don't *care*, man. I seriously don't give a shit. I don't give a shit about you, either. I'm not *actually* sorry. It just came out, I didn't actually mean it. You're a fucking idiot".

"Fine".

For a bit, they were silent again.

"I wanna die," Owen finally said softly.

"Well, I want you to be dead, so that works out".

"No, I mean . . . I want to be dead. All the time. I . . . when I'm busy, I can suppress it. But sometimes, I'll just be walking down the street and just get this overwhelming desire to . . . to fall down on the ground, curl up, and shrink into a tiny little dot. Or else I lie in bed at night, and I fantasize about taking a knife and stabbing myself over and over again, carving out my heart, until I pass out".

Unkillable didn't answer.

"Don't you . . . ever feel like that?"

The killer sighed. "Yeah, sure. I do. But it's like you said, I keep busy so I don't have to think about it. I think about other things. Drug deals, killing people, people trying to kill me . . . I don't know".

"I sometimes think, this would be a lot easier if I was dead. Just . . . it'd be less painful. You know?"

"I think about that every day, every fucking hour. But I can't die. So what can I do?"

There was another minute in which the two men just sat, musing. "Can I ask you," started Owen, "do you think we're human?"

"What?"

Owen wasn't sure where the thought came from, but here, for the first time, was someone who might be able to understand. Someone he could really talk to. So he spoke. "You know. Are we *human*? Philosophically speaking. I think . . . I've been thinking about evolution a lot lately. One of my therapists taught me—"

"You had *therapists*?"

"Sure. A whole bunch".

"Fuck, you really are privileged. I couldn't even imagine affording therapy".

"You're in a penthouse, you've got drug money. Pretty sure you can afford it now, you just choose not to".

"Fuck you".

"Right," said Owen before continuing. "Well, anyway, like I was saying, you know how everything we experience is the product of thousands of years of evolution? As in, sadness is really our mind's way of telling us to slow down, analyze our situation? So maybe . . . maybe what we have, this unkillable thing, it's a form of random mutation that's embedded in evolution. It obviously benefits us—it's a beneficial trait in terms of survival. So from that perspective, the idea that we're a next step in evolution would make us *very* human, extra-human.

"But then I think . . . what if, I don't know. I just . . . I've always felt like I'm missing something. Something vital, you know? That bit most people have that lets them be happy, be normal, enjoy their lives, not worry. I don't have that. And it sounds like you don't either. So, what if that's . . . what if that missing bit is our humanity? What if we're inhuman?"

Unkillable sighed. "Look, you're talking to a guy who's got no compunction about killing people. You really want to talk about being inhuman?"

"You make a good point," said Owen, and the two fell into another silence.

"Why are you *here*?" Unkillable asked again, sounding exhausted.

"I'm here to stop you, like I said".

"Why? What does it matter? Are you seriously on some sort of crusade for justice? Will it give you joy and satisfaction to bring me down?"

"I'll be saving people".

"Sure. You know, most of the people I kill are criminals. What if, by taking me down, you'll actually be dooming the city? I mean, think about it. I've consolidated all crime in this damn city under one roof. If I'm out, what do you think is going to happen? There'll be a power vacuum so big, it'll trigger a bigger gang war than you can imagine".

"I'll just have to fix that problem when I get there".

"You really believe that?"

"You really expect me to believe that taking you down is going to result in more crime, more death, than letting you roam free?"

"I could be right".

"Come on. What you did at that police station . . . you want to know why I think you're irredeemable? That station, you know who their captain was? It was the same police captain who recruited me as a hero in the first place. Her name's Dinah Borst".

"Ohhh, I get it. I killed your little friend".

"You didn't, actually. She's the only one you missed. But you killed her entire squad. I don't . . . it hasn't hit her yet, but it will soon, and I don't know how she's going to recover from it. She's going to be in so much fucking pain, and guilt, and . . . and I understand pain and I can't . . . I don't want her to . . . "

Owen trailed off.

Unkillable was pissed off again, becoming animated. "Oh, come on! If you tell me the whole reason you're up here busting my nuts is because you're in love with some lady cop, I'm going to jump off the fucking balcony. Is that it? Seriously? Are you at least fucking her?"

Wait. Something started gnawing at Owen, something at the back of his mind—an idea . . .

"Huh?" he asked, not focused on Unkillable.

"This chick you're talking about. The cop. You two doing it?"

"No, no. I mean, once, but now we're . . . no".

"Oh, god. You're in love with her or something, aren't you? I actually *am* gonna fucking puke. Don't tell me you're in love with her?"

"I don't . . . I don't know. I think, maybe—maybe I was, sort of . . . yeah. But things kind of . . . changed. She didn't trust me, and . . . I don't know".

"Fucking high-school drama, I swear".

What was it? An idea . . . what were they talking about?

"Makes me want to shoot myself. You're just sad, man".

Oh.

Right.

Oh!

Suddenly, it all clicked.

Owen knew how this was going to end.

He just needed to figure out how to get to that endpoint.

Owen stood up.

"Where the fuck are you going?"

"Bathroom. I have to pee".

"Do you think I'm stupid? You're going to call the cops in on me or something".

"I'm not going to. If I did, you'd just shoot them. I'm not an idiot. Also, if I wanted to call anyone you wouldn't be able to stop me".

"Fucking . . . you know what, you're right. If cops do storm the place, I am going to slaughter them all. I've already done that. And it'll be on you this time".

"If *you* kill cops, it'll be on me?"

"I'm warning you".

"Well, good thing I'm just going to use the bathroom," Owen said, walking out of the study. He found the bathroom down the hall. Owen washed his face, peed, and texted Dinah.

When he walked out, Unkillable was in the kitchen. Perfect.

"Tell me the truth—did you text the cops from in there?"

"I did, actually. They want to come in. I told them not to bother. No need".

"No need? You still think you're going to take me down?"

Oh, the beautiful irony in that question, Owen thought to himself. Aloud, he said, "That's exactly what I'm going to do. Take you down. Stay there".

He went back to the study and picked up the gym bag with all the cuffs.

When he came back, Unkillable was pointing a gun at him. "You think I'm letting you come near me with that? Nobody's putting cuffs on me. Least of all you. Even if you did, I'd just find a way to chew my hand off or something. It'll grow back, and then I'll fucking kill you, and your lady cop friend, and every-fucking-body. So, you just stay six feet away, okay?"

"Oh, I don't need this stuff anymore. In fact, come with me. I'm going to toss this off the balcony".

"Seriously?"

"Come watch".

Owen walked out of the kitchen and into the adjacent balcony. He looked down.

Wow.

They were fifty-six floors up. Fifty-five if the thirteenth floor wasn't marked. Dumb superstition. Oh well, what can you do? One floor less wasn't going to matter at this height, anyway.

"Come out here!" Owen called. Unkillable was still in the kitchen, gun tentatively pointed at Owen. It was hot out. The fucking heatwave. "Come see".

"Why do you need me out there?"

"Symbolism," Owen answered.

Begrudgingly, Unkillable stepped out onto the balcony, though he stayed out of Owen's reach. "You know, I *so* wish you were killable right now".

"I could say the same thing".

"You could. You're really tossing the bag? With all the handcuffs, guns . . . what else is in there?"

Owen held the bag over the balcony's railing. Then he let it fall.

The two men leaned slightly, following the heavy black gym bag with their eyes as it fell to the ground.

"Fuck. So, what's next?" asked Unkillable mockingly.

He was so . . . Owen couldn't tell if it was confidence or if he genuinely didn't give a shit. The truth was probably somewhere in-between.

Unkillable wasn't anything like him. Not really. Sure, they both had the *unkillable* thing going on, but whereas Owen's depression made him hate himself, Unkillable hated the rest of humanity. He had nothing but disdain for anyone other than himself. Killing people meant nothing to him—he was just a fucking psychopath.

Maybe Owen could have gone down the same path, given the wrong circumstances. But he hadn't. And that's what mattered. He still cared about people. He valued life as a general concept, even if he didn't value his own.

So, he held no compunction nor guilt over what he did next.

He grabbed Unkillable, who was standing next to him on the balcony, still holding a gun. Panicking, Unkillable squeezed a couple of shots at Owen but missed. The two grappled for a few seconds, but Owen managed to hold on tight, almost hugging Unkillable.

Then he leaned over and let gravity pull his body down, taking Unkillable down with him.

Owen and Unkillable tumbled off the Accountant's balcony on the fifty-sixth or fifty-fifth floor, falling towards the ground, accelerating at 9.82 m/s/s, their heart rates accelerating at an even faster pace. They both blacked out before they hit the ground, Unkillable passing out about a second before Owen did. Then they hit the ground at roughly the exact same instant, about six metres apart.

And all that was left of them was the splatter.

11 – *It's going to be shit*

OWEN came-to all at once.

Everything hurt. Every bit of him was tingling with a sharp, white-hot, pins-and-needles sensation—the worst he's ever felt. Trying to move any muscle sent an electric shock to the base of his spine. He couldn't see, and there was a loud, high-pitched ringing in his ears.

Through the ringing, he heard a voice. *Her* voice.

"You're waking up. You're okay. Thank God".

Borst. Dinah. She was there.

Of course she was there. She was always there.

Foggy shapes started to form in his eyes. Better than the blackness.

He croaked. His voice almost worked, somehow. "Did . . . you . . . get him?"

"Yes, don't worry. He's bound, fully secured. We've got the full Hannibal Lecter gear on him, everything. You got him, Owen". She patted his arm, he thought, not fully recognizing the sensation through the excruciating pain it was causing him. "You did it".

The pain was sharpening, as were his vision and hearing.

"Good," he managed to say.

Then he didn't say anything. He didn't move for a minute.

"We . . . I've got a stretcher. We're thinking of putting you on it. There's an ambulance. We'll take you to Dr. Larner—"

"Don't".

"Owen, you need to be looked at. I mean—"

"Not yet. Don't touch. Too much pain . . . to move".

"Okay. Okay, we'll wait a few minutes".

"Thanks".

He saw her straighten up. She was crouching over him, but had walked off to talk to some fellow officers.

Owen saw *him*. He really did get the Hannibal Lecter treatment, wearing some sort of straitjacket. Was that what it was called? Owen couldn't remember. The important thing was, Unkillable was secure. There was no way he was getting out of that—even chewing an arm off wouldn't help.

He could breathe a little bit easier. Figuratively *and* literally, as it were.

His muscles were starting to cooperate too. He tried to sit up and managed it, for the most part.

"Woah, there!" said Borst when she noticed. "Take it easy".

"It's fine".

"You just fell—"

"I know".

"Well, of course you know, but . . . look, we got him. *You* got him. Just like you said you would. You did good".

"Good," he echoed. It came out kind of dismissive, for some reason. He could tell she noticed that.

"Are you sure you're okay? I mean, not okay physically, just . . . how are you doing mentally?"

"Honestly? Not great".

Borst nodded. "Was it bad up there? What was he like?"

"A psychopathic murderer".

"So, he shot you?"

"A few times. At one point, he attacked me with a sword. But he figured out pretty quickly that trying to kill me wouldn't do any good. Then we just . . . talked. For a good while there".

"Anything we could use?"

"Tons. I should've been wearing a wire, he confessed to a lot".

"That's fine, Owen. We've got that Lincoln kid—I'm getting him into witness protection. We've got the FBI involved now. The fact that he hit the station . . . it's insanity. We have clear footage from the surveillance cameras, and we're working on getting more witnesses. Major Crime is all over it—they lost men too. We'll have more than enough evidence to convict him without you having to get involved any further".

"That's good to know".

"So . . . you two just talked?"

"For a while. Eventually, I think it was something he said, or maybe I just remembered that one girl I talked out of jumping off a roof—right before I agreed to do this thing with Richardson, you remember? Back then I said, 'If you jump, I jump'. That just popped into my mind, and then it clicked".

"I got your text and kept my officers out of sight".

"Yeah. Getting him to the balcony wasn't hard. I guess that's the whole story".

"So . . . you said you're not okay. What's on your mind?"

"Few things. For one, I threw a guy off a balcony".

"It was a smart idea. I never would have thought of it".

"No, I mean . . . I basically committed murder".

"No, you didn't. You didn't kill anyone. You knew he wouldn't—"

"I didn't *know*. He could have died. But . . . I think, honestly, I might have been okay with that. And that scares the fuck out of me," Owen said, staring at the ground.

"Owen, I'm a cop. I've been in action. I've had to shoot people. I know what it's like . . . and there's not much I can say. You know you did the right thing. You helped us catch one of the worst killers I've ever come across. You did the right thing, the good thing, and you didn't even kill him".

"I know that, logically, but—"

"Yeah. Takes a while to do that mental math and forgive yourself. I get it, believe me".

"I know you do. Look, I'm feeling . . . I can sort of feel my legs now. I want to try and get up".

"Are you sure?"

"Yeah. Just let me . . ."

"Here—"

Borst offered her arm. He took it and managed to pull himself up.

"I can't believe you're okay. It's been . . . not even an hour. You were literally a splatter of goo. I could have sworn you didn't make it".

"Yeah. I'm fine. Dinah, I'm gonna go home".

"I really think we need to get you to a hospital. Or Dr. Larner, at least".

"Tomorrow. I'll go see him tomorrow".

"You promise?"

"Yeah".

"Okay. If you think that's the best thing for you. And listen, maybe tomorrow we could have dinner again. You know, I—"

"No".

"I'm . . . sorry?" asked Borst, surprised.

"I don't think we should have dinner. I don't . . . I don't think I want to".

"Umm . . . okay. Is . . . can I ask why?"

Owen sighed. "I think I'm very mad at you. Very . . . disappointed".

"Because . . . because I arrested you?"

"Yes".

"But you said you *understood.* I thought—"

"I do understand. I do, I get why you did what you did, but . . . Dinah, you should have trusted me. The fact that I understand doesn't mean I'm not hurt, or that I forgive you. Not yet, anyway".

Borst didn't know what to say to that.

"I'm sure that hurts," Owen said.

"It really fucking does," she mumbled.

"I'm sorry. I just have to be honest with how I feel. Look, Dinah, it's going to be shit. You're going to need space. Your squad, the entire station . . . the survivor's guilt is probably going to hit like a truck. You haven't processed any of it yet. You're going to go through hell".

"Don't you think I need a friend to help me through that? Don't you think I need *you*?" she said, pleading, practically shouting.

"I'm sorry. I have to figure out my side too before I can be there for you. It's selfish, and it's shitty of me, but . . . I think we both have to take some time to deal with our own shit. For now".

Dinah nodded, but her expression remained one of deep resentment. She looked around, made sure no one else was looking at them, and carefully took out her flask.

Owen took a step forward and grabbed it while it was still in her hand.

"You need to stop that. All that drinking. It's not helping, it never has. I really think—"

"You don't get to say that. Not right now. Fuck you," she said, snatching the flask back and taking a long, hard drink.

"Fine. You're right".

"Sorry. I'm angry too, now".

"It's okay. You probably should be".

The two stood across from each other.

"You're gonna go?" she asked.

"Give me your gun".

"Why? So you can shoot yourself in the head again, like that one time? What are you trying to do—prove that you're a miserable, depressed, pathetic little man? Prove that you're in more pain than anyone else? Owen, fuck off. Seriously".

He nodded for a second. "Yeah. Yeah, you're right. I already jumped off a fifty-sixth-storey balcony. That's probably enough for one day".

He turned around and started to walk away.

Both Owen and Borst half-expected her to call out after him, or for him to turn around.

Neither one did.

He just kept on walking away from her.

Depresso III:
War on Drugs

Won't it be dull when we rid ourselves
Of all these demons haunting us
To keep us company?
Won't it be odd to be happy like we
Always thought we're supposed to feel
But never seem to be?

— *War on Drugs*, S. Page & E. Robertson, 2003

1 – *A person, first*

TERRY and Marco were in the cafeteria having lunch.

It was late September, a few weeks into a new term, a new year. On the surface, everything was the same, but Terry could sense some changes, and he didn't like them.

"I got the new *Headbasher* game. You want to come over tonight?" he asked Marco, who's been his best friend since forever.

"Man, it's Friday night. We should go out".

"Like what, a movie?"

"No, man. Parties. Girls. Alcohol".

Terry sighed. Over the summer, his best friend changed. He became obsessed with partying, drinking, cars, and girls. Maybe Marco was growing up while Terry was getting left behind. At least, that's what it felt like. Terry was perfectly happy gaming and focusing on schoolwork—he was a good student, while Marco was average but falling behind this year. And Terry was disappointed his friend had these new priorities.

"Come on, man, you know I hate parties".

"Yeah, you got *social anxiety*. You really have to work on that," said Marco. "Come on, just try it. Come out and have fun".

"Why can't we just chill at my place, play some games? I can maybe sneak us some beers, I don't think my dad will notice," Terry suggested. He hated beer, it was bitter and gross, but he was hoping Marco might be convinced.

Instead, Marco gave him a pitying look, shaking his head.

Then suddenly something happened that distracted him, something that's never happened to Terry before. Two girls came over to their usual cafeteria table, the one by the wall, where they'd sit by themselves every day for lunch.

"Hey, Marco," said one of the girls. Terry thought her name was Trisha. She stood next to Marco, leaning over the table, and Terry's eyes were involuntarily drawn to her cleavage. He averted his gaze quickly before anyone noticed.

"What's up?"

"Are you coming to Stacy's party tonight?"

"Yeah. I was just trying to convince my friend Terry here to come with".

"Who, this nerd?" said Trisha. "Who cares about him?"

"He's my friend, Trish. Don't be a bitch".

"Yeah, Trish. He's kind of cute," said the other girl, who was standing next to Trisha.

"Whatever. So, party? You're coming, right?"

"Yeah, I'll be there".

"Cool. Hey, by the way, what do you think of Gwen?"

"Who?" Marco asked. Trisha pointed, and both boys turned in their seats to check out Gwen.

"I don't really know her," said Marco.

"I think we have calculus together," said Terry. In return, he got a look from Trish that said, 'No one gives a shit about what *you* think'.

"Do you think she's cute?" Trish's friend asked Marco.

"Yeah, she's hot".

"You should talk to her at the party tonight," said Trisha in a suggestive tone. Then she straightened up. "I better see you there".

After the two girls left, Marco turned back to Terry. "So, are you coming to the party or not? I'll give you a ride, maybe I can finally convince my brother to let me borrow his car".

"What's the point?" asked Terry. "You'll be busy with Trisha and Gwen and their friends".

"Dude, come on. First off, that's not a bad thing. You can get busy with them, too. You heard Angie, she thinks you're cute".

"Man—"

"Oh, stop being such a virgin, Terr. You've got to grow up sometime. I'm going to the party. Text me if you want me to pick you up," said Marco, leaving in a huff.

Terry felt like crying. He wasn't sure why. He didn't want to go to the party, but now he felt like he was being forced to. Goddamn Trisha and

Angie and . . . and goddamn Marco. All they cared about was making out and drinking beer and being assholes.

Terry missed last year. The simpler days of video games and TV marathons and no awkward bullshit about girls. But then, maybe his friend was right. Maybe that's what growing up meant—life changes, and you've got to leave the old you behind and move on to girls, driving, partying, drinking, and being a dick. Life sucks.

He got up, picking up both his and Marco's trays and depositing them by the bin, then headed off to the library where he could read his manga in peace before it was time for his next class.

. . .

Dr. Larner was in a rush. He had a hell of a morning, starting with a two-hour degenerative diseases seminar that was moved last-minute into a larger lecture hall in the Biochem building. The beginning of fall term was always chaotic, with frequent venue changes as class sizes shifted due to students adding and dropping their courses. As a result of the lecture seminar getting moved, Dr. Larner was only just now walking to his office, which was up on the fifth floor of the CUH, the City University Hospital building. He was rolling a suitcase with him because he was supposed to travel straight to the airport in the afternoon, heading to a major conference where three of the grad students he was supervising were presenting spotlight papers.

Life as a renowned medical researcher was never dull.

It's taken him ages to get there, of course. He used to be a practicing physician for a decade before discovering his true passion. Medical practice these days was way too political, driven by money, with insurance and big pharma pushing drugs left and right. It sickened him. Larner knew that if he wanted to make the big bucks, there was a room for him running drug trials for major pharmaceutical corporations. But money was never his motivation.

Larner was interested in the *science*.

So, he joined CUH, first as a faculty lecturer while still seeing patients, and later as a full-time professor. He published multiple influential papers, got tenure. He didn't even mind the teaching—in fact, every once in a while, he reflected that instructing students was the best way to impact the field, inspiring future doctors and researchers. Sure, some of them would disappear into big pharma's backrooms, but others would save lives—either on an individual basis or by developing medicine, equipment, and procedures for curing diseases.

That's what he wanted to do. Cure. Save. Help.

Sure, the administrative duties of having to grade classes with sixty-plus students were a pain. He much preferred smaller seminars or working one-on-one with grad students on experiments and publications that impacted the field. But, ultimately, after decades in medicine, Larner had lived a life he could be proud of. He was getting close to retirement age but had no plans to slow down anytime soon.

As Larner rolled his suitcase down the hallway, he saw someone waiting by his office door. On top of everything else, he had forgotten about the appointment he had with his patient today.

Though no longer a practicing physician, Larner would occasionally consult on colleagues' cases having to do with his specialty—neural degenerative diseases. These days, he also had exactly one patient of his own, a very special case.

"Owen! I completely forgot. I apologize, my seminar got moved, and I had to run all the way across campus. Sorry, give me one minute," said the old professor, unlocking his office door. "Come in, come in. Have a seat".

Larner's office was a cross between a typical university professor's office—full of textbooks and paper drafts—and the plastic models and medical charts of a doctor's office. Larner rolled his suitcase into a corner and sat down, turning his chair towards Owen, who sat uncomfortably between the door and a coat rack.

"How are you?" asked Larner.

"I'm . . . I'm okay," Owen said tentatively.

Larner nodded. "Good, good. I'm sorry for forgetting the time, but thank you for coming in. I just thought, it's been about six months since our first series of tests. Perhaps now would be a good time to retest and see if there have been any changes in your unique physiology".

"Sure. Do you need to cut off my finger again?"

"No, no," smiled Larner. "I'll just need some bloodwork this time. You know, I checked your original samples just last week—we've kept them. It's quite remarkable, no degeneration whatsoever. After six months! I've never seen anything like it. Your cells could hold the secret to curing any number of diseases, my lab is hard at work at finding the key. No success so far, I'm afraid. It seems that whatever makes your cellular structure so unique—its resistance to stimuli—also makes it highly inappropriate as a template for study or treatment, but I'm sure if we stare at it long enough, we'll strike gold in some form or another. Oh, I'm rambling. Let me just . . . hmm," he paused, looking in his drawer for some equipment.

"I haven't drawn blood in ages . . . usually get nurses to do that. But I suppose it's best if we still keep things between us, yes?"

"I think so".

"Then I apologize in advance, this might hurt a pinch. Hold still," Dr. Larner said, proceeding to prick Owen's arm with a needle connected to a test tube. Owen averted his eyes. "This will take just a minute. I want to make sure I'm drawing enough blood, so I won't have to call you back in next week," laughed the doctor.

"I should have asked—any changes in your health? Are you on any medication?" he inquired after a minute.

"No. But I may start taking antidepressants again. My psychiatrist thinks it's a good idea, and I think I might give it a shot".

"That's wonderful. Remind me, in the past, you've been on antidepressants?"

"Yes, multiple times, different pills, different doses. For years. But they've never done anything".

"It'll be really interesting to study the impact on your hormone levels. We might learn something new about how your body operates".

"Sure".

"That would require regular blood tests. Bi-weekly, I would say, once you start on the drug regime".

"That's fine. My current psychiatrist is here at CUH, two floors down. I can drop by after my appointments".

"Fantastic! I don't know if I've emphasized this enough, but you're making a significant contribution to medical science".

"That's good," Owen said distractedly while Larner concluded drawing blood and corked his test tubes.

"All done. And look at that, no bleeding. You're already clotted up, and the skin's repairing right in front of our eyes. Fascinating".

Owen didn't respond.

Dr. Larner checked the dusty, faded clock on his office wall. "I still have some time before office hours. So, how are you physically? No new symptoms, nothing interesting to report?"

"Nothing new. I'm a little constipated".

"Really? Interesting. Any new physical trauma?"

"No, other than some gun wounds and burns, there hasn't been much. Not since . . . the time I jumped down fifty-six floors".

"Right. That recovery had been nothing short of miraculous. I really wish I'd have been there to measure, document . . . I mean, your bones, they've recovered to the *same* state, the same age, density. It defies everything we know about physiology".

They were both silent for a moment.

"I apologize," Dr. Larner suddenly said. Owen didn't expect that. "I know I talk like . . . it must sound as if I'm treating you like a lab rat, some sort of experiment. You're a person, first. I can get very excited about the science, and I sometimes forget that".

"It's okay—"

"No, no, it's not. Tell me, how is your, uhm, your crime-fighting operation going these days?"

"It's going well, actually. We're doing good".

"That's great to hear! I had a call with Sharon Richardson the other day, or it might have been a few weeks ago, actually. She also mentioned things were going well. But you know, I haven't heard anything from Dinah in a long time. Dinah Borst? Not since the Purple Massacre, in any case".

Owen nearly flinched at the mention of the Purple Massacre. That was the name the papers eventually settled on for the carnage at the 16th precinct station, the one Owen had witnessed. Boys in blue bloodied red—hence purple. He found it distasteful, to say the least.

"How *is* Dinah?" continued Larner.

"I don't know, actually. I haven't heard from her lately either. I know Richardson checked with some of her contacts on the force . . . she's gone on paid leave with mandated psychiatric treatment. That's all I know".

"I see, I see. And how's your own psychiatric treatment?"

"It's helping a lot, actually," Owen answered candidly. "It's been a pretty difficult time, after the Unkillable incident. But I've been dealing with it in a pretty healthy way, I think. I'm doing better than expected. And like I said, we're considering medication, which I haven't tried in years. Who knows, maybe it'll help".

"I certainly hope so," the doctor said before getting interrupted by a knock on his office door. "Oh, I'm sorry, that must be some of my seminar students. Their office hours are just about to start. Would you like to stay, or—"

"Oh, it's okay, I should get going anyway".

"Right, well, it was very good to see you".

"You too, doctor".

"I'll text you when I get the results of your new bloodwork, and do let me know when you've commenced treatment with any medication. We can monitor your body's reactions from a chemical and hormonal perspective, and maybe learn a thing or two".

"Sounds good. Have a nice afternoon," said Owen, leaving the office.

2 – *Let's not worry*

AS soon as he got to the ground floor, Owen's phone buzzed.

"Hey".

"Owen? Where are you?" asked Richardson.

For the past six months, Owen and Richardson have been partners, working together to tackle crimes, respond to disasters, and undertake operations where no one but Owen—thanks to his unique inability to die—could make a difference and save lives. Captain Dinah Borst used to be part of their crew, but since the Purple Massacre and the subsequent capture of the criminal known as Unkillable, she's dropped off the radar, refusing to return Richardson's calls.

"I'm at the City University Hospital. Was just visiting Dr. Larner".

"Perfect, that's perfect. Look, I've got Donoghue on the other line, I'm going to add him to the call. We need you on an op. Are you free the rest of the day?"

"I am, yes".

"Great, let me just . . ." said Richardson, before a loud beep confirmed that Captain Donoghue joined the line.

A gruff man but a good police, Donoghue was recruited by Richardson to essentially take over Borst's role in the operation. Years ago, Donoghue and Borst worked under Richardson in her old precinct, but he was now working in Central, overseeing both the Drug Enforcement and Organized Crime taskforces.

Since the fall of most of the city's criminal organizations as part of Unkillable's spree of violence, the city's drug problem essentially decentralized, with localized small-scale operations popping up everywhere. Donoghue saw this as an opportunity to hit them hard, instituting a whack-a-mole anti-drug strategy while doubling his units' budget and personnel. The Mayor and

City Council were more than happy to react to the massacre by allocating funds to combat organized violence, and Donoghue's profile rose suddenly and precipitously.

In public, Donoghue was the face of the city's renewed and enthusiastic war on crime. Secretly, he also served as the bridge between the city's police force and Richardson and Owen's unsanctioned, underground operation, providing enforcement and requesting assistance when appropriate. For instance, today.

"Owen, that you?"

"Yes, sir," answered Owen. He knew Donoghue liked formality and was proud of his rank.

"Good. We've got a situation, and we need you on it. You up for it?"

"What's the situation, sir?"

"I have an undercover operative who's just identified a lab ready to supply half of Church Village. I'd love to raid it, but that'd blow his cover. There's no way for my officers to get in without tipping anyone off, and I can't afford these assholes running to the wind. Best solution, the way I see it, is to have you go in and confiscate-slash-destroy everything. We protect the city *and* the operative. In fact, if it's staged like a break-in, they may lead us to uncover a rival gang. My man agrees—it's our best course of action".

"You just want me to go in and . . . what? Steal their drugs?"

"Confiscate product, break equipment, make sure the lab's no longer operational. That's the number one goal, to cut them off and decommission the lab. But at the same time, it's vitally important that you grab at least some of the product, the drugs. I'll need those for evidence. Grab what you can and destroy the rest, flush it down the drain. Got it?"

"Yeah, I think I got it".

"Good. Now listen, I'm in contact with my operative, he's in the lab right now. They're ready to send a major shipment out tonight, so we've got to act soon. My man will make sure there's a window when the lab would be empty. Can you make it in a couple of hours?"

"What's the location?"

Donoghue told him the address. It was nearby. City University was stationed right in the middle of the city's downtown core, surrounded by government housing and less affluent neighbourhoods to one side and a giant park bordered by luxury high-rises on the other. Owen himself didn't live too far. It was a lively, central part of the city that was a mishmash of different cultures and socioeconomic strata.

The drug lab was in the garage of a townhouse about twenty minutes away by foot.

"I can make it".

"Good. Get there in two hours, and wait outside until you see them leave. Then give them a few minutes, and get in and out as fast as you can. I'll text if my operative raises any flags".

"You know," opined Richardson, "this will be much smoother if we could communicate with your operative directly".

"For security reasons, you know I can't do that. His identity stays private, I'm the only go-between. It's an undercover operation—you know the stakes, Richardson. You were on the force".

"Yeah, yeah," she grumbled. "I just don't like that we're putting *my* man at risk".

"I don't mind risk," said Owen. "It's fine. We're taking drugs off the street, neutralizing a new gang. It's worth a little risk. Besides, even if I'm caught, it's nothing I can't handle".

"That's what I like to hear. Good luck," said Donoghue, hanging up.

"You got it?" Richardson asked.

"Got it," Owen confirmed.

"How's Larner?"

"He's fine. He hasn't heard anything from Dinah either".

"Right. Shit. Well . . . nothing we can do about her right now, Owen. She'll get back to us when she's ready. Let's not worry about her—she's strong, I'm sure she's fine. Let's just focus on the op right now".

"Right, yeah".

"Let me know if you need me, I'll be on standby".

"Thanks. I'm not too worried about it," said Owen. The op sounded straightforward enough, nothing he hadn't done before.

. . .

He had time to kill. Owen sat down at a coffee shop at a random university building.

Years of living with depression had taught him the art of staring at a wall and waiting for time to pass. A lot of it had to do with accepting that all sorts of thoughts would enter your mind—some of them will be negative thoughts—and that was *okay*. You had to let them pass through, hold them, then let them go. Thoughts don't have to lead to actions, and thoughts don't have to affect feelings. It's still useful to acknowledge them, but at the end of the day, they're just thoughts.

Owen had a variety of thoughts go through his head while he waited. First, he thought about being old. Owen *was* old, compared to all the fresh undergraduates around him, busy talking about their new classes and making new friends. He thought about his own university life—ages ago. He had moved out to a faraway school to get away from home. He made some friends, and he remembered being semi-interested in a few classes. But his undergraduate experience was tainted with a prolonged depressive episode and an early suicide attempt. Looking back, his memory of the time was pretty foggy.

Was it depression that fogged his mind or the antidepressants he was on back then? He was strongly considering going back on medication. It felt like a safe time to try it, but he was still worried. Antidepressants can make depression feel worse, or bring on suicidal ideation. He's had experience with that. But nowadays, he was doing pretty well mentally. Which was surprising.

He expected to be a lot worse with Dinah out of his life. It had been a couple of months since he last saw her, and he expected to miss her, to think about her all the time. But the truth was, he was more focused than ever, and life had become easier, in a sense. Lighter.

Sure, he still worried about her as a friend every time he thought of her. How was she coping? *Was* she coping? The carnage at her precinct was too much for anyone to come to terms with without help. He had needed help, and he got it—he began to see a therapist as soon as the Unkillable episode was over. Being trapped in a cell while cops and killers were warring all around him was traumatizing, and he recognized that he needed someone to listen and offer support as he worked through the trauma. Years of therapy helped him differentiate helpful from harmful coping mechanisms, but an ordeal of that level required ongoing therapy, there was no way around it.

Was Dinah seeing a therapist? And what about her alcohol dependency? Owen had seen it. He tried to ignore it, but the last time he saw her, he grabbed her flask away from her. Maybe that was presumptuous, maybe he was projecting inappropriately, but he had seen his own mother. He'd seen his sister. Alcohol, drugs . . . he knew how that ended. Maybe that's why he felt comfortable with Donoghue targeting drug rings, even though his methods and politicking were . . . questionable.

Those were a lot of different thoughts, Owen realized. He tried to empty his mind and checked his watch. Enough time had passed. He got up.

On the way to the suspected meth lab, he stopped by the campus store and bought two of their largest university-branded gym bags. He figured if he was grabbing drugs out of a lab, he needed a way to carry them. He walked the rest of the way. It wasn't far.

. . .

The house Donoghue indicated was on a residential street. This close to City University, half the houses were shared off-campus student accommodations, with the rest full of young families attracted by reasonable rent and the proximity to downtown. Hard to imagine these two very different demographics surviving side-by-side, Owen reflected. Working families with kids living next to hard-drinking, hard-partying university students, and in-between, garage labs manufacturing crystal meth or heroin or whatever other drugs you made in a garage lab. Owen wasn't an expert.

There was no bench, no park, nowhere on the bright street where he could stand inconspicuously. He needed to wait for Donoghue's contact to leave the house, signalling that it was safe for Owen to infiltrate. Owen wasn't sure what to do. He just stood across the street, trying to look nonchalant. It probably wasn't working.

Instead of standing there like a creep, he started pacing up and down the street, stopping at the corner, then turning back around. Nothing was happening. He felt extremely awkward.

Finally, he heard noises. A loud group of young people, mostly men, left the house in question and got into three cars, driving away. No one paid him any attention. Owen gave it five minutes. He initially intended to give it ten, but he got impatient. Following the instructions passed to him via Donoghue from the undercover operative, Owen jumped the old, locked wooden gate leading to the backyard of the target house. He walked around the house, finding the backdoor unlocked.

"Hello?" he called out. "Anybody home?"

Hearing no response, he entered. The house was a mess. It was either a hideout for low-level criminals, or just a normal house occupied by immature university students. The living room was full of cheap furniture, a large screen TV, multiple gaming systems, and endless empty beer cans. The kitchen was similarly stocked with alcohol, pizza boxes, and chip packets—no food of measurable nutritional value in sight. No weapons or drugs either, though.

Owen made his way through the house and into the garage.

There we go, he thought.

While the house was a sad mess, the garage was a proper lab. It was spotless, with lab coats, goggles, and gloves hanging near the door. The equipment seemed high-grade to his untrained eye—lots of pipettes and beakers, chemical vats, shiny silver bowls, and various yellow-and-red containers.

Owen wondered whether this was an actual drug ring involved with organized crime or a bunch of chemistry students from City University trying to make a quick buck.

He soon found the product. There was a lot—the entire wall was blocked by large boxes, twenty in total, each with about fifty small sandwich-sized sealed plastic bags.

Enough drugs for half the Church Village neighbourhood. Donoghue wasn't kidding.

Owen got to work.

He knew he had to be fast. The last thing he wanted was to get caught. He hadn't seen any weapons around, but if there was a way to avoid violence, he wanted to take it. Besides, it would make things tough for Donoghue's undercover cop. So Owen moved briskly.

He started by taking photographs of everything on his phone and sending them over to Richardson. The lab setup, the product, all of it. Next, he removed as much of the finished meth as he could, stuffing plastic bags into his university-branded gym bags. He could only empty one and a half of the cardboard boxes.

He spent a minute trying to think of what to do with the rest. He decided to focus on the raw ingredients first. He made it a little tougher to make any new batches by pouring the yellow-and-red containers down the drain.

At one point, he stopped, wondering whether this was safe—not for him, he knew he'd be fine—but for the pipes and the neighbourhood sewers. What if these chemicals were corroding the environment, seeping into water sources, poisoning the whole of Church Village and University Heights? Then Owen shrugged off the thought. He decided to ask Richardson later. He stopped handling the chemicals, noticing his hands showed discoloured chemical burns. They'd heal in a bit, he knew.

Next, he got rid of the rest of the drugs. Initially, he continued pouring things down the drain, but then he decided to grab the boxes and take them to the washroom, dumping the drugs down the toilet bowl. This worked a little faster, but opening each individual bag was still frustrating to no end. All in all, it took over an hour to get rid of everything.

The grand finale was smashing some of the equipment. Owen felt conflicted over this since any kind of activity that was essentially *wrong* filled him with a disproportionate amount of guilt, which stemmed from patterns developed from his father overreacting to even minor transgressions when he was very young. But he knew this sanctioned act of property damage would ensure that making new drugs and selling them around the city would be much more challenging for this gang. It would also make it look more like the work of a rival gang rather than the work of a secret operative directed by undercover police. It was safer that way. So, trying to overcome his guilt patterns, Owen tossed beakers around, tore pipes, dropped a large mixer-looking machine onto the floor and hit it with a test-tube rack, denting and cracking both. When he felt like he had done enough damage, he grabbed the gym bags and left through the backyard, leaving the gate unlocked on his way out.

A neighbour was walking a dog as Owen left. He tried to turn his head away and walked off quickly, feeling like a criminal.

This whole thing felt wrong.

. . .

"Owen?" Richardson answered on the first ring.

"Yeah, hi".

"How did the op go? I got your photographic evidence".

"Good, yeah, it went okay. I smashed stuff up, grabbed some of the . . . the *product*," Owen said. He was passing people on the street and was too worried to say drugs. "I dumped the rest down the toilet. Uhm . . . yeah. Whole thing felt really weird, to be honest. We gotta talk about that".

"Absolutely. What do you need right now? Where are you?"

"I just left the place. I've got two giant bags full of the stuff on me. Where am I taking them?"

"That's a good question. Let me think . . . you can bring them here, or, well, you're pretty close to your place, right?"

"Yeah. I was thinking of going home first. I kind of want to shower and change after all the chemical stuff".

"How about you do that? Go on home, I'll check in with Donoghue. Then I'll let you know whether you should bring the evidence over here or maybe straight to him someplace. I'll ask. Does that sound okay?"

"Yeah, that's great. Oh, also, I spilled some of the chemicals down the drain, and I wasn't really sure . . . like, I don't know if I should have done that. I mean in terms of chemical safety or . . . I don't know".

"Do you remember the names of the chemicals?"

"No, but we have photos of the whole setup".

"Right. Well, we can look into that together when you come here. I'll do some checking online. I think it's probably fine, though," said Richardson, though she didn't sound very reassuring. "You did good, you did what Donoghue asked. Don't worry".

"Okay".

"Great, you head on home then, and we'll reconnect maybe in about an hour or so?"

"Yeah, that sounds good".

. . .

Owen hung up. He felt like the call didn't really accomplish anything. Why did he call Richardson in the first place again? Probably just seeking reassurance and trying to alleviate his guilt. Or was he right to feel this way? He shrugged and kept on walking towards his own apartment building.

Along the way, Owen had to cross a bridge. It was a viaduct, actually, crossing over a ravine. And in this city, this viaduct was infamous.

It was a suicide bridge, a spot well-known for the multitudes—hundreds—of people who had, over the years, committed suicide by jumping into the ravine below. It was particularly problematic in the heat of summer and right around the holidays. But throughout the year, there used to be multiple suicides each month off this single bridge, causing it to be ranked as one of the most fatal standing structures on the continent.

The bridge, just a couple of blocks from Owen's apartment, held a personal meaning for him. He had jumped off this very bridge, attempting suicide, on two separate occasions, including the attempt following his sister's death. That was a particularly difficult and dark time for him.

A few months after that attempt, the city finally acted. They put up a barrier, which was partially funded by taxpayers and partially by a fundraising campaign. Owen contributed to the campaign, though he felt conflicted at the time. Construction took ages, like all construction projects in this city. The noise and dust clouds made living in his apartment difficult, particularly since Owen used to have nothing to do all day. That wasn't a good year. But once it was put in place, the barrier effectively lowered incidents of suicide attempts by jumping off this viaduct. So it seemed like it was worth it.

Owen reflected on this as he crossed the bridge carrying two heavy gym bags full of drugs on his way home.

3 – *I felt a lot of things*

"HOW are you today?" asked Dr. Griffith.

Dinah Borst was seated on a cushiony armchair that was altogether too soft. It practically swallowed her whole body. She wasn't comfortable. She was at her therapist's office, a specialized police psychiatrist who was an expert on post-traumatic stress disorder and other mental hazards prevalent in police work. This was an assigned weekly session, one of the conditions of her mandated paid leave.

She didn't want to be on leave.

Leave was the worst thing she could be on.

She needed work. She needed *something*. Something to do, to keep her mind busy. Anything. She was losing it. She was going crazy. But instead of being understanding, her superiors, guided by the recommendations of some bullshit investigative committee, decided what she needed was time off and time on the couch of this so-called expert.

She had nothing but disdain for Dr. Griffith. But she needed the doctor on her side, because Griffith had the final say on formally assessing whether Borst was ready to go back on active duty. So Borst had to play nice.

"I'm okay," she lied.

"That's good to hear. Let's go through our usual questionnaire? You know it's just a formality, but I have to ask these".

"Sure".

"Have you had any thoughts about harming yourself this week?"

"No," lied Borst.

"Harming others?"

"No". This one was true.

"Good. Any trouble sleeping?"

"Nope".

"Concentrating?"

"A little," admitted Borst. She had to give her something, make it believable.

"Alright, we can talk about that. Any drug use?"

"No".

"Alcohol?"

"Yes".

"Still drinking a glass of wine a day?"

"And the occasional beer," smiled Borst. She established this lie about a pattern of light, reasonable alcohol consumption in previous sessions. Of course, the truth was very different. She was downing entire bottles of wine daily, not to mention the harder stuff. With nothing else to keep her occupied all day, what was she expected to do—refrain from drinking? It was the only thing that helped.

Her days started around 1:00 p.m. when she would wake up and finally force herself to get out of bed because she had to pee. Since it was already after lunch, drinking was acceptable. Not that she gave a shit what time it was. So Borst would get up, piss, browse some news, park herself in front of the TV, and open a bottle, always starting with the cheap stuff. An hour or two into the day, she'd sometimes call someone, a colleague, just to check-in, see if they might want her advice on any active cases. Not that there were any important cases lately. Crime died down with the end of the summer heatwave and Unkillable's arrest.

That occasional conversation with a colleague, lasting a few minutes, was the highlight of her day. It was also the greatest challenge of each day—she had to sound sober, composed. Once that was over with, she'd order some food, drink, and keep on watching random crap as her brain atrophied. Then she would doze off on the sofa until it was time to drag herself back to bed.

Another day wasted.

But if her therapist asked, she had a far healthier routine—eating well, exercising, working on arts-and-crafts projects, and drinking in perfect moderation. Lies, lies, lies.

"Good," continued Dr. Griffith. "Well, it sounds like you're doing well. What would you like to talk about today, Dinah?"

"I . . . don't really have much to say. Nothing new. I'm just anxious to get back to work," said Borst, trying to smile.

"I understand. But you're only two months into your leave".

"Two months can be a long time. I mean, I feel like I'm getting close to being ready to go back, you know?"

"Yes, I understand you might feel that way, but you've been assigned this leave for a reason, Dinah. You experienced very serious trauma. You need to recover".

"I know that, but I just . . . I really feel that I'd make a better recovery if I had something to occupy my time. I think that being unproductive, feeling inactive, it's made things more difficult for me".

"That's perfectly reasonable. Have you been trying to do little things throughout the day, like we discussed last time?"

"Yes, I . . . you know, I have my daily routine. Uhm, painting, and . . . working out. You know".

"Are you still trying to write your memoir?" smiled her doctor.

"I am," lied Borst. There was no *Memoir of a Policewoman*. But a few weeks ago, Dr. Griffith asked what progress she's made, and Dinah had to make something up, some project. Owen once told her he used to write. Maybe that's what made her think of this particular lie.

Owen. She hadn't discussed him yet. And she wasn't about to.

"Well, that's a productive activity, don't you think?"

"I do, of course. But . . . look, I'm a cop, not a writer or . . . or anything else. Keeping a routine, working out, it's all great, but . . . I miss active duty. I miss my job. I . . . look, I *am* a cop. We talked about that last time—I define myself by my work, it's who I am. I just *really* want to get back to it already".

"But given the trauma you faced, the massacre . . . well, it *must* take time to recover, don't you think?"

"Well—"

"We really haven't discussed it much. Let's make that the focus of today".

"I don't . . . uh, well, sure. We could".

Dr. Griffith tapped her notepad with her pen. "I know going over the actual details may be painful, but I do believe that's an important part of the process. Do you think you're ready to tell me what happened when you entered the station that day?"

No. Borst *wasn't* ready. She didn't want to relive it. It was the last thing she wanted. But if she was ever going to convince Dr. Griffith she was fine and ready to resume duty, she'd have to. *Fuck it. This doctor wants to talk about it? Let's talk about it*, she thought.

"Well, I remember . . . I drove into the parking lot. Everything was . . . was quiet, which was already very unusual. No cars going in or out of the lot, no one going in or out of the building. I think . . . I think I could tell something was wrong. Then I saw blood. I think there was like a stain, pooling blood, on the ground just outside the door".

"So, you knew something was wrong? Do you remember how you felt?"

"Not really. I don't know if I *felt* anything, I think I just operated by instinct. It all happened so fast . . . I walked into the station and saw all the blood, and . . . bodies, everywhere. I saw the kid, Fredericks. He was alive, he—he told me what happened. Uhm, then I . . . I secured the station, made sure no assailants were left. I walked through the scene looking for survivors, I called for backup. Yeah".

"And you don't remember what you felt at any point?"

"I mean, of course, I . . . I felt a lot of things".

"Such as?"

Borst really didn't want to explore this. She decided to keep making stuff up instead.

"Well, I must have been scared. Terrified, obviously. A lot of people were dead, there was blood everywhere. I didn't know whether the assailant was still around, so . . . yeah. I was scared. And . . . and I felt *angry*. I mean, my squad, the 1-6, they were . . . almost like family, you know? So there was loss, anger".

"What were you angry about?"

"Angry they were dead!" Borst said, incredulous that Griffith dared question it.

"Were you angry at anything else?"

"No. Yes. I mean . . . I was angry at—at the motherfucker who killed them, angry that . . . I don't know. Maybe I was angry at myself, feeling guilty, actually. Or maybe that came later".

"Guilty about what?"

Borst was getting irritated at all these probing questions. "Guilty that . . . I wasn't there".

"You mean, you felt guilty that you weren't at the 16th precinct station while the massacre took place?"

"Yeah".

"What would have happened if you *had* been there?" asked Dr. Griffith, taking dumb notes with her dumb pen again.

"I would have died, same as the whole station. I don't have any delusions that I could have saved them all or anything like that. I know I couldn't have saved anyone, but it's just . . . I *should* have been there".

"Why do you say that?"

Borst didn't respond right away. Why did she need to know everything? Fucking psychiatrist bitch.

"Dinah, that point had been missing from every report I've seen. Where *were* you while the massacre was taking place?"

"I was . . ." Borst started, then trailed off.

"This could be important. It could help us pinpoint why you've been feeling guilty".

"No, it's . . . I . . ." Borst stumbled. Was she going to explain about Owen? Arresting him, then feeling so guilty, so shitty about it that she had to take a break for an hour and seek guidance?

"Yes?"

"I . . . I had just arrested someone. I put him in a cell in connection with some gang crime. I wasn't sure he was guilty, but I had some evidence, a witness, and . . . I was conflicted about it, feeling really . . . look, at the time, it was difficult. For a while. The whole summer, the heatwave, there . . . we thought there was a gang war going on, it was exhausting. And that arrest . . . anyway. So, I took an hour off, just . . . *one* hour. I needed to clear my head".

"Where did you go?"

"It's . . . dumb".

"Dinah, it could be important".

"I went to . . . I went to see my father's grave".

"Oh!" proclaimed Dr. Griffith, raising an eyebrow. "I'll be honest, when people feel as guilty as you do, and get so evasive . . . I expected you might have been having an affair or, well, doing something illicit. You were just visiting a grave?"

"Yes," Borst nodded. "My dad was a cop, and he passed away not too long ago, and . . . well, actually, I guess it's been years. I used to go to his grave a lot, just to think, to ask . . . I kind of pretended to talk to him, like he gave me advice. I know it's stupid, but it helped. So, on that day, I left my cell phone at my desk, and I drove to the graveyard. When I came back . . . that's when I saw what happened".

"So, you feel guilty for visiting your father's grave? Do you feel like that was wrong of you? It doesn't really sound like a bad thing to do, Dinah".

Borst shook her head. "No, I guess I don't feel guilty about visiting his grave".

"But you *do* feel guilty?"

"Well, of *course* I do. They were . . . it was *my* squad. I was their captain. Santiago, Dawson, everyone. Like I said, we were closer than family in a sense. We had each other's backs. You have to trust your people, build the relationships. And now they're gone, and . . . I should have been there, I should have been with them. It's just . . . it doesn't seem fair".

"It isn't fair," agreed Griffith.

"Right? It isn't. So . . . yeah. I feel . . . angry, and powerless. I know I couldn't have stopped it. I would have died with them. And I didn't, and I'm glad about that, I guess, but I feel . . . guilty. Because maybe I *should* have died that day. And . . . yeah".

The doctor nodded. "Those are all very natural things to feel, don't you think?"

"I do. I get it. It's survivor's guilt".

"It doesn't affect your day-to-day?"

Borst thought of what she should say. "Maybe a little. I think about it sometimes, I . . . yeah. If I'm honest, I don't have a lot to do, which is why I keep asking about getting back on the force. Without . . . like, with nothing to keep my mind busy, sometimes . . ."

"You find yourself overwhelmed with the guilt?"

"Yeah. Yeah, exactly".

"Any nightmares?"

"No, not so far". Lies again. Back to those.

"And no trouble sleeping?"

"No". That part was true—the copious amount of alcohol she'd been consuming helped ensure she could get consistent sleep each night. But she wasn't about to share that caveat with her therapist.

"That's . . . good. Very good," said Griffith, though she didn't sound convinced. "I think we made some progress here. How do you feel, having shared a little of what you're going through and what happened?"

"Uhm . . . I don't know. I guess it's good to say it out loud, but . . . I don't know that it makes much of a difference, if I'm honest. I'm really okay. Sure, I feel guilty and angry sometimes, but it's not like . . . it doesn't *really* affect me. It's not like I wake up in the middle of the night with visions of the station floor covered in blood, or . . . like, ghosts of my old squad or whatever. I mean, I'm not . . . I'm not crazy. I'm coping".

"Yes, those are all good signs. I do worry that perhaps you're bottling some of your emotions, but I feel like we're finally beginning to process. Let's continue down this path next week, Dinah. For now, I wanted to go through some ideas on more things you can do day-to-day to make sure you're feeling busy and productive".

. . .

Borst was back in her apartment. She felt angry.

Therapy was stupid. Dr. Griffith was insistently refusing to recommend that she return to active duty early. The bitch.

She opened up! She told her about . . . about that day, about her feelings and all that crap. Borst didn't *mean* to share, but she did, and . . . what more did the doctor want from her?

She wasn't traumatized. She wasn't catatonic. She wasn't mentally ill. She wasn't an alco—

Borst stared at the bottle of cheap red in her hand. When had she opened that one?

Okay. Maybe the alcohol was starting to get a *little* out of control. But that was only because she was out of work. Once she got back on duty, she'd slow it down again, no problem.

No problem. Exactly. She didn't have a *problem*. She was sane, sound, and healthy. Perfectly fine.

Borst sighed.

She shouldn't have talked about that day. She'd have the nightmares again tonight. At least she didn't have them every night. Maybe that was another reason she drank so much—when she had enough booze to pass out on the couch, sometimes she didn't dream about it. The blood, the faces on the floor. All those cops, *her* cops—

No. Don't think about it, she told herself.

At least she didn't tell Dr. Griffith about Owen.

She checked her phone, even though she knew. No messages. No calls. Nothing from him. Oh, other people tried to call, check up on her. Her superiors, D'Alfonso, Richardson, even Dr. Larner once. She ignored their calls.

She was determined to ignore his call, too, when he finally broke down and called her. It'd be soon, she knew it. Owen would call.

Fuck him, anyway. Asshole.

She flung her phone onto a chair, drank a mouthful of wine, and sank onto the couch. *Her* couch. Nice and hard and comfortable. Nothing like Dr. Griffith's soft piece of crap.

Another week until the next session. And nothing much to do till then. Dinah Borst sank back into the nothing, the boredom, the anger, the guilt, the nightmares, the alcohol, the depression, the waiting, the nothing-to-do, the hopelessness, the helplessness, the pointlessness, the sleep, the sleeplessness, the sighing, the shouting, the crying, the giving up on it all.

Her life now. Or lack thereof.

4 – *Didn't really think it through*

OWEN walked into the Control Room, also known as Richardson's basement. He brought the bags full of drugs over.

The whole way, Owen was paranoid that he'd get questioned by a random cop or that one of the bags would burst open for some reason. Ridiculous, but, well, he didn't enjoy walking around with large quantities of meth in university-branded gym bags.

"So, the op went okay? You're all right?" asked Richardson.

"It went fine, but . . . well, I don't know".

"What is it?"

Owen sighed. "I, look . . . I don't like this. I know what Donoghue's trying to accomplish, but it felt like I was breaking into somebody's house, smashing stuff. It's . . . I felt like *I* was the criminal, you know?"

"You were breaking into a *meth lab*. You smashed their stuff and confiscated their product. Donoghue explained it, he's protecting his undercover asset, and we're tackling the city's drug problem. You know what's been going on since Unkillable murdered half the city's organized crime and dismantled their infrastructure. All these small amateur operations started popping up, and the leftover gangs are trying to consolidate. We're preventing a potential turf war from escalating by dismantling these nests, one at a time".

"I know, I understand *that* part. I know we're doing the right thing, but . . . it just doesn't feel right. Being in there, in the moment".

"So you're saying you don't have a problem with Donoghue's mission, but you don't like his methods?"

"Exactly. His methods, and his . . . his attitude".

"I agree," said Richardson.

Owen paused. "You do?"

"I thought you were fine with it. You didn't voice any concerns, so I didn't say anything either. But yeah, I have a problem with how Donoghue operates. His ops are . . . they feel impulsive and poorly thought-out. I don't mind sending you out to decommission a lab, I think that's great. But why isn't Donoghue sending his own men to not only decommission the lab but make arrests? Keeping an undercover operative safe is an excuse—he could've figured out a way around that. I figured, if you like getting into action, why not send you in. But if you're not cool with it, then forget it".

Owen nodded.

"Not to mention, with Donoghue . . . you don't know him like I do. He's gunning for Commissioner, and it shows. He's always played his own political game. He used to be on my squad, you know, and he's good police, even if he's an asshole. But this?" she asked, lifting one of the gym bags off the ground. "You know why he wanted you to nab a sample? It's got nothing to do with evidence—he's not arresting anyone. No, I bet you he just wants to take credit for it, publicly. Show off all the drugs his force is taking off the street just so he gets clout, recognition".

"So *that's* why he wants it".

"Otherwise, why not just have you destroy it all?"

"Yeah, exactly, I was asking myself the same thing. I could have destroyed all of it. Taking a couple of bags with me as samples or whatever never made any sense. So I just carried it around all over town just because he—"

"For his *optics*. Yeah".

Owen clenched his fists. "That actually kind of pisses me off. I really don't like that".

"Well, look, I'm not a huge fan of the guy either, but . . . what can we do? He's my best contact still on the force. I thought he had vision, but . . . he's not Dinah".

"No, he's not".

Richardson sighed. "We can try to focus on more of our own ops instead. I mean, look, now that summer's over we have fewer fires, accidents, and a lot less violent crime. That's in part because Unkillable's gone, in part because of the police cracking down after the massacre, and . . . I don't know, maybe it's partly seasonal too, could be. There's just less for us to do. And that's . . . I mean, it's boring for us, but for the city, I guess it's great, actually. Right?"

Owen nodded. "Of course. Less crime is good. Just, um, you know. It's frustrating".

Richardson scratched her head. "I was going to suggest something, but . . . "

"What is it?"

It took a minute for Richardson to come out with it. It was a simple idea, really. "Well, I was thinking, you know . . . you can always join the force proper. Become a cop".

"But won't that defeat the purpose of me operating on the margins? As an independent . . . I mean, the whole idea was that I can enter situations that cops can't. That was Dinah's idea from the beginning, and Donoghue seems to want the same thing".

"Exactly. Donoghue . . . I trust him, he's a good cop. I just think . . . look, if we can't think of a way to use you effectively as is, maybe it means we're going about it the wrong way. Maybe doing it through the formal channels is the right thing to do at this point. I just wanted to put it out there".

"I know. I know. It's just . . . with Dinah, I always felt like . . . she had a plan, you know? She always knew what the next step was. And now we sort of lost that".

After a moment of awkward silence, Richardson asked, "Have you heard from her?"

"Nothing".

"Have you *tried* to reach out?"

"No," Owen shook his head. "I'm just not ready".

"Owen, she—"

"I know. I just . . . I'm not ready. I'm still angry. I'm working through it".

"She did what she thought was right".

"And I completely understand that! But it still hurts. She threw me in a cell. And I had . . . I ended up witnessing a fucking *massacre* because of that. It was traumatic. I know it's not her fault—she wasn't the one killing anybody, she didn't even know about Unkillable at the time, but honestly, I have nightmares about it".

"Yeah, of course—" Richardson started, but Owen kept talking.

"Do you remember the trafficking ring bust? The first op Dinah asked me to go on, before you were involved. You remember me telling you about it?"

"I think so".

"I rescued some girls from, yeah, a trafficking ring. They shot . . . at one point the criminals shot at the girls who were running out of that basement and . . . for ages, I had nightmares about it. Every single night. And nobody died, no one even got seriously hurt back then. So, with the . . . the police station shoot-out, whatever you call it, the purple fucking massacre . . . it just . . ."

"Owen, I get it. It must have been hell. And you lived through it. And . . . Owen, I'm a cop, too. I've seen death, I've been in action. Nothing like that massacre, I know, but . . . I just, I *do* have some understanding".

"I know you do. That's why I feel like I can talk to you. And I talk to my therapist, too".

"Is it helping?"

"A lot. I knew I was going to need it. I told Dr. Larner about it. He wants to test my blood once I go back on antidepressants. Maybe we'll figure out something that helps".

"That great, Owen. That's really good".

"I know. Dr. Larner tried to contact Dinah too, by the way. She's not replying to him, either".

"Shit. I'm really worried".

"I'm worried about her too, Sharon. But, you know, a few of my therapists said this over the years, and it's true—you can only be responsible for your own feelings, your own shit. We don't . . . we can't hold ourselves responsible for what Dinah is going through. We're concerned, and that's because we're . . . we're her friends. But she . . . well, there's no point spiralling into guilt over it. That's it".

"You're right. You know, for someone your age, you're pretty smart".

"Well, I've been through my fair share of shit".

"I know. Look, you can leave those bags with me. I'll get them to Donoghue. I'll talk to him".

"Don't. Don't bother. I don't know. Don't . . . I mean, it's not like we're quitting, or like we don't want to work with him anymore".

"No, of course not. I'll just let him know that we care about doing the right thing the right way, and we want to focus on doing good when it really matters. You have a set of skills and… they should be used for the right sort of operation, not just to . . . anyway, I won't be confrontational. Don't worry, I've been on the force long enough, I know how to handle boys like him".

"Good. Thanks, Sharon".

"I don't think we're going to get anything on the radio tonight. Why don't you head on home? Take it easy".

Owen nodded and got up. He turned to leave, but then turned back towards Richardson.

"You know, why don't we have a training session? I could use some practice. And I don't think either of us has anything important to do tonight. *I* don't, anyway".

Richardson smiled. "All right, then. Let's do us some training".

. . .

It was good, the training. Like old times—well, just a few months ago, really, but it felt like another lifetime. Those days before the massacre, before Unkillable, back when Richardson started training Owen to be an operative who can save lives. Being in that basement again, just training, not thinking about Donoghue's problematic missions or about Dinah being gone, was nice. They focused on core muscle training and a bit of hand-to-hand combat. Then they shared dinner, which was rare. But the truth was, they were both lonely. Owen knew that Richardson was now a retired widow. She probably needed the distraction of being his controller as much as he needed to feel useful as an operative. It gave them both something to do. It gave their lives meaning, a reason to wake up in the morning.

Without the ops, Owen was worried he'd regress back to the sad, depressed man he used to be. But maybe . . . in therapy, they've discussed the possibility that maybe it wouldn't be the case. Maybe he could find something else that would give his life purpose. He had been considering retaking control of his board position at the media conglomerate he inherited from his father and resuming work on some of the mental health initiatives he started at the company. Now that he had more energy and a better outlook on life, maybe he could make a difference that way.

Owen was thinking about that as he walked back home from Richardson's. It was late, but he was used to late-night walks around the city. It was almost October, and the weather was getting colder. He didn't mind, though. The weather was pretty similar to the day, back in February, when he went to the bank. That fateful day, he thought to himself, when he met Dinah for the first time. Dinah . . .

His hand reached into his pocket for his phone. Maybe he ought to try . . . maybe she did deserve . . .

Before he could finish the thought, the phone buzzed.

It was Richardson. Did he forget something back in the basement, or did Donoghue want something new? Or maybe it had to do with those drugs he left behind. He answered.

"Hello?"

"Hey, how tired are you?"

"Not very," Owen answered.

"Good, I have an op I can send you on. Feel up to it?"

"Is it Donoghue?"

"Nope. We have a genuine situation. Some idiot climbed up a scaffolding on a construction site. They're stuck up there".

"I'm on it. What's the address?"

. . .

The construction site was at a major intersection in midtown. Owen rode the subway a few stops, ran a couple of blocks, and found a gate that should have been locked but wasn't. Two uniformed officers were already on the scene.

"What's the situation?" he asked them.

"Who are you?"

"I'm on Donoghue's squad," said Owen, bending the truth a little.

"Donoghue? All right . . . well, we called the fire department. Going to need a ladder for this one. Whoever they are, they climbed way up," said one of the cops, pointing upwards.

On a metal scaffolding, at least ten floors off the ground, Owen could make out the figure of a person, backlit by some ground torches.

"We tried to communicate, but they haven't said anything. Could be a jumper, we don't know," continued the officer. "Not much we can do from down here".

"Right. I better get up there".

"Excuse me?"

"I'm going up. Wait down here for the ladder," said Owen.

"How are you going to get up there?"

"If they got up there, I'll get up there".

"It's your skin, man".

And so, he climbed.

Owen couldn't help but think of that girl . . . why couldn't he remember her name? The one he happened to notice by chance months ago. She was up on a rooftop, about to jump, and he managed to talk her down, sort of. It was the moment that basically marked the beginning of his new life as someone who tries to do good and save lives.

So maybe this was appropriate. Maybe tonight was also an important night, one that would mark a new beginning for him.

Climbing the scaffolding was difficult. The lower floors had enough boards and beams to climb off of, but it was slow going, and his hands quickly started to chafe and ache. Owen had to twist and push his body from one level to the next. He was glad his upper body strength was substantial now, thanks to months of training with Richardson. But the farther up he got, the fewer supporting structures there were for him to get a foothold and keep pushing. He found himself teetering at a couple of points. He wasn't afraid of falling—he knew it wouldn't kill him—but he didn't want to have to start over, so he went at it slowly, deliberately.

"Hey!"

Finally, the other climber spotted him. It was a woman, based on the voice.

"Stay there!" he yelled back.

"No, *you* stay down! Why are you climbing here?"

"I just want to talk! Don't move," said Owen. But he was worried. What if his climbing was going to freak this woman out? What if she jumped before he could get there?

"Please, don't jump! I'm almost there". He had two or three more levels to go, but at this stage, the building was basically just metal beams—there wasn't anything to hold onto anymore. How did this girl make it up there? The only thing he could think of was to try and jump, catching onto the beam above him to pull himself up. But if he missed or slipped, he'd fall.

Well, here goes nothing, he figured.

Somehow, he made it. They were now on the same beam. The woman was standing on the edge of the horizontal beam, holding onto a perpendicular one for support. In the dim illumination coming from floodlights around the base of the construction site, she looked scared.

"Hi. My name is Owen," he started.

"Why the hell did you climb up here?"

"I'm just here to talk".

"Talk about what?! I just want to come *down,*" she said.

That gave Owen pause. "You don't . . . you're not going to jump? You changed your mind? That's good—"

"I wasn't going to jump! I'm just stuck".

Owen was confused. "You're . . . stuck? Why did you come up here?"

"I was streaming a live video. For my channel".

"For your . . . you're streaming this?"

"Well, not anymore. I *was*. I'm an extreme climber. I climb stuff, cliffs, structures. I have a shit-ton of followers".

So, she wasn't suicidal.

"Anyway, how do we get down?"

Owen had not thought of that.

"I don't know".

"What do you mean, you don't know? Then why the hell did you come up here?"

"Well . . . I thought you were about to jump. I was going to talk you down".

"Down *how*? That's my problem—I don't know how to get down".

"I . . . yeah, I don't either".

"So what was your plan? I don't get it," said the climber.

"Yeah, I guess I didn't really think it through," Owen admitted. "The cops are down there—"

"They're going to arrest me?!"

"No, they're . . . well, I don't know, actually. You're probably trespassing. But I don't think you'll get charged with anything more than mischief. You didn't damage anything, right?"

"No!"

"Yeah, then it'll be fine. Anyway, they've got the fire department coming with ladders".

"Okay. But I don't get it. Why did you climb up if they're bringing a ladder?"

"I don't know," Owen said. He was growing frustrated. Where was that ladder?

They didn't speak much after that. It took the fire department another fifteen or so horribly awkward minutes to show up. They lowered the girl down first, and the cops let her off with a warning.

"So, why'd you go up there, anyway?" they asked him when he finally got on the ground.

"Just wanted to make sure she wasn't going to jump".

"Good thing she didn't. Still, you really risked your neck up there, I watched you climb. Was sure you were going to fall at a couple of points there. That jump was nuts!"

"Yeah . . . look, I'm going to head home. Good work out here, guys," Owen said, scurrying off.

. . .

He didn't feel like he could face calling Richardson, so he just sent a short text instead. *All good, just a climber who got stuck. She's down now, all safe, no danger.*

Fuck. Fucking . . . fuck.

What the hell was that? He asked himself on the subway, heading back towards his part of town. He wasn't *needed.* He just assumed . . . it was dumb. It was dumb of him to climb up there, to respond. He must have been projecting—she wasn't suicidal at all. It was . . .

What was the point of him anymore?

It's been *weeks* since he'd done anything that mattered, since he saved any lives, helped anybody. The drug stuff with Donoghue was helpful, sure, but it didn't . . . it didn't feel like it mattered. Any cop could get it done. It wasn't life-or-death stuff. It wasn't a situation that required Owen, like the Unkillable case.

What was he *doing*?

Fuck it. As he walked from the subway station to his apartment, he decided it was time. He knew what he wanted to do.

He wanted to talk to her. Dinah. He . . . he missed her. He worried about her and wanted to check up on her. He'd been thinking about it for weeks. But more than that, he wanted . . . he needed to talk to her, to . . . to hear her tell him that he mattered. That he could be doing good, making a difference. The whole thing was her idea, and he knew Dinah would set him straight again. Remind him what the point was, then help him get back there.

He called her. Found her number on his phone and hit dial.

It rang. Again. And again. And again.

And a few more times after that.

She didn't pick up.

Owen sighed. He was feeling down, lower than he had in a while, he realized, as he walked up the steps to his apartment, unlocked the door, took a quick shower, and went to bed, trying not to think too much about anything.

There'd be time to think tomorrow. Tonight, well, he had a long training session, and he climbed an under-construction building without falling once. He was drained, physically and emotionally. Owen earned his rest.

But then, why was it so damn hard to fall asleep?

5 — *I need help*

UGH. This guy.

Donoghue was on the news. Borst remembered him well—they'd gone through the academy together as two of the older students in their cohort, she entering it with a law degree, her father having just passed away, and he with a background in political science. They graduated together, and both served in Richardson's squad for a number of years.

Donoghue was decent police, but he didn't really care about the badge. He kept moving around, playing angles, trying to get reassigned to different divisions—major crime, illegal substances, tech and response strategy, cadet training. While she put her head down and did the work, rising through the ranks until she became a captain, Donoghue had developed a network of allies throughout the entire force. Borst felt as if Donoghue was always chasing the next promotion, looking to play politics rather than solve crime and serve the city—he just wanted to get to the top as quickly as possible. Actual boots-to-the-ground police work was beneath him.

Look at him now, his smug face on TV. Heading the drug and organized crime squads, boasting about some bust. "My team is busy cleaning up this city. If the recent decline in crime rates is any indication, our focus on tackling the city's drug and trafficking operations head-on has contributed to a significant reduction in gang violence. The city's ongoing war on drugs has been nothing but a resounding success".

Oh, bullshit. The decline in crime had *nothing* to do with his drug busts. It had everything to do with Unkillable, who single-handedly took out half the gangs in the city. Gangs are out, so crime's down, and drug-related incidents are down too, making Donoghue's job easier for him. And somehow, he managed to take all the credit. What a dick.

Borst was angry. She was angry at Donoghue, angry at herself, angry at the whole damn world. It was late, the TV was tuned to a local news channel, and she was on the sofa, feet up, head foggy.

Then her phone buzzed.

She couldn't think of who it might be. It was too late for anyone from the force to ring her. She looked at the caller ID.

Shit, she thought.

Owen.

What the fuck?

It's been . . .... months. Literally months since he basically abandoned her, walking away. He hadn't called her since. Richardson had, even Larner had, but Owen hadn't. He made it clear that he wanted nothing to do with her anymore.

And now he was calling? Fuck him, she thought. *Seriously.*

She wasn't going to answer.

Should she answer?

No. No, she . . .

But . . .

No. She shouldn't. She just let it keep on ringing until he gave up.

Fuck. Why? Why did he call?

She wanted to talk to him. But . . . fuck, he didn't deserve it. And besides, this wasn't . . . wasn't the right time for it. It was late, and she was buzzed. Not answering was the best thing to do.

Unless . . . what if he was in trouble?

No. No, come on. Owen couldn't die, he couldn't be hurt. No way he was in trouble. And he had Richardson, anyway. He didn't need *her*.

Nobody needed her.

Borst realized she was shaking. Was she that angry?

She needed a stiffer drink. She got off the couch, but too quickly, almost falling down again after getting lightheaded. *Woah. Okay. Slowly now. Stiff drink, here we go*, she thought to herself.

She rummaged through empty bottles. So many empty bottles. When did she manage to drink all of these?

There wasn't much left. Just the cheap wine. She needed something stronger.

Okay. Well, it was late, but the corner store would be open and have some alcohol she could purchase. And she could use the air. She could use . . . she could use a minute outside, trying to forget that Owen called. Trying to . . . yeah. And she'd get her alcohol, and that would help her sleep.

Good plan.

She grabbed her phone, her card, made sure she had pants on, grabbed a jacket, shoes, keys. Borst walked out, locked her door, and walked down the steps, out of the building.

Wow, it was cold out. When did it become so cold out at night? It was summer just . . . well, weeks ago, she realized. *What month was it? September, right? It's amazing how time can move so fast and yet not at all. Doesn't matter. Okay, turn right, towards the corner store.*

Borst started walking. Her head was all fogged up.

She had her phone out in her hand, nearly stumbling as she walked. She didn't even notice the guy on the bike coming up behind her. When he grabbed her phone, she didn't realize what was happening. One minute, she was just walking along, phone in hand. The next, some guy had snatched her phone out of her hand and was biking away at top speed.

Borst instinctively burst into action. She was a trained cop, and her years and years of training and active duty kicked in. She started running after the guy.

Normally, she might have had a slim chance of catching up. But after weeks of inactivity, not to mention the alcohol she drank throughout the day, there was no chance. In another minute, the thief was too far gone, along with her phone.

Fuck.

Part of her just wanted to keep going, get the booze. But . . . no. Chalk it down as a lost cause. Best to get back home.

Get back home. Sleep it off.

It was lucky her keys were in her pocket and not in her hand with the phone. She turned around, walked up the stairs, stepped through the door—

And immediately tripped, slipping on a bottle lying on the floor. She fell down hard, hitting her back with a thud.

Borst found herself lying prone, flat on her back in her own doorway, her phone having been stolen literally out of her hand.

Finally, the tears came.

It had been months since she let it out, but just at that moment, feeling so low, so *defeated* . . . she broke down.

It felt like it took an hour for her to calm down again and get back up, slowly, because her back hurt. She definitely strained a muscle or possibly threw her back out completely. Who knew whether she'd be able to stand upright tomorrow.

She waddled straight to bed, fell down on top of it, still wearing her clothes and shoes. She couldn't remember whether she locked the apartment door behind her but decided that fuck it, it didn't matter.

Nothing mattered.

Her face felt puffy from the crying. Her head hurt like hell. Her back was throbbing violently.

Sleep. Just let me sleep, please, she prayed to no one in particular.

Just before she drifted off to sleep, a thought popped into her head. As it happened, it would be a thought that would turn things around for her. Just three words.

I need help.

. . .

"Are you okay?" asked Dr. Griffith as Borst limped gingerly into her office.

"I hurt my back a couple of days ago. Slipped and fell. I'm fine, it's just a spasm".

"I see. And how are you emotionally?"

"I . . . think I mostly hurt my pride," lied Borst dismissively. She still didn't trust Griffith.

"Mmhm. How did it happen, exactly?"

"Oh, it was nothing. Actually, it's . . . a bit embarrassing. I was out on the street, holding my phone out, not really paying attention. And some jerk on a bike grabbed the phone out of my hand and cycled away with it".

"Wow. That's terrible".

"No, no, it's fine. Really. I mean . . . well, the hard part is I lost the contact information of some people I really care about. I don't know how I can contact them again, and that actually . . . I'm upset about that," Borst admitted.

"You didn't have the contact info backed up?"

"Well, it was a work phone, connected to my laptop at work. I could get the data from there, but I can't go into the precinct while I'm on this leave, so I'm stuck".

Dr. Griffith nodded a couple of times. "Let me see what I can do about it".

"What do you mean?"

"I'll talk to some people. I have clout. If I recommend that it'll be helpful for your recovery, maybe they'll let you have the laptop. You'll have to promise not to use it for work, obviously".

"You could do that?"

"Well, I can't make any promises, but I can try. Recovering contacts when your phone gets stolen . . . you should at least be allowed to do that".

"I really appreciate that," said Borst. And she meant it. Griffith surprised her. Maybe the doctor *was* on her side after all. "Thank you".

"You're welcome. Now—"

"Doctor?" Borst cut her off. She made a decision. It was spur-of-the-moment, but as a cop, Borst was used to making sudden calls based on what her gut was telling her. She decided she may as well try and trust Dr. Griffith. It couldn't hurt, anyway. And she needed help, she knew that now.

"Yes, Dinah?"

"I think I finally hit my rock bottom," she said.

"What makes you say that?" asked her therapist.

"Well, for one thing, I literally hit bottom. I fell on the floor pretty hard when I hurt my back".

"Mmhm".

"But, uhm. . ." Borst continued, "well, I think . . . I better tell you the honest truth. Because I realized . . . I need help".

"That's very good, Dinah. The first step towards recovery is always admitting you need help, I'm sure you've heard that before. But why do you believe you need help? And why now?"

"I think . . . well, I probably *do* have some form of PTSD. The—the massacre . . . I haven't been sleeping well, I've been having nightmares. I didn't tell you about them because I was hoping you'd sign off on getting me back to work faster if I pretended I was okay. But I'm *not* okay. I feel guilty, I mean it's probably survivor's guilt but . . . I do have things to be guilty for, and it's . . . it's confusing. I'm also angry. I'm so angry, all the time, I'm all alone, I'm . . . "

Borst trailed off. Griffith made some notes.

"Is that all?"

"No. That's just the start, I'm . . . I think the bigger issue might be the alcohol".

"You've told me you drink a glass of wine a day".

"Yeah. That, uhm, that was a lie. I drink several bottles a day. I'm basically constantly drinking".

"This started after the incident at your precinct?"

"No. I've been drinking more than I should have since before that, but . . . well, it's gotten worse now that I've got nothing to do all day. I guess . . . at some point, it became a dependency, but I think it's a long-running issue. I always have a flask on me. I keep bottles in my desk at work".

"Did you drink while on duty?"

"No. Um, well, actually, yes. Sometimes. I mean I wouldn't get *drunk* on duty, but . . . I would drink a little to steady my nerves. Just a mouthful at a time, but . . . then at night I'd drink more".

Griffith nodded. "Why are you telling me this now?"

"Because of what happened. When I got my phone stolen, I was walking out of my apartment . . . I was actually going out to get some alcohol. That's why I was outside. It was late, and I was already buzzed, but I needed something stronger, I was running low, and I thought it would be a good idea to go buy some liquor. And, as I walked out, almost right outside my door, this guy on a bike stole my phone out of my hand. I thought I could chase after him, but I got so winded almost immediately. I was so dizzy, I almost fell down. When I was in shape, when I was on duty, I maybe could have caught up to him, but . . . well, I walked back upstairs, and I . . . ha, it's almost funny when I think about it. I slipped on an empty bottle of wine that was on the floor just as I walked back into my apartment, and that's how I hurt my back".

"Wow. There's certainly some irony to you getting hurt by alcohol in that particular manner," said her therapist.

Borst nodded. "So here I am. I need help".

"Dinah, I'm glad you feel like you can admit to some of your faults now. That shows a lot of trust. And I hope you really *do* want my help. Because, I'll be honest with you, I knew all along you were hiding things from me. No one would get out of a situation like the Purple Massacre without serious scars. It's important to deal with those, and I'm going to try and help you with that. And by trusting me, and by being honest, we can make progress much more quickly. If we know that turning to alcohol is your pattern, your coping mechanism, well, that's very useful information".

"Right".

"But that doesn't mean this is going to be easy. You've been through serious trauma, and you've been self-medicating using alcohol for what sounds like a long time. There are likely other issues deep down—last session, you mentioned your father's passing. We'll need to explore all of that. This is going to be tough, Dinah. Getting better will take work".

"I'm not afraid of work. I *want* work, I want something to do. The toughest thing for me is to be stuck like this, not knowing what to do. And I just . . . I want to be better. I want to . . . to not feel like shit. I've been sober for two full days now, and I *hate* it. I hate being sober, I hate . . . I hate how unhappy I feel. I guess alcohol made me numb to it, and now I'm just so miserable. And I don't know what to do, how to make it stop, how to . . . to . . ."

Borst broke down. Again. Over the past two days of sobriety, she broke down crying every few hours. It's been a hellish time.

"We'll work on it. It'll take time, it'll take effort. But we'll work on it. Together. And it will get better," promised Dr. Griffith. Borst nodded. She wasn't sure she believed the doctor, but . . . what did she have to lose?

"Let's start by talking about your drinking. When did you first start to notice you were drinking a lot?" the doctor asked.

And the therapy truly began.

. . .

That same night, there was a knock on Borst's door.

She opened it to find a uniformed officer.

"Hi, Captain Borst? I was told to deliver this here". The officer was carrying her work laptop sealed in a plastic evidence bag.

"Oh, thank you".

"You're welcome, ma'am," said the junior policeman, who turned away.

Attached to the laptop was a note: *Borst, your account's locked so you can't log onto the server, but you'll be able to extract your contacts and local files if you need them. Ring me if you need tech support. – Everett.*

Borst smiled. So, Griffith came through. Borst was glad she had chosen to trust her. She placed the laptop on her coffee table and went back to reading the cognitive behavioural therapy guide Griffith recommended. She had to admit, it wasn't as dumb as she thought it would be.

She wished she could have a glass of wine as she read. She drank water instead.

6 — *Barely*

IT was a few weeks later. The needle's prick didn't bother Owen. He'd suffered through far worse pain. Needles were nothing.

"All done," said Dr. Larner, who had just finished extracting some blood from Owen's arm.

"Good".

"Now, as I was saying, so far we haven't observed any change whatsoever. Your hormone levels have not been impacted at all by the antidepressants you're on, which is quite contrary to what you'd expect in a usual case. My hypothesis is that your body is capable of maintaining perfect stasis. It somehow manages to eliminate any externally-introduced disequilibrium—that would explain why poisons don't work on you. Have you ever been exposed to any toxins?"

"I don't think so . . . oh, carbon monoxide. Also a whole bunch of pills taken all at once that would normally kill most people, I guess. They gave me charcoal water at the hospital afterwards, but I was fine anyway".

"Right, well, this supports the hypothesis. Let's continue monitoring how your body reacts to the medication for now. Perhaps in a few months we'll run an experiment where we introduce other compounds into your bloodstream and observe the reaction. That'll be quite fascinating, I'll have to consider the best . . . hmm, perhaps a cytotoxic agent like cyclophosphamide . . . now that's a *very* interesting thought," said the doctor, mostly to himself. Owen let him talk.

"At any rate," continued Larner, "you can put your jacket back on. You're dressed quite formally today, what's the occasion?"

Owen was wearing a suit, for once. It's been nigh on a year since he's worn his suit. He was glad it still fit, though truth be told, his body shape had been fairly consistent since high-school. His shoulders were a bit more defined these days, so the jacket was a little tight, but even after months of training with Richardson, he hadn't changed much physically. The perks of being superhuman, he supposed.

"I had a board meeting before my appointment today".

"Oh? I didn't know you were a member of any board".

"I'm on the Kline-Laurie board. I was trying to convince them to set a higher budget for their annual mental health campaign. They actually donate quite a bit already, but I think in recent years they've focused too heavily on investing in start-ups and tech ventures that are supposed to promote wellness and mindfulness. Meditation apps and things like that. I guess it sort of fits the company's mission, since we're running a media conglomerate, but I think we could do a lot more if we were supporting grassroots programs and especially anti-stigma campaigns".

"Absolutely, absolutely. You know, the hospital could use support too. Since we're affiliated with the university, our budget is limited," hinted Larner, smiling.

Owen nodded. "I'll definitely take a look at that. I'm hoping to take a more active role in directing our philanthropic efforts".

"Wonderful! I have to say, you seem well. Less stressed, more energetic. Much better than you've looked in past months, despite the antidepressants only having a negligible chemical effect. I wonder if there's a placebo effect here, or perhaps it's something else?"

"Thanks, doctor. I think I *am* better. Therapy's helpful, even if the drugs don't do anything. And being more active professionally is pretty healthy too, I guess".

"And you're still, uh, fighting crime and all that?"

"Well, not so much, actually. It's been a few weeks since I've done anything like that," Owen said. Ever since the climber incident, he hadn't been out on any ops. Richardson called him a couple of times with possible Donoghue-sponsored drug busts, but Owen turned them down. He just didn't feel like going on another meaningless, uncomfortable mission.

"I'm actually having dinner with Sharon Richardson tonight," he continued.

"Please give her my regards," said Larner. "It's been too long since we've spoken".

"I'll tell her she better give you a call soon. Maybe we can all have dinner one evening".

The doctor smiled genially. "That would be lovely. Well, I'm sorry, but if you'll excuse me, I do have to rush across campus. Let me know next time you're at CUH for an appointment, and we'll keep monitoring and studying you".

Owen nodded, thanked Dr. Larner, and left his office. He walked downstairs, towards a bagel and coffee shop on the ground floor. He wanted to think.

Was he doing better? Honestly, Owen wasn't sure. When he thought of Richardson, of Dinah, of his recent life as an operative who actively tried to save people, Owen felt frustrated and disappointed. Nothing was happening—there were no opportunities to do meaningful work there. It was upsetting.

He was also upset about Dinah not picking up. Upset, and worried. There were two possibilities, really—the first was, she *couldn't* answer. That felt unlikely. Owen was more worried about the second possibility—that she *wouldn't* answer. In his head, he could imagine that Dinah succumbed to her alcoholism, that the trauma of Unkillable's murderous rampage finally caught up to her. He was probably projecting, but . . . what if that *was* the case?

Truth was, if she wouldn't let him in, he couldn't help. As much as he cared about her, Owen had to remind himself that he wasn't responsible for her well-being. It was hard not to feel responsible—not to feel guilty—but the best he could do was acknowledge these feelings, recognize that they came from a good place, and try his best to let the feelings go because they weren't useful.

Dinah . . . Owen couldn't help but wonder if his current apathy towards his *hero mission* had something to do with her absence from his life. It was all intertwined. He spent some of today's therapy session examining his relationship with Dinah, what it meant to him, and why he was ready to let go of it at the first sign of betrayal or doubt. He was just protecting himself. It was one of his patterns, a pattern he had picked up from growing up with emotionally withdrawn parents, but a pattern he was hoping to break.

Maybe he should try giving Dinah another call some time.

Meanwhile, while heroism was stalled, his professional work at Kline-Laurie felt like it was progressing. And that made him feel better.

He had his therapy, helping him deal with his complicated thoughts and keep any unproductive feelings at bay.

He had Dr. Larner's support, which was scientifically meaningful, if nothing else. Owen supposed it didn't actually benefit him much personally, but if his blood did eventually lead to the discovery of any sort of cure or scientific breakthrough, he probably owed it to the world to get pricked every few weeks. Besides, Larner was a decent guy.

And he had Richardson. Even if he didn't go out on any more ops, they could still train together, share an occasional dinner. She was a friend. He was looking forward to seeing her tonight.

He had a lot of good things going on.

Yeah. He was doing better.

Right?

. . .

They had a long training session, two hours of full-body exercises, plus some self-defence. Then they each showered and ordered some dinner.

"This was good, Sharon. Thank you for taking the time".

"Thanks for suggesting it. God knows I'm bored as heck lately".

Owen nodded. "I understand".

"There's been *nothing*! This city is as quiet as a mute mime—which obviously is excellent, crime is down, couldn't be happier about that—but that does mean there's nothing much for me to do. I'm honestly reconsidering offering personal training sessions again," Richardson sighed. "But enough about me, how have you been?"

"I've been okay, actually".

"That's good. Still nothing from Dinah?"

"I actually tried to call her . . . that night of our last op, a couple of weeks ago. She didn't pick up".

"Damn".

"Larner says hello, though. I suggested we all do dinner some evening, but . . . well, you know his schedule".

"Right. He's a busy man. Wish I could say the same," complained Richardson.

"Actually, I wanted to talk to you about that".

"Me too. Look, I know you're not a fan of Donoghue, but he's been calling a lot. He has a big op in mind, apparently. It's another drug bust, but . . . well, he says his undercover operative identified it as an absolute key link in the network. Take this one out, and the rest of the tower falls down, according to him".

"The last one wasn't enough?" grumbled Owen.

"I guess not. He was kind of weird about it. When I brought the bags over to him, he seemed annoyed. He expected you to hold on to them, I think. I don't know what that's about. Maybe he just wants to meet you . . . he asks about you each time he calls. The guy's getting obsessed, but maybe that's a good thing, maybe he honestly believes he can put you to good use".

"He hasn't so far".

"I know, Owen, but . . . maybe we should consider it anyway? It's . . . I mean, the only reason we came together, the two of us and Dinah, was to clean up the city. This is one way of doing that. It's not glamorous or, you know . . . I mean I get it. It doesn't feel great. But sometimes you have to do the dumb, boring, tedious things. It's how we make a difference. We can't have an Unkillable every week".

Richardson could immediately sense she shouldn't have said that. "Sorry, I didn't mean—"

"It's okay, Sharon. I know what you mean. Yeah. Maybe an op every once in a while, even if it's just another sneaky drug bust, isn't a bad idea. I mean, you're right. We're still doing good, getting dangerous substances off the streets".

"Exactly. Anyway, sorry, what was it *you* wanted to talk about?"

"Oh, right. So, uhm, do you remember, I told you how I'm trying to streamline the philanthropic activities at Kline-Laurie?"

"Sure. I still can't believe I had no idea you're the Kline-Laurie heir. That's crazy".

"Yeah, well, I've been a pretty absentee heir for the most part, but I'm still on the board, and I'm hoping to take a more active role. The previous director of philanthropy was focusing on activities like . . . you know, things like sponsoring hackathons and providing seed investments to start-ups that have a focus on mental health. It's an interesting strategy, but I'd like to bring things back to their roots, give more support to established organizations that are doing good. I also think, as a media company, Kline-Laurie should be leveraging their core competencies. For example, giving ad space to charity organizations or running awareness campaigns. That's the type of thing the company's not really doing but absolutely should be".

"That makes sense," nodded Richardson, though she couldn't quite follow all the jargon Owen threw at her, and she couldn't exactly see where he was going with this.

"We've been focusing very heavily on mental health, and I'd like that to stay the focus, but I also think—to be honest, the reason mental health and addiction were such a focus was because . . . well, my father started it after my mother's car crash. He started a partnership with organizations that lobby against drunk and distracted driving, and then he helped out charities that assist with addiction, drugs and alcohol. And when he . . . after the plane crash, and after my sister, I really wanted the company to use some of its profits to support similar initiatives.

"And I still think that should be the number-one priority, but . . . I think my time working with you and Dinah helped me realize, there are other ways to do good in the world, too. So, I guess what I'm saying is, I want to expand the scope".

"Right".

"Anyway, I'm building out teams to explore all of these ideas. What we can invest in, how Kline-Laurie can contribute more than just financially. And . . . well, I was thinking . . . I could use you on the team".

Richardson was flabbergasted. "Me?!"

"Yeah".

"I'm . . . Owen, I've been a cop all my life. I'm not a corporate person".

"I know. But you're a great manager of people. You have so many transferrable skills. And this wouldn't be . . . it's not a full-time desk job, it's a part-time advisory position. You'd be hired as a consultant, just to help keep us on track, give a different perspective. Your expertise in directing people, teams, your ties with the force . . . you understand what this city needs, Sharon. You'd be an asset".

"I think you want Donoghue," Richardson joked. "He's the politician".

"No. I want you".

"Did you make the same offer to Larner? Are you just asking everybody you know?"

"No. Dr. Larner's a great academic, but he wouldn't fit a team trying to raise and allocate funds. His head is too . . . nebulous, full of scientific ideas and ways to test them out. I need somebody with organizational and operational skills, not just ideas".

"Owen, I'm flattered. I honestly never thought you'd come to me with this sort of offer. All I can promise is that I'll think about it, but I have to be honest, it really doesn't sound like my thing".

"You were complaining about being bored. This could take up as much or as little time as you'd like, and you'd be doing good—"

"I understand. I'll think about it".

"Okay".

The two ate in silence for a minute. The awkwardness was cut short by a buzzing sound.

"Hello?" Richardson answered her phone.

Owen concentrated on his food. On some level, he felt disappointed, maybe even a little resentful, at Richardson's reaction. He tried to let go of that feeling. After all, she was entitled to say no. The position he was thinking about seemed to make sense to him, but she had no idea what he had in mind—she had her own ideas. She probably felt this was very far out of her comfort zone. And while Richardson complained about being bored, people complain about things all the time. It didn't always mean they were looking for someone to solve the issue, sometimes they just wanted somebody to listen.

By the time Owen's thoughts led him to accept that it was perfectly okay for Richardson to reject his offer and that he didn't have to be upset over it, she was trying to get his attention while still on the phone.

"Hey, it's Donoghue. He's asking about the op. He says he can try and put something together for tomorrow".

Owen had a board meeting in two days, but he was pretty much prepared for it—he already knew what he wanted to say to the board. He even put together some presentation slides.

"Tomorrow should work," he said.

Richardson wrapped up the call. "Okay, he'll work it all out and give us the details tomorrow morning. Are you sure about this?"

Owen nodded. "You're right. I want to do good, and there are different ways of doing that. This is one way I can contribute. Sort of. So, I guess I should. We'll just see what Donoghue needs tomorrow".

. . .

"Got it, 9:00 p.m.," confirmed Owen.

The instructions were simple and remarkably similar to the previous drug bust. Donoghue provided the address, and Owen was to destroy equipment, dump chemicals—yes, this was environmentally safe, Donoghue assured him—grab some of the drugs as evidence and do his best to destroy the rest. Donoghue's undercover contact guaranteed the place would be empty tonight for at least three hours, more than enough time for Owen to decommission a lab and set the suppliers back a few months.

Donoghue kept highlighting how they'd be dealing a blow to dealers, closing off supply lines. Owen could see the point. He just didn't feel very comfortable trespassing onto private property and destroying things that didn't belong to him.

"Look, this isn't strictly-speaking legal. Obviously, if you get arrested, I'll sort it out," Donoghue reassured him. "Don't worry about that. From an ethical standpoint . . . these drugs are killing people. At the end of the day, that's what it's about. These are illegal, dangerous substances, they lead to gang violence, overdoses, they kill people a dozen ways over. So yeah, ethically, I'm okay with it".

Owen understood. He just wasn't *as* okay with it. He wasn't sure why. But he'd already told Richardson he'd do it. He wasn't going to back out now.

That night, just before 9:00, Owen approached the house in question. It was another small townhouse on the fringe of midtown, on the west side of the City University campus this time. It wasn't exactly walking distance from his place, but he walked it anyway. Once he got there, Donoghue said the sign would be the porch lights—if they were off, it would be safe to sneak in.

There were no cars in the driveway, and the lights were off.

He made sure no witnesses were looking and jumped the fence. The backyard was full of weeds and grass so tall it reached his shins. The backdoor was broken off its hinges. The house looked abandoned, seemingly far more likely to house a drug lab than the previous private residence he broke into. For some reason, that made Owen feel a little more at ease.

Once he made it inside, he noted a lack of any and all furniture. An empty, unplugged fridge stood open in the kitchen. There was a musty smell that made Owen gag. He hurried to identify the door leading to the garage. He found a toilet first, another room empty except for an old, stained mattress, and finally the door to the garage, where the lab was supposed to be.

The garage was empty.

No cardboard boxes full of drugs in little plastic bags, no vats of chemicals, no sink full of beakers, no equipment . . . nothing at all.

What was going on? Was the lab upstairs, maybe? Or . . . was there a basement, or—

The door leading from the house to the garage slammed shut behind him.

Owen turned to find himself facing a very large man.

"Hey," he started to say before a fist slammed into his stomach, sending him to his knees. Then the stranger kicked his face. Owen was on the cold, hard garage floor as the very large man continued to pummel the living shit out of him. It went on and on—kicks, stomps, mostly targeting his abdomen and head. He definitely heard ribs crack, and his jaw got dislocated pretty early on, possibly from a kick to the head or maybe even the impact with the floor. The pain hit like a tidal wave and failed to diminish.

Owen had never been beaten like that. Sure, he'd been shot many times, but this was violence on another level. As much as it was physically painful, what really got to him was the impotence, the humiliation of it all. There was nothing he could do—he was powerless—all he could do was cower on the floor and wait for it to be over. It had to be over at some point. It had to be. It had to be.

Finally, the man let up.

It was over.

Owen was in a massive amount of pain, his vision blurred, his muscles twitched, his breathing laboured. There was an acrid taste in his mouth, so he coughed, which actually hurt quite a bit, and spat blood onto the floor, and possibly a tooth. He gave himself a moment to just lie there and not move.

His assailant said nothing, did nothing, while Owen recovered.

"Who are you?" Owen asked, still on the floor.

"You are alive?" asked the man. He had an accent Owen couldn't quite place.

"Barely".

"That is not good. I am to kill you".

"Because of the drugs?"

"What drugs?" asked the stranger.

"I'm here to decommission a meth lab. Get rid of your drugs," said Owen, getting confused. Since the large man seemed willing to converse rather than just hit him, Owen figured he might as well try to sit up. The pain was dulling rapidly, his vision returning to normal. He wiped blood from his face and moved to a sitting position, looking up at the guy who was at least six-and-a-half feet tall.

"No drugs," said the giant.

"No drugs? So . . . this was a setup?"

"I do not know this, setting up. I have to kill you".

"Please don't".

"Sorry. I do not have choice".

"Wait, listen. You *can't* kill me".

"I do not have choice," repeated his assailant, who proved far more polite than Owen expected.

"No, I understand that you have to *try*—I mean you won't be *able* to. I'm . . . . " Owen was about to say unkillable but couldn't bring himself to use that word. "I can't be killed," he said, which wasn't really any different.

"I do not understand".

"Look . . . do you have a gun?"

"Yes," said the man.

"Give it to me".

"I am not stupid".

"No! Okay, don't give it to me. Shoot me in the head".

"The man said not to shooting".

"You have to kill me, right? Just shoot me and see what happens, okay? Please".

The large man considered this. Finally, out of his pocket, he produced a gun that looked comically small in his huge hand. "I will shoot you. It is respectful, yes?"

"Thank you. Go ahead".

"You want in the face?"

"Shoot me in the head, yeah. Just go for it".

The man hesitated but then pointed the gun at Owen's face. Owen felt an inappropriate sense of relief at the prospect of getting shot instead of facing another beatdown. "Goodbye now," the giant said, shooting Owen in the face.

Now *this* was familiar.

The ringing in his ears, the dull ache oddly similar to a sinus infection. Owen shook the bullet out, wiped off the new splotch of blood, and looked up.

"See? I can't be killed".

The giant stared at Owen for a moment. Owen couldn't tell whether his expression was one of fear or just bewilderment.

"The man said you cannot. But I have to kill you".

"What man?" asked Owen. This must have been a setup. Did Donoghue's man blow his cover? Or did . . . did *Unkillable* . . .?

The stranger paced, shaking his head. Owen stayed seated. He finally stopped, addressing Owen again. "If I hit you more, you will die?"

"No. Sorry".

The giant nodded. "Shoot? No?"

"No".

"Then how to kill you?"

"I'm sorry, there's no way. I've been cut, stabbed, drowned, poisoned . . . nothing works. I have a sort of superpower".

"Supreme power? This . . . I do not know what I to do".

"Look, you can't kill me. Why don't you just let me go? You can say we fought, but I ran away".

"No, this I cannot do," said the giant defiantly.

"Well, you can't kill me. So . . . what choice is there?"

"I think. You wait here".

The giant left the garage. Owen wasn't about to wait. He stood up as quickly as his weak legs would let him, and walked towards the garage door, trying to pull it up. One of his arms barely functioned, but he still managed to grab the handle and start sliding the far-too-heavy door upwards, ever-so-slowly.

Too damn loud.

The giant came back. "I told to wait," he said. He sounded hurt.

"Sorry," Owen apologized reflexively.

"I keep you here," said the man, and Owen realized what he brought back to the garage with him—a bunch of metal spikes, or stakes, the kind you use to secure tents to the ground, plus a long metal chain.

"What are you going to do with those?" Owen asked, but the man provided no explanation.

Instead, he lifted Owen off the ground with one hand, walked him across the garage, pinned him to the wall separating the garage from the house, and started shoving one of the spikes through his chest and into the wall.

Owen screamed.

The second spike went through his stomach. It hurt like hell. By the fifth or sixth, Owen was in too much pain to scream or protest.

Finally, Owen's body was held up solely by the spikes, like he was stapled to the wall. The giant proceeded to bind Owen's hands together with the chain, flinging it over a beam hanging off the roof, then securing it with more spikes that he shoved into a side wall across the garage. Owen was trapped, stuck to the wall, his hands hanging away from him so that he was unable to push himself off or remove the spikes.

"This . . . hurts," he complained, barely able to speak. His face was stained with blood and tears.

"I am sorry, but I do not have choice. I make sure you not run away," said the very large man. "I go to ask what is next. Now, goodbye".

He left the garage.

"Wait! Come back here!" shouted Owen, weakly.

But the man didn't come back. And Owen was left alone, hanging.

7 – *A pretty shitty coping strategy*

SHE didn't know what had startled her awake at first.

Borst may have quit drinking, but her days still felt empty and unstructured. She would still pass out on the sofa and wake up at noon some days. That's where she found herself—the living room sofa. The clock said 10:00 a.m.

Her apartment doorbell rang again. So, that's what woke her up. "Just a minute!" she yelled, running to the bathroom to wash her face and make sure she looked halfway presentable, enough to answer the door. Who could it possibly be?

Pants. She was not wearing any. She hurriedly put some on and finally opened the door, only to immediately regret not taking more time to fix her appearance.

Against all expectations, there stood Division Inspector D'Alfonso, her boss.

"Sir," she said, her face and voice clearly communicating her surprise.

"Borst. May I come in?"

"Of course, of course, just, uhm . . . give me a second, have a seat," she said, gesturing towards her kitchen table. The living room area was a mess. *She* was a mess. She left to find a hoodie to cover the wrinkled t-shirt she had slept in. What a disaster.

D'Alfonso himself was dressed casually, which was odd. Borst wasn't used to seeing him out of uniform. Was it his day off? Did he randomly decide to check in on her?

She joined him in the kitchen. "Can I get you anything? Coffee?"

"That'd be lovely," he said, and Borst began hastily brewing two cups. "How have you been, Borst? I have to admit, I've been worried about you. I probably should have visited or at least contacted you earlier. I'm sorry about that".

"Oh, no, sir—"

"Jules, please".

"Jules, you don't have to apologize. I've been . . . recovering. It's been difficult, but I'm doing a lot better now. A little better every day". She tried to smile.

Why was he here? Was he going to invite her back to active duty? Borst allowed herself a glimmer of hope.

"That's good to hear. You know, I'm not sure you've heard, but the reason I haven't contacted you—"

"It's okay, really, you don't have to explain".

"Right. Borst—"

"Dinah," she tried smiling again. He returned the smile for once, and she got back to the coffee, finding one clean mug and washing another.

"Dinah. What I was trying to say is, I've been . . . struggling, myself. We lost . . . so many good officers that day. Of course, I've never blamed you. I know you've done everything . . . everything you could. I saw the files, the video, all the testimonies. I . . . how do I put this?"

"Sir?"

"Sorry, I've been thinking about this conversation again and again in my head, but it's hard to find the right words. I can't imagine what it's been like for you . . . no officer could ever be ready for something like that. And I can say that because I've been feeling it myself. I tried my best to get . . . get my head back . . . into the job. But after . . . things have . . . things have gotten worse".

D'Alfonso paused. Borst wasn't sure what he was trying to say.

"I'm not sure you've been told. I've resigned from the force".

She nearly dropped the coffee mug she was holding.

D'Alfonso . . . quit? He . . . he wasn't here to invite her back?

For a second, she thought she'd burst into tears, but she composed herself before turning around and placing both mugs, intact, on the table.

"I haven't heard, no".

Her now-former boss nodded. "I'm sure you have some questions".

"Why did you . . . was it the massacre, or . . .?"

"That was a big part of it. It took a major emotional toll on me, as it has on everyone, and I can't even imagine how you've managed to pull through. But it's more than that. And I . . . I know you and I, we've often seen eye-to-eye, perhaps more so than some of the other captains and squad leaders I've worked with".

"I used to think that too, but . . . sir, Jules, I . . . well, I don't want to speak out of turn, or—"

"No, please, speak your mind".

"With respect, sir . . . for the past few months I've been sitting on my ass getting agitated, angry, just waiting to get back to work. To serve and protect. When I saw you today, I thought . . . I figured maybe you're here to tell me I'm coming back. I was *hoping*. So . . . it's just disappointing, I guess, to hear you say you quit. You gave up".

D'Alfonso shook his head. "I understand the disappointment, but please, I want to share my point of view. Recently, I've been seeing things differently, and I've been thinking . . . if I can explain it, maybe you would want to join me on this new journey I'm looking to start".

Borst sipped some of her coffee. They both took it black. "Okay, then please, explain".

D'Alfonso took a minute. "Well, you're familiar with the general atmosphere in this country. How cops . . . how racism has pervaded police forces in cities all over the nation, how folks are asking politicians to defund the police".

"That's not a *police* problem, it's a *racism* problem. Not all cops—"

"Dinah, please. I know. I used to think that way, too. But then I saw some statistics. Do you know, since the . . . massacre and the aftermath, crime in the city has been falling. Reports of gun violence, gang-related crime, have dropped thirty percent".

Borst nodded. Of course, with Unkillable having disposed of most organized crime in the city, violence was bound to fall.

"And yet arrests have *increased* by ten percent," D'Alfonso continued. "Mostly related to drug charges. And the demographics . . . I don't have to tell you how the arrests trend by neighbourhood, you can guess it yourself.

It's got nothing to do with actual crime, actual serving-and-protecting. It's city-sponsored tasks forces, most of which were created following the massacre, targeting the drug problem, the gang problem".

Donoghue, thought Borst. She remembered seeing his smug face on TV.

"The city's been throwing money at the force to arrest more people, show results. Well, there are people on the force who would happily take advantage. And the easiest people to arrest just happen to be black folks in poor neighbourhoods. It's not a coincidence, it's . . . it's self-perpetuating. It's the way the system was set-up".

"Yes, but . . . sir, again, it's a few bad, dumb assholes who—"

D'Alfonso sighed. "I know. But also . . . your dad was a cop, wasn't he?"

"He was. What does that have to do with anything?"

"My father was a policeman, as well. That's my point. We're too . . . you know how it is. Cops take care of other cops first. Not everyone, but . . . look, I know you love the force. We've been conditioned to. I want to turn a blind eye, say it's a handful of racist, violent, or corrupt individuals. But the truth is, the police force is a closed network. It feeds itself.

"I was sitting in my office, staring out the window, slowly realizing . . . Borst, I will never be able to fix things from the inside. It's too broken. *I* felt broken. After losing good cops like that, and seeing the force become more corrupt, the bad cops taking advantage of the situation to prop themselves up . . . it made me sick to my stomach".

Borst nodded again. There was nothing she could say. She was starting to get it.

"I was thinking, hell, maybe we *should* defund the police. Fire everyone and start over. Find a new way to serve. Instead of cops carrying weapons and acting like they have immunity from the law because they carry a badge . . . employ officers who value responsibility, who are proud to be accountable. I don't know, maybe that's too vainglorious, or . . ."

"It's how it should be. But it feels really far away".

"Yes. Exactly. But . . . well, we can move towards it, maybe. The reason I'm here," D'Alfonso perked up, "is to ask you to join me. I'm starting something new. It's . . . we're still in the planning stages, brainstorming. It's going to be somewhere between a think-tank and a consultancy, I imagine. But we may also move towards offering actual security services. We're looking at funding models. I have a few contacts in the mayor's office who have expressed interest, and . . . we can make something, together. Build something".

"But . . . why me?" Dinah asked. Was it just pity? Did D'Alfonso feel responsible for the massacre? Did he think she was too broken to get back onto the force?

"You have a law degree. You're more qualified than most people on the force. And like I said, the two of us, I feel, we have a good rapport. And I suppose I've always suspected . . . I know your values. You genuinely care about police work, about helping people, protecting them. I thought this could be something you would care about doing".

"It . . . would," Borst confirmed. "Actually, I've . . . before the massacre, I had this, uhm, side-project. I've been trying to make the city safer, it's—it's hard to explain. But you know, I think there's a guy you should meet. His name's O—"

D'Alfonso cut her off. "I'm not looking to meet people, Dinah. It's not just talk for me. I want to make this happen. Will you join me?"

Borst stood up, placing her empty mug in the sink. "Sir, I . . . I appreciate it. I don't have an answer for you right now. I don't know. I'm not well, to be honest. I'm still working on my, uh, mental health. So, I think . . . I'll need time to . . . to think about it. But I do appreciate you coming to me".

The former inspector rose too. "I understand, of course. I'm sorry, I didn't mean to be presumptuous. Whenever you're ready, if you'd like to join this project, there'll be room for you at the table".

"Thank you".

"Is there anything . . . anything I can help with? I'm asking unrelated to what we just talked about, but as a former colleague, and a friend".

Borst smiled. "Thank you, no. I'm . . . I'm getting by".

"Right. Well, if you need anything—"

"I'll give you a call".

After he left, Borst sat back on her sofa. Oof. That was a heavy conversation, and she had a lot to think about. It was a good thing she had some hours to kill before . . .

Oh, right. *That* was tonight.

. . .

My name is Dinah, and I'm an alcoholic.

She never did end up saying that sentence in front of anyone, even though she had practiced it multiple times in front of the mirror. Walking into the AA meeting at a church across town was a big step for her, one suggested by Dr. Griffith, and one that, after a lot of consideration, she decided to undertake. D'Alfonso's unprompted visit earlier that day may have thrown her off, but at the same time, maybe it gave her a bit of courage, too. It reminded her there were things for her to work towards.

Borst felt very nervous, arriving early and selecting a seat among the plastic chairs arranged in a circle. It was just her and the organizer, a non-descript middle-aged man.

"You're new," he smiled.

"It's my first meeting".

"Welcome. I'm Peter, I'm a pastor at the church, and I help run these meetings. What's your name?"

"I thought this is anonymous".

"It is, absolutely. You can use a fake name if you'd like. It just helps facilitate discussion, and there's an agreement that whatever is discussed in this room stays here. That's the promise of anonymity, which is very important to everyone here. It's a critical part of the process".

"I'm Dinah".

"Nice to meet you, Dinah. I won't ask you any more questions. You can choose to share with the group if you're comfortable, or you can just listen, since this is your first time. Let me give you some of the literature, if that's okay? Are you Christian?"

"I am, but I'm not very religious".

"That's fine, we welcome all religions here. I just like to ask because the twelve-step process, which you may have heard of, is based on Christian beliefs, and it does help if you believe in God or any power greater than yourself".

"I see," said Borst noncommittally.

"Don't worry," Peter smiled, "you've already completed the first step—by coming here, you've admitted that you're powerless over alcohol and that you need to get your life back on track. Only eleven steps to go".

Borst nodded. She wasn't sure she liked Peter.

"Well, folks should start arriving shortly. We keep the meetings pretty informal. You don't have anything to worry about".

Peter left her to arrange some crackers and a pot of hot water for tea or coffee. A minute later, others started to arrive, some in pairs, most alone.

She was surprised to see the diversity—every age, gender, and ethnicity was represented. Borst kept to herself, nose buried in her newly-purchased phone, trying to avoid conversation with strangers. Soon, just over half the seats were full. An Asian lady, a little younger than her, sat to her right, while the seat to her left was empty.

The meeting began. Peter stood up, welcomed Borst, though not by name, as a new member, and asked if anyone had anything they wanted to share to start the session. With the attention away from her, Borst spent the session listening.

Borst listened to a middle-aged woman complain about her struggles balancing work and family life and how proud she was to be a year sober. She used to be unable to function without drinking and had missed her kids' recitals and activities. Now, she was spending a lot more time with them, and her husband was faithful to her again. But she was still worried about his fidelity and was afraid that if he cheated again, she'd start drinking again.

Borst listened to a university kid who was planning to re-enroll next term. His drinking got so out-of-hand that he was hospitalized and had to go back to living in his parents' basement for two terms. He hated how his parents were constantly on his case, and he had nothing to do while his studies were paused. He felt hopeful but knew that going back to school would re-introduce the pressure to party and drink, and he wasn't sure he was strong enough.

Borst listened to a stage actor who had a relapse during a major production of *Little Shop of Horrors*. The show felt like a step down from his previous roles in more artistic and less commercial productions, even if the recent paycheque was twice the size. He felt down and started drinking until he blacked out for a whole day, missing a matinee, and he was feeling remorseful and full of self-hatred since then.

Borst listened to a disgraced lawyer, an unemployed designer, and a mortgage broker.

Finally, Peter turned to her.

"I know it's your first meeting, but we're almost out of time. I just wanted to check if you wanted to share anything with the group".

She turned to the woman next to her, who gave her an encouraging nod. There was something vaguely familiar about this woman. Borst was confused.

She didn't . . . she didn't feel ready. She was so relieved when she thought she wouldn't have to speak.

Borst shook her head. She felt a little ashamed, a little cowardly.

"That's okay," Peter said. "Coming here today was the first step—we all went through it. You can come next time and maybe speak then. There's no judgement here. Do have a look at the literature, and feel free to stick around later, I'm sure some of our members would be happy to speak to you and help you through the process based on their experiences".

As no one had anything to add, Peter concluded the meeting. "Very good session, everyone. Thank you to everyone who shared and everyone who listened. We'll meet again in two weeks' time".

Borst grabbed her stuff and walked out with the crowd. She thought she heard Peter call after her, but she didn't want to stop and chat with him. She was annoyed at him for singling her out, and annoyed at herself for not speaking. She just wanted to get out of there.

"Hey," she felt a tug at her sleeve. It was the young woman who had sat next to her. "Do you have a couple of minutes? Maybe we can grab a tea".

"Uhm . . . it's okay, I—" Borst stammered.

"You don't remember me, do you? You're Captain Borst, right?"

Borst nodded, her confusion intensifying.

"I'm Jennifer Ng. I'm . . . I *was* . . . Becky Chen's fiancée".

Oh. Shit.

"I'm . . . wow, I'm so sorry, I didn't . . ."

"Let's have some tea," said Jennifer.

There was a coffee chain across the street. Borst followed Jennifer and mimicked her order for chamomile tea. They sipped in silence for a minute or two.

"I'm sorry, I genuinely didn't recognize you at all. I—"

"That's okay. We only met a couple of times in passing when I picked Becky up from the precinct. The 1-6, she always called it. I just . . . I've seen your photo in the papers, so . . . it was easier for me to recognize you".

Borst nodded. She thought back on Chen. As a captain, she wasn't supposed to have favourites, but she saw a lot of herself in Chen. She had pushed her along. And when she heard from that kid, Lincoln Fredericks, that she was killed, that was one too many gut-punches that day. She felt guilty for each and every death at the 1-6, but *she* had sent Chen up to that penthouse. She felt responsible. It haunted her more than the others, every night when she couldn't stop herself from thinking about it.

Borst braced herself, then spoke. "Right. Listen, I'm . . . I'm so sorry. What happened to Chen, it was . . . it was entirely my fault, my responsibility, and . . . I'm just, I'm sorry—"

"No," said Jennifer, shaking her head.

"But—"

"Look, Captain . . . do I call you Captain? That's what Becky always called you".

"Call me Dinah, please".

"Dinah. You know, Becky, she loved her job. She loved being a cop. And she admired the hell out of you. She told me you basically fought for a promotion for her?"

"I just suggested that she take the Sergeant's exam, I didn't—she did it all herself. She was an exemplary officer, and—"

"Well, she appreciated it. She thought the world of you".

There were tears in Borst's eyes. "But . . . but I . . . she . . ."

"How did she die?"

"Huh?" Borst blinked, confused.

"They never told us. Me, Becky's parents . . . they just said she died in the line of duty. They said she wasn't at the Purple Massacre, but it happened on the same day, and . . . I'm just confused. We never got closure, and . . ."

Jennifer sighed, looking down at her tea. "I'm struggling. When they told us . . . it took me a week to even understand it, intellectually. The penny hasn't really dropped, emotionally. I moved out of our apartment, I couldn't stand staying there any longer. I'm seeing a therapist. I'm going to meetings. But I'm not *better*. But maybe if I knew . . ."

Borst sobered up. This woman was grieving, and Borst had information that could help. Jennifer deserved to know. Borst wiped the tears away and tried to speak in a clear and steady voice. "Chen was killed by the same perpetrator of the Purple Massacre, a man who called himself Unkillable. This was earlier in the day, before the incident at the precinct station. Chen was . . . I assigned her to a squad of armed operatives who infiltrated the apartment where the perp was holed up, based on an anonymous tip that came in. They weren't ready for him, and the entire squad was murdered. I wasn't there, and I can't say for sure, but . . . Chen was the only officer on the op from the 1-6, and that's the precinct Unkillable targeted. Based on that, I believe that Chen carried herself with particular valour and acted bravely. She deserved the posthumous commendation she received, and far more than that, if it were up to me".

Now it was Jennifer who was tearing up. "Th-thank you".

"I'm sorry I never reached out. I'm temporarily off the force, and . . . technically, I'm not allowed to, right now. I wouldn't have been able to access your contact information. But I wish I could. My precinct, my squad . . . they were like family to me, and what happened, it's killing me. I can only imagine what you, her actual family, feels".

Jennifer nodded.

"I'll be happy to . . . speak to Chen's parents. Or . . ."

"They'd love to hear from you. I can give you their email".

"Good. Yeah, I think I'd feel . . . I'd feel good about that too".

Jennifer sniffed loudly. "Becky was right. You're a good captain".

"I'm not, I'm . . ."

Borst trailed off, and for a few minutes the two women went back to their tea.

"This was your first AA meeting?" Jennifer asked.

"Yes".

"Was it the . . . the massacre that made you . . . drink?"

"It . . . drove me over the edge, I guess. But I was already drinking".

Jennifer nodded. "I get it. I used to drink a lot too. Well, it started with a little, then it was more. Then it just got out of control after . . . some bad shit happened, years ago. That's when I first started with AA, and I've been sober for a long time. But then Becky was gone, and . . . well, yeah".

Borst didn't know how to respond to that.

"Did you . . . what did you think about the meeting?"

"I . . . don't know," Borst answered.

"I don't like them much. They kind of give your week structure, and the talking helps, I guess. It's just, I was raised very Christian, but I fell out of it. Coming out as a lesbian kind of . . . does that. And I don't . . . I'll be honest, I don't really like how religious the meetings can get sometimes".

Borst appreciated that she said that. The religious overtones bothered her, too.

"Yeah, that kind of turned me off," she admitted.

"Don't let it. These meetings *can* help. Really. I think . . . you should read the brochure, but only pay attention to the parts that make sense to you. Skip all the God stuff if you don't believe in it".

"Jennifer, can I . . . can I ask a question about the sobriety stuff?"

"Yes, absolutely," Jennifer said encouragingly.

"Did you . . . when you first quit alcohol, did you also struggle with . . . hating being sober, and wanting to drink again, and not feeling sure why you were trying to avoid it?"

"Of course! I think everyone does, even if they don't admit it. It's still so hard some days. Even with Becky around, sometimes I would lie in bed next to her and ask myself, why *shouldn't* I sneak out of bed to have just one glass of wine? Just to help me fall asleep. What's wrong with that?"

"How do you stop yourself?"

"I don't know. I guess I just . . . deep down, I know drinking isn't good for me. It just masks things, so I don't have to deal with them. It's like, drinking is my coping strategy, but it's a pretty shitty coping strategy".

Borst nodded. That resonated with her.

"Alcohol masks the pain, numbs it. Maybe it's the same for you. When Becky died, there was so much pain I couldn't deal with it, so I started drinking again. But the thing I remembered pretty quickly is . . . pain isn't something you can really run away from. Physical pain, maybe, but not the deep-down emotional stuff. If you don't deal with it, if you don't let yourself feel it, then I don't think you can get better".

Borst nodded.

"So, that's what helps, just knowing that, I guess. Knowing that if you choose to drink, then you're choosing to be numb. And numbing the pain gets *really* addictive. Instead, I want to choose to feel the pain, but get better, be better".

"Jennifer, that's really helpful," said Borst honestly.

"I'm glad! It's good to . . . to articulate it, actually. Do you have a sponsor yet?"

"A what?"

"Part of the program, at AA, is having a sponsor. Just someone, a friend you can call when you're feeling weak, who can help talk you out of it, or just remind you why you shouldn't have that drink".

"Oh. I don't . . . I don't have a sponsor".

"Well, do you want to be one another's sponsor? We can . . . even if meetings aren't your thing, we can keep checking in with each other, and . . . I just think it could be helpful," said Jennifer, looking at her now-cold tea.

"I think so too. Yeah. I'd like that," said Borst.

The AA meeting left her with mixed feelings, but now that she got a chance to speak to Jennifer, Borst was grateful she had taken that step. There was something serendipitous about running into Chen's fiancée at a meeting all the way across town. And a big coincidence that it happened on the same day when D'Alfonso decided to visit and maybe give her a new reason to keep going. Maybe this was the universe telling her that it was going to be okay, that she *deserved* to be okay. She had already quit drinking. Step one done.

Borst smiled as she sipped the last of her tea.

8 — *This is going to hurt*

OWEN was stuck hanging.

He was still attached to the garage wall with stakes shoved through his body, his arms chained away from him and secured against the opposite wall.

He tried everything—wriggling, using his feet to push himself away from the wall, trying to free his hands—nothing worked.

Initially, he expected the man who had stuck him in this position to return after a while. He waited and waited. And nothing. No very large man. No one at all.

It was about 9:00 p.m. when he first entered the house. He could tell it was dark outside by the lack of light coming through the gaps on the sides of the garage door. He stayed hanging through the night, the hours passing. He was awake the whole time. Owen never needed much sleep, possibly as a side effect of his unique powers, or else just something his body had gotten used to after years of sleeping poorly due to his mental health issues. Either way, it wasn't like he could have fallen asleep easily—the spikes driven through his body sent constant jolts of pain through him. He was sure the man would come back, and he lost track of time.

Then he saw light through the gaps—the sun was rising.

Shit. It must have been at least nine hours of hanging.

What if the man *wasn't* coming back?

Owen started a renewed attempt at gaining his freedom, struggling against the spikes and chain. He was weaker now, though, and could tell it was hopeless. He started screaming for help instead. It was the only thing he could think of.

After screaming for what felt like a couple of hours, he gave up.

What was he going to do?

His phone was in his pocket, but there was no way to reach it.

What else did he have? What were his options?

Owen didn't see any. His head felt fuzzy. He couldn't think of anything. He couldn't think. He started screaming again but no one came.

Would anyone come to the house to check on him? Someone had to, surely. The big man. Or . . . his boss. Or somebody.

Somebody.

The light outside was growing brighter. It must have been getting on mid-morning, or early afternoon, even. It . . .

Oh, shit. His board meeting.

He was missing it, or had already missed it. It was a really important meeting, too. He was going to request budget approvals from the board. He had a slide deck all prepared, outlining his key proposals—he sought to be appointed as Director of Philanthropy and Community Partnerships, replacing the recently-retired director. He had big plans, diverting a lot of resources away from current projects that focused too heavily on a small number of risky ventures, and balancing support for media campaigns that more closely aligned with the company's core activities. He'd done his research, he knew what sort of team he wanted to put in place, and was ready to propose fund allocations and control processes.

That was the life he wanted to live now, focusing on business—Kline-Laurie was his family's legacy, after all. And he knew he could make an impact. He felt motivated. For the first time in his life, his depression felt under control and, more importantly, he had proven to himself that he was capable of doing good, that his life could mean something.

Those months working with Dinah and Richardson taught him that. For years, Owen operated under the belief that there was no way for him to be happy. Therefore, he reasoned, there was no point to anything, really. If there's no way to be happy, if he was doomed to be miserable, why bother? He wound up falling into lengthy depressive episodes and repeatedly attempted suicide, which of course, never worked.

In the past, there had been periods when he was in therapy, actively trying to be better, and feeling relatively okay. He had tried to run philanthropy at Kline-Laurie before. He tried a number of other professions too, other lives—as a writer, freelance journalist, web designer . . . he tried a bunch of options. But each time, sooner or later, life started to feel pointless again, the depression would set back in, and he would quit, or else get fired, and end up spending his days staring at walls yet again.

But then everything changed . . . with Dinah. She showed him that his life could be meaningful. He could save lives. And he had. Many lives. And that was important, it was good. And through their operations, he learned that he was capable of . . . of *not* feeling like shit all the time.

He realized that being miserable didn't mean his life was doomed to be worthless. He could still do good, even if he didn't feel happy about it, even if sometimes he still wanted to kill himself.

One way to make his life matter was to be an operative who supported the police and went out and saved lives. That wasn't the *only* way, though. Owen felt pretty convinced that, through his family's company, his father's legacy, he could do good in a different way, too. Potentially *more* good than he could accomplish by saving one life at a time.

No, he wasn't sure he was equipped for it yet, but he started looking at applying to business schools, which he thought might help him learn how to effectively run an organization and develop a network of useful connections.

Maybe the whole idea was a pipe dream, but lately, it felt more real to him than *this*. This hero crap. It just wasn't working anymore.

Case in point—he was fucking *stuck*.

And now he missed the damn meeting, and . . . fuck. Helping Donoghue had cost him a chance at a different, possibly better, life.

Fueled by anger, Owen struggled again, trying to push his body forward using momentum, sort of jumping in place. It wasn't working. It was impossible.

What was he going to do?

Stuck.

It was physically painful, but also mentally demeaning. Dehumanizing. There was something about it . . .

If he was being honest, Owen had always seen himself as invincible. He couldn't die. He could be hurt, sure, but he always recovered. He'd beaten Unkillable.

So *this* . . . it was a defeat that served to teach him humility. Some random large guy conclusively defeated him just by pinning him to a wall. That's all it took.

Fuck, it hurt.

He wanted to scream some more, but his throat was parched. He hadn't had any water in hours. He would probably be fine. He wasn't going to die from it . . . right?

What if he was?

What if he could die from dehydration? He never tested it . . . so, who knows. Maybe his body needed water to repair itself. Or what if he was just left here forever?

Could that happen? The large guy knew he was here, but . . . who else did? This house was clearly abandoned, but at some point, someone would have to come here. Right? Well . . .well, maybe not. If the house was privately owned, who gave a shit if it stood empty?

So, Owen was fucked.

At a couple of points, he thought he felt his phone vibrating in his pocket. Nothing he could do. He couldn't get to his phone and call Richardson, or Dinah, or anyone. That goddamn fucking Donoghue. It was all his fault, chasing stupid drug deals for self-promotion. Asshole.

Owen started to cry but stopped after a bit. It wasn't doing any good, and he was dehydrated anyway.

What if he *did* die?

It used to be all he ever wanted. Death. Rest. Respite. He just wanted to escape this world. It was tough, it was *so* tough, every day, every morning, just getting out of bed could be so damn difficult. Once he died, he would be free of it, of the pain, the pointlessness.

He always imagined he would welcome death with open arms.

And now—would he welcome it with bound, hanging arms?

Owen was kind of shocked to realize something.

He didn't really want to die. Not just then. Not yet.

For the first time in his life, a part of him hoped he would live past this experience.

He wanted to try and make a difference by funding organizations and supporting initiatives that did good in the world, that battled the mental health stigma, that changed and saved lives. He wanted to try and preserve the legacy of his family's company. After that, if and when the pain, the mental anguish of his depression, came back, then yes, please, he wanted to die. But first . . .

He wanted to see if he could be a better person.

He wanted to still save lives himself, if he could find a better way to do that, a way that felt as authentic as Dinah's original plan.

He wanted to see Dinah again. To speak to her, make things right.

He wanted all those things . . . just a tiny, fractional, marginal bit *more* than he wanted to die at that moment.

Wow. This was new.

The light outside was dimming. The sun must be setting. How long had he been tied up there? Nearly a full day, surely.

He wriggled again, as hard as he possibly could, driven by this new realization, a new desire to go on.

Come on! He urged himself. The spikes had to give at some point, right? Gravity had to mean something. *Come on!*

Nothing.

Owen felt tired. Maybe he could try to nap, just a little . . . maybe . . .

. . .

No answer.

Borst frowned.

She finally bothered to program her new phone with the data stored on her work laptop, downloading her contacts.

There was only one contact she wanted to call, though.

The previous day had opened her eyes a little.

D'Alfonso's visit reminded her of *purpose*. Of why she joined the force in the first place. She spent time just thinking about things, imagining how it might be. Working with smart, good people, D'Alfonso, but also Richardson, and . . . if there was a way to combine what she's been doing, the secret ops, with his ideas about consulting and political influence, maybe they could genuinely change things for the better.

And then, talking to Jennifer had been helpful, too. It showed her that she wasn't the only one in this position, turning to alcohol for help in dealing with heavy situations. Plus, the fact that she was Chen's fiancée gave an extra dimension to their connection, a shared grief. That was one good thing that came out of the AA meeting.

She read the Alcoholics Anonymous literature that morning and threw it straight in the recycling bin. She just wasn't interested in what they were selling. Giving herself up to God, accepting she had no power . . . that wasn't the solution for her.

Borst needed to feel in control. She needed to know she was making a choice in staying sober. Otherwise, it was pointless. She wasn't going to let God or anyone else take control of her life—she forged her own path.

But . . . that didn't mean she had to go at it alone. Friends were important. Support systems were important. The brochures had a point there. Dr. Griffith had said so too, and she was right. Her therapist turned out to be pretty smart after all.

Maybe Borst *could* do it alone . . . but she didn't have to.

Now she had Jennifer to call if she ever felt weak. She had D'Alfonso, who might be interested in directing her professionally.

And then there was Owen.

In less than a year, they've been through so much together. Lives have been saved because of the two of them.

She felt a connection to him, one that went deeper than any superficial attraction or their one night together. Thinking about it made her realize she didn't have to give up on it. She didn't want to.

He *did* call her. That day, just before she hurt her back, hitting rock bottom. She panicked and didn't answer. She didn't know why he had called, but now that she thought about it, it didn't matter. Ultimately, he must have wanted to talk, to reconnect.

And Borst wanted that too.

So, she bit her pride, held her breath, and dialled.

No answer.

Disappointed, she flung her phone on the sofa and crossed her arms.

Why didn't he answer? Was he okay? Did he need her help?

No, of course not. He was Owen. He had to be okay. He was probably busy, or . . .

Borst thought about drinking.

It was okay to think about it, as long as she ended up deciding against it.

She decided against it.

She picked up a book instead, another of Griffith's recommendations.

So, he didn't answer. He was probably just tied up. Maybe he was out on an op. Or maybe he was like her, unsure of what he wanted, worried and scared of what talking to each other might mean.

Either way, she'd wait for him to call, or maybe she'd try again at some point.

For now, the best thing she could do was . . . well, read this book, she guessed.

And not drink. Definitely not drink.

. . .

He wasn't sure whether he had passed out. He might have, at one point.

But he was awake when he heard the noise from the back of the house.

It was dark out, as far as he could tell. Hopefully, it was still the same night. The sounds came suddenly, the creak of a door opening, footsteps. It must have been the very large man who pinned him to the wall in the first place. Or perhaps it was his boss.

Even if it was the large man, calling for help couldn't hurt.

"Help!" Owen called out. His voice cracked. His throat was very dry.

A minute later she was there.

Thank God.

Richardson.

"Holy shit, Owen—I'm so sorry. Are you okay?"

She looked at him and saw what looked like a corpse. Owen's face was ashen, his face and torso soaked in dried blood, his eyes bloodshot, his limbs dangling pathetically. He could barely lift his head.

"Not really," he croaked.

"Let me try and get these off," Richardson said, and pulled on one of the spikes stuck through Owen's body. It came out, with effort, and blood. Owen winced with obvious pain. "I'm sorry," said Richardson. He was still stuck, and bleeding now.

"Is there . . . water?"

"No, um . . . let me check the kitchen".

Richardson rushed to the kitchen, and Owen heard the sound of rummaging. She came back almost immediately. "I'm sorry, I couldn't find a cup. I—"

"It's fine. Just . . . get me . . . down," he struggled to say.

"Of course. Let's start with your arms," she said.

Richardson removed the chains holding Owen's arms. As soon as they were free, Owen attempted to pull a spike out himself. He could barely lift his arms—they wouldn't obey him.

"I can't . . . move . . . arms. You have . . . to pull".

"Okay. Owen, this is going to hurt".

"Hurt is . . . fine. Just . . . hurry".

Richardson went to work.

"Who did this?" she sighed, pulling hard. "They really stuck these in there! Shit".

Another spike came out, and another.

Owen whimpered. "Are you okay?" asked Richardson.

"Keep . . . going".

Finally, there were two stakes left.

That's when his body started to slip downwards, the spikes carving through him.

He moaned softly.

"Shit, shit, shit. Let me find . . . there's got to be something for you to stand on—"

Richardson looked around the garage, but it was practically empty.

"No time . . . please, jusss—"

He was slipping slowly, two vertical gashes grotesquely running through his abdomen.

With great effort, Richardson pulled the final two spikes out of him.

Owen's body slumped to the floor. The wall was covered in red streaks, and blood was pooling underneath him.

"Owen? Are you . . . fuck, are you—"

"Give me . . . a minute," he said, breathing hard.

Richardson stood there, not sure what to do. Owen looked like he was dying.

But a minute later, colour started flowing back to his face. He started coughing, spitting blood onto the floor. A couple of minutes after that, he looked up at her.

"Thank you," he said, his voice barely audible.

"Of course, you don't . . . you don't have to *thank* me. I . . . I'm just sorry I didn't come earlier. I could tell something was wrong when you wouldn't return any messages or calls, but Donoghue said his undercover man saw you off and . . . he said it was all okay, the lab was dismantled".

"There was no lab".

"What happened?"

"I don't know," Owen said, pausing to cough. "I walked in, no lab, nothing. Just a big guy who beat the shit out of me, then did this".

"I don't understand . . ."

"Me neither. I don't care. I'm just glad you came".

"Me too. I'm glad we put that tracer on your phone. Donoghue never shared the address. I'm starting to think . . . you don't think you were set up?"

"Probably. I . . . look, I really don't care right now. I just want some water, I want to go home, shower, and sleep. And then I have to fix things with the board. Shit".

"Oh, right, you told me about your important meeting, did you miss it? I'm so sorry, Owen. Yeah, let's . . . let me drive you home. We can talk about Donoghue and everything later. It's just . . . what if . . ."

"What?"

"Unkillable. What if he wasn't working alone back then? And Donoghue's undercover contact, what if there's a connection? I know I'm conjecturing, but . . . I'll have to do some proper detective work. Let me worry about that, I owe you that much".

"Sharon, don't. You just saved me. You don't owe me anything. Honestly, I think . . . maybe you should drop it. Don't look into anything, don't . . . don't risk it. Just let it go. I think I'm done, anyway".

"Done? Owen, don't make any rash—"

"I'm not. Anyway, it's not the time. Let's . . . I just want to go home. We can figure it out later".

"Yeah. Yeah, exactly, let's . . . we'll figure it out later. Yeah. Can you walk?"

Owen stood up. Other than his stained and torn clothes, and his slightly pale face, he looked fine. "Yeah. Just really parched".

"We'll stop on the way and get you a drink," said Richardson.

She supported him on the way out of that cursed, abandoned house.

. . .

He was tired but couldn't sleep. He was finally home, having had some food and water and a shower. He was lying in bed, staring at the ceiling.

He checked his phone for the first time in over twenty-four hours.

He had plenty of missed calls from Richardson, and several from board executives' assistants looking for him that morning.

And one call . . . from *her*.

He called back.

She picked up.

"Wow. Hi".

"Hi".

"I wasn't sure you'd call back," she said.

"Sorry, I was . . . you might not believe this, but I was stuck to a wall, pinned up, for the past twenty-four hours".

"What?!"

"Literally, I was trapped. Some guy, some huge guy, shoved me up against a wall and stuck spikes through me. I couldn't get down until, finally, Sharon came by to check up on me about a day later. She saved me".

"That's . . . Owen, I'm so sorry".

"It's okay. Not your fault".

"I know, but . . . fuck".

"Yeah. So, that's been my day".

"Sounds like I've missed a lot".

"You missed some, yeah. Anyway, Dinah, it's been . . . how are you?"

"I'm okay".

"Are you *really*?"

There was a pause. "No, I'm not. But, I'm . . . well, I'm finally moving in the right direction, so . . . I think I will be. Eventually".

"That's really good, Dinah".

"Yeah. It's . . . yeah".

An awkward pause followed.

"I'm sober," she said.

"I am so glad to hear that".

"Yeah. I guess you realized I had a problem before I ever did. I see it now, and I . . . I've even been to an AA meeting".

"Wow, that's good progress".

"Yeah. To be honest, I don't think I'll be going back. I don't really like that it's, uhm . . . it's very religious. Preachy. But some of the stuff isn't bad . . . well, anyway. I guess the reason I wanted to call yesterday was . . ."

Borst trailed off.

"Yeah?" he asked.

"Owen, I never properly apologized for arresting you. I think . . . well, you know, I was just trying to do my job, being a good cop, you know, with the evidence I had and . . . and everything. But . . . it's not an excuse. I wasn't being a good friend, I never gave you a chance to explain. And I'm just . . . I'm sorry about that. Really".

A shorter pause this time.

"I . . . Dinah, I get it. Thank you. It wasn't . . . I mean, having to choose between being a good friend and a good cop, that's not a position you deserved to be put in. And I don't . . . I guess, okay, what I'm trying to say is, it was shit for both of us. I'm sorry too, and I forgive you. And I hope we can move past it".

"Yeah. Yeah, exactly, I hope . . . we'll move past it".

"Thanks, Dinah. I, uhm . . . I've missed you".

"I missed me too. And you. And . . . just, everything in my old life, really".

"I get that".

"I . . . to be honest, I'm struggling. Not having work, nothing to distract me, it's really tough".

"That part will pass, though. I'm sure they'll let you back on the force soon".

"Yeah, I hope so. My therapist is a police psychiatrist, she's qualified to certify when I'm ready to go back. And actually, my division inspector, well, former inspector, he had some ideas that I think are worth thinking about. But I guess I'm probably not ready yet, to be honest. Unkillable's attack really shook me. It was traumatic, and my therapist and I uncovered . . . well, let's just say I've had a lot of emotional baggage to unpack. I'm still unpacking it".

"Hey, I've been unpacking mine for over a decade. The important thing is to be committed to it, do the work. I'm also back in therapy. I've even started taking medication. Dr. Larner is monitoring me, chemically. It's not . . . I mean, you know. Hopefully, it'll help, but we'll see".

"Yeah. So, you're doing well? Still saving lives, being a superhero? Depresso?"

"Not so much anymore, actually. I'm . . . I think I just quit".

"Oh. Really?"

Owen sighed. "After the past twenty-four hours, I guess I have a lot to process. But I think I recently found new ways to . . . to make a difference, live a meaningful life. So, I might do that. And stop . . . stop with the whole hero thing. It's just . . . it made sense at one point, when the city really needed it, but now, it just doesn't feel like I'm making a difference".

"I guess that makes sense".

"Sorry, you're probably disappointed".

"No, no, it's . . . I just want to know what's going on with you, and . . . I mean, it's good to know. I'm just sorry it's . . . it sounds like things aren't great".

"Some things are, some things aren't. It's life, I guess. But mentally, I'm doing okay. Although, after the past day, stuck to that wall, I'm going to . . . yeah. I'm going to need more therapy, I think," Owen said in an ironically humorous tone.

"Good. I can now say first-hand that it helps".

"Yeah. It does".

"Hey, um . . . listen, it's pretty late, and . . ."

"Right, yeah. I guess we should both go to bed".

"Yeah. But I'm really glad you called".

"I'm glad you picked up".

"Let's talk again soon".

"Absolutely. We'll . . . I think we'll get past things, and—yeah. I hope we'll be good again".

"Me too, Owen. Have a good night".

"Good night, Dinah".

9 – *He's out*

"SORRY, I missed the vein, let me just . . . *there* we go".

A couple of weeks later, in late October, Owen visited Dr. Larner again.

"You didn't even wince," commented the doctor. He was taking another blood sample.

"I've had worse pain than needles".

"Of course you have, forgive me. Well, in the meantime, I can update you—the medication you're on continues to have absolutely no effect. I've seen no fluctuation in hormone levels. It's as if your body recognizes the antidepressants as a foreign entity and breaks them down immediately with no adverse effects—I suspect there's no receptor binding whatsoever. Your biology is remarkable".

"So . . . I should stop taking them?"

"At this point, you may as well. I won't dismiss the placebo effect . . . you're weighing that against the financial factor. You'd do just as well with sugar pills".

"Right".

"I'm sorry. I just realized I'm basically telling you the medication you're taking is ineffective. I guess I was viewing it from the perspective of an experimental scientist and forgot the medical doctor aspect. I apologize. How *is* your mood?"

"It's . . . stable. Which is good. I've been through another sort of trauma a few weeks back," he said, referring to the wall incident, "but I'm in therapy, and I have friends I can talk to, which helps. Even if the pills don't".

"Good, very good. And you know, even if the SSRIs don't work, you can still try tetracyclics or—"

"Do you think those would work?"

"Hmm . . . honestly, my hypothesis would be no. At a base level, all anti-depressants work on blocking inhibitors. If your body is smart enough to somehow prevent foreign elements from doing that . . . I'm not sure if there's a backup plan at this stage".

"I understand. It's okay. To be honest, pills have never worked for me, so I can't say I had a lot of hope in them this time around. As long as I can manage my depression in other ways, it's fine".

"Right, that sounds sensible. And how have you been otherwise?"

"Well, I've been . . . you know, the past couple of weeks, they've been pretty okay," Owen started.

He didn't know it at the time, but they would be the best couple of weeks he was going to have for a long time to come.

"I've had a bit of a hiccup at work, but I smoothed it over. I've been working on the philanthropy stuff. The board's happy, they approved my proposal, so we're moving forward".

"Any money coming the hospital's way?"

Owen almost smiled, expecting the question. "We'll see. We're currently building out the processes for evaluating and approving different causes. I'll let you know when applications are open".

"I'd appreciate it, Owen. Your company's money could make a big difference".

"Absolutely, there may even be an opportunity for some media partnerships. Look, I'm not ruling anything out, but City University Hospital will have to apply like everyone else. The process has to be fair".

"Of course, of course. I understand," said Larner. Owen suspected he didn't, but he didn't say anything.

"Besides that, I've actually reconnected with Dinah Borst. She sends her best".

"Oh, that's fantastic! I've been worried about her".

"Yeah, she's been in a bad state, but she's getting better now. She's getting the help she needs".

"That's very good to hear!"

"I agree".

"And I trust Sharon is well too?"

"I . . . haven't been in very close touch with her lately," Owen admitted. He'd been avoiding Richardson's calls since the wall incident. He did text occasionally to assure her he was fine. She kept mentioning there were some big developments with Donoghue that she wanted to discuss, but he kept blowing her off with lame excuses. "I'm sure she's fine, though".

"Good, good," said Dr. Larner. For a moment, neither of them had anything to add. "Well, I'll get your blood to my lab, and I'll let you know if I find anything interesting. So far, your body is as healthy as ever".

"That's good to know".

"Yes. Now . . . I should probably get back to revising my students' papers. We're submitting three to one of the major conferences this year, and I have to make edits".

Owen rose. "Good luck. I guess I'll head out. I'll let you know next time I'm at CUH".

"Great. Have yourself a nice day," said Dr. Larner, turning his chair towards his desk again.

Owen walked out of Larner's office. He was having a pretty decent day. His earlier therapy appointment was a particularly effective one—he spoke about the experience of feeling helpless and ineffectual. He was specifically referring to the feeling of being stuck to a wall, but there were a lot of parallels to be drawn to the general experience of depression.

Reliving his trauma so soon was horrible but important at the same time. He didn't want to keep it inside, where the feelings of humiliation and loss of control would fester and grow out of proportion, leading to self-resentment. He remembered feeling so powerless, so weak . . . Owen's response was to slowly reclaim the feeling of control in his life, in part by avoiding Richardson and focusing on what he wanted to focus on. Still, talking with his therapist helped. She reminded him that it wasn't his fault, that being weak in certain situations didn't necessarily imply that he had no value in others. They also covered how, in the big picture, he ultimately survived a difficult situation, and looking at it from that lens made it seem much more positive.

It wasn't an immediate fix, but therapy never is. For Owen, therapy was just about discussing ideas and trying to find insights that made him feel a tiny bit less shitty, a tiny bit stronger. And in that sense, today's session helped a lot.

It also helped that he was active and had productive, meaningful things to keep him busy. That mostly had to do with his work at Kline-Laurie.

The board was definitely disappointed that he was a no-show at the big meeting, but they afforded him another chance to make his case. Being a namesake of the corporation probably helped with that. He was nervous before the second chance, knowing it could be his last. But he prepared, revised the presentation, practiced it, contacted some of the key team members he was counting on both inside and outside the organization to see if they had any comments. He came in ready, and shockingly, he knocked it out of the park.

The board unanimously approved all of his suggestions. He was installed as a new vice-president and given a budget to oversee. For the past week, he held down a proper 9-5 job, actually working much longer hours than that, but then he was glad to. He felt engaged building out his team, setting strategy and targets, giving them tasks to research, outlining the processes they'd need to develop.

Owen never imagined that when he wasn't in the midst of a depressive episode, a proper job could seem so meaningful, almost exciting, even. His team was dedicated to the mission, working hard at putting everything in place—the processes for receiving, evaluating, accepting, and monitoring proposals, plans for mental health media campaigns, and a new program offering volunteer opportunities for corporate employees. Once they were up and running, Owen knew they could have a real impact.

As an operative working with Borst and Richardson, Owen saved one life at a time. But there were fewer lives who needed saving these days, with the city more peaceful than ever. There were, however, plenty of lives who needed help, and there were so many causes—from mental and physical health problems to income-based education gaps to racism-fueled violence. There was no shortage of suffering.

With his huge bag of privilege, Owen had the opportunity to help with that. Why would that mean any less than breaking into a house and dismantling a meth lab?

It was good to be busy with a mission that felt authentic, purposeful.

Besides working normal business hours, Owen was also studying for the GMAT, the graduate management admission test. He planned to take it and apply to local business schools, figuring an MBA would help him on his newfound mission.

In the past, as recently as a year or so ago, Owen spent most of his days in bed. He didn't need much sleep, so most of his time was occupied by staring at the ceiling and trying to combat negative thoughts. He wouldn't really do much else with himself—he'd take care of chores like groceries or the bank, try a bit of creative writing, or just sit and stare at a wall or a screen. Days would go by and he wouldn't get out of bed, let alone his apartment. It was a depressive existence.

Well, look at him now. He still didn't need much sleep, so he woke up early, got to the office, put in a long, productive shift, got home, studied. It was normal, real. It was good.

And he was in touch with Borst again. He and Dinah exchanged text messages each night. She . . . understood. They were going through some of the same stuff. It was nice to have someone who could offer that type of support. Someone he could just text and say, *I've been feeling down today. I know I'm being hard on myself but I don't know how to stop.*

And she'd say the same, writing something like, *I know. I've been so tempted to drink and I feel so angry at myself. I know I'm supposed to let it go . . . maybe I'm hard on myself too. How do we stop?*

And he might answer, *I guess it starts by recognizing that it's okay to feel tempted, or down, or weak. Just as long as we don't let it affect what we do. For what it's worth, I think you* are *hard on yourself. You're on a very tough journey, and you've been really strong so far. Give yourself some credit.*

Finally, she'd text, *Thanks. You too. With everything you've been through . . . I think you've grown a huge amount, and I hope you can recognize it too and be a little easier on yourself.*

Conversations like that were helpful. They didn't call or meet for coffee or anything like that. And it wasn't romantic or anything. It was just two friends texting, supporting each other through difficult times.

It was positive. He was glad she was back in his life.

So when she called him that night, he was a little surprised, but of course, he answered.

. . .

"Hello?" he answered.

"Hi".

"Hi. How, uh . . . how's it going?"

"Good, it's . . . it's okay," she replied. Then she paused.

"What's up?" he finally asked.

"I've been talking to Richardson, catching up. I think the three of us need to talk".

"What, uhm . . . what about?"

"She . . . Owen, have you been avoiding her?"

Owen considered for a moment, then decided to come clean. "Yeah, I have, actually".

"How come?"

He sighed. "Dinah, it's . . . it's complicated".

"Does it have to do with the fact that you were stuck to a wall for about a day?"

"It's got something to do with that, yeah," Owen admitted.

"Well, that's sort of what the two of us wanted to talk to you about".

"Oh?"

"Look, let me just tell you. Richardson did the legwork. You've been set up. Donoghue . . . at first, she thought his undercover contact turned, or that it was *him*, Unkillable, somehow. But it became pretty clear that it's Donoghue himself who's been trying to get to you".

"Get to me? What does that mean?"

"Well . . . we're not sure exactly. It sounds like . . . there was something about you and bags of drugs?"

"Yes, he had me carry some drugs over to Richardson's".

"But you had them at your place first?"

"Yeah, right".

"Well, we suspect he didn't actually mean for you to bring the drugs to Richardson's. Donoghue wanted the drugs at your place, and he was planning to bust you for possession and arrest you".

"What?"

"Yep. And when that didn't work, he staged the fake meth lab bust that turned into . . . well, you on a wall".

"But what was the point of that?"

"Richardson suspects he was trying to incapacitate you while building up some case he could use to frame you up. She talked to a couple of officers on his task force, and they confirmed that . . . anyway, look, I'm here with Richardson, it'd be easier to explain in person. Why don't you come over?"

"Wait, I don't understand. What's Donoghue's goal here?"

"We don't know yet, but we *do* know he's trying to get you. So, we've got to take him down".

Owen paused.

"Hello?" Borst asked after Owen failed to respond.

"Yeah, no, I'm here, it's just . . . Dinah, what do you two want?"

"What do you mean? We want you to come down here. Richardson and you and I, the three of us . . . we're gonna make a plan and take this asshole down".

"No".

It was Borst's turn to pause.

"What do you mean *no*?"

"I mean no. I don't . . . I don't want to do that. I'm done, Dinah".

"Done with what?"

"With the . . . the operations, with . . . you know. Fighting crime half-assed, trying to cobble together . . . whatever it was. It was good for a while, we made a difference. But it's not needed anymore, and it's . . . *I* don't need it anymore. I'm finding my own ways to do good. And it's working for me, I feel good about it. So yeah, I'm done, Dinah. Sorry".

"I can't . . . wow. Okay. But . . . Owen, he's after you. You can't just . . . you can't ignore that. Right?"

"Why not? I don't really give a shit".

"If he's trying to frame you—"

"He can try. I'll deal with it if he does. I haven't done anything illegal, and I . . . look, I know I'm lucky in that regard, but I *do* have money, access to lawyers. And I'm not that dumb. I can figure things out".

"So, you're just . . . that's it? You're giving up?"

Owen sighed. "Dinah, I'm sorry. I don't really see it as giving up. I spoke with my therapist about that. It's more useful to think of it as moving on to the next stage of my life".

Dinah didn't know what to say.

"You're really not coming?"

"No. Dinah, I already told Sharon, just drop it. If some dickhead wants to come after me, let him. There's no point in you two getting involved. Just let it go".

"I don't know if we can do that, Owen".

"Okay, well . . . I can't make you. But . . . I told you what I think".

"Yeah".

"Well, um . . . I'm sorry, I can tell you're disappointed. It's just . . . I've got to do the right thing for me".

"Right, yeah. I get that".

"Yeah. So . . . we'll talk soon. I'll text you".

"Have a good night, Owen".

"You too, Dinah".

. . .

"He's out".

"What?" asked Richardson, surprised.

"Yeah. He said . . . he said no," said Borst, putting her phone away.

"Huh. I did *not* expect that. I know he's been avoiding my calls, but . . . did he say why?"

"Not really. He just doesn't want to do it anymore—he's moving on. I don't know".

"Shit. Okay, so . . . we lost Owen. Now what?"

"I still think we should go after Donoghue," Borst said firmly.

"The two of us? But Owen's—"

"Owen's got his special powers, but we're still cops. And Donoghue's crooked. We can get him".

"Maybe you're right. I'm so damn pissed at myself. I genuinely thought he was good police—"

"I *hate* that phrase," interrupted Borst.

"What phrase?"

"Good police. Good cop. It's so . . . *ingrained* in us. Like the few bad cases, the racist cops who kill innocent black people, who use unsanctioned violence, like they're the exception".

"You don't have to lecture me about cops killing blacks," said Richardson, who was mixed-race.

"I know, I know. I just mean . . . I've been talking to D'Alfonso, the division inspector who used to be my immediate supervisor. He left the force. He's been sending me these studies, statistics . . . the concept of *bad* police and *good* police is completely skewed. I'm not saying it's not about individuals, about race, but also it's also situational. Data shows that officers who have gone through an emotionally difficult case, domestic abuse or anything like that, are far more likely to use unnecessary violence. It's not all about bad officers, it's about . . ."

Borst trailed off for a second, but Richardson didn't interrupt.

"It's about a broken fucking system. Look at me—it took me this long to go to therapy. I used to think it was for wusses, cowards. I thought therapy was dumb, a sign of weakness. You know what I did instead, to cope with the trauma and pressure I was exposed to in the course of routine police work? I drank. Sometimes I drank on duty. I'm a fucking alcoholic, and I refused to get help because of dumb ideas about weakness and . . . it just shouldn't be like that. *Every* cop should be in therapy. The police force should be organized in a way that minimizes these patterns that are more likely to lead officers to open fire. Or . . . well, not to even mention the need for better training and internal enforcement when it comes to racist incidents or . . . just basic fucking human decency".

Borst realized she was breathing hard. She had worked herself up into a bit of a fury and just caught hold of it. She stopped.

"I'm sorry, Sharon".

"It's fine. What you said, it's all true. Most cops, decent cops anyway, have these thoughts to struggle with, I think. I know I have".

"Yeah. And yet, nothing ever gets done. D'Alfonso, he's got some ideas. About . . . starting some sort of organization that tackles these problems in modern police forces. I think . . . I don't know. I might join his cause. Then again . . . it also feels like I'm betraying the part of me that's always wanted to be a cop, ever since my father—he was a cop, so—I don't know what the right thing is".

"Well, it sounds like this D'Alfonso guy might be on to something interesting. I'd like to meet with him, chat. Maybe we could all work together," said the former deputy chief.

"Yeah. Maybe".

"In the meantime, we've still got to deal with Donoghue. He's been after Owen personally, trying to frame him, or . . . hell knows what. And on top of that, he's been on a crusade, trying to boost his numbers by enforcing minor drug violations and targeting black communities. We need to take him down, and we have to do it without our main asset".

"We don't need Owen. I told you, look, it's not about overpowering a criminal or whatever, we don't need superpowers here. Donoghue's just a man. We just need . . . what we really need out of him is a confession".

"Right," agreed Richardson. "If we can get him to admit he's been chasing arrests—or better yet, if he admits to setting Owen up . . . but he'd never do it".

"Not knowingly, sure. But if he thinks I'm on his side, he might".

"You can't entrap him, Dinah. You're a cop".

"Not at the moment, I'm not. I'm off the force, suspended. I just have to wear a wire and go to Donoghue, pretending like I want Owen taken down too, and we'll see what he says. There's nothing to lose".

"I don't know, Dinah—"

"He doesn't know we're on to him, right? Those officers you talked to, would they tip him off?"

"No, I don't think so. There's plenty of people on the force who hate Donoghue".

"You can say *that* again. Fucking prick. So yeah, he doesn't know we're coming, I doubt he'd suspect a thing. I say we go for it".

"I guess . . . yeah. If you can get a confession . . . I just don't know if it'll work. And I'm worried—"

"It's worth a shot, though. It's Donoghue. Even if it goes sideways, what's he going to do? He's not going to shoot a fellow cop. It feels pretty safe to me".

"Donoghue paid off some guy to nail Owen to a goddamn garage wall, Dinah. He's . . . look, we both knew him back when you two were detectives on my squad. I can't believe I trusted the fucker. He was always too clever for his own good, too opportunistic, reckless. If he's gotten worse, he's a dangerous man".

"Sharon, it's me. I can handle myself".

"*Owen* could—"

"Owen's out. Look, here's how we do it. You have all the equipment we need, right? Wires and transmitters? Good. So, you call Donoghue up, tell him I want to meet him. His place, so he'll be off guard. Just tell him I'm about to be reinstated and that you've updated me on the Owen situation. Tell him I have some concerns about Owen that I wanted to share. Don't say anything more than that. Let's see what he says".

Richardson sighed. "Okay. Okay, I guess . . . I hope you're right. He may be corrupt, but Donoghue's not a murderer. Fine. You want to meet him tonight? It's a Thursday, traffic shouldn't too bad. You could get there by 8:00".

Borst gave it some thought. "You know what, let's say tomorrow night instead. It'll give us time to run through scenarios, make sure we both feel more confident. What do you think?"

"Okay," said Richardson. She would end up regretting that one word for the rest of her life.

. . .

Borst made one stop on the way back home. Planning had gone well, and the meeting was set. Donoghue took the bait, and they were ready to take him down the next night. Before that, there was someone important she wanted to talk to.

"Hi, Dad".

She hadn't visited his grave since the day of the massacre. She's thought about him a ton, discussed the relationship in therapy, but she hadn't felt ready to visit again. Not until today. Planning to take Donoghue down made her feel like she was finally getting back to being her old herself again.

No, not her old self. A better version of herself. A sober version of herself.

"I've missed you. Sorry I've been away for so long, things have been . . ." she chuckled. "I don't even know where to start".

Borst was lost in thought for a bit in the cold October night air.

"Dad, do you remember that night? It was around this time of year. The cancer was so advanced you were barely awake. But that night, you were lucid, and that old crappy TV in the hospital room was showing one of those old cowboy movies you used to love. We just sat and watched, and you turned to me and said, 'You're gonna be one of the good guys, Dinah. A lawyer. Catching the crooks, like your old man'. You had this smile on.

"You know, I never realized how much you loved me, not really, not until I saw you smile at me like that. And it broke my damn heart. Because I didn't want to be a lawyer, I never did. You pushed me into it, and I was terrified of disappointing you, but . . . I knew it wouldn't work. I could only ever be a criminal lawyer. I mean, come on. It was never gonna be contract law or some bullshit. But I knew if I was going to be a prosecutor, I'd end up putting some innocent men behind bars, and if I was going to be a defender, I'd sometimes have to defend guilty criminals. And I couldn't do either.

"Everything was simple for you. Well, it looked simple, anyway. I guess now I know it wasn't. But when I was a kid . . . you were a cop, and you arrested bad guys. Like the movie cowboys. That was it. And I wanted . . . wanted you to be proud, wanted you to look at me like you did that night, but to see *me*. The real me, not the perfect lawyer daughter you had in your head. I never got that, and I guess I never will".

Borst held back tears.

"Sorry, I . . . I don't know what I'm saying".

She breathed again.

"I told you that night at the hospital that I loved you. But it was more than that. I idolized you, you know. My therapist says it's normal for a girl to idolize her dad, especially if he's a single parent. But I guess that means I never really knew you as a man, just as this super-cop dad. I recently started to look back, and I realized, every memory before you got sick . . . there was always a glass or a bottle in your hand.

"I mean . . ." she chuckled again, "what kind of girl has a flask? I was copying you. And I guess . . . I wish I had the time to talk to you about *that*. About pain. Addiction. I'm pretty sure you were just as dependent on the juice as I am. Was. I'm sober now. I think you'd be proud of me for that, Dad. I am.

"It's hard. Every day. But I guess it's always been hard. I was just hiding behind a bottle. Now I'm facing it, and it's hard but it feels brave. I don't know—I can't explain it. I miss you, but . . . actually, for a while, I was really angry at you. Because you were my dad, but you didn't equip me for . . . for sobriety, for . . .

"I remember another time, back when I was maybe twelve. I had a friend from school over, and we were working on an assignment, but then we were heating up a frozen pizza and just chatting and watching TV, and before we knew it, it was 11:00, and Amanda was like, 'Oh, shit, I should be home'. Then she turned and asked me where my dad was, how come I was alone so late at night. It seemed normal to me—you were probably on a late bust or something, but I guess most kids go to bed with their parents tucking them in. You finally got back, and you drove Amanda home, and then you came back, probably around midnight, and I was so mad, so embarrassed, I imagined my friend thought I came from this crazy broken home with no parents around, and . . .

"I love you, but you weren't a perfect dad. And . . . it's taken me some time to make peace with that. I mean, nobody's perfect, and hell knows you had it tough—a single parent and a cop and all that. But still, like I said, I used to idolize you, so it was hard to admit you were . . . well, normal. Flawed.

"Anyway, yeah. I wanted to say that. I'm feeling more like myself now and . . . I *am* at peace with it. With you. And I do miss you and love you, and all that. But I'm going to get better. Be a better me. Both because of you and in spite of you. And I think . . . I *know* you'd be proud".

Borst shivered. It was getting late, growing colder outside.

"Dad, I have more to say, but I'm really cold. I'll see you soon, I promise".

She suddenly realized that every previous time she visited her dad's grave, she'd reach for her flask and have a drink to his memory. She needed a new gesture.

Awkwardly, she saluted the gravestone. "Bye, Dad".

. . .

She got back home. Standing in her apartment, Borst felt . . . what *was* she feeling? Satisfaction? Contentment? Pride? Yeah, maybe that was it.

She finally managed to tell her dad's spirit the things that had been preying on her mind. That felt like a real step forward. And she was back to fighting the good fight. Donoghue was trying to frame an innocent man—her friend. Well, maybe she had a little something to say about that.

So why did she want a *drink* so bad?

She better talk to Dr. Griffith about that. Borst thought that having too much free time was triggering her these days. But maybe nerves had something to do with it, too. She used to drink to steady herself even as a cop, after all. Now, her mind was back on Donoghue and the preparations with Richardson—she was a day away from a major operation, and there was no alcohol to help her relax.

She *was* nervous. She would need to devise a strategy, a coping mechanism, to deal with her nerves before she could rejoin the force. Luckily, her therapist would probably have some ideas. Griffith had been very helpful the past few weeks, and with the support from Jennifer and thinking about D'Alfonso's ideas, things felt like they were finally moving in the right direction. However long it might take to get there.

Borst's phone buzzed. It was a text from Owen.

Hi. Sorry about earlier. I know I said no about helping with ops, but I hope we can still be friends.

She sat down. Again, the urge to drink struck her. Would it ever go away? She sighed. Owen . . . she was disappointed, maybe even hurt, when he said no. In her mind, when she was sitting with Richardson and learning about Donoghue, she thought it would be a perfect chance to get the gang back together. She was excited about planning an operation with the three of them, like old times. Then Owen had to spoil it by saying no.

But then . . . he had a right to say no. She wasn't going to force him to be something he didn't want to be. It sucked, and she was frustrated, sure, but . . . they *could* still be friends. Right?

Of course. Disappointed but still friends, she texted back.

How about dinner tomorrow night? he asked.

That gave her pause. The last time they had dinner, she drank too much, they were both vulnerable and ended up. . . and, well, things went to hell after that. But . . .

Were they friends? Or were they . . . *could* they be . . . more?

What did he want? What did *she* want?

Better talk to Dr. Griffith about that, too, she supposed.

Busy tomorrow, she replied, thinking about the Donoghue op. *Saturday night?*

Let's do Saturday, he wrote back.

She was hoping he smiled as he typed those words. *She* smiled as she read them.

Ugh, shit. What was she doing?

10 — *If you have the balls*

"BORST".

"Donoghue".

"Come in".

He greeted her at his apartment door, then stepped aside, welcoming her in. Richardson tried to convince her to set the meet at a bar or a coffee shop, somewhere public, safe. But Borst wasn't afraid. Doing it at his place would make him more comfortable, and therefore more likely to incriminate himself. Presumably. *Let's hope*, she thought.

"Didn't expect you to come, I have to admit," Donoghue started.

His apartment was stupid. He had a huge-ass TV, a whole bunch of electronic gadgets, framed landscape photos on the wall, a tacky globe—generic décor that was as tasteless as it was overpriced. A robot vacuum was traversing the floor emitting a mild hum, bumping into a well-stocked liquor cabinet that gave her pause. Everything about Donohue's place screamed *I have money, and I feel the need to show it off in exchange for validation.*

The dick.

"Well, you knew I'm involved in the Owen situation. I was out for a while, but I'm coming back in".

"I know. The Purple Massacre. It must've been hard on you. Well, I'm glad you reached out, we can catch each other up. Richardson mentioned you had concerns, and I do too. We'll discuss. Can I get you a drink?"

"Thanks, but I'm off alcohol at the moment. Maybe some water?"

"Coming right up," Donoghue said, making a show of fixing himself a gin and tonic first.

The fucking dick.

"There you go," he said, handing her a glass. They both sat down, she on a leather chair, he on the sofa. "So, how's your sabbatical been?"

"It's been . . . helpful. I needed the time to process, deal with the trauma. I'm not sure you can imagine what it's like, walking into your squad room and finding a bloodbath".

"Oh, I can imagine," he said cryptically. Was he just being an asshole on general principle?

"Right, well, I'm in therapy, dealing with it. I may be ready to go back to active duty soon—"

"Really? I'm not so sure that's gonna happen. Not that soon".

"What are you talking about?"

"Borst, you know I was on the committee that reviewed your case? The rest of the committee felt that three months would be sufficient for your mandated leave, but I suggested you'd need a year, at least. I'm not sure I'll be ready to sign off on your return so soon. But, well . . . we'll see how things go tonight".

The fucking dick bastard.

"How the hell did *you* get on the committee?" Borst demanded. She couldn't help herself.

"I've got my connections. I have a lot of connections these days, thanks to you".

"I don't know what that means".

"You fucking bitch. You really don't know?"

Borst stood up. "What did you call me?"

"Sit down," he said with the creepiest, most obnoxious, disgustingly entitled smile on his face. Borst hesitated. Her instincts told her to get out, but she needed the confession. It was all set up. So she did as he asked and sat down.

"Good," Donoghue continued. "Now we're on the same damn page. You cost me a promotion. It took me *years* to recover from that".

"How exactly did I cost you a promotion?"

"You don't remember? It should have been *me* that made lieutenant. Instead, Richardson promoted you, because you're a woman. You think I don't know—"

"You're an idiot. I deserved that promotion—"

"Like hell you did. My closing rate was far superior".

"Sure, because you never picked up a case that required actual detective work. How many kidnappings or violent crimes did you ever solve? No, you always went for the easy—"

"I'm head of a drug and organized crime taskforce, Borst. I—"

"Yeah, which you only got thanks to your *connections*. Kissing ass left and right, you were always more interested in networking than doing any actual legwork. Richardson saw right through you".

"Oh, screw you. Let me tell you the truth, so you can stop wallowing in your little delusions. You got where you are for exactly two reasons—your daddy's name has some clout, and you're a woman. That's it. You got promoted and fast-tracked, but you're a career cop, and you're never going to be more than that. You hit your glass ceiling, and that's where you'll stay, head of a precinct squad, captain rank. If you're very lucky, you'll get promoted to inspector in five years. Meantime, I actually know what I'm doing. I'm making connections, leading taskforces, finding out what people need and giving it to them, making a name for myself. While you're stuck in your little 1-6, I'm on the route for the commissioner's office, and the only thing that'll prevent me from getting there would be diversity and gender hires like you. So fuck you, *cunt*".

Borst forced herself to stay calm. It wasn't all that hard. Donoghue was an ass, and she was bringing him down. Okay, let's play. "That's a nice little rant, Donoghue. But you want to know something? I'm happy being a captain, actually leading people. I know the names of everybody on my squad. I know them, I care about them, and they know I do. I'm doing *real* police work, I'm out on the damn streets, and I love it. I don't give a shit if I ever get promoted because I'm not chasing meaningless titles. I became a cop because I want to help people—"

"*Please*. We both know you found this guy, this Owen guy, because you were hoping to pull ahead".

"I found him because I was tired of red tape and union bullshit, tired of trusting a police force that doesn't always get things done. Owen lets me do the things I can't do because of the legal crap, and we've been saving lives".

"I don't believe that for a second. Owen's been helping you make a name for yourself. He's been letting old Richardson feel relevant again. I get it. That's what Unkillable was all about".

"You have no idea what you're talking about, Donoghue".

"Sure I don't," he mocked her. "First you and Richardson screwed me over a promotion back when we were both detectives. Then you cooked up a whole pot of bullshit with this Owen situation, and now you both need *my* help. Well, fuck the both of you. You should just be glad I didn't blow the whole thing wide open, take it public".

"Blow *what* open? You know I got promoted on merit, no one's going to believe that you were discriminated against".

"I'm not talking about the promotion anymore—that's ancient history. No, I'm talking about your nuclear weapon. This Owen guy".

"You were going to expose *him*? What does that mean?" she asked, hoping Donoghue might already spill the beans.

Donoghue took a sip. A part of Borst wanted to grab the glass from his hand and drink it herself. A greater part wanted to smash it in his face. He just looked so smug, the fucker.

"I'll explain, you idiot. You've been playing with fire. A couple of months ago, I got the call from Richardson. She's been looking for someone to coordinate some unsanctioned operations. She came to me because she needed somebody discreet who's got good connections. She trusted me—"

"That was a mistake. You only care about yourself".

"Fuck you. Yeah, I look after Number One, but I also care about this city. I guess most of the old guard's retired because I don't think the old bitch had much choice. Who else was she going to call? And I am well connected. So, she came to me. And she told me . . . oh boy, the shit she told me".

"What?"

"You found this guy who couldn't die? A fucking superhero. And you were deploying him on secret operations, taking down mobsters, saving the city".

"Sure".

"Borst, how fucking stupid are you? *I* investigated the Purple Massacre. I was on the committee. I know all about this Unkillable character. I saw the footage. I spoke to the protected witness, that Fredericks kid.

"Here was a guy who went by the name Unkillable—a guy who couldn't die, who could get shot as many times as you like, who was apparently thrown off a high-rise balcony, squashed to a pulp, and survived like nothing fucking happened. And this guy took it upon himself to murder a whole squadron of officers, demolish a SWAT team, not to mention the criminals he personally executed in front of eyewitnesses. I know all about Unkillable and what he's capable of.

"And now here's Richardson calling me, telling me there's another guy just like him?"

"Owen's *nothing* like Unkillable".

"You don't know that!"

"I *know* him".

"I don't fucking care if he's your long-lost brother, I don't care if you sucked his cock, you *don't* know him. He's a nuke, a ticking time bomb. *He can't die*. He can do anything—he can kill, he can murder, with no consequences. And you've been deploying him? You lost your mind, Borst. You're endangering the fucking public, and as far as I'm concerned, you shouldn't *just* be off the force, you should be in jail".

"So that's it? You're scared of the guy?"

"You're damn straight I'm scared, and you should be too".

"Is that why you tried to frame him for possession*?* Because *that's* pathetic".

"I've been trying to—" Donoghue started, then abruptly paused. His eyebrows furrowed. "Stand up," he said.

"What?"

He walked over to her, and without asking permission, patted her shoulders, her upper chest, her stomach. "You fucking—"

She tried to protect herself, curling up while grabbing at his arm. He slapped her hard, making her recoil back. Then he reached down her blouse.

He grabbed the recording device and yanked it off. The tape stung as it peeled off her skin. She yelped despite herself.

"A *wire*?" he threw it to the floor and smashed it with his foot. "You're unbelievable, you know that?"

She stood up. "I had to protect myself. That was just insurance".

"For what? You're trying to fucking set me up or something?"

Borst had to improvise, but that was fine. She was alert, awake, more sober than she'd been in a decade or longer. She was doing this for herself, and she was doing this for Owen. She could do this.

"Look, you're right. Owen needs to be shut down. I *was* insane when I started up the whole thing. I must have been. Truth is, I was drunk. I'm an alcoholic, Donoghue. You want to pull me out in front of a tribunal, go ahead. I'll answer for my actions. But first, we need to fix it. And honestly, I didn't know where you'd stand. You're so concerned about your own ass, I figured you might side with Owen, maybe you'd want to keep him for yourself. Based on what Richardson's been telling me, you've been happy enough using him for drug busts and then proudly bragging about it on TV. So no, I didn't trust you to be with me on this, and I needed some assurances to cover my ass. That's why I wore the wire".

"You . . ." Donoghue was confused. "*You* want to shut him down too?"

"Yeah".

"But I thought . . . Richardson . . ."

"She doesn't know anything about it".

"*She* told me you're coming over. She obviously knows you're here".

"She thinks we're just coordinating some future ops. She doesn't get it".

"Doesn't get what?"

"She wasn't there!" Borst shouted. "Richardson didn't see what happened at the 1-6, she didn't see those two bodies falling . . . she doesn't get it. I didn't for a second imagine she'd keep it going with him, without me, but . . . as soon as found out she did, I tried to shut it down".

"So, that's why they've gone quiet on me the past couple weeks?"

"That and the fucking . . . what was it? You got someone to stick him to a wall in some garage? That's fucking psychotic. They suspect you now".

"I didn't . . . that wasn't me. It wasn't my idea".

"What wasn't?"

"The wall thing. I just told my guy he needed to hurt Owen bad enough so he`d pass out. Then we were going to come in and plant the lab shit around him and bust him red-handed".

"Owen heals in minutes, you were never going to get him unconscious".

"Well, I didn't know that! My guy—"

"Who's this guy?"

"I told you, I'm well connected. He's technically an informant, but I've used him in unsanctioned ops, same as you did with this Owen guy. Except my guy isn't a freak who could turn on us at any moment, and we'd have *no way* to take him out".

"I still don't fucking get it. What was your plan?"

"Arrest the guy! It's the only way to keep the world safe—put him behind bars. I tried, but I couldn't find anything to charge him with. He's never committed a crime, at least nothing I could find. So, I figured I'd have to . . . you know . . ."

"Frame him?"

"Yes. Frame him. Plant drugs. I'm head of a drugs taskforce, what else am I supposed to do? No easier way to set him up and take him down. I figured, same as Unkillable, as long as he's in jail, the city's safe".

"So that was your plan? Bust him on fake drug charges?"

"Well, you tell me—was he guilty of anything? Was there anything else I could bring him down on?"

"He's clean. Trust me, I looked".

"Exactly. So, you have a better idea?"

"Donoghue, look at yourself. You've been fabricating evidence, planting crap . . . you had Owen carry bags of meth across town for you, you had a guy, an informant of yours, commit assault and illegal detainment all on your order— and you didn't even manage to charge Owen with anything because he's done nothing wrong. You did all of that for *nothing*?"

"I . . . yeah, that's what I did—trying to frame him, to find any way I could to get him off the streets. It didn't work, but that's the best I could come up with. I didn't know what else to do. Now, what do you got? How do we shut him down?"

Borst got up, shook her head, and punched Donoghue in the nose.

"That's for slapping me earlier. Boys, you heard him, he admitted to it. Come in", she called out.

"What? Fuck you, you bitch. What's happening? We need a plan. We've got to take this guy down".

"No, we don't, you asshole," said Borst as uniformed officers entered Donoghue's apartment. "Owen's already shut down, he shut himself down. He doesn't want anything to do with this bullshit you put him up to. He's out of the game. It's safe".

"It's *not* safe, not until he's in a cell. A guy like him, who can't die, the power's going to go to his head. He'll fucking kill people, sooner or later, and—"

"You want to talk about power going to somebody's head? Looking at your fucking self. Trying to frame an innocent guy just because you're afraid of him? You've always been a fucking coward. *That's* why you didn't get that promotion. But we got you now, you dick".

"What the fuck, who are these officers?" Donoghue asked indignantly.

"Cuff him," Borst ordered.

The uniformed officers approached Donoghue, who tried to get away. "Get the fuck off, you can't . . . do you know who I am?"

"You have the right to remain silent," said the detective placing him under arrest.

"Borst, what the *fuck*—"

"You admitted to it. The framing, sanctioned assault, all of it. You just confessed".

"What are you talking about? Your wire—"

"My phone's been on in my pocket since I walked in. Richardson's on the line, recording this whole damn conversation. The wire was a decoy. So, you're under arrest, and I don't know if you'll see a cell, but at the very least you'll be sanctioned. It's a damn sight more than you deserve".

"None of this will stand up in court—it's coercion, and you know it".

"I'm not a cop right now. I'm a citizen, thanks to *you*. And even if it doesn't hold up in court, it'll hopefully be enough to earn you a suspension. And I'm willing to bet that once they start digging into you, anti-corruption will find a thing or two. D'Alfonso already gave me some pretty damning stats. You're enough of a scumbag to hang yourself without my help".

"You . . . you fucking *bitch* . . ." Donoghue walked towards her, trying to act threatening with his hands cuffed behind his back. "You're not getting—"

"What? I'm not getting away with it? I think I just did. But go ahead, if you have the balls, threaten me. I don't have to record anything anymore, I've got witnesses".

"Fuck . . . fuck you," mumbled Donoghue, but he finally accepted defeat.

"Yeah, well, fuck you too," answered Borst. "Take him away, boys," she commanded, and it felt pretty damn good.

. . .

Once Donoghue was in the back of a squad car and the officers assured her they'd book him straight away, Borst got into her own car. Her heart was beating fast, and her vision was blurry. What was happening to her? Was it a heart attack?

She tried to breathe. This had never happened before.

A few agonizing minutes later, her vision refocused, and she could breathe again. Maybe it was a panic attack. The sight of those uniformed cops . . . did it trigger something?

Borst wasn't ready for active duty. She knew it with certainty now. She'd have to talk to Dr. Griffith about it.

Fuck.

What if she would never be okay again? What if this panic was her new reality?

Her father would be ashamed, she thought for a moment. Then she realized, no, he wouldn't. Of course he wouldn't. Her father would be *proud*—proud of her for fighting, for trying, for getting clean, getting better.

And besides, there was always D'Alfonso's new organization. A new purpose. That could be the answer—a better way to serve and protect.

Borst nodded to herself, alone in her car. Her heart rate slowly dropped down to normal. The future was bright. There was hope. Yes.

In her rear-view mirror, she saw that the officers had driven Donoghue away, and for a moment, Borst's heart skipped a beat. This was a different sort of panic, a more concrete one—what if she messed it up somehow? What if the call had dropped or if Richardson couldn't clearly hear the conversation from her pocket?

What if the whole thing was a bust, and they didn't have anything?

She took her phone out of her pocket and dialled.

"Tell me you got it?" she asked.

"All of it. We're golden," said Richardson. Borst could hear the smile on her face as she said it, sitting in that basement across the city.

Borst laughed out loud, relief palpably washing over her. "See? Who needs immortal superheroes, anyway?"

"That's right. You were amazing, Borst. Good improvisation there. We got a clear confession—any court would uphold it. Union will make a fuss, but he's going to get reprimanded, fined, probably suspended for a long time. No more dreams of commissioner, that's for sure".

"Thank God for that".

"Amen. And you played your part perfectly. I tell you, if I was on the committee, you'd be back on the force tomorrow".

"Thanks, Sharon. That means a lot. I'm . . . my heart's still racing, but it's such a relief. We took down one more dick who's only out for himself, giving the police force a bad name in the process. I think we ought to be proud of that". She checked the time. "Shit, it's late. Hey, is it okay if I drive over? I want to hear that tape".

"Absolutely, I'll wait up. We can listen together, then send it to the prosecutor's office. You did good, Borst".

"Thanks," she said, smiling. She *felt* good. She nailed the bastard.

She couldn't wait to tell Owen everything over dinner tomorrow evening.

11 – *Dead*

"DUDE! You are *not* okay to drive," argued Terry.

"Nah, don't worry, I'm cool. Besides, I didn't borrow my brother's BMW to *not* drive it".

"Yeah, but—"

"Shut up, Terry," said Marco.

"Yeah, stop being a bitch, Terry," added Gwen. "Just get in".

Terry wasn't sure what to do. He was standing outside Ryan's house where the party still raged on. People were puking out on the front lawn. It was a Friday night, late fall term, and Terry really didn't want to be there.

Marco so badly wanted to be cool this year, hang out with the cool kids. But Terry didn't give a shit. He came to the party even though he hated parties just because, yet again, Marco had pressured him into it. He didn't drink, but Marco did—Terry saw it.

Terry had hoped Marco would improve through the school year, get back to the old friend Terry used to know, the one who liked the same things he did—video games, manga, superhero shows—but over the past weeks, his friend had only gotten worse. Ever since Marco got together with Gwen, he started going to parties every weekend and usually guilted Terry into coming with. Terry was always so damn uncomfortable in that sort of situation, awkwardly trying to avoid conversations and sidestepping asshole jocks who would make fun of him because he wasn't drinking and he wasn't cool. Maybe he genuinely did have social anxiety? He wasn't sure. He just wished he could be back home playing a game or watching a movie.

Instead, he spent his whole damn Friday night watching his semi-drunk best friend try to convince Gwen to make out with him in the middle of a party. Finally, she had enough and talked Marco into leaving. Terry walked out with them.

Marco and Gwen got into Marco's brother's car, but Marco had been drinking, and Terry wasn't comfortable with him driving. At the same time, he didn't want to start a fight or anything. It was such a shitty situation.

"Come on, I'll drive you home," Marco said.

"No, it's okay. I'll walk," Terry decided.

"Just get in, you pussy!" shouted Gwen and honked the BMW's horn. She and Marco started laughing, and Terry was getting upset. When did his best friend become such an ass?

Oh great, and now Kevin and his buddies were leaving the house, too.

"Yo, whose car is this?" asked Kevin. He was on the football team, loud, popular, and a total douche.

"Marco, that you in there? Where the fuck did you get this nice car from?" Kevin joked while his football friends gathered around. Terry just wanted to get out of there and walk home.

"You jealous?" beamed Marco.

"Yo, we should race!" said Kevin, animated.

"Yeah! Terry, get in here! Let's do this—we're gonna race!"

"Marco, man, you're drunk. You shouldn't even be *in* the car," Terry pointed out.

"Oh, fuck off. Let's just ditch this loser," suggested Gwen.

"What's the matter? This kid bothering you?" Kevin asked, pointing towards Terry.

"Kevin, man, Marco's drunk. He shouldn't be driving," Terry pleaded.

"He doesn't look drunk to me. You wanna drive instead? I bet you drive like my grandma," said Kevin, triggering a round of laughter from his buddies.

"Oh, forget it," proclaimed Terry. He ducked under the arm of one of Kevin's large football teammates and started walking away.

"Terry! Terry, come on!" he could hear Marco and Gwen shouting after him, honking the horn some more.

He could also hear Kevin. "Let him go, he's a pussy. Come on, we've got to race this BMW. I want to see what speed it can hit".

Terry rolled his eyes as he started walking. He didn't live far, and besides, he wanted to clear his head and get some air before he got home and his parents started questioning him. He hoped he didn't smell like beer just from being in the vicinity. It wasn't even that late on a Friday night. He was kind of hoping they would go grab some fries or something at a burger place nearby, him and Marco, like they used to. But his friend was too busy impressing that bitch Gwen, so . . . whatever. It wasn't worth it.

He grumbled to himself as he walked, thinking it was time for him to find some new friends.

He'd have to, once he recovered from the shock.

. . .

Sharon Richardson listened to dispatch transmissions out of habit more than anything. There were few exciting calls these days, but every once in a while, she'd catch something and think about texting Owen.

Truth be told, Richardson was disappointed. She was disappointed both at his decision and how it came about—it was basically ghosting. But she knew that even if Owen had tried to talk to her about it, tried to explain, she probably wouldn't have given him the courtesy of listening. Richardson enjoyed being on active duty, deploying her operative and saving lives. Sure, maybe it was unfair of her—after all, she wasn't the one putting herself at risk, she was saving lives from the comfort of the Control Room, her safe, remote basement. But still.

She and Owen had been doing good, saving lives. Maybe that wasn't as critical anymore now that the city was no longer on fire like it was over the summer, literally and figuratively, but they could still do good.

She could still do good.

She could still do *something*.

Because otherwise, without Owen . . . she wasn't doing much.

He did ask her to take up a role on some board, some sort of management position, whatever it was. But that wasn't her. Richardson wasn't a corporate shill. She had spent her entire life on the force, retired honourably, and . . . and was bored out of her mind ever since. Losing her life-partner didn't help. She had the pension, was well-off financially and in good health, but . . . there was no one to talk to, nothing to do.

She hated it.

Six months. That's how long it's been, really. March, when Borst introduced them, to September, which was when he started ghosting her. Six or seven months of operations, of having a goal, a meaning, something to do with her days.

What was she supposed to do now? Go back to offering private training sessions to rich assholes? Sit with Owen, managing some fund that decided which charity his money goes to? Oh, heck no.

Richardson had hoped that once Borst came back, *she* could convince Owen to come to his senses and get back to action. And with the Donoghue thing just staring them in the face—he was obviously trying to take Owen down—surely, he'd be engaged again, ready to take revenge for being pinned to a wall for a day, ready to take the bastard down.

But Owen wasn't interested, and Dinah didn't push him. No. She just went and did it herself.

Well, good for her. Who knew, maybe the two of them could be the new team—Borst and Richardson, action heroines. But it wouldn't be the same without Owen. He *couldn't die*, for crying out loud! All the things he could do, the people he could save, and instead he chose to hide behind a desk like some corporate stooge.

Richardson sighed. She was disappointed, angry. She tried to tell herself to relax. Borst had taken Donoghue down tonight, that was the important thing. It was a positive development, a good day. Getting angry was pointless. Just calm down.

There it was, now. She was just about to reach over to turn the comm off when a dispatch communication came over, calling out about a car crash. Street racing, some kids hitting a civilian car. They were probably drunk. Fucking rich kids . . . the car was on fire. It was just a few blocks away.

If Owen was there, she would've sent him out. He could have gotten the bodies out, see if they were still alive with no risk of getting hurt by fire or an explosion. He might have even rescued someone.

But he was at home, and by the time he'd get to the scene, it'd be all over. What was the point?

Richardson sighed. She was frustrated and a little tired. It wasn't very late on a Friday night, but it was getting there.

She didn't even wonder about Borst until a good twenty minutes later.

What was taking so long?

She didn't start *worrying* about Borst until another half an hour after that.

She didn't put two and two together until it was far too late.

. . .

A couple of blocks away from Owen's apartment there was a viaduct.

It used to be a suicide bridge—a popular spot for lost, broken people to toss their lives away and jump into the ravine below. Owen himself had done so in the past, twice. He didn't die, of course. He can't die.

But a lot of other people did die. So, the city finally put up a barrier with beautiful lights, and once construction concluded, the viaduct became safe. People could no longer climb over the edge, and suicide rates from that bridge fell dramatically.

The city's overall suicide rates, however, remained flat.

It turned out that the city had treated a symptom, but not the disease. The people who were depressed and suicidal enough to jump off the viaduct didn't suddenly become happy and fulfilled and mentally healthy. No. They just walked a few blocks south to the next bridge over.

That's where Owen was standing.

It was the middle of the night on a Friday. Just a short while ago, Owen was in bed, but he couldn't sleep, so when Richardson's call came through, he heard his phone buzz. He hesitated for a moment. *Probably some last-minute op she wanted to send me out on,* he thought. But then he saw the time. It was late, and he didn't think Richardson would be calling so late at night if it wasn't important. So, he picked up.

And she told him.

"Borst is dead. I'm so sorry".

He didn't get it at first. She gave him the details—some drunk kids were street-racing and hit Borst's car head-on. She was probably killed on impact. No suffering. Like that was any consolation.

Dead. Dinah. Dead.

She *couldn't* be dead. They were having dinner tomorrow night. He was just thinking about that. He was going to suggest Thai food again, like last time. How could Borst be dead?

It wouldn't register. Death didn't register. *He* couldn't die. How could Borst?

Except that wasn't quite right. Death did register. His parents were dead, his sister. All those cops in the precinct station gunned down in front of his eyes. Dead. All those ghosts. And now . . . Borst.

"Owen? Are you there?" that was Richardson, asking, on the phone. Back then. A few minutes ago? An hour? A lifetime?

"What do you mean, dead?"

She explained it again, and again.

Just some drunk kids. Borst had just gotten sober. She finally stopped drinking. Something about that was so unfair.

Fuck.

"You don't have to worry about the Donoghue stuff anymore, by the way. We got him. *She* got him. She got him to admit he was trying to frame you, set you up. I have it all on tape. He's been arrested. She did it, Owen. Her last act was a heroic one, taking down a bad guy, just like she would have wanted. She was just driving back here from Donoghue's apartment when . . ."

The realization, the thoughts, the feelings—they hit all at once, like a goddamn brick wall.

Donoghue—

She—

Guilty. Owen was guilty.

Borst went after Donoghue for *his* sake. If only . . . if he hadn't refused to help . . . if he was part of the op, if . . .

It was all his fault. His fault Dinah was dead.

Dead.

He felt—

It didn't matter. Nothing did.

Richardson was still talking. Or maybe she wasn't. Owen stopped listening, stopped hearing. He wasn't capable anymore. He disconnected the call and got out of bed, out of his apartment.

And walked here.

He knew this bridge well. He stood over it before, contemplating jumping.

All those people who used to jump from the viaduct. All they had to do was walk a little farther.

Owen stood there, on the edge, looking down.

He'd been doing so well. Mentally. He was better, he was . . .

It didn't matter.

He looked down.

He wasn't going to die. So, it didn't matter.

Or was he? Maybe, this time . . .

Owen stood on the bridge.

And Borst was dead.

And everything was shit. And everything was over, done.

And there was no point, and nothing mattered anymore.

And Borst was dead.

And it hurt, *he* hurt, so bad.

And he looked down.

And Borst was dead.

And Owen jumped.

Epilogue

"HEY! You got a visitor".

The man known as Unkillable rose, intrigued. Other than his court-appointed lawyers, he'd never had a visitor before. He followed the guard. As he walked through the halls, other prisoners instinctively shied away from him. Unlike most weeks, he happened to be out of solitary confinement, so the general populace had reason to be afraid of the short, skinny man.

He was ushered into a room with a plastic chair seated in front of a clear, reinforced divider. On the other side was the man who was simultaneously the last person Unkillable expected to see, and the only person it could have possibly been.

"Motherfucker!" he exclaimed. "What do *you* want?"

On the other side of the divider sat Owen, hunched over. He didn't look like he was all there.

"She's dead," he said in a soft voice.

"Who's dead?"

"Her name was Dinah Borst," Owen said, finally raising his gaze to meet his former nemesis. "She was your arresting officer. I told you about her, you might remember. She was the one who recruited me, who—"

"I don't give a shit," Unkillable cut him off. "So, how'd she die? Was it your fault?"

Owen looked hurt. It was about much pain as Unkillable could inflict on him from the wrong side of the partition.

"It feels like it's my fault," Owen sighed. "But no. It was just random chance. She was hit by a drunk driver".

"Wow. Well, tough luck. What the fuck do you want from *me*?"

"I just . . . there's no one else who gets it. Who *could* get it. No one I can talk to. I'm seeing a psychiatrist, talking to people, friends, but it's . . . it's not doing anything. It's not helping".

"And you think *I'd* help you?"

"When we were in that apartment," Owen explained, "you told me there was a girl once. A girl who died".

"Buddy, there were *plenty* of girls who died".

"No. Before you became . . . Unkillable". The way Owen uttered the name made it sound like the word was a chunk of mucus stuck in the back of his throat. "She was special—you mentioned her".

"Oh, her. Sure. A lifetime ago. Jenny. She got shot in front of me. Yeah".

"What did you do? What did . . . I'm just, I'm so angry. So unbelievably angry, and I don't know . . . I don't know what to do with that anger".

"You want to know what I did? I already told you, didn't I? I shot the guy who killed her. And that helped with the pain, a little, so I went on to shoot a whole bunch of other guys. You want to try that? I highly recommend it".

Unkillable expected Owen to look at him in disgust. He didn't. He just continued to look . . . lost.

"You're seriously thinking about it? Go shoot the guy who killed her. See what happens".

"He died in the crash".

Unkillable smiled. "Ah, so you can't even get revenge. Well, I guess you're fucked. And you know what? I don't give a shit. Far as I'm concerned, she was the bitch who put me here. Good fucking riddance to her".

This time, Owen raised his head. He looked a little angry.

Unkillable continued. "Actually, you know what? I was wrong. This *does* affect me. Because now I have to change my plans".

Owen just shook his head.

"You want to know what I've been doing here since I got locked up, waiting for my trial?"

Unkillable wasn't in prison. He was in jail, awaiting processing, judgement. He was probably going to end up with a life sentence at the very least, but for now, he was stuck in a weird purgatory.

"I've just been planning. Picturing it. Because we both know I'll be out of here soon enough".

"You're not getting out".

"Wanna bet? One way or another, I'll get free. I've got it all worked out. It's all I do here, plan it out. Just yesterday, for example, I had this brilliant idea. If I could just make my way into the kitchens, I can jump into one of those giant blenders they've got there. I'll get turn into mush, and guess what? They'll just throw me out, like garbage. Well, surprise-surprise! I'll recover, and I'll be out. Then, oh, then I'll come for *you*. I'm going to kill everyone you've ever loved, everyone you've ever touched, your parents, your siblings, lovers, your favourite fucking barista—"

"My family's all dead. And my . . . Borst's dead. Everyone's dead. And I don't drink coffee. So, do your worst," said Owen in a flat voice.

"Fucking . . . shit. You are just . . . you're ruining all my illusions! Fuck you. Well, I'll just torture *you* then. I had this amazing thought—I'm going to dig a hole, thirty feet, just dig underground. And then I'll shove you in there and bury you alive. How about that?"

"Go for it. But you're not getting out of here".

"I *am*, buddy. Mark my words, sooner or later I'll be out, and I'll be coming after you".

Owen rose.

"Where are you going?"

"I don't know".

"What the fuck? Why'd you even come here? Are you seriously that desperate and lost that you were hoping *I* would help you?"

Owen looked at him but didn't answer.

"Fuck you!" Unkillable rose, too, his anger finally boiling over. "I'm in here because of you! Why the fuck . . . what did you think I would say to you? You thought I'd help? Console you? I want to *kill* you! That's what I fucking want! *You*! *Dead!*"

"Yeah. Me too," Owen mumbled.

"You fucking—no! Get the fuck . . . get off me!"

The guards finally reacted, four of them trying to restrain Unkillable and succeeding quite handily. He was indeed unkillable, but he wasn't invincible, nor even particularly strong.

"I'm gonna fucking kill you! You hear me!? Look at me! I'll fucking—"

But the guards were cuffing Unkillable and marching him away from the visitors' room, probably back to solitary confinement for the time being.

Owen walked away, feeling as empty and in just as much pain as he did when he came in. The visit had been pointless. Life felt pointless. But he couldn't end it, as much as he wanted to. He couldn't go on, and he couldn't die. He could only . . . be.

About the Author

O. W. LÁAV is a Canadian writer from Toronto. A graduate of the Universities of Waterloo, Toronto, and Oxford, Láav worked as a financial analyst, machine learning researcher, and high-school teacher. He's lived on three continents, and will probably keep moving around and reinventing himself whenever he gets bored.

Láav currently resides in Newark, NJ and works in data science, but finds the time to write whenever he can.

The Depresso Trilogy is Láav's first full-length novel. His first book, *Modern Sadness: Short Stories*, was released in 2020.

CPSIA information can be obtained
at www.ICGtesting.com
Printed in the USA
BVHW070822130423
662287BV00015B/633/J

9 781039 128323